A Slice of Heaven

SHERRYL WOODS

A Slice of Heaven

MIRA®

ISBN-13: 978-0-7783-2415-7
ISBN-10:   0-7783-2415-X

A SLICE OF HEAVEN

www.MIRABooks.com

Printed in U.S.A.

10 9 8 7 6 5 4 3 2 1

Dear Friends,

Welcome back to Serenity! I hope you're enjoying the Sweet Magnolias and are looking forward to discovering more about these wonderful women who've been friends through thick and thin since childhood. This time you'll learn more about Dana Sue Sullivan and her daughter, Annie, and the man who broke both their hearts. And you'll spend more time at The Corner Spa, in the kitchen at Sullivan's restaurant and with Maddie and Helen.

As those of you who read *Stealing Home* know, Dana Sue and Annie are each facing very complicated and serious issues related to food. Dana Sue has a family history of diabetes and is at high risk herself. Annie is anorexic, a problem faced by an increasing number of girls at earlier and earlier ages.

To be sure that I fully understood the gravity of this problem, its risks and treatment, I turned to a couple of experts. I immediately got in touch with a college friend, Charlotte Stall, a registered dietician who's worked with children in Denver hospitals for many years, though not in an eating disorders program. Like the characters in this series, Charlotte's been a friend for so long she knows way too many of my deepest, darkest secrets, and despite her best efforts, she still can't get me to eat my vegetables. She, in turn, introduced me to Cinda Nab, a registered dietician at The Children's Hospital of Denver, who works with their eating disorders unit. I am deeply indebted to her for her thoughtful responses to all of my questions. There are some differences between the kind of program that might be found in a small-town hospital such as the fictional one in Serenity and the extensive treatment program at The Children's Hospital of Denver. I've tried to adapt in a reasonable, responsible way. Any mishandling of Annie's treatment rests solely on my shoulders.

I hope you'll enjoy visiting once again with everyone in Serenity and that you'll be back when Helen finally meets her match in *Feels Like Family*, coming in April 2007 from MIRA Books.

All best,

Sherryl

1

The smell of burning toast caught Dana Sue's attention just before the smoke detector went off. Snatching the charred bread from the toaster, she tossed it into the sink, then grabbed a towel and waved it at the shrieking alarm to disperse the smoke. At last the overly sensitive thing fell silent.

"Mom, what on earth is going on in here?" Annie demanded, standing in the kitchen doorway, her nose wrinkling at the aroma of burnt toast. She was dressed for school in jeans that hung on her too-thin frame and a scoop-neck T-shirt that revealed pale skin stretched taut over protruding collarbones.

Restraining the desire to comment on the evidence that Annie had lost more weight, Dana Sue regarded her teenager with a chagrined expression. "Take a guess."

"You burned the toast again," Annie said, a grin spreading across her face, relieving the gauntness ever so slightly. "Some chef you are. If I ratted you out about this, no one would ever come to Sullivan's to eat again."

"Which is why we don't serve breakfast and why you're sworn to secrecy, unless you expect to be grounded, phoneless and disconnected from your e-mail till you hit thirty," Dana Sue told her, not entirely in jest. Sullivan's had been a huge success from the moment she'd opened the restaurant's doors. Word-of-mouth raves had spread through the entire region. Even Charleston's top restaurant-and-food critic had hailed it for its innovative Southern dishes. Dana Sue didn't need her sassy kid ruining that with word of her culinary disasters at home.

"Why were you making toast, anyway? You don't eat it," Annie said, filling a glass with water and taking a tiny sip before dumping the rest down the drain.

"I was fixing you breakfast," Dana Sue said, pulling a plate with a fluffy omelet from the oven, where she'd kept it warm. She'd added low-fat cheese and finely shredded red and green sweet peppers, just the way Annie had always liked it. The omelet was perfect, a vision suitable for the cover of any gourmet magazine.

Annie looked at the food with a repugnant expression most people reserved for roadkill. "I don't think so."

"Sit," Dana Sue ordered, losing patience with the too-familiar reaction. "You have to eat. Breakfast is the most important meal, especially on a school day. Think of the protein as brain power. Besides, I dragged myself out of bed to fix it for you, so you're going to eat it."

Annie, her beautiful sixteen-year-old, regarded her with one of those "Mother! Not again" looks, but at least she sat down at the table. Dana Sue sat across from her, holding her mug of black coffee as if it were liquid gold. After a late night at the restaurant, she needed all the caffeine she could get first thing in the morning to be alert enough to deal with Annie's quick-thinking evasiveness.

"How was your first day back at school?" Dana Sue asked.

Annie shrugged.

"Do you have any classes with Ty this year?" For as long as Dana Sue could remember, Annie had harbored a crush on

Tyler Townsend, whose mom was one of Dana Sue's best friends and most recently a business partner at The Corner Spa, Serenity's new fitness club for women.

"Mom, he's a senior. I'm a junior," Annie explained with exaggerated patience. "We don't have any of the same classes."

"Too bad," Dana Sue said, meaning it. Ty had gone through some issues of his own since his dad had walked out on Maddie, but he'd always been a good sounding board for Annie, the way a big brother or best friend would be. Not that Annie appreciated the value of that. She wanted Ty to notice her as a *girl*, as someone he'd be interested in dating. So far, though, Ty was oblivious.

Dana Sue studied Annie's sullen expression and tried again, determined to find some way to connect with the child who was slipping away too fast. "Do you like your teachers?"

"They talk. I listen. What's to like?"

Dana Sue bit back a sigh. A few short years ago, Annie had been a little chatterbox. There hadn't been a detail of her day she hadn't wanted to share with her mom and dad. Of course, ever since Ronnie had cheated on Dana Sue and she'd thrown him out two years ago, everything had changed. Annie's adoration for her father had been destroyed, just as Dana Sue's heart had been broken. For a long time after the divorce, silence had fallen in the Sullivan household, with neither of them wanting to talk about the one thing that really mattered.

"Mom, I have to go or I'll be late." A glance at the clock had Annie bouncing up eagerly.

Dana Sue looked at the untouched plate of food. "You haven't eaten a bite of that."

"Sorry. It looks fantastic, but I'm not hungry. See you tonight." She brushed a kiss across Dana Sue's cheek and took off, leaving behind the no longer perfect omelet and a whiff of perfume that Dana Sue recognized as the expensive scent she'd bought for herself last Christmas and wore only on very special occasions. Since such occasions had been few and far between since the divorce, it probably didn't matter that her daughter was wasting it on high school boys.

Only after she was alone again and her coffee had turned cold did Dana Sue notice the brown sack with Annie's lunch still sitting on the counter. It could have been an oversight, but she knew better. Annie had deliberately left it behind, just as she'd ignored the breakfast her mother had fixed.

The memory of Annie's collapse during Maddie's wedding reception last year at Thanksgiving came flooding back, and with it a tide of fresh panic.

"Oh, sweetie," Dana Sue murmured. "Not again."

"I'm thinking for tonight's dessert I'll make an old-fashioned bread pudding with maybe some Granny Smith apples to add a little tartness and texture," Erik Whitney said before Dana Sue had a chance to tie on her apron. "What do you think?"

Even as her mouth watered, her brain was calculating the carbohydrates. Off the chart, she concluded, and sighed. Her customers could indulge, but she'd have to avoid the dessert like the plague.

Erik regarded her worriedly. "Too much sugar?"

"For me, yes. For the rest of the universe, it sounds perfect."

"I could do a fresh fruit cobbler instead, maybe use a sugar substitute," he suggested.

Dana Sue shook her head. She'd built Sullivan's reputation by putting a new spin on old Southern favorites. Most of the time, her selections were healthier than some of the traditional butter-soaked dishes, but when it came to desserts, she knew her clientele preferred decadent. She'd hired Erik straight out of the Atlanta Culinary Institute because the school's placement officer had ranked him the best pastry chef candidate they'd seen in years.

Older than most graduates, Erik was already in his thirties. Eager to experiment and show what he could do, Erik hadn't disappointed her or her customers. He was such a huge improvement over her last sous-chef, a temperamental man who was difficult to work with, that Dana Sue counted her blessings every single day that Erik could double as a sous-chef and pastry chef. He'd quickly become more than an employee. He'd become a friend.

Moreover, there was already a high demand in South Carolina for Erik's wedding cakes. He'd raised the traditional cake to an art form that rivaled anything seen at fancy celebrity weddings. Dana Sue knew she'd be lucky to keep him for another year or two at most before some big-city restaurant or catering company lured him away, but for the moment he seemed content in Serenity, happy with the latitude she gave him.

"We did plenty of fruit cobblers over the summer," she told him. "The bread pudding sounds great for tonight. You're cooking for the customers, not me."

When was the last time she'd allowed herself so much as a teaspoonful of any of Erik's rich desserts? Not since Doc Marshall had given her yet another stern lecture on losing the fifteen pounds she'd gained in the past two years, and warned her—again—that she was putting herself at risk for diabetes, the disease that had killed her mother. That should have been warning enough for Dana Sue without the doctor reminding her constantly.

She'd thought that working with her two best friends to open The Corner Spa would keep her so busy she'd stay on her diet. She'd also convinced herself that the spectacular surroundings they'd created would give her an incentive to exercise. So far, though, she'd gained five more pounds testing all the healthy drinks and low-fat muffins they'd put on the spa menu. There was a peach-pear smoothie that might be worth dying for.

Putting on weight might be an occupational hazard for a chef, but Dana Sue laid some of the blame on the collapse of her marriage two years ago. When she'd kicked Ronnie Sullivan out of her house for cheating on her, she'd consoled herself with food—unlike her daughter, who'd chosen to avoid it.

"You're not the only person in Serenity worrying about sugar," Erik reminded her. "I can adapt."

"So can I. It's not as if I'll starve, sweetie. Tonight's menu will have plenty of vegetables and three healthy main courses. Now, go work your magic. Our regulars expect something amazing from you every time they come in."

"Okay," he said finally, then gave her a penetrating look. "You want to tell me what else is on your mind?"

She frowned at him. "What makes you think there's something else on my mind?"

"Experience," he said succinctly. "And if you won't talk to me, then go call Maddie or Helen and get it off your chest. If you're as distracted during the dinner rush as you were during lunch, I'll have to spend the whole evening bailing you out."

"Excuse me?" she said tightly, not one bit happy about the accuracy of his comment.

"Sweetie, half a dozen meals came back in here because you'd left off some part of the order. It's one thing to forget to send out French fries. It's another to leave off the meat."

Dana Sue moaned. "Oh, God, I was hoping you hadn't noticed that."

Erik winked at her. "I notice most everything that goes on in here. That's what makes me a good backup for you. Now, go make that call, you hear?"

Dana Sue held in a sigh as Erik went to gather his ingredients from their well-stocked storeroom, and her own thoughts returned to her daughter. It was impossible for her to go on denying that Annie was getting skinnier by the day. She claimed she was no thinner than the models she saw in magazines and on TV, and that she was perfectly healthy, but Dana Sue thought otherwise. Her clothes hung loosely on her bony frame, Annie's ineffective attempt to disguise just how thin she really was. Dana Sue was convinced she was starving herself so she wouldn't turn out like her mom—overweight and alone.

Despite a frantic pace with the lunch crowd, which usually energized her and kept her focused, today Dana Sue hadn't been able to shake the image of that abandoned brown sack. Usually Annie made a pretense of eating *some*thing just to keep her mother off her case. Now Dana Sue wondered if that left-behind paper bag, with its turkey sandwich on whole-grain bread, celery and carrot sticks and a banana, was a cry for help.

Satisfied that Erik could watch over the dinner preparations in the state-of-the-art, stainless-steel kitchen, Dana Sue slipped into her small, cluttered office to follow his advice and call Maddie at the gym. Whenever her world seemed to be crumbling, she turned to her two best friends—Maddie Maddox, who was managing The Corner Spa, and attorney Helen Decatur—for sensible advice or a shoulder to cry on. Over the years they'd grown adept at providing both. Nobody in Serenity messed with one of the Sweet Magnolias without tangling with the other two, as well.

They'd bolstered each other through schoolgirl crushes, failed marriages and health scares. They'd shared joys and sorrows. Most recently they'd gone into business together, which had brought them closer than ever, their various skills complementing each other nicely.

"How are things in the world of fitness?" Dana Sue asked, forcing a cheery note into her voice.

"What's wrong?" Maddie asked at once.

Dana Sue bristled at being so easily read for the second time that afternoon. She obviously wasn't as good at covering her emotions as she'd like to be. "Why do you automatically assume something's wrong?"

"Because it's less than an hour till your dinner rush starts," Maddie said. "You're usually up to your eyeballs in preparation. You don't make casual, just-to-chat calls until after nine when things start to settle down again."

"I am way too predictable," Dana Sue muttered, making a vow to change that. Once, she'd been the most reckless and daring of all the Sweet Magnolias. But since the divorce, knowing she had a daughter to raise and send to college—her ex-husband made the court-ordered child support payments, but that was all—she'd turned cautious.

"So, what is it? What's wrong?" Maddie repeated. "Did somebody complain about their quiche at lunch? Were the salad greens from the produce vendor not crisp enough?"

"Very funny," Dana Sue said, not the least bit amused by Maddie's reference to her perfectionism. "Actually, it's Annie. I really think she's in trouble again, Maddie. I know you and Helen have been worried all along about her eating habits and weight loss. The collapse at your wedding freaked all of us out, but that was almost a year ago and she's been getting better since then. I made sure of it." Suddenly overwhelmed by a wave of unfamiliar helplessness, Dana Sue added, "Now, I just don't know. I think I've been deluding myself."

"Tell me what happened," Maddie commanded.

Dana Sue related the morning's incident. "Am I making too much of her ignoring the breakfast I'd fixed, and leaving behind her lunch?" she asked hopefully.

"If that was all you had to go on, I'd say yes," Maddie replied. "But, sweetie, you know there are other signs that Annie has an eating disorder. We've all seen them. When she passed out at my wedding, it was a warning. If she's anorexic, that kind of thing doesn't miraculously go away. She's probably just gotten better at hiding it from you. She needs counseling."

Dana Sue still clung to the hope they'd gotten it all wrong. "Maybe it's just back-to-school jitters, or maybe she's eating the cafeteria food at school," she suggested. She wondered if Maddie's son might have noticed something. "Could you talk to Ty? He might have some idea. They don't have any classes together, I know. Annie told me that much today, but maybe they have the same lunch hour."

"I'll ask him," Maddie promised. "But I'm not sure teenage boys pay the slightest bit of attention to what girls are eating. They're too busy scarfing down everything in sight."

"Try," Dana Sue pleaded. "Obviously I'm not getting anywhere talking to her. She just gets defensive."

"I'll do my best," Maddie promised. "I'll ask Cal, too. You can't imagine the kind of gossip my husband overhears in the locker room. Who would have guessed that a baseball coach would know so much? He may be the school's best resource for staying on top of what the kids are up to. Sometimes I think he knows when students are in trouble before their own parents do. He certainly did in Ty's case."

"I remember," Dana Sue said, recalling how concern for Ty had drawn Maddie and Cal together. "Thanks for checking into this, Maddie. Let me know what you find out, okay?"

"Of course. I'll give you a call later tonight," her friend promised. "Try not to worry too much. Annie's a smart girl."

"But maybe not smart enough," Dana Sue said wearily. "I know this kind of thing can happen because of peer pressure and all the role models these girls see on TV and in the movies, but Annie also has a lot of issues thanks to her dad running around on me."

"You think this has something to do with Ronnie?" Maddie sounded skeptical.

"I do," Dana Sue told her. "I think she convinced herself it wouldn't have happened if I'd weighed a hundred and five. Of course, I haven't weighed that since seventh grade."

"You're also five-ten. You'd look ridiculous," Maddie said.

"Probably, but it might be kind of fun to test the willowy look on the men in Serenity," Dana Sue said with a wistful note. Then she added realistically, "But it's never going to happen. No matter how hard I try these days, I can't seem to lose more than a pound, and that never stays off long. I'm destined to be tall, but frumpy."

"Sounds as if Annie isn't the only one who could use a body image lecture," Maddie said. "I'll get Helen over here first thing in the morning. When you come by to drop off the salads for the café, we'll fix that thinking of yours right up. You're gorgeous, Dana Sue Sullivan, and don't you forget that for a single second."

"Let's just focus on Annie for the time being," Dana Sue replied, dismissing her own food issues, as well as Maddie's loyal attempt to bolster her spirits. "She's the one who could be in real trouble, not me."

"Then Helen and I will help you deal with it," Maddie assured her. "Have the Sweet Magnolias ever let each other down?"

"Not once," Dana Sue admitted, then hesitated as a distant memory came back to her and made her smile, temporarily wiping out her anxiety over Annie. "Wait. I take that back. There was that time you two left me twisting in the wind to deal with a cop after we played a prank on our gym teacher."

"That prank was *your* idea, and we didn't intentionally leave you behind," Maddie corrected. "We thought you could run faster. We came back for you, didn't we?"

"Sure, right after the cop called my folks and threatened to haul me off to jail if he caught me doing anything that stupid again. I was so scared I was throwing up by the time you came back."

"Yes, well, there's no need to dwell on ancient history," Maddie said briskly. "We will be there to help with Annie, whatever she needs. You, too."

"Thanks. I'll talk to you later, then."

When Dana Sue placed the portable phone back in its charger, she felt the first faint stirring of relief. She'd faced a lot of turmoil, and had triumphed with Maddie and Helen by her side. They'd gotten her through her divorce and helped her open her restaurant when she hadn't been convinced she could do it. Surely this crisis—if there even was a crisis—could be tackled just as easily if they all put their heads together.

Annie hated her physical education class. She was a complete and total klutz. Worse, Ms. Franklin—who weighed about a hundred pounds soaking wet and had boundless enthusiasm for anything athletic—was always scowling at her, as if there was something wrong with her. Usually Annie scowled right back at her, but today she couldn't seem to summon up the energy.

"Annie, I'd like to see you after class," Ms. Franklin said, once she'd tortured them all by making them jog around the track. Twice.

"Uh-oh," Sarah said, giving Annie a commiserating look. "What do you suppose she wants?"

"I doubt she's going to ask me to go out for the track team," Annie joked, still trying to catch her breath. She'd never been athletic, but lately even the slightest bit of activity left her winded, unlike Sarah, who looked as if the run had been no more than a stroll between classes.

Sarah, who'd been Annie's best friend since fifth grade and knew most of her deepest, darkest secrets, studied her worriedly. "You don't think she's going to say something about you being out of shape, do you? Grown-ups get all freaked out if they think we're not ready to compete in some marathon or something. I mean, who'd want to do that?"

"Not me," Annie agreed, relieved that the odd racing sensation in her chest had finally eased a little and she was able to breathe more normally.

"Maybe she found out about you passing out and ending up in the hospital."

"Oh, come on, Sarah. That was last year," Annie griped. "Everyone's forgotten all about it."

"I'm just saying, if Ms. Franklin thinks you're going to crash in her class, maybe she'll let you out of it."

"As if," Annie scoffed. "Nobody gets out of P.E. without some kind of doctor's note, and Doc Marshall will never give me one. Not that I'd ask. If I did, my mom would have a cow.

She still gets all weird about me not eating the way she thinks I should." She rolled her eyes. "Like the way she eats is so healthy. She's packed on so much weight since my dad left, no man will ever look at her twice. I'm never letting that happen to me."

"How much do you weigh now?" Sarah asked.

Annie shrugged. "I'm not sure."

Her friend regarded her with disbelief. "Oh, you are, too, Annie Sullivan. I know perfectly well you weigh yourself at least three or four times a day."

Annie frowned. Okay, maybe she was a little obsessive about making sure that she never picked up an ounce, but she couldn't trust the scale at home to be accurate. So she weighed herself again on the one in the locker room. And sometimes again, if she stopped by The Corner Spa to see Maddie. Even if she knew her weight to the last ounce, it didn't mean she wanted her best friend to know. Besides, it wasn't the number on the scale that mattered. It was the way she looked in the mirror. She looked fat and that was all that mattered. Sometimes when she saw herself in all those mirrors at the spa, she wanted to cry. She couldn't figure out how her mom could even bear to walk into that room.

"Annie?" Sarah said, her expression worried. "Are you below a hundred? You look to me like you weigh less than ninety pounds."

"What if I do?" Annie said defensively. "I still need to lose a couple more pounds to look really great."

"But you promised you'd stop obsessing about your weight," Sarah said, an edge of panic in her voice. "You said passing out when you were dancing with Ty was the most embarrassing moment of your life, and you'd never be in a position for that to happen again. You told everyone you'd keep your weight at least at a hundred pounds, and even that's pretty skinny for your height. You *promised*," Sarah emphasized. "How can you have forgotten all that? And you know it happened because you weren't eating."

"I hadn't eaten *that day*," Annie countered stubbornly. "I eat."

"What have you had today?" Sarah persisted.

"My mom fixed me a huge omelet for breakfast," she said. Sarah gave her a knowing look. "But did you eat it?"

Annie sighed. Sarah evidently wasn't going to let this go. "I don't know why you're getting so worked up over this. What have *you* eaten today?"

"I had cereal and half a banana for breakfast and a salad for lunch," Sarah replied.

Annie felt like throwing up just thinking about eating that much food. "Well, good for you. Don't come to me when you're too fat to fit into your clothes."

"I'm not gaining weight," Sarah said. "In fact, I've even lost a couple of pounds by eating sensibly." She gave Annie a chagrined look. "I'd give anything for a burger and fries, though. To hear my mom and dad talk, that's all kids ever did back in the day. They went to Wharton's after football games and pigged out. They went there after school and had milk shakes. Can you imagine?"

"No way," Annie said.

The last time she'd eaten a burger and fries, she'd been having lunch with her dad. That was the day he'd told her he was leaving, that he and her mom were getting a divorce. Of course, after she'd witnessed her mom tossing all his stuff on the front lawn it hadn't come as a huge shock, but it had made her sick just the same. She'd left the table at Wharton's, run into the restroom and lost her lunch right there.

Since that awful day, nothing had appealed to her. Not the

burgers and fries she'd once loved, not pizza or ice cream, not even the stuff her mom had on the menu at the restaurant. It was like her dad had yanked her appetite right out of her, along with her heart. Finding out that he'd cheated on her mom, then watching that huge, embarrassing scene on the front lawn, had pretty much killed any desire to ever eat again. Annie knew her mom had been right to do that, but it had left her feeling all alone and empty inside. Her dad had been the one guy who'd always thought she was the most beautiful, special girl in the world. She supposed he still did think that, but he wasn't around to tell her. Hearing it on the phone wasn't the same. No matter how many times he said it, she dismissed it because there was no way he knew how she really looked these days. It was just so much *blah-blah-blah*.

"It would be kinda nice to hang out at Wharton's, though, wouldn't it?" Sarah said wistfully. "A lot of the kids still go after school."

"Go ahead and do it," Annie said. "Don't let me stop you."

"It wouldn't be any fun without you," she protested. "Couldn't we go just once? We don't have to order what everyone else is having."

Annie was already shaking her head. "Last time I went with my mom and Maddie and Ty, they all stared at me when I ordered water with a slice of lemon. You'd have thought I'd asked for a beer or something. And you know Grace Wharton gossips about everything. My mom would know in an hour that I was in there and didn't have anything to eat or drink."

Sarah looked disappointed. "I guess you're right."

Annie felt a momentary twinge of guilt. It wasn't right that her hang-ups were keeping her best friend from having fun. "You know," she said at last, "maybe it would be okay. I could order a soda or something. I don't have to drink it." Her mood brightened. "And maybe Ty will be there."

Sarah grinned. "You know he will be. All the cool guys go there after school. So, when do you want to go?"

"Might as well be today," Annie said. "I have to go see Ms. Franklin now. I'll meet you out front after I'm finished and we can walk over."

Wasting money on a drink she wouldn't even sip was a small price to pay to spend an hour or so around Ty. Not that she was fooling herself by thinking he would pay the slightest bit of attention to her. Not only was Ty a senior, he was a star on the baseball team. He was so beyond her reach. He was always surrounded by the most gorgeous girls in his class. He seemed to like the tall, thin ones with long, silky blond hair and big boobs. Annie, at only five foot three, with chestnut curls and no chest to speak of, couldn't compete with them.

But she had one thing none of those girls had. She and Ty were almost family. She got to spend holidays and lots of other special occasions with him. And one of these days, when she was thin enough, when her body was absolutely perfect, he was going to wake up and notice her.

2

It was hotter than blazes working on the roof of yet another house in yet another new subdivision, this one outside of Beaufort, South Carolina. The sun was pounding down on Ronnie Sullivan's bare, sweat-drenched shoulders, and under his hard hat, his head was soaking wet. His work boots felt as if they each weighed a hundred pounds.

In the past two years Ronnie had worked more construction jobs around the state of South Carolina than any man with good sense ought to. The more physically demanding, the better. He was pretty sure if he kept it up much longer, the sun would bake his brain completely, especially since he'd decided to concede defeat to his receding hairline and shave his head.

After all these months of taking any job that was offered, then going back to a cheap motel room for a cold shower, and out to some bar for an icy beer and greasy food, he was exhausted, physically and emotionally. But no matter how exhausted he was when he tumbled into bed, it was never enough to chase away the nightmares and regrets.

There was no question in his mind that he'd blown the best thing that had ever happened to him—his marriage to Dana Sue. Worse, he'd done it stupidly and carelessly, not even once thinking of the consequences until it had been too damn late.

Years of heat exposure, from a lifetime of working construction, was the only possible explanation for his idiotic decision to have a fling back in Serenity—the gossip capital of the South—practically under his wife's nose. It had taken about a nanosecond for her to find out he'd slept with some woman he'd met in a bar after work. One time, dammit, but nobody in Serenity was handing out passes for freebies. Once was more than enough to rip his life apart.

Dana Sue hadn't given him even a minute to explain and beg her forgiveness. She'd tossed two suitcases filled with his belongings on the front lawn, not even caring that half the contents were falling out all over the place. She'd screamed that he was lower than pond scum, that she hated him and never wanted to see him again. The entire neighborhood had witnessed his downfall. A couple of women, showing their solidarity with Dana Sue, had actually cheered her on.

Ronnie had wanted to stay and fight for their marriage, but he'd known Dana Sue long enough to recognize that stubborn, fiery glint in her eyes. He'd left, knowing he was making the second-worst mistake of his life. The first had been that tawdry, meaningless, one-night affair.

Before he'd gone, he'd taken his little girl out to lunch to try to explain things to her, but Annie hadn't wanted to hear his explanations. At fourteen she'd been just old enough to understand exactly what he'd done and why her mother had been so furious. She'd listened to him in stony silence, then gone into the restroom and stayed there until he'd had to send Grace Wharton in after her.

Since he'd left, not a day had gone by when he hadn't regretted hurting Dana Sue or putting that devastated look in his little girl's eyes. Falling off the pedestal Annie'd put him on had just about broken what was left of his heart.

During the divorce proceedings he'd fought for visitation rights, but Helen had kept them to a bare minimum. Not that it had mattered. He'd spent more than a year trying to maintain some kind of contact with Annie, but she'd hung up on every call and refused to see him when he'd tried to arrange a visit. He knew some of that was out of loyalty to her mom, but a good bit more was her own disappointment and anger. For a few months now, she'd at least taken his calls, but the conversations still tended to be stilted and uninformative, nothing at all like the heart-to-hearts they used to have.

Since Dana Sue and Annie weren't that eager to see him, Ronnie hadn't set foot in Serenity again, coward that he was. But lately he'd been thinking more and more about going home. He wasn't cut out for a vagabond's life. He hated living in motel rooms and moving from place to place in search of work. He'd been on this last job for the better part of a year, but it still wasn't the same as settling down. Even the freedom to make a play for a woman when he felt like it had worn thin. He figured there was a certain amount of irony in that.

The truth was, he missed being married, especially to Dana Sue, who'd stolen his heart when they were fifteen and hadn't let loose of it yet. Why he hadn't had the sense to realize that a couple of years back, before he'd done something so totally stupid, was beyond him.

Thanks to his recent talks with Annie, he knew his ex-wife hadn't found someone else. Of course, that didn't mean she'd take him back. If he did return to Serenity, he was going to have his work cut out for him trying to win her over, but maybe two years was long enough for her to have cooled down just a little. She might not pull a shotgun on him on sight. At least he hoped not. He knew for a fact she could hit a tin can at fifty feet. If she aimed for him, she wouldn't miss.

And even if she hit him, as long as she didn't hit anything vital, so what? He had it coming. And, hell, he thought with a grin, what was life without a little excitement and risk from time to time? He just needed an excuse to get his foot in the door. If winning Dana Sue back was meant to be, he figured one would come along sooner or later.

At quitting time, he climbed down off the roof, grabbed a bottle of water and took a long swallow, then doused himself with the rest of it.

Thanksgiving, he decided, with the first real anticipation he'd felt in two long years. If fate hadn't handed him the right excuse by then, he was heading home and taking his chances.

Dana Sue and Maddie took their iced tea—unsweetened for Dana Sue, which was practically a crime in these parts—onto the shaded brick patio out back of The Corner Spa. At eight in the morning the air was still a reasonably pleasant seventy-five, but the humidity and bright sun promised a scorcher by day's end. It would be another couple of months before that humidity loosened its grip on South Carolina, probably just in time for Thanksgiving.

Inside, a half dozen women were already working out, and a few more were in the café, having Dana Sue's no-fat, high-fiber raisin bran muffins with bowls of fresh fruit.

"Where's Helen?" Dana Sue asked when she and Maddie were settled.

"Taking a shower upstairs," Maddie said. "She's been here working out since before the doors opened."

Dana Sue regarded her friend with disbelief. "Helen? *Our* Helen?"

"She had another appointment with Doc Marshall yesterday," Maddie explained. "He read her the riot act about her blood pressure again. It's way too high for a woman who's only forty-one. He reminded her she was supposed to cut down on stress and get more exercise. So, for today at least, she's determined to stick to her workout regimen."

"Want to lay odds on how long it lasts this time?" Dana Sue said. "She was totally committed a couple of months ago, but then her caseload got heavy and she was back to working fourteen-hour days. There were a few weeks there when we didn't even see her."

"I know," Maddie said. "She's a type-A personality through and through. I'm not sure she can change. I've talked to her till I'm blue in the face, but she certainly isn't listening to me."

"Who won't listen to you?" Helen asked, grabbing a chair and sitting.

"You, as a matter of fact," Maddie said, without the slightest trace of guilt about talking behind Helen's back.

"I've been in the gym for the last hour, haven't I?" she grumbled, obviously guessing the topic. "What more do you want?"

"We want you to take better care of yourself," Dana Sue said gently. "Not for one day or a week, but from here on out."

Helen frowned. "Isn't that the pot calling the kettle black?"

"Yes," Dana Sue readily admitted. It was so much easier to tackle Helen's health issues than her own or Annie's.

"I'm not discussing this," Helen said. "Doc Marshall gave me a piece of his mind. I took it to heart. End of story."

Dana Sue exchanged a look with Maddie, but neither of them said a word. If they pushed any harder, Helen would only dig in her heels and start avoiding them. It would be just the excuse she needed to stay away from the gym entirely, even if she did have a major financial stake in the place.

Helen nodded in satisfaction at their silence. "Thank you.

Now then, on a far more pleasant subject, I looked over the books last night," she said. "Memberships are up."

"Ten percent over last month," Maddie confirmed. "Spa treatments have nearly doubled. And the café business has tripled. We're running well ahead of the projections in our business plan."

Dana Sue regarded her with surprise. "Really? Are we getting more café business at breakfast or lunch?"

"All day long," Maddie said. "We have one group of women who come in three times a week at four o'clock to work out, then have tea. They've been begging me to ask you to come up with a low-calorie, low-fat scone for them. They all went to London together a couple of years ago and got hooked on afternoon tea. They keep telling me what a civilized tradition it is to have a late-afternoon snack with pleasant company and conversation."

"Now there's an idea," Helen said thoughtfully. "Late afternoon is probably dead a lot of the time, right?"

"So far, and it's worse now that school's started again," Maddie agreed.

"I suppose some women are picking up kids from school," Helen suggested. "Others are at work or starting dinner preparations. An afternoon-workout-and-tea promotion might encourage a few more women who think a gym's not for them to give us a try. It might appeal to some retirees, who think they don't fit in with the younger crowd."

"I like it!" Dana Sue said eagerly. "Maybe we could even add in a mother-daughter promotion. That might lure in some of the moms who do car pool. It would save them from going home and fixing some snack for the kids, or leaving the kids to grab a fistful of cookies or some junk food. We can staff the day care room so the little ones will be out of their hair, while moms and daughters work out together."

Maddie and Helen exchanged a look.

"Are you thinking you and Annie could share something like that?" Maddie asked.

"Why not?" Dana Sue asked.

"Because, for one thing, afternoon must be the worst possible time for you to be away from the restaurant," Maddie said realistically.

"I could make it work for an hour," Dana Sue insisted. "It would just mean more prep work in the morning or letting Erik and Karen do a little more. She's only been at the restaurant for a few weeks, but Karen's turning into a very capable assistant. She picks up everything I tell her in no time. And, of course, Erik could run the place with one hand tied behind him. The only reason he doesn't is out of deference to me."

"Deference?" Helen inquired with a raised eyebrow. "Or fear for his life? I've got to say, I don't see you relinquishing that much control. That kitchen is your domain. You flipped out when somebody moved the refrigerator two inches while you weren't around. You claimed it threw off your stride when you were in a rush."

"I'm not *that* much of a control freak," Dana Sue said irritably.

"Oh, really? Since when?" Helen taunted.

"Okay, maybe I am, just like both of you," she conceded. "But it would be worth the sacrifice if it meant getting my daughter back on track and the two of us communicating more."

"I hate to say it, but I'm not sure I see a teenage girl wanting to spend time at a gym with her mother," Maddie said.

"Even one who's obsessed with her weight?" Dana Sue asked, disappointed, but trusting Maddie's instincts when it came to her daughter. Both Maddie and Helen seemed better able to read Annie these days than she was. Maybe it was their objectivity.

"Especially then," Maddie said. "This place is filled with mirrors, for one thing. People with body-image issues hate that. I've seen the way Annie shies away from looking in them whenever she stops by here."

"Then what do I do?" Dana Sue demanded. "You talked to Cal and Ty, Maddie, and they both said Annie's not eating, right? If she's not eating at home and she's not eating at school, then she has a problem. Am I supposed to let her starve herself before I do something?"

"Of course you can't ignore what's happening," Maddie soothed. "But you have to be smart about it. You need real proof before you confront her."

"Aside from her weight?" Dana Sue said. "I bet she doesn't weigh ninety pounds. Her clothes just hang on her. Maybe I should take her back to Doc Marshall and let him deal with her. Maybe he could scare some sense into her."

"Has he scared you?" Helen asked pointedly. Not waiting for an answer, she said, "No, because you've known him forever. All of us have known him forever. Heck, he used to give us lollipops. You don't listen to him. *I* don't listen to him."

"Which is a whole other issue," Maddie commented pointedly.

Helen shrugged off the warning. "Whatever. My point is that he's a big ole teddy bear who smokes in secret and probably has high blood pressure, high cholesterol and all the other stuff he warns us about. Who's going to take him seriously?"

Maddie frowned at her. "Just because he doesn't intimidate you doesn't mean he couldn't get through to Annie. Unfortunately, though, he'd only be speculating about whether she has an eating disorder, the same way we are. We need some sort of proof so Dana Sue can confront her with real evidence Annie can't possibly deny."

"Such as?" Dana Sue asked, frustrated. "Isn't the fact that she doesn't touch any food I put in front of her evidence enough?"

"She'll just claim she's eating when you're not around," Maddie said. "She might even toss food down the garbage disposal to make you think she's eaten it. I'm sure there are a lot of sneaky ways she can think of to reassure you, especially since you're not always there at mealtime."

"The scales don't lie," Dana Sue said. "Not that she'd let me get within ten feet of her when she's weighing herself."

Helen's expression turned thoughtful. "Maybe we're going about this all wrong. We're focusing completely on Annie, which probably makes her feel as if she's under a microscope."

Maddie nodded slowly. "I think you have a point. Do you suppose Annie's friends have eating disorders, as well?" she asked Dana Sue.

Dana Sue thought about that. She'd overheard some of them talking about dieting from time to time, but none were as painfully thin as Annie. To her they didn't seem any more obsessed about their weight than Dana Sue or her friends were.

"Not that I've noticed," she replied eventually. "Sarah Connors is around the house the most and she looks perfectly healthy. She and Annie talk about whatever fad diet is in the news, but Sarah eats the meals and snacks I fix for them. So do most of the others."

"You're sure of that?" Maddie asked.

"Well, I don't stand over them every second and watch, if that's what you're asking."

"Maybe you should," Helen countered.

"Are you crazy? Annie would flip out if I insisted on hanging out with her and her friends."

"Goodness knows, *we* would have," Maddie agreed. "But

could you suggest a sleepover? Maybe order pizzas, have a ton of snacks available, and bake some brownies and see how they handle it? Just stick your head in from time to time to see who's eating and who's not?"

Dana Sue regarded her quizzically. "You want me to spy on them?"

"Okay, it sounds ridiculous," Maddie admitted. "But it might give you some idea if this is just Annie's problem or if she's responding to peer pressure. And spying is a very under-rated tool for parents. We *need* to know what's going on with our kids. Period."

"Okay, let's say I buy that," Dana Sue said. "What will I really find out? If the food's gone, sure, then someone ate it. Or they flushed it down the toilet. Or they binged and purged. There's more than one eating disorder, you know."

"I agree with Maddie. I think it's worth a shot," Helen said. "What have you got to lose?"

Considering how little she knew about the eating habits of Annie's friends, maybe it would give her some much-needed insight, Dana Sue decided. "I suppose it could work," she conceded eventually. It might be a pretty flimsy lifeline, but she was desperate. She'd grab on to anything at this point.

Maddie beamed at her. "That's the spirit. Now let's talk about you."

Dana Sue frowned. "No can do. I've got to go."

"Not so fast," Helen said, latching on to her arm until she sank back down in her seat. "What has Doc Marshall told *you* lately?"

"That I'm still borderline diabetic, that I need to exercise, watch what I eat and check my blood sugar on a regular basis," she recited dutifully.

"And you're doing all that?" Maddie pressed.

"Yes," she said, though she didn't look either of them in the eye.

"Really?" Helen's skepticism was plain. "You must be using all this lovely, expensive exercise equipment we bought when I'm not around." She glanced at Maddie. "Is that right? Is Dana Sue in here, say, midmorning? Midafternoon?"

"Maybe I'm sneaking in after the place is closed!" she snapped. "And I don't know what gives you the right to question my exercise routine. Yours is no better."

"Agreed," Helen said at once. "Which is why I've come up with a suitable challenge for each of us."

"This isn't good," Maddie mumbled.

Dana Sue grinned. "No kidding."

"Okay, you two, I'm serious," Helen said. "I think we should each write down our goals, whatever they are, and a plan for reaching them. Whichever one of us sticks to the plan and achieves the goal wins something spectacular, to be paid for by the other two."

Maddie's eyes immediately lit up. She'd always loved a competition. And she loved winning almost as much as Helen did. "Do we each get to pick out our own prize?"

Helen nodded. "Seems only fair, don't you think?"

"Any price limit?" Dana Sue asked. "You're the only one of us raking in big bucks."

Helen grinned. "Which should be excellent motivation for each of you to want to beat me. However, I happen to know Sullivan's is way ahead of your financial projections, and if this place continues at its current pace, your cries of 'poor me' won't hold water. The Corner Spa is going to make us all rich. We deserve to splurge, and none of us is going to go bankrupt if we do. The profits from this place will see to that." She turned to Maddie. "So, what's your dream prize?"

"The sky's really the limit?" she asked, looking thoughtful.

"Why not?" Helen said with a shrug. "The whole idea is to motivate ourselves to work at this. The promise of a new dress or a pair of shoes won't cut it."

"Then I think a trip to Hawaii for my first anniversary would be wonderful," Maddie declared. "We probably couldn't take it till spring break, but I'd be willing to wait for that."

Helen made a note on her ever-present legal pad. "So, a first-class trip for two, or three counting the baby, since I can't see your mother looking after an infant. She's only recently adjusted to babysitting your other three and two of them are in their teens."

"Yes, it would definitely be for three," Maddie confirmed. "Cal would never agree to leave Jessica Lynn behind. He can barely make himself go out the door to work."

Helen turned to Dana Sue. "How about you? Any dream vacations you've been denying yourself? A new car? A fancy new kitchen at home?"

"I spend all day in a fancy new kitchen at the restaurant," Dana Sue said. "That's enough stainless steel for me. And I think travel's highly overrated."

"Only because you got lost on our senior trip to Washington, D.C.," Maddie teased. "No one's ever let you live that down, and you haven't left South Carolina since."

"Okay, no kitchen, no travel," Helen said. "What, then? Dream big."

There was only one thing Dana Sue really wanted for herself. She wanted a man in her life, the right man, one who would respect her and treat her as if she was the best thing that had ever happened to him. And, in the deepest, darkest corner of her heart, she wanted that man to be Ronnie Sullivan. Unfortunately, as much as Helen and Maddie loved her, they couldn't give her that. And as furious as they were with him, it wasn't a fantasy they'd encourage, anyway.

"I know what she wants," Maddie said quietly.

"What?" Helen asked.

Maddie's eyes locked with Dana Sue's. "She wants Ronnie back."

"I most certainly do not," she sputtered indignantly, out of habit or maybe self-defense or embarrassment. How shameful was it to still want a man she'd made such a huge production out of throwing out? "How could you even say such a thing, Maddie? You know what that man did to me. You were there to pick up the pieces. Ronnie Sullivan is the last thing I want. If I never see his sorry face again, it will be too soon."

Her two best friends regarded her with knowing expressions.

"Emphatic," Helen said.

"Too emphatic?" Maddie asked.

They both grinned, thoroughly pleased with themselves.

Dana Sue scowled. "Well, all I have to say is that if Ronnie Sullivan is your idea of a spectacular prize, then one of *you* take him. I don't want him. And the prospect of having him back certainly wouldn't motivate me to do anything except order a large pizza every single night for the rest of my life."

"Maybe she means it, after all," Maddie said, though she sounded doubtful.

"Okay, then, a spiffy little convertible," Helen suggested. "Red, maybe?"

Dana Sue grinned, relieved to have the topic of Ronnie behind her. "Now you're talking my language. And it better have a top-of-the-line stereo system, plus that navigational gizmo."

"That's definitely important," Maddie agreed, "since you have absolutely no sense of direction—thus the problems you had on the senior trip."

"Stop reminding me of that," Dana Sue retorted good-naturedly. "I get where I'm going."

"Eventually," Helen commented.

"Okay, smarty-pants, what about you?" Dana Sue asked her. "What's your big prize?"

"A shopping spree," Helen said without any hesitation.

"Was there ever any doubt?" Maddie asked wryly.

Helen scowled at her. "In Paris," she added.

"All right!" Maddie said enthusiastically. "And we all get to go."

Dana Sue laughed. "I'm liking this more and more. Now I almost don't care if Helen wins."

"No fair," Helen said. "You have to promise to really try to win your own prize."

"When does this contest start?" Maddie asked.

"As soon as we set our goals," Helen said. "And they need to be meaningful goals, ambitious but attainable, okay? Shall we meet same time tomorrow to share them and decide how long we have to attain them?"

"I'm in," Maddie said.

Dana Sue thought of the nifty little red sports car she'd seen the last time she and Annie had gone to Charleston. It had reminded her of a car Ronnie had had a long time ago, before they'd gotten married, long before things between them had gone so terribly wrong.

"Me, too," she said at once.

Maybe she'd never be thin and willowy again, but perhaps she could recapture that carefree, confident feeling she'd had at eighteen, when everything was right with her world. And maybe if she felt better about herself, she could find a way to teach Annie how to do the same thing.

3

Any thought of goal-setting flew out the window that night when a grease fire started in the kitchen in the middle of the dinner rush.

As soon as Karen shrieked, "Fire!" Erik grabbed an extinguisher and started spraying. Meanwhile, Karen raced for a phone and dialed 911, even though the small blaze was already mostly contained.

Assured that Erik had things under control in the kitchen, Dana Sue headed into the dining room to soothe the rattled patrons, then went outside to the patio to explain to customers there and to await the arrival of the firemen, whom she hoped to prevent from dragging their hoses through the restaurant. Thanks to Erik's quick reaction, there was no need for all those men and their equipment to plow through the place. In fact, by the time the volunteer firefighters arrived on the scene, there was little evidence of the blaze beyond frayed nerves, the lingering scent of smoke and the mess in the immediate vicinity of the greasy pan that had caught on fire.

Though she wouldn't really be able to tell until morning, it appeared there'd been no smoke damage at all to the dining room, with its pale-peach walls and dark-green trim. A trip to the laundry would take care of any lingering scent in the tablecloths and napkins.

"It was my fault. I am so sorry," Karen said for at least the tenth time after the fire chief had signed off and let them get back to business.

A struggling single mom in her midtwenties, Karen had tears streaming down her pale cheeks. She'd been a short-order cook at a local diner when Dana Sue discovered her. Seeing the waste of cooking talent, Dana Sue had offered to train her to handle the high-quality meals at Sullivan's.

"I just turned away for a second," Karen said. "I didn't realize the flame was so high. Then I panicked. I've never done anything like this before, I swear it."

"Hey, it's nothing," Dana Sue reassured her. "It's happened to all of us, right, Erik? There was no real harm done."

"I've never had a grease fire," Erik said, "but I've burned my share of pies and cakes and smoked up the kitchen."

"I'll stay late and clean up," Karen offered. "By the time you come in tomorrow, you won't even know it happened."

"We'll all pitch in," Dana Sue corrected. "We're a team. Now let's get back to work before all our customers stage a rebellion."

"I need to do something," Karen insisted. "Let me buy a glass of wine for every customer. It'll take me a while to pay for them, but it's the least I can do."

"It's already done," Dana Sue told her, "and you're not paying. The money comes out of our PR budget. Now, cook. We have ten backed-up orders for the grilled salmon, three for the pork chops and five for the fried catfish. Let's go, people."

The teamwork on which Dana Sue and her staff prided themselves kicked back into high gear. By nine o'clock all the customers had been fed and most were lingering over coffee and one of Erik's desserts.

As Dana Sue made the rounds of the tables in the dining room, almost everyone commented on the delicious meal, but most were eager to congratulate her on the way her staff had dealt with the crisis.

"If I hadn't heard the sirens and seen the firemen myself, I'd never have guessed you had a fire in the kitchen," the mayor told her. "You handled yourself really well, Dana Sue."

"Thank you," she said, surprised. She and Howard Lewis hadn't always seen eye to eye, particularly during the controversy over Maddie's relationship with the much-younger Cal Maddox. Now that the two were respectably married, apparently the mayor had forgotten all about the old animosity. Either that or his desire for a good meal had overcome his disapproval of her association with Maddie and Cal.

"Well, of course she handled the crisis just fine," Hamilton Rogers, chairman of the school board, said. "Those Sweet Magnolias always knew how to wriggle out of a tight spot." He winked at Dana Sue. "It was a trait they certainly needed growing up."

Dana Sue laughed. "We certainly did."

"Just how many times did you and Ronnie get caught trying to play hooky?" Hamilton asked.

Dana Sue gave him her most innocent look. "Why, I don't believe we ever got caught doing such a thing," she said.

The school board chairman chuckled. "You can admit it now, Dana Sue. We won't take away your diploma."

She shook her head. "Still not talking."

"Well, you definitely added a little excitement to our meal tonight," the mayor said. "Things have been a little too quiet in Serenity lately."

After the last of the customers was gone, Dana Sue joined her staff in the kitchen to do the cleanup. In two hours every surface was spotless, every inch of steel gleaming. Under even the best of circumstances, she was a fanatic about Sullivan's kitchen being ready for a health department inspection. She'd been doubly exacting tonight. By the time she finally got home, she was exhausted.

Spotting a light on in Annie's room, she tapped on the door. "Sweetie, you still awake?"

Annie glanced up from her computer and blinked, then looked at her clock. "Mom, where have you been? It's late. And you smell like smoke again. What did you burn this time?"

"We had a grease fire tonight. It turned out to be nothing, but it created quite a mess in the kitchen."

Annie's eyes widened in alarm. "You're okay? You're sure? Why didn't you call me? I would have come in to help you clean up."

Dana Sue heard the worry in her daughter's voice. Annie knew that any calamity at Sullivan's could turn their world upside down yet again, so Dana Sue sought to reassure her. "I know you would have, but Erik, Karen and I were able to handle it. Besides, it's a school night. I'm sure you had homework."

"Some," Annie agreed.

"Did you get something to eat?"

"Mom!" Annie protested, immediately on the defensive.

"It was just a question," Dana Sue said, her own hackles rising. "You didn't stop by the restaurant after school, so I wondered if you'd fixed something here."

"No, Sarah and I went to Wharton's with some other kids, just to hang out," Annie told her in a calmer tone.

Dana Sue relaxed and grinned. She perched on the edge of the bed, hoping for the kind of girl talk she and Annie had once shared. "I remember doing that when I was your age. I'll bet not a day went by that Maddie, Helen and I weren't there, along with whomever we were dating at the time."

"You were always with Dad, though, weren't you?" Annie said, then hesitated, as if trying to gauge her mother's reaction. When Dana Sue said nothing, she continued, "I mean, you guys were a couple when you were younger than me, right?"

Dana Sue nodded, lost for a second in the good memories. There had been a lot of them, but she'd buried most under the anger she'd needed just to keep going after Ronnie left.

"Dad was a hunk, huh?"

"He was," Dana Sue admitted. "The first time I saw him, after he and his family moved here from North Carolina, I thought he was the sexiest boy I'd ever seen. He had *danger* written all over him, from his coal-black, too-long hair to his leather jacket."

"Was that the only reason you liked him?" Annie asked. "Because he was so sexy-looking?"

"No, of course not," Dana Sue said nobly. "He was sweet and smart and funny, too."

Her daughter grinned. "I always thought it was because every other girl in school wanted him and you wanted to prove *you* could get him."

Dana Sue laughed. "Did your father tell you that?"

"Nope. Maddie did. She said you were so single-minded when it came to getting Dad to notice you."

"Yeah, I probably was," Dana Sue confessed. "He was the first boy who wouldn't even give me a second look. Naturally, that made him an irresistible challenge. And I knew he would make my folks a little crazy." She leaned closer and confided, "He had a tattoo, you know."

Annie giggled. "Maddie said he gave you a tough time on purpose, because if he'd made it easy, you'd have lost interest."

Dana Sue thought back and tried to imagine losing interest in Ronnie. She couldn't. Her feelings for him had been all-consuming for a long time. Not even nearly eighteen years of marriage had turned down the heat between them. An affair and two years of separation had only driven her to bury the attraction.

"I don't know," she told Annie. "I fell pretty hard, pretty fast."

"And you never regretted it, did you?" her daughter asked. "I mean, not till the end, when he was with that other woman."

Dana Sue didn't like even thinking about the day she'd found out about Ronnie's affair, much less reminiscing about it, but it was evident that Annie had been wanting to ask these questions for a long time. It was as if she'd been saving them up for the right moment. It was also evident she'd been turning to Maddie to find some of the answers she wanted. Dana Sue felt incredibly guilty that Annie hadn't been able to ask her own mother for the details of her parents' courtship.

"No, until the day he cheated on me—or the day I found out about it, anyway—I never regretted a single second with your dad." She felt Annie deserved total honesty, not an answer colored by far more recent bitterness and resentment.

"So, he made, like, this one huge mistake and that was it?" Annie said, frowning. "None of the rest mattered anymore?"

"That's the way I saw it," Dana Sue said. "Some betrayals are just too huge."

"Do you still feel that way?"

Dana Sue regarded her daughter with a puzzled look. "Why do you ask?"

"I just wondered how you'd feel if Dad came back to town. Could you forgive him now?"

It was the second time in one day that people Dana Sue loved had suggested it might be time for her to get over the past and move on, maybe even with that scum-of-the-earth, cheating ex of hers. She told herself that could only happen if she let her heart—or her hormones—overrule her head. Once Burned, Twice Shy was her motto.

"Sorry, baby. I know you'd like that, but it's not going to happen," she said. "When you're a little older and have fallen in love, maybe you'll understand why some things are simply unforgivable."

Before Annie could press her on it, she stood up. "You need to get some sleep, young lady. So do I."

She brushed a kiss across Annie's forehead. "Lights out, okay?"

To her surprise, her daughter's arms came around her waist. "I love you, Mom."

"Oh, sweetie, I love you, too," Dana Sue whispered, tears in her eyes. "And wherever he is, I know your dad loves you, as well. More than anything."

"I know," Annie said with a sniff. "Sometimes, I just wish he was here, you know?"

Dana Sue bit back a sigh. "Yeah," she admitted. "I do know."

There were times when she felt as if someone had carved out her heart and left her aching and empty inside. But that feeling paled compared to the anger she'd felt when she'd found out about his fling with some woman whose name he didn't even remember. Weighing the two emotions and adding in a healthy dose of pride, she'd had only one choice. Maybe someday she would even get used to living with it.

The phone rang, waking Dana Sue from a sound sleep. She slapped at the alarm, blaming it for the offending noise. When the shrill ringing continued, she fumbled for the phone.

"Where are you?" Helen demanded. "It's eight-thirty. Maddie and I have been waiting for half an hour."

Dana Sue sat up in bed and rubbed her eyes. "Why?" she mumbled.

"Our challenge," Helen reminded her. "Our goals."

"I don't have any, except to go back to sleep," Dana Sue muttered, and hung up.

Of course, the phone immediately rang again. "Get up. We're on our way over," Helen said crisply. "You have ten minutes to get the coffee brewing. You might want to squeeze in a shower, too. You sound like you could use a cold one to kick-start your brain."

This time when Dana Sue slammed the phone back in its cradle, she resigned herself to getting up. Helen had a key and wasn't afraid to use it. Nor would she hesitate to toss Dana Sue into that icy shower herself. Bossy woman!

She didn't bother with putting a robe on over her oversize Carolina Panthers T-shirt, one of the few things of Ronnie's she'd kept. She'd told herself she'd simply forgotten to add it to the pile of his clothing she'd stuffed haphazardly into suitcases and tossed onto the front lawn, but the truth was she'd slept in it for a long time after he'd gone because his scent had clung to it. Many washings later that was no longer the case, but some sentiment she didn't care to identify kept her wearing it every night.

She padded into the kitchen and put on the coffee, then went into the bathroom and brushed her teeth and splashed water on her face. She'd barely made it back to the kitchen when the back door opened and Helen and Maddie strolled in.

"Shouldn't you both be working?" Dana Sue inquired testily.

"We should be," Helen agreed. "But we had an important

appointment with our third partner at eight o'clock this morning. We thought finding out why you didn't show up took precedence over work." She wrinkled her nose. "And why does it smell like smoke in here?"

Dana Sue winced. "Actually, that's me. We had a little grease fire in the kitchen at the restaurant. No big deal, but I was there late, cleaning up the mess. I haven't had a chance to take a shower and wash my hair."

"You had a fire?" Maddie looked dismayed. "Why didn't you call us?"

"Before or after we called the fire department?" Dana Sue said. "Or perhaps you two have become volunteer firefighters without telling me."

"Why didn't you call us *later*?" Maddie asked. "We could have helped you clean up."

"My staff did that," Dana Sue said. "And before you ask, I have not even had time to think about my goals or my action plan."

"Not a problem," Helen said briskly. She got out cups and poured coffee for all of them. "We'll help."

"But this is supposed to be my goal and my action plan," Dana Sue protested.

Helen gave her a chiding look. "Surely you don't mind a little input from the two people who know you best."

"Do I get to critique your plans?" Dana Sue asked suspiciously.

"Absolutely." Maddie nodded.

At the exact same moment, Helen said, "No."

Dana Sue grinned. "I thought so. In that case, Maddie, you can help with mine. Helen, keep your mouth shut."

Maddie laughed. "You are such a dreamer. Don't you remember? Helen is the biggest control freak of us all."

"Which is exactly why I want her to butt out," Dana Sue said.

"This whole challenge was my idea," Helen reminded them. "That gives me the right to butt in." She whipped a legal pad out of her briefcase. "Now tell me what your primary goal is, Dana Sue. Losing weight? Keeping your blood sugar in check?"

"Getting you out of my kitchen so I can get ready to go to work," she countered. "As you noted when you called here, I'm running late. I can't send all my customers to McDonald's just because you've set some deadline for getting this challenge of ours under way. Why are you in such a rush, anyway? It's not as if we haven't needed health goals for ourselves for months now."

Helen flushed guiltily. "I promised Doc Marshall I would give him a concrete plan by next week with proof I'm sticking to it, so he wouldn't insist on starting me on medication to bring down my blood pressure. I figured sworn affidavits from the two of you would do the trick. He's a little jaded where I'm concerned these days, but he trusts you two." She grinned at Dana Sue. "Well, Maddie, anyway."

"It might be more effective if you actually got your blood pressure down a little bit," Maddie commented wryly. "Have you considered, oh, taking a day off, perhaps? Having a relaxing massage at the spa? Trying a little meditation?"

"How can I do any of that?" Helen demanded. "I have two trials scheduled this month. Should I just hand my clients a note from my doctor, then tell them I'm not prepared because I needed a day off?"

"You know, I was reading about exactly that kind of thing the other day," Maddie said. "It was about the whole concept of the Sabbath, not necessarily in a religious context, but just in terms of people needing more than ever to take time for themselves to reflect and relax. Remember when we were kids and no one did anything on Sunday except go to church and hang out with family and friends? Now it's just another day to be crammed with things to do from morning to night. No wonder we never feel refreshed."

"Maddie's exactly right," Dana Sue said. "Your mind would probably be a lot clearer and sharper, Helen, if you gave it a break once in a while." She pointed at the legal pad. "Write that down. It needs to be one of your goals."

"We were not discussing my goals," Helen said.

"Actually, we were," Maddie stated. "And your need to have them so Doc Marshall will let you off the hook. You want testimony from the two of us, you better write down 'one day a week of actual relaxation' and stick to it."

"Oh, for heaven's sake," she grumbled, but jotted it down.

"Very good," Dana Sue said. "Now I really do have to get ready for work, you guys. I promise I'll work on my goals today and we can compare notes tomorrow, okay?"

"I suppose it will have to do," Helen said reluctantly. "I'm due at the office in a few minutes myself. I have a new client coming in for a consultation."

Dana Sue walked the two of them to the door. "I'll see you tomorrow morning," she promised.

They'd already stepped outside when Maddie turned back. "I don't suppose you had time to talk to Annie about a sleepover, did you?"

"No, but last night we did have one of the best conversations we've had in a long time. I'll bring up the sleepover thing when I see her tonight."

"Don't put it off," Maddie stressed.

"I won't." Not only was it important, but as Dana Sue already knew, her two best friends would hound her until she did it. It would be easier just to get it over with.

* * *

"Mom, that is so lame," Annie declared when her mother came up with this crazy sleepover idea. "I mean, how old do you think I am—six?"

"When I was your age, girls got together all the time. We ate pizza and popcorn, experimented with makeup and talked about boys."

"You and Maddie and Helen?" Annie guessed.

"And a few others," her mom said. "It was fun."

"What about boys?" Annie asked.

"We talked about them," her mother said, looking faintly puzzled.

"I mean, could I have boys over, too?"

"You mean for a couple of hours?" her mother asked.

"No, for the whole sleepover. We'd play music, dance, whatever. It would be really cool."

"Not a chance! Not under my roof, anyway," her mom said, as if Annie had suggested some kind of orgy or something. "Are you crazy? That's just asking for trouble."

"Mom, it's not like we'd *do* anything. You'd be right here."

"I don't care. It's a terrible idea. I can't imagine the other parents would go along with it."

Annie studied her mother speculatively. Ever since her dad had left, her mom could be talked into a lot of things if Annie played her cards right. "What if the other parents said okay?" she coaxed. "Would you let us do it then?"

"Absolutely not," her mother said, holding firm.

"Then forget it! I don't want to spend the night with a bunch of girls. Like I said, it's totally lame."

Now it was her mother's turn to give her an odd, curious look. "When you went to Sarah's a couple of weeks ago, were there boys there that night?"

Oops! Annie thought. No one was supposed to find out about that. No parents, anyway. "Of course not," she lied.

"I will find out if you're not telling me the truth," her mother warned.

Annie just rolled her eyes. Her mom was clueless. There were at least a dozen things she'd done that her mom would flip out about if she ever found out about them.

"Don't give me that look," her mother said. "I can make a few calls and your goose will be cooked."

"Not likely," Annie said. She couldn't think of a single soul who'd blab. Just in case, though, she probably ought to get her mother off on another track. "Maybe having Sarah over would be okay. And Raylene," she added. "But that's it."

"Friday night," her mom suggested, looking pleased. "And if you decide to ask a few more girls, it would be okay."

Perfect, Annie thought. Her mom never got home from the restaurant before midnight on Fridays and Saturdays. If the guys stopped by, she just had to get them out the door by eleven forty-five. And if she could convince Ty to be one of those guys, even if she got caught, maybe her mom would think of Ty as a chaperone or something. Even though Annie didn't think of him that way, her mom always said she was lucky to have him as kind of a surrogate big brother. *As if,* Annie thought.

She gave her mother an impulsive hug, noting once again that she'd probably gained another five pounds just since she'd opened the spa with Maddie and Helen. It wasn't a very good recommendation for the place, in Annie's opinion.

"Mom, I thought you were going on a diet," she said accusingly.

"I am on a diet, but at my age it's harder to lose weight," her mom said, immediately on the defensive, which was where Annie liked her to be.

"I thought that's why you guys opened that gym, so you could exercise and kick your metabolism back into gear. I'll bet you don't even spend ten minutes a day on the treadmill there, do you?"

"I do when I can," she responded, her expression tense.

"Well, if you don't lose it, you're going to get sick and die like Grandma," Annie said. "And I will not go and live with Dad." She said it matter-of-factly, but the truth was the possibility terrified her—not of getting to be with her dad, but of her mom dying.

"I don't think you need to worry about that," she answered. "I have no intention of dying anytime soon, and we don't even know where your father is."

"*I* know," Annie blurted without thinking. "He's working down in Beaufort and living in some dump."

Her mom looked stunned. "How do you know that? He sends his support checks through his attorney."

Seeing the dismay on her mother's face, Annie immediately felt guilty for keeping her dad's calls a secret. "He's phoned once or twice," she admitted, unwilling to say it had been that many times just in the past couple of weeks. It wasn't like her mom had ever said she couldn't talk to him, or even see him if she wanted to. But initially Annie had made such a big deal about not taking his calls or visiting him that she hadn't wanted to admit it when she'd finally started talking to him. It would have felt as if she were betraying her mom.

"When?"

"While you're at work. He calls me on my cell phone, mostly."

"I see," her mother said, looking suddenly weary.

Annie could tell she wanted to say more, but she just turned and left the room…probably to get something to eat, if Annie knew anything about her. That was exactly why Annie had kept the calls a secret.

"I swear to God, if I could have gotten my hands on Ronnie right that second, I would have strangled him on the spot," Dana Sue declared to Maddie the next morning in the gym. "I know I'm being ridiculous, that Annie has a right to talk to her dad, but I know he talked her into keeping it a secret."

"Are you sure about that?" Maddie asked. "Maybe Annie was afraid it would hurt you to know they were talking again."

Dana Sue scowled. "So now my own daughter's afraid to be honest with me? Isn't *that* great. Just one more giant gap between us. And before you ask, no, I have not set my goals. I was too furious to sit down and think about it last night, and I came straight here first thing this morning. You might as well call Helen and tell her, because I'm not up to her bullying me about it."

"You need to work off some of that anger," Maddie said, her tone soothing. "Why don't you tell me the rest while we walk on the treadmills?"

"I hate the damn treadmill!" Dana Sue snapped. "I'm getting a blueberry muffin. I'll be out on the patio when you finish being noble."

Maddie merely sighed. "I'll come with you."

After they were seated, Dana Sue picked the blueberries out of the muffin and ate them, managing to leave most of the muffin on the plate. "I know I have no business eating this stuff, so don't even say it," she muttered.

"Not saying a word," Maddie responded mildly.

Dana Sue pushed the plate away. "It's been two damn

years," she said heatedly. "How can the mere mention of that man still get me so worked up?"

"Do you want an honest answer or was that a rhetorical question?" Maddie asked.

"An honest answer, please."

"You're still in love with him."

"Don't be absurd!"

Maddie shrugged. "You asked for honesty. Try being honest with yourself. And to be brutally honest, I'd say your reaction last night was just plain jealousy."

Dana Sue stared at her friend incredulously. "You think I was jealous that my daughter has been talking to Ronnie?"

"Weren't you?"

She bit back her inclination to snap out a denial, then frowned at Maddie. "You know me too damn well."

Maddie grinned. "Yes, I do." She studied Dana Sue for a moment. "What are you going to do about it?"

"Nothing. Are you nuts? The man cheated on me. I wouldn't let him back into my life if he crawled on his knees."

"Yeah, right," Maddie murmured, her skepticism plain.

"I have my pride," Dana Sue added.

"In spades," she concurred.

"Well, then, you know I mean what I say."

"I know you *want* to mean it," Maddie said. "But if Ronnie Sullivan walked through that door right now, looking all sexy and sassy the way he always did, I wouldn't want to bet against him."

Unfortunately, if she was being totally honest, neither would Dana Sue. Fortunately, she doubted she'd ever be put to that test. If Ronnie had even half a grain of sense left in that handsome head of his, he'd never set foot in Serenity again.

Of course, if he'd loved her the way he'd claimed to, he

never would have cheated on her. And—this was the kicker she always came back to—he would have stayed and fought for her. Sure, she'd made it plain she didn't want him here. She'd even had Helen lay down all sorts of ground rules about his having only limited contact with Annie, which the idiot had actually agreed to. He should have known she was reacting in the heat of the moment, making outrageous demands because she was hurt. He knew her better than anyone, even better than Maddie or Helen, which was saying something. He knew she blew sky-high when her temper kicked in, then simmered for a while, then cooled down. But he'd gone anyway. He hadn't waited around to see if she'd give him a second chance. That had told her all she really needed to know. He'd wanted to go. That was the bottom line.

She'd never admit it to a living, breathing soul, but that was what had hurt more than anything—Ronnie hadn't loved her enough to stay. And that was his most unforgivable sin of all.

4

Ronnie was sitting in some dive of a bar with Toby Keith in the background singing a song about a "Dear John" note. Every time the singer repeated in a low, sad tone, "She's gone," Ronnie thought of Dana Sue. She was gone, all right, and he still didn't have the first clue about how to win her back. He'd spent two years pondering the problem and, beyond his decision to do something by Thanksgiving, he was no closer to an action plan now than he'd been on the day he'd left Serenity.

Funny that twenty-seven years ago, when his family had moved to Serenity, he'd seen exactly what he needed to do to win Dana Sue's heart. Even at fourteen he'd noticed how the boys swarmed around her, drawn not only to her long legs and developing chest, but to her easy temperament and laughter. He'd also realized that the only way to stand out from the crowd would be to feign indifference. Sure enough, that had caught her attention. He hadn't pursued Dana Sue. She'd come after him. He wondered if that technique would work again.

Probably not, he concluded sadly. He'd been gone two years, and as near as he could tell, she wasn't pining for him. She certainly hadn't chased after him.

As he continued pondering a strategy, a thirtysomething

woman wearing tight jeans, a low-cut tank top and spike heels slid onto the stool next to him. Her black hair was long and straight and her lipstick was as red as her tank top. She was a stark contrast to Dana Sue's leggy, wholesome appearance. Most men would have found her sexy, but to Ronnie she was simply trying too hard.

"Hey, sugar, you look like you could use some company," she said in a low purr that should have set his pulse racing.

He met her gaze, took a long, slow sip of his beer and tried to work up some enthusiasm for whatever she was offering. But pretty as she was, she wasn't the woman he wanted.

Still, he forced a smile out of sheer habit. "Buy you a drink?"

"Sure," she said. "A light beer."

He beckoned the bartender over and placed the order, then swirled his own beer around in the glass, wondering why not one of the women who'd come on to him since his divorce had held any appeal. Maybe what he should have been asking himself was why one woman had managed to sneak through his defenses back when he'd still been very much married. To his everlasting regret, he couldn't even remember what she'd looked like, or any highlight of their conversation.

"You want to talk about it?" his companion inquired, taking a sip of her beer. "My name's Linda, by the way. Folks say I'm a real good listener." She leaned in closer. "Among other things."

Ronnie gave her another speculative once-over, but the attraction just wasn't there for him.

"Come on," she prodded. "Every man has a story he's just dying to tell."

"Not me," he insisted.

"Broken heart, then," she concluded. "Men hate talking about being dumped."

"The broken heart wasn't mine," he corrected, then thought about it. In the end, his heart had been just as shattered as Dana Sue's, and he'd had a load of guilt to go along with it.

"What did you do?" Linda asked. "Sleep around on her?"

"Something like that," he admitted.

"Then I imagine you'll do it again. Men always do."

"Is that so?"

"In my experience, anyway."

Amused by her world-weary attempt at wisdom, he said, "Then you must have real bad taste in men."

She laughed. "Says the guy I've been coming on to for the past five minutes."

"Like I said, bad taste," he agreed. "But your luck's about to change, because I'm going to do you a favor and take off." He put some bills on the bar, then met her disappointed gaze. "And just so you know, if I ever convince my ex-wife to take me back, she'll have nothing to worry about. I learned my lesson. She's the only one for me."

"You gonna try to sell me some of that swamp land east of here next?"

"Nope. I'm just gonna wish you better luck with the next guy who comes along," he said, and walked away.

"I wonder if this ex of yours knows she's a lucky woman," she called after him.

Ronnie chuckled at that. "I most seriously doubt it, unless she considers herself damn lucky that I'm gone."

"Then she's a fool," his new friend said.

Ronnie shook his head. "No," he said in an undertone not meant to be heard, "that was me."

And sometime in the next couple of months, he was going to try to convince Dana Sue of that.

Back in his dingy room at the motel his boss had made a deal with for the out-of-town construction crew, Ronnie checked the time, figured Dana Sue would still be at the restaurant and called Annie on her cell phone. After the first few months of sounding either angry or distant or both, she'd finally let down her guard. They'd almost recaptured the closeness they'd once shared. He treasured these calls and he was pretty sure Annie did, too. He missed his daughter as much as he missed Dana Sue. The months when Annie had frozen him out had taken a real toll on him, but he'd kept calling.

"Dad!" she said eagerly, sounding like her old self. "How are you?"

"I'm good," he lied, then listened to the loud background noise on Annie's end of the line. "Where are you, baby? It sounds like you're at a party."

"Wait a sec. I'll go in the other room so I can hear you," she said.

It was suddenly quiet on the other end of the line. "Where are you?" Ronnie asked again.

"At home. I have a few friends over."

Ronnie might not be in line for any parent-of-the-year awards, but that didn't sound good. "Isn't your mom at work?" he asked.

Annie hesitated for a long moment, then said, "Yes, but she said I could have a sleepover tonight. In fact, it was her idea."

"That's great," he enthused, but a vague suspicion that Annie was bending the truth continued to nag at him. He finally put his finger on it and asked, "Didn't I hear some male voices?"

"Must have been the music," she said glibly. "How are you, Dad?"

"I'm fine, and don't try to change the subject, young lady. I seriously doubt your mother would be happy that there are boys over when she's not there."

"Ty's here," she said excitedly. "You always liked him."

"Of course I did, but not at home with my daughter and her friends when there's no adult in the house," Ronnie said. "Is he the only guy there?"

"No," she admitted.

"Sweetie, you know that's not a good idea. Does your mom know about the boys coming by?"

The long silence that greeted the question pretty much answered it. He let it go on, knowing that Annie was incapable of lying to him. She might avoid the truth, but she wouldn't outright lie.

Eventually she asked, "Are you gonna call Mom and tell her?"

Though she'd tried to sound meek, Ronnie heard the knowing tone in her voice and figured she was counting on him not to do that. He debated surprising her by making the call, but he doubted Dana Sue would be happy about the news or about his being the messenger. Maybe he could settle this himself and save them both a lot of grief.

"You have them out of there in the next five minutes and it'll be our secret," he told Annie. "Deal?"

"But, Dad—"

"That's the deal. Take it or leave it."

"How will you even know if they're still here?"

"I suppose I won't know for sure. But I'm trusting you to keep your word. You going to give it to me, or do I call your mom?"

"I should go ahead and let you call her," Annie said. "At least it would get the two of you talking again."

"Okay with me," he said. "What's it going to be, kiddo?"

Again, he let the silence build, knowing she was struggling with herself over doing the right thing.

"I'll tell the boys they have to leave," she finally said grudgingly. "But we weren't doing anything wrong, Dad. I swear it. You know Ty always looks out for me. He would never let things get out of control."

"You had them over without your mom's permission," Ronnie said. "You were doing something wrong the second you let them in the door."

"When did you get so strict?" she grumbled.

"Last five minutes," he replied, chuckling. "Up till now, you never gave me any reason to think I needed to be strict."

"If you came home, you'd know what I was up to all the time," she said.

"I imagine you'd see that as a mixed blessing in no time at all," he responded.

"Probably," she admitted, then added, "But it would be worth it, Daddy. I miss you."

"I miss you, too, angel. Now, go send those boys packing. Then you and your girlfriends can talk about them all night long, the way you did when you were a few years younger."

"Did you and Mom actually listen to us?" Annie asked indignantly.

"Never," he said piously. "We just interpreted the giggles coming from your room. Those were a dead giveaway, at least to your mom. Don't forget, she was your age once. There's not much you could do or think that she didn't do before you, including breaking the rules."

"That's what you think," Annie muttered.

"What?" he said sharply, not liking her tone.

"I love you, Daddy."

He sighed and let it go. Long-distance parenting pretty

much sucked. "Love you, too, baby. Take care of yourself and give your mom a hug. Just don't tell her it's from me."

"I wish things were different," Annie said wistfully. "I wish they could go back to the way they were."

"Me, too. Now, go shoo those boys out before your mom catches them there and we both end up in hot water."

"'Night, Daddy."

"'Night, angel."

Ronnie clung to the phone for a long time after Annie had hung up. She was growing up so fast and he was missing it. Maybe it was his own fault. Maybe he even deserved to be shut out of Annie's life. According to Helen, Dana Sue had wanted him gone completely from both their lives, but he'd balked at that. He'd demanded visitation rights. What he hadn't guessed was how hard it would be to get Annie to go along with them. His teenage daughter was every bit as stubborn as her mom, but she, at least, was mellowing.

He realized now what he should have seen two years ago. He didn't have to let things be that way forever. Dana Sue might not be happy about him moving back to town, but she'd just have to get over it if he and Annie wanted to reestablish their relationship. And while he might not know that much about teenage girls, he knew a whole lot about teenage boys. Annie could use a dad around to keep her from making the kind of mistakes that could ruin her life.

Once again, he resolved to figure out some way to go back to Serenity before he missed out on even more memories.

Dana Sue was ninety percent certain that the car pulling away from her house as she drove up was filled with teenage boys. Cursing under her breath, she turned into the driveway. It was a good thing she'd decided to leave the restaurant half an hour earlier than usual. She was sure Annie must have calculated the boys' departure based on her usual time for getting home.

When she walked into the kitchen, Sarah regarded her with a startled expression that bore a trace of guilt. With her basic honesty and pale, freckled complexion, she lied poorly and blushed easily. Her cheeks were a telltale rosy pink right now.

"Hi, Mrs. Sullivan," she said with obviously forced cheer. "Great party. Thanks for letting us stay over."

"Anytime," Dana Sue said. "I'm glad Annie decided to make it a big party, instead of just asking you and Raylene. Everyone having fun?"

"Absolutely. We all brought over some CDs and we've been dancing. We'll probably watch a DVD after a while. Annie says you guys have a whole bunch of chick flicks."

"Our favorites," Dana Sue confirmed. "Is there enough food?"

"Plenty," Sarah confirmed. "I can't remember the last time I stuffed myself with pizza, and those brownies you brought home from the restaurant are fabulous. I've had two."

Dana Sue fought the urge to ask whether Annie had indulged in either the pizza or the brownies. Sarah took it out of her hands.

"You want to know if Annie's had any, don't you?" she asked.

Dana Sue nodded. "You know why it matters, don't you, Sarah? If it weren't so important, I would never ask you to rat on her. I'm afraid she's in real trouble."

"I know. I worry about her, too," Sarah admitted in a low voice. "I think she's—"

"Sarah, what's taking so long?" Annie called out, walking into the kitchen. When she spotted the two of them together, her eyes immediately narrowed in suspicion. "Hi, Mom. You're early. How come?"

"Erik said he could handle things, so I decided to make an early night of it," Dana Sue said, disappointed that Annie's untimely interruption had kept Sarah from answering her question. She forced a smile. "Having fun, baby?"

"We're having a great time, aren't we, Sarah?"

"The best," she confirmed, avoiding Dana Sue's eyes.

"You're not going to hang out with us, are you?" Annie demanded.

"Of course not," Dana Sue said, noting her daughter's flushed cheeks and wondering if that was due to excitement or guilt about the boys who'd been there. "I'm heading up-stairs to bed."

Annie nodded. "Okay, then. Sarah, I'll help you grab those sodas. Everybody's hot from dancing."

Dana Sue waited while the girls took half a dozen cans of diet soda and bottled water from the refrigerator. As they left the room, Sarah glanced back and gave a subtle shake of her head to say that Annie hadn't been eating along with every-one else. Dana Sue felt like sitting down at the kitchen table and crying.

She'd wanted so badly to believe that all her instincts were wrong, that Annie wasn't anorexic, after all. She'd watched her so closely for the past year, redoubling her efforts after that fainting spell at Maddie's reception. But obviously Annie was more clever at hiding her eating disorder than Dana Sue was at detecting it. She could blame it on her schedule, being away from home for too many meals, but she'd tried to supervise Annie's diet, she really had. She'd insisted she come by the restaurant for dinner. She'd packed nutritious lunches. But the honest-to-God truth was she hadn't been there to see that every bite went into her daughter's mouth. As for the obvious signs that Annie was in crisis, she'd obviously been in deep denial.

No more, though. They were going to have to confront this head-on. It was time. Past time. Add in the fact that Annie had apparently had boys over in direct defiance of Dana Sue's instructions, and tomorrow was going to be a tough day. She and her daughter were going to have a heart-to-heart, and Annie wasn't going to like the outcome—a visit to Doc Marshall's office and then being grounded for a month—one bit.

With the music downstairs playing at a deafening volume, Dana Sue finally managed to fall into a restless, troubled sleep around two in the morning. She'd barely closed her eyes, it seemed, when someone started frantically shaking her.

"Mrs. Sullivan, wake up!" Sarah commanded, sounding panicked.

Dana Sue's eyes snapped open. "What's wrong?"

"It's Annie," the girl said, tears streaking down her face. "She's passed out and we can't wake her up. Hurry, please."

Dana Sue tore down the stairs with the sobbing Sarah on her heels. The other girls were kneeling around a prostrate Annie.

"I don't think she's breathing," Raylene said, looking up at Dana Sue with wide eyes. "I've been giving her CPR, just the way we learned to in health class."

"Move," Dana Sue said, drawing on some inner reserve of calm, even though she was terrified. "Someone call 911, okay?"

"I already have," one of the girls said, sounding scared.

"Thanks. Keep an eye out for them, please?" Dana Sue said, focusing on Annie's pale face. Her lips were turning blue and she was still. So damn still. Kneeling beside her, Dana Sue began doing chest compressions as she'd been taught in her own CPR classes, then trying to force breath into her lungs. The girls stood around in stricken silence, holding hands, their faces damp with tears.

Time seemed to stand still as Dana Sue tried desperately to breathe life back into her daughter. She was only dimly aware of the sirens when the ambulance arrived. Then the EMTs were there, forcing her aside, taking over, talking in a code she didn't understand as they barked information about resting heart rate and other vital signs into a cell phone that apparently linked them to the emergency room. Sarah slipped up beside Dana Sue and clung to her hand.

"She's going to be okay," Sarah whispered. "She's going to be okay."

Dana Sue squeezed her hand. "Of course she is," she agreed, though she was certain of no such thing.

Raylene approached. "I called Mrs. Maddox," she said. "Is that okay? She said she'd phone Ms. Decatur and have her come by and pick us up. Mrs. Maddox is coming straight here to go with you to the hospital."

Dana Sue gave Raylene a grateful look. "You did exactly the right thing," she told her, impressed by the girl's ability to act so quickly in a crisis. She had a cool head and good instincts. "Thank you."

"We want to go to the hospital with you," Sarah said. "Can we do that? Our folks aren't expecting us home, anyway. Please, Mrs. Sullivan. Ms. Decatur can take us there just as easily as she can take us home."

Dana Sue knew what it was like to wait for information when someone was seriously ill. She'd waited all alone in a hospital emergency room when her mother had been taken in that last time. She'd been only a few years older than these girls were now. Annie had been little more than a toddler, and Ronnie had stayed home with her. Maddie and Helen had rushed over the second Dana Sue had called them, but the wait for them and for news had seemed interminable. Maybe it would be easier for Annie's friends to wait together at the hospital, where they would have news as soon as it was available.

"Okay," she said at last. "But as soon as it's morning, I want you to call your folks and tell them where you are, okay? Then it will be up to them whether you go home or stay."

"I'm sure Annie will be fine by then," Sarah said staunchly.

"Of course she will be," Raylene agreed.

The next half hour was a blur as the EMTs loaded Annie, who was breathing now, but still unconscious, into the ambulance. Helen briskly piled the girls into her car, and Maddie saw to it that Dana Sue pulled herself together, then wrapped an arm around her waist and guided her into her car. She still wore Ronnie's shirt, but had at least added a respectable pair of jeans.

"Annie's going to be fine," Maddie said, giving Dana Sue's hand one last squeeze before she started the engine and pulled out of the driveway.

"She wasn't breathing," Dana Sue said, shivering despite the warm night. "It was as if her heart had just stopped. It's this damned eating disorder, I know it. God, Maddie, what if she…?" She couldn't even voice the question.

"She's breathing now," her friend reminded her. "Focus on that. You heard the EMTs. She was breathing okay on her own when they left the house."

Dana Sue frowned at her. "Don't make it sound as if this was nothing. It's not like when she fainted at your wedding. People don't lose consciousness and stop breathing unless it's serious. She could have had a cardiac arrest or a stroke or something. What kind of mother am I to let things get this bad?"

"Stop thinking the worst," Maddie commanded. "You're a wonderful mother, and whatever happened, she's in good hands now. There are specialists on call at the hospital and I'm sure they'll be there by the time the ambulance arrives."

Dana Sue nodded, but she wasn't consoled. What if the damage was already done? What if whatever had happened was so terrible her beautiful girl never fully recovered?

Dana Sue wanted to pray, wanted to bargain with God to save her baby, but she couldn't find the words, couldn't think at all. It was as if she'd awakened from a deep sleep to find herself living a nightmare.

"Dana Sue?" Maddie repeated, finally getting her attention.

"What? Did you say something?"

"I asked if you'd given any thought to calling Ronnie," her friend said quietly. "He deserves to know what's going on. Annie is his daughter, too, and whatever you think of him, he always adored her."

"I know," Dana Sue whispered, tears stinging her eyes as she remembered the way Ronnie had doted on Annie from the moment she was born. In the early days he'd been as eager as she was to get up for the middle-of-the-night feedings. More than once, she'd found him rocking Annie back to sleep with a look of such profound awe on his face it had made her cry. There was an entire album filled with pictures of the two of them. Dana Sue had shoved it to the back of a closet and buried it under blankets after he'd gone.

"I know I should call him," she conceded, "but I don't know if I can cope with this and seeing him, too."

"I don't think you have a choice," Maddie said. "Besides, you're stronger than you think. You can cope with whatever you have to as long as you keep reminding yourself that getting Annie well is the only thing that matters."

"Knowing her dad was here would mean the world to her," Dana Sue admitted. Before the divorce, the bond between father and daughter had been one of the things she'd loved most about Ronnie. That bond had deepened as Annie had gotten older and gone from pleading for piggyback rides to learning to ride a bike or to hit a baseball in an attempt to impress Ty. It was Dana Sue's fault that bond had been broken. She was the one who'd dragged Annie into the middle of her pain and resentment. And when she should have been relieved to discover that those two were talking again, she'd been jealous, just as Maddie had said.

"Call him," Maddie urged. "Do you know how to reach him?"

"I know he's somewhere around Beaufort. I can probably reach him on his cell phone. I doubt he's had the number changed. And if that doesn't work, I'll bet Annie has his number tucked away somewhere."

"Try his cell," Maddie instructed. "If you don't get him, I'll go back to the house and look through Annie's address book."

"I'll wait till we get to the hospital and find out how she's doing," Dana Sue said, wanting to put off making the call as long as possible. She didn't want to hear Ronnie's voice, didn't want to hear even the slightest accusation that she'd somehow failed as a mother, or else how could this have happened? It was one thing to blame herself, but to see the blame in his eyes would destroy her.

Maddie regarded her with a disappointed expression, but said nothing.

Dana Sue sighed at her unspoken disapproval. "Okay, I'll try him now."

But how on earth was she supposed to tell Ronnie that his precious girl had nearly died tonight, could still die tonight? In all the scenarios she'd ever imagined for speaking to her ex again, this was one she'd never thought of. Maybe because it was so awful she'd never dared to contemplate it…or maybe because it was the one guaranteed to bring him roaring back into her life.

5

The ringing of Ronnie's cell phone jarred him out of a deep sleep and a dream about Dana Sue. When he heard her voice on the other end of the line, he thought he must still be dreaming. Only dimly aware that he clutched the cell phone in his hand, he closed his eyes and hugged the pillow a little more tightly, hoping to sink back into the dream. The phone fell from his hand.

"Dammit, Ronnie Sullivan, don't you dare go back to sleep!" Dana Sue shouted in his ear. "Ronnie, wake up! I wouldn't be calling if this weren't important. It's about Annie."

Even though her shouts seemed to be coming from a great distance, they were enough to snap him awake. "What about Annie?" he muttered groggily, digging around in the covers until he found the phone. "Talk to me. What about Annie?"

His heart was pounding in his chest as he considered all the terrible possibilities. An accident? Had those boys come back to the house and stirred up trouble? It had to be bad, for Dana Sue to break two years of silence to call him.

Dana Sue, who could talk as slow as molasses when she wanted to sweet-talk him into something wicked, could also manage to squeeze a ten-minute conversation into ten seconds when she was worked up. She was clearly very worked up. She was talking so fast he could barely pick up every fifth word.

"Hey, slow down, sugar," he said. "You're waking me out of a sound sleep. I can't understand a word you're saying."

"It's Annie!" she said, sounding hysterical. "I don't care where the hell you are, Ronnie, or who you're with, or what your priorities are these days. Your daughter needs you."

That was all he had to hear. He could find out all the rest when he got there. With the phone clamped between his head and shoulder, he fished around in the pitch-dark room until he found the switch on the lamp beside his bed.

"I'll be there in under an hour," he promised, "but you're going to have to tell me where you are."

"At Regional Hospital," she said, her voice catching on a sob.

His heart seemed to flat-out stop in his chest. "Baby, can you tell me what happened?"

"I don't know. Not exactly, anyway. She had some girls over for the night. It was going to be just Sarah and Raylene, but then she decided to invite more. I'd told her that was okay. In fact, I encouraged it. It was all part of a plan, you see."

"Sugar, you're rambling," he said. "Get to the point."

"Right. Sorry. I'm just such a wreck."

"It's okay," he soothed. "Just take a deep breath and tell me."

For once she actually listened to him. He could hear her slow intake of breath, then a sigh.

"Feeling better?" he asked.

"Not really. Anyway, a little while ago one of the girls woke me up and said Annie had collapsed. Raylene was doing CPR on her when I got downstairs. I took over for what seemed like forever till the EMTs came." Dana Sue paused, then gave a choked sound he didn't even recognize. "I tried and tried, Ronnie, but I couldn't wake her up."

He was hopping on one foot, trying to pull his jeans on without letting go of the phone. "And now? Is she awake now?"

"No," Dana Sue said. "At least, I don't think so. I just got to the hospital. I wanted to call you before I went inside, but couldn't get a signal for my cell phone till now."

"It's okay, baby. Everything's going to be okay. It has to be. I'm on my way. Is there anybody there with you?"

"Maddie drove me over and Helen's probably already inside."

Now *there* was a confrontation he'd prefer to avoid. Those two hadn't minced words when they'd raked him over the coals for what he'd done to Dana Sue. He knew, though, that they were exactly the support system Dana Sue needed right now. If he wanted her back, he was going to have to face them sooner or later, anyway. Maddie, at least, might be reasonable. Helen was bound to have her claws out, but so be it.

"Good," he told Dana Sue. "And I'll be there before you know it. I promise," he added, knowing that his promises probably weren't worth a hill of beans, but he didn't know what else to say.

"Just hurry, please. I need to get inside and see if the doctors can tell me anything yet," she said, and disconnected.

Ronnie was slower to disconnect. *Well, there you go,* he thought. *Fate has just stepped in.*

But if anything happened to his little girl, he didn't even want to think about what the future might hold.

"Okay, I called him. Are you satisfied?" Dana Sue said to Maddie.

Her friend had stayed right by her side, almost as if she feared Dana Sue would renege on her promise to call Ronnie and tell him just how serious the situation was.

"Is he coming?" Maddie asked, following her into the E.R.

waiting room, with its bustling activity, icy temperature and antiseptic smell.

"He says he is," Dana Sue answered, not entirely sure how she felt about that. Ronnie had sounded genuinely distraught, and she had no reason to doubt that he was. She'd never questioned his commitment to their daughter, only to her. He'd stood up to Helen in court and insisted on having visitation rights. She knew how hard he'd tried to keep in touch with Annie. It must have killed him to be rejected again and again. Enough time had passed that she could almost feel sorry for him. Now, hearing his voice, needing his strength, made her remember too many things she'd been trying frantically to forget.

"It's good that he's coming," Maddie said. "Annie needs both of you right now."

"I need to see her," Dana Sue said, heading to the desk to plead for permission to go into the cubicle where the doctors were working on her baby.

Even before she got there, Maddie intercepted her. "What you need to do is let the doctors do their job," she said, guiding her to a seat away from the other families crowded into the waiting room. Only after she was satisfied that Dana Sue would stay put did she leave her alone long enough to let the nurse on duty know they were there.

Before Dana Sue could muster up the energy to make a desperate dash into the treatment area, Maddie was back, and then Helen came in with all the girls, explaining that she'd detoured to take one of them home.

"Any news?" she asked.

Dana Sue shook her head, then burst into tears. She turned away from the obviously terrified teens and buried her head on Maddie's shoulder. "I don't know how much longer I can bear this," she whispered.

"I know it's hard," Maddie said. "Waiting is the worst part."

"What if—?"

Maddie cut her off. "Don't you dare say it," she said sternly. "Only positive thoughts, you hear me?"

"Maddie's right," Helen said, though her normally composed face showed traces of the same gut-wrenching fear that was eating at Dana Sue. With no children of her own, Helen felt a special connection to Maddie's children and to Annie. And now that Annie was in her teens, Helen loved to indulge her in shopping trips to Charleston.

Pushing her own fears aside, Dana Sue reached out and took Helen's hand. Seeing her normally unflappable friend so deeply shaken was most disconcerting.

"Why don't you two go to the chapel and say a prayer for Annie?" Maddie suggested. "I'll stay here with the girls."

Dana Sue regarded her with alarm. "But what if there's news?"

"The chapel's right down the hall. I'll come get you the instant the doctors come out," she promised.

Dana Sue glanced at Helen, noted the tears welling up in her eyes, and knew her friend was close to falling apart. She needed a distraction. They both did.

"Come on, Helen," she said, getting to her feet. "Let's go see if you can use your excellent powers of persuasion where they'll really count."

Helen gave her a wan smile. "God might give me a little more trouble than the typical jury," she commented. "Especially since we haven't been on the best of terms recently."

"You and me both," Dana Sue admitted. "Hopefully He'll forgive us for our lapses."

"He won't take our sins out on Annie," Helen said confidently. "I know that much."

As they found their way to the tiny chapel, Dana Sue was already praying, asking God to heal her daughter and to give her another chance to be a better mother. Inside the quiet, dimly lit room, with the scent of burning candles filling the air, an amazing sense of serenity stole over her. She almost felt as if God had heard her silent plea and was enfolding her in His reassuring arms.

She and Helen sank onto a hard, wooden pew and looked up at the small stained-glass window behind the altar.

"Do you think He hears everyone who comes here?" she asked Helen.

"I don't know," Helen replied. "But tonight I really need to believe He does. I need to believe that He won't let Annie suffer, that He'll heal her and bring her back to us." She glanced over at Dana Sue, her cheeks damp with tears. "I think I love that girl of yours as much as you do. We simply can't lose her."

The sense of peace that had come over her when they walked into the chapel brought Dana Sue comfort. "We won't," she said, with a level of confidence that astounded her. "We won't lose her."

Helen gave her a startled look. "You sound awfully sure."

"I am. I'm not certain why I'm so positive, but I am." She sighed. "If I'm right, things will be a lot different from here on out. No more sticking my head in the sand about her eating disorder. No more convincing myself that she's eating when I know in my heart she's not. Annie's going to get whatever help she needs. She's not going to leave this hospital till we know exactly what to do to make her well. I won't fail her again."

Helen regarded Dana Sue with dismay. "You didn't fail her."

"I did," she said emphatically. "She's here, isn't she?

Whose fault is that, if not mine? I saw the signs. We all did. But did I take her to see the doctor? No. Did I realize that she was really in crisis? No. What is wrong with me? Was I just too busy to see it?"

"Absolutely not." Helen shook her head. "Like a lot of parents, you just didn't want to believe what you were seeing. The choice was Annie's, Dana Sue. She's not five years old or even ten. She's almost a grown woman."

"But she's still way too young to fully understand the consequences of her actions," Dana Sue argued. "I knew, but I kept putting off doing anything about this, because I didn't want to confront her and upset her with my suspicions. I wanted her to like me, instead of being the responsible parent she needed. If ever there was an occasion that called for tough love, this was it. I've read probably a hundred articles. I knew all the signs and symptoms of anorexia. I even knew the dangers, and yet I kept telling myself that it couldn't happen to Annie, not to the girl with the sunny disposition who'd always embraced life. She was going out with her friends. She was active. I just didn't believe we'd reached a crisis stage."

"Well, that's water under the bridge," Helen said pragmatically. "We'll all work together to fix this now."

Dana Sue closed her eyes and tried to imagine Ronnie's shock when he saw Annie for the first time in two years. Somehow she'd gotten used to seeing the thin shadow of the girl Annie had once been. Ronnie only had memories of an exuberant, healthy teenager with glowing skin, shiny hair and the first hint of a woman's curves.

"What?" Helen asked, studying her worriedly.

"Ronnie's going to be furious when he sees her," Dana Sue said. "He's going to wonder how on earth I let something like this happen to our daughter without trying to fix it. He's going to want to talk to teachers and counselors about why they didn't see it and intervene."

"It's not as if he was here to do his part," Helen said heatedly. "So of course he'll want to spread the blame around."

Dana Sue regarded her with a wry expression. "He wasn't here because that's how I wanted it, remember? I was the one who insisted on limited visitation and then secretly rejoiced when Annie refused to see him at all."

There was a faint flash of guilt in Helen's eyes, but she continued her defense of Dana Sue's actions. "Come on, hon. Don't you dare let him off the hook and take all the blame on yourself."

"I had full custody," Dana Sue reminded her. "You fought for it and got it."

"There wasn't much of a fight," Helen scoffed. "Ronnie was anxious to leave and get on with his life. He was only too eager to send support checks and forget all about her."

Dana Sue didn't usually cut Ronnie a lot of slack, but now she did. "You know better than that, Helen. Whatever his issues were with me, he loved Annie. He only agreed to limited visitation because you convinced him it would be best if Annie wasn't pulled in two different directions. In the beginning he called almost every night, but Annie hung up on him. He invited her to visit him over and over again, but she turned him down. She told me. Lately, though, they've been in touch, probably even more than I know."

"Maddie mentioned that," Helen said. "Why are you defending him all of a sudden?"

"I'm not defending him. I'm just trying to prepare myself for how he's going to react when he gets here." She shuddered. "Something tells me all hell is going to break loose."

In fact, there was a very good chance that Ronnie would

take one look at his daughter and head straight for the courthouse to argue for a new custody arrangement, one that would
give him the day-to-day responsibility for his daughter. Given
tonight's events, Dana Sue wasn't sure she had the strength—
or the right—to fight him.

Ronnie spotted Maddie the minute he walked into the hospital. She was in the midst of half a dozen teenage girls, but
her gaze immediately clashed with his. To his surprise, her
eyes held warmth and compassion.

She stood up and crossed the waiting room to where he
stood uncertainly just inside the door. Places like this freaked
him out under the best of conditions. He'd been a wreck the
night Annie was born, and her birth had gone smoothly
enough. Based on what Dana Sue had told him, it was anything but certain that tonight would turn out as happily.

"Ronnie, it's good to see you," Maddie said, surprising him
again. "I just wish it were under different circumstances."

"Me, too," he said, risking a kiss on her cheek that would
have come naturally a few years back. She'd always been his
champion with Dana Sue, at least until he'd betrayed his wife.
Then she'd turned into a protective best friend with little good
to say to or about him. But she, at least, had apparently mel-
lowed, even more than he'd dared to hope.

"How's Annie? Is Dana Sue with her?"

Maddie shook her head. "We don't know anything yet.
Dana Sue's in the chapel with Helen. Maybe you should go
in there. Let her know you've arrived."

"I think I'll wait here," he said, dreading this first meeting
almost as much as he desired it. "Is she holding up okay? She
was a mess when she called me."

"She still is, unless the visit to the chapel has helped.

Helen's just as bad. She doesn't often let anyone see her soft side, but she loves Annie as if she were her own."

"She certainly fought like a mother hen to keep her away from me," Ronnie said bitterly, then shrugged. "I was lucky to win visitation rights. Little did I know that Annie was so mad at me that she wouldn't even speak to me for the better part of a year, much less come to visit."

Maddie smiled. "Well, that's in the past. She's forgiven you, hasn't she?"

"She's speaking to me, at least," he responded. "That's something. I probably should have stayed right here in town so Annie couldn't avoid me, but I thought maybe if I left the way Dana Sue wanted, both of them would start to miss me, maybe give me another chance."

"How'd that work for you?" Maddie inquired dryly.

He smiled grimly. "You know the answer to that."

Just then he spotted Dana Sue and Helen coming down the hall. His heart seemed to stop in his chest. Damn, she looked good, even with her hair a tangled mess, her Carolina Panthers T-shirt—no, *his* T-shirt, he realized with a pang—wrinkled and way too big, her feet jammed into an old pair of sneakers. Her complexion was too pale and her incredible deep-green eyes were shadowed by fear.

Ronnie started to go to her, but stopped himself and waited for her to come to him.

"Old patterns might not be the best on a night like this," Maddie said in an undertone. "Reach out to her, Ronnie. She needs you. Whatever else has happened, that child in there belongs to both of you."

It was all the encouragement he needed. He strode across the lobby, and almost before he knew it, Dana Sue was in his arms. Her whole body shaking with sobs; she clung to his neck.

"I'm sorry," she said over and over.

Not sure what she had to be sorry for, he just held her tightly and tried to keep himself from bursting into tears, too.

"Shh, baby, it's going to be okay," he promised, though he knew no such thing. "Annie's going to be fine."

Before the words were out of his mouth, Dana Sue wrenched herself from his arms, as if she'd suddenly remembered how angry she was at him. Pushing away, she wrapped her arms around her middle and looked at the floor.

He regarded her with concern. "Dana Sue, what is it you're not telling me?"

"Nothing," she stated, but her guilty expression said otherwise.

"Have the doctors been out? Have they told you what's going on yet?"

She shook her head.

Ronnie pressed her, sure she was keeping something from him. "But you know more than you've said, don't you? What happened tonight?"

Dana Sue opened her mouth, but before she could speak, Helen was between them. "What is wrong with you?" she demanded. "She's upset enough without you getting in her face."

Despite his frustration, Ronnie backed off at once. "You're right. I'm sorry. I just want to know what's going on."

"We all do," Helen told him.

"Well, maybe I can get some answers you haven't been able to get," he said.

Ignoring Helen's skeptical look and Dana Sue's shattered expression, he stalked over to the desk and demanded to speak to a doctor.

"He'll be out as soon as he's able," the nurse told him, her expression so grim that another wave of panic washed over him.

"Isn't there *something* you can tell me?" he pleaded. "That's my daughter in there."

"I'm sorry," the nurse said. "If I knew anything, I'd tell you."

"How long will it be before the doctor comes out?"

"That depends on how your daughter is responding to treatment. She's his first priority right now."

"Of course," Ronnie said, backing down, but wanting to scream in frustration.

Maddie appeared beside him. "Why don't we go get coffee for everyone?" she suggested. "It's going to be a long night."

He started to snap that he didn't want coffee, he wanted answers, but stopped himself before he could utter the words. They *all* wanted answers.

"Sure," he said at last, then cast one last look at his ex-wife. "Maybe I should stay with Dana Sue."

"Give her a little time," Maddie said. "She's dealing with a lot of conflicting emotions right now."

"And I'm not?" he retorted sharply, then winced. "Sorry."

She smiled. "You don't need to apologize to me," she told him. "But you might want to work on a really, really good one for Dana Sue. Despite what happened a few minutes ago when she threw herself into your arms, she's still not in a forgiving mood."

Despite the tension and the serious nature of the situation, his lips quirked. "You think?"

Maddie tucked her arm through his and led him toward the cafeteria. "Can I ask you something?"

"Have I ever been able to stop you?"

"I know you came because of Annie, but what about Dana Sue?"

He paused in midstride and faced her. "What are you asking me, Maddie?"

"I suppose I'm asking if you still love her," she said bluntly. "Do you?"

"Do you really think this is the time for that discussion?" he asked.

Her expression was grave as she met his eyes. "Yes."

"Okay, then." He met her gaze evenly. "I never stopped loving her, not for a minute."

Maddie seemed to breathe a sigh of relief. "Thought so."

They started to walk again, but before they'd taken half a dozen steps, she stopped and punched him in the arm. "Then why the heck did you walk away without a fight?"

"Stupidity?" he suggested.

"Was that a question or a statement? Because if you ask me, only an idiot would walk away from the woman he loves just because she tells him to go. And you, Ronnie Sullivan, were never an idiot. I couldn't believe it when I found out you'd left. If I'd known where to find you, I would have hunted you down and tried to talk some sense into you."

"Helen knew where I was," he pointed out.

Maddie gave him a wry look. "Helen wasn't in a forthcoming mood at the time. She'd have been happier if you'd disappeared off the face of the earth."

"She made that clear," Ronnie said. "As for me being an idiot, I surely was for one night. I guess that mistake was such a whopper that it convinced me I didn't deserve another chance. It was like I said a minute ago—I thought if I went, Dana Sue would start to miss me. Took me by surprise that she didn't."

"And now?"

"Now I'm going to fight for another chance with both my girls."

Maddie nodded in satisfaction. "About damn time."

Ronnie grinned. Wasn't *that* the truth?

6

It seemed to Dana Sue they'd been waiting a lifetime. She'd prayed, she'd paced the hallways and she'd fought off tears more times than she could count. She'd lost it only once, when she'd been wrapped in Ronnie's comforting arms, but then she'd remembered how furious she was with him, and had pulled away. She would not allow that man to think he had the right or the ability to ease her pain.

They'd finally settled on opposite sides of the waiting room. She had Maddie and Helen on either side of her, and they were surrounded by Annie's friends, who'd refused to leave despite the hours that had passed. The sun was already up. Dana Sue glanced guiltily across the room, saw Ronnie sitting all alone and felt a moment's sympathy for him. Then she reminded herself that he'd *chosen* to be an outsider.

"Don't you think you should talk to Ronnie?" Maddie asked gently. "He was right earlier. You do know more than you've told him. It might be best to prepare him for whatever the doctor has to say."

Dana Sue shook her head. "I can't just walk over there and say that Annie is anorexic and has probably messed up her whole body. I tried before, but I couldn't get the words out."

"It won't get any easier," Maddie said.

"Leave her alone!" Helen snapped. "If it had been up to me, she wouldn't have called him at all."

"Then it's a good thing you weren't the one who was with her earlier," Maddie chided. "Ronnie has a right to know that Annie's in the hospital. He's her father."

"I don't remember you being all that anxious to involve Bill when Ty was in trouble a few months ago," Helen retorted.

"Ty made some mistakes. His life wasn't at stake," Maddie said pointedly.

"Stop it!" Dana Sue commanded. "Why are you two arguing about this now? For better or worse, Ronnie's here."

"Which is it?" Maddie asked, studying her curiously. "Better or worse?"

She sighed. "For a minute, seeing him felt really good," she admitted. "He was always so calm in a crisis, so supportive. When my mom died, he took care of everything, even though he'd loved her, too. When I saw him tonight, all I wanted was to draw on all that strength." She shrugged. "Then I remembered how mad I am at him."

"So rather than lean on him, even under these circumstances, you pushed him away." Maddie shook her head. "Sometimes I'm not sure which of you is the bigger idiot."

"Way to be supportive, Maddie," Helen said sarcastically.

"That's enough," Dana Sue exclaimed.

"Of course it is," Helen said, sounding surprisingly meek. "I'm sorry. You don't need the two of us bickering with each other."

"That's right," Maddie agreed. "I'm sorry, too."

Just then a weary-looking doctor finally emerged from the treatment area, paused at the nurses' station to speak to the receptionist, glanced their way and nodded, then came toward them. His grim expression had Dana Sue reaching for Maddie's hand.

"I'm Dr. Lane. You're here with Annie Sullivan?" he asked.

"I'm her mother," Dana Sue said, tightening her grip on Maddie's hand.

"And I'm her father," Ronnie announced, joining them, but avoiding Dana Sue's gaze. "How is she?"

"I won't lie to you," the doctor said. "It's been touch and go all night, but her age is on her side. I think she's stable now. We've gotten her electrolytes balanced for the moment and her labs are improving, but she's not out of the woods. If she holds her own for another twenty-four hours and we can start getting some nutrition into her, then she's got a good chance at recovery."

All the color had drained from Ronnie's face as the doctor spoke. Dana Sue felt so shaky she could barely stand. She sank onto the hard, plastic chair, Maddie right beside her.

"What the hell happened?" Ronnie asked. "She's sixteen. Kids that age don't have…" His voice faltered. "What did she have?"

"A cardiac arrest," the doctor said. "Quite a bad one. I imagine she'd been having incidents of arrhythmia for some time now, given her overall condition. Had she mentioned anything? Any odd sensations in her chest?"

Dana Sue shook her head. "Not a word."

Sarah stepped up and said in a small voice, "I think she might have been having some trouble in gym class. She was getting winded real easy. And she didn't say it, but I think her chest hurt. One time she admitted she felt kind of funny, like she might pass out, but then she sat down and a few minutes later she said she was okay."

The doctor nodded. "That fits."

Ronnie regarded all of them with confusion. "Why would she be having arrhythmia?" he asked. "This doesn't make any sense. Are you sure?"

"I'm sure," Dr. Lane said. "I'm the cardiologist on call for this kind of thing. I have to tell you I haven't seen a heart muscle in such bad shape in a while. It had gotten so weak it was barely pumping." He looked from Dana Sue to Ronnie. "She was sleeping when this happened, right?"

"She was having a sleepover," Dana Sue said. "I don't know how much sleeping was going on." She looked to Sarah and Raylene.

"Just before it happened, she said she was really tired and wanted to take a quick nap," Sarah said. "But she wanted us to wake her when we were ready to watch the DVD."

"But we couldn't wake her up," Raylene said.

"Because her heart rate had gone way down," the doctor said, his expression grim. "Be thankful these girls were with her. If she'd been in her room alone and no one had checked on her before morning, we wouldn't be having this conversation at all."

Dana Sue sagged against Maddie. "You mean…"

"She could have died," the doctor said bluntly.

Dana Sue gasped. Even though the possibility had crossed her mind, hearing the words was devastating.

Ronnie shook his head as if he couldn't quite process the information. "I don't understand. She's sixteen," he repeated. "She didn't have any birth defects. Her heart's always been just fine. The pediatrician would have said something if it wasn't."

The doctor regarded him with a sympathetic expression. "Obviously you're not aware of her eating disorder."

"Her what?" Ronnie said incredulously. He stared hard at Dana Sue. "Annie has an eating disorder?"

The doctor's gaze was on Dana Sue, as well. "I'd guess she's anorexic. Isn't that right, Mrs. Sullivan?"

Numb, Dana Sue could only nod. There would be no denying the truth after tonight, even if she'd wanted to.

Ronnie looked as if he wanted to hit something. "How the hell did something like that happen?" he demanded. "I can't say I know a lot about eating disorders, but to get to this point, it doesn't happen overnight, does it?"

The doctor shook his head. "No. It takes time to put this much strain on the body's organs."

"Dammit, Dana Sue, I've been gone for two years. Where were you while this was happening?" Ronnie asked.

"Where were *you?*" Helen snapped back when Dana Sue couldn't seem to think of a reply.

The doctor held up a hand. "That's not the issue right now. I think we all need to focus on getting Annie through this crisis, getting her lab work back to normal. Then we'll bring in a team of experts. Anorexia is a complicated disorder. There's no quick, sure fix. Together we'll decide what needs to be done to keep this from happening again. We may recommend that Annie go into a treatment facility where they can monitor her more closely. You should prepare yourselves for that possibility."

Shattered, Dana Sue nodded.

"Sure," Ronnie said, but his scowl remained firmly in place. "Will she have damage to her heart from this?"

"Not the same kind of damage she'd have if she'd had a heart attack caused by a blockage. That can destroy some of the heart tissue. Right now, the muscle's simply weak and her electrolytes are all out of whack. Those are things that can be corrected, assuming she deals with the underlying cause—the anorexia."

Ronnie seemed to be struggling to take it all in. "Can I see her now?"

"We've moved her to a room in ICU. You and Mrs. Sullivan can go in for five minutes. Not a second longer," he told them firmly. "And whatever issues you two have with each other, leave them at the door, understood? She's asleep right now, but even so, she might hear what you're saying or be aware of any tension between you. She doesn't need the added stress."

Ronnie nodded. His gaze softened slightly as he turned to Dana Sue. "You ready?"

She hesitated for an instant, but then Ronnie held out his hand. Unable to resist, she took it, steeling herself for the jolt of awareness the contact was destined to bring.

Then all that mattered was the strength that seemed to flow through her as they followed the doctor to the elevator. For this one brief moment, it didn't seem to matter that Ronnie had betrayed her, then left her. All that mattered was Annie and that the two of them were there for her…and for each other.

The instant she felt stronger, though, Dana Sue pulled away and strode on ahead. She could not allow herself to count on Ronnie's support. The last time she'd trusted him, the last time she'd relied on him for anything, he'd cheated on her. If she needed to remind herself of that a thousand times a day, she would. She would never let herself be in a position to get her heart broken like that again.

After what he'd just learned in the E.R., Ronnie wished he'd been able to see Annie on his own, but he could hardly deny Dana Sue the right to be there when they'd both been waiting half the night for the chance to see their little girl. At the very least, he wished they'd been able to lean on each other for support, but aside from that one moment of weakness when he'd first arrived, and the brief contact she'd permitted in the elevator, Dana Sue had kept her distance. Even now, she was walking ahead of him as if determined to reach Annie's side before he did, as if it was some sort of contest.

He had so many questions it took every ounce of restraint he possessed not to let them come pouring out. The doctor was right. There would be time enough for questions and accusations later, once he'd seen Annie and developed a real sense of just how bad things had gotten in his absence.

At the door to Annie's ICU cubicle, Dr. Lane paused. "Remember what I told you both," he said sternly. "Five minutes and no arguing."

Ronnie nodded. "We understand."

He held the door and Dana Sue walked in ahead of him, then swayed backward. He steadied her with a hand on her waist.

"You okay?" he asked, regarding her with concern.

She squared her shoulders and met his gaze. "Of course," she said, then moved quickly to Annie's bedside.

Ronnie was slower to approach. The room had the same antiseptic smell as the emergency room, which was disconcerting enough. But here there was an odd stillness, as well. Annie was never still, never quiet. The silence was broken only by the steady beeping of some monitor and Dana Sue's barely contained sigh as she sat down beside the bed.

"Hi, sweetie," she whispered, taking Annie's hand in hers. "Mom's here. So is your dad."

Ronnie finally managed to propel himself forward, but when he caught sight of his daughter's wan, gaunt face and the IV hooked up to her arm, the oxygen being fed through her nose, he almost stumbled.

"Oh, my God," he gasped, horrified not just by all the

tubes and monitors, but by the teenager who was so thin she barely made a ripple in the sheets.

Dana Sue cast a warning look in his direction and he managed to smother the damning accusations on the tip of his tongue. Instead he moved to the other side of the bed and sat. Since the IV was attached to that hand, he settled for stroking a finger along Annie's thin, icy arm.

"Hey, angel. You've given your mom and me quite a scare, but you're going to be fine. The doctor says you just need a little rest. Mom and I will be right here, okay? We'll be in the waiting room right outside. If you need us, all you have to do is tell the nurse and she'll get us. And we'll be in to talk to you every time they let us."

"That's right," Dana Sue confirmed. "We're not going anywhere. All your friends are here, too. Sarah's mad as heck at you for spoiling the sleepover. She says she's expecting you to throw another one ASAP. And Raylene says she'll keep track of all your assignments at school, so you won't fall behind. I think she said it because she's jealous you're going to miss a few classes, and wants to be sure you don't get out of any of the homework."

Ronnie couldn't be sure, but it almost looked as if Dana Sue's words stirred a faint hint of a smile on Annie's face. He glanced up and saw the nurse motioning to them. He walked around the bed and laid a hand on Dana Sue's shoulder, then leaned down and pressed a kiss to Annie's forehead.

"We have to leave you for a little while—they won't let us stay," he told her. "See you later, kiddo."

Dana Sue stood reluctantly, her eyes filled with tears. "You're going to be fine, sweetie. I promise. We'll be back soon."

Outside the room, she wobbled on her feet. As furious as he was at his daughter's condition, Ronnie took her elbow and steadied her.

"We need to talk," he said tightly.

"Not now," she pleaded.

"Yes, now. We'll go to the cafeteria. You look like you're about to pass out. You need some food."

"I can't eat."

"You can," he said firmly. When her chin jutted stubbornly, he asked, "Do I have to throw you over my shoulder and carry you down there? I will, you know. As mad as I am, the prospect of causing a scene doesn't bother me in the slightest."

Her defiant gaze clashed with his, and for a second he thought she might test him. But she finally gave him a disgusted look and started down the hall on her own.

He followed her to the cafeteria, got a tray and began piling on food. Juice, fresh fruit, a bagel and cream cheese, scrambled eggs, pancakes and two cups of coffee.

"You feeding a lumberjack?" Dana Sue asked when he reached for a second plate of pancakes.

He studied the array of food on the tray and decided there was enough for the two of them. He knew Dana Sue. Despite her claim that she wasn't hungry, she always ate in a crisis. And it had been a very long time since that fast-food dinner he'd had the night before.

"I guess this will do," he conceded, paying the cashier. Then he led the way to a table just being vacated near a window. After all those hours in which time had seemed to drag, he was surprised to see the sun well up in the morning sky.

The cafeteria was bustling with visiting families and staff. It was a far cry from the few exhausted customers who'd been here when he and Maddie had come down for coffee earlier.

Ronnie put all the dishes on the table, then placed the empty tray on a neighboring one. He divided the eggs and pancakes between them, put a plate in front of Dana Sue and began to eat. When she continued to sit perfectly still, her food untouched, he grinned at her.

"You're going to need fortification to fight with me," he commented. "Eat. The pancakes are good. The eggs are edible. They won't be once they get cold."

"Now there's a reason to dive in," she retorted, but she picked up her fork and tasted the pancakes.

"Well?" he asked.

"Not as good as the ones I do for Sunday brunch at Sullivan's."

He bit back a smile. Even under these circumstances, her competitive streak kicked in.

"Once Annie's well, I'll have to come by and try yours," he said, taking a sip of orange juice. "I seem to recall they were pretty spectacular when you made them for us on holiday mornings."

"Don't start dredging up ancient history, Ronnie," she said. "I have no desire to stroll down memory lane with you."

"Okay, then, let's talk about something more recent," he said, looking directly into her eyes and removing the kid gloves with which he'd been treating her. "How the hell did Annie get into the shape she's in?"

"A lot of teenage girls have eating disorders," Dana Sue said defensively.

"I only care about *our* teenage daughter. How did things get this bad without your taking some kind of action?"

Dana Sue dropped her fork and burst into tears. "I don't know," she whispered. "I honestly don't know. I thought I was on top of it. I fixed good food for her. She swore to me she was eating it. I guess I just didn't want to believe she would lie to me about something so important."

Ronnie was too angry to allow himself to feel even a

moment's pity for her obvious anguish. "You were here. You had to know there was something wrong. Good God, she can't even weigh ninety pounds."

Eyes blazing, Dana Sue glared right back at him. "Don't you think I know that? Don't you think I've asked myself a thousand times why I didn't force the issue sooner? I did the best I could, Ronnie. I talked to her. The whole sleepover was supposed to give me some idea if she was doing this on her own or if her friends were just as obsessed with dieting as she was."

"Too little, too damn late!"

"Don't you dare blame all this on me!" she said. "Where were you?"

He dismissed a momentary pang of guilt and retaliated with a barb of his own. "I was where you wanted me to be—gone."

"Because you cheated on me!" she said furiously. "And that's what started this whole mess."

He stared at her incredulously. "You're blaming Annie's anorexia on me because I cheated on you?"

"Yes, I am," she said fiercely. "She convinced herself that if I'd been thin enough, you wouldn't have cheated, so she decided to starve herself so she wouldn't wind up alone like me."

"That's absurd," Ronnie declared. "Did she tell you that?"

"Not in so many words, but it was right there every time she got on my case about my weight. She hated you for cheating on me, Ronnie, but she hated me just as much because she thought it was my fault."

Ronnie sank back in his chair and raked a hand over his head. It was an automatic gesture he hadn't stopped even after he'd shaved his balding head. Some habits die hard.

As Dana Sue watched him, her stark despair faded for just an instant. "I like the new look," she said. "You still getting used to it?"

Ronnie nodded. "I saw little point in pretending I wasn't going bald, so I figured what the hell."

"It suits you. On you bald is very sexy."

"Really? That's quite a compliment coming from you."

Her expression promptly closed down. "Don't let it go to your bald head," she said.

"Wouldn't dream of it," he assured her.

"Maybe we should limit our conversation to Annie," Dana Sue suggested.

"It would be safer turf," he agreed. "Although you never used to take the safe route, sugar."

"I've changed," she said tersely. "Let's stick to what Annie needs."

Despite his desire to continue to spar with Dana Sue, if only to put some color in her cheeks, he sighed. "That poor kid," he murmured. "I honestly thought she was doing okay. She sounded fine when we talked." He glanced warily at Dana Sue. "You knew we'd been talking, right?"

"I just found out a few days ago," she admitted. "How long has it been going on?"

"I started calling from the beginning." He shrugged. "She hung up. A while back, maybe six months ago, she finally started talking. To be honest, I don't think she wanted you to know."

"Then it wasn't your idea that she keep it from me?"

"No, of course not. I figured she'd know the best way to handle it."

"You left it up to a sixteen-year-old to decide whether to lie to her mother?"

"Omit the truth," he contradicted. "I wasn't violating our agreement, Dana Sue. I'd had the right to talk to her and see her all along. If she didn't say anything to you, it's probably because she didn't want to upset you."

Dana Sue regarded him with surprise, as if she hadn't expected him to understand that. "You're right," she conceded with obvious reluctance. "I suppose on some level I needed to believe you didn't give a damn about either of us anymore."

"Well, you were wrong," he said flatly.

To buy himself a couple of minutes to think about the mess they'd made of things, he stabbed a fork into a chunk of cantaloupe, then offered it to Dana Sue. She shook her head. He popped it into his mouth and chewed.

"Not bad," he said, then stabbed another piece. "Try it."

"Ronnie!" she protested.

He continued holding out the fork until she finally took it and tasted the cantaloupe.

"You're right. It *is* good."

He grinned at the admission. "Told you so," he said, then fell silent. Finally he lifted his gaze to hers. "What do we do now?"

"About?"

"Annie, of course."

She regarded him with a bewildered expression. "I honestly don't know. I suppose we'll have to let the doctors guide us through the next couple of weeks."

"You're willing to relinquish control to the doctors?" His tone was skeptical.

"When I'm at a loss, I am," she said.

"You *have* changed."

"Mostly for the better, I think."

"I'd like to hear about what's going on in your life," Ronnie said, knowing he was pushing the limits they'd agreed to. "I can't wait to see the restaurant. Annie says it's awesome. She sent me a review from the Charleston paper."

Dana Sue looked startled. "She did?"

"I was real proud of you, not just for getting a rave review, but for making a real success of yourself doing something you love."

"Thanks," she said, clearly uncomfortable with the praise. "We'd better get back upstairs. It's almost time for us to see Annie again."

"You go ahead," he told her. "Have a couple of minutes alone with her. I'll finish my coffee, clear this stuff away and join you."

"Are you sure?"

"Go on, Dana Sue."

"Thanks," she said again, and set off eagerly.

He sighed and took one last sip of his coffee just in time to hear Maddie comment, "That was very gracious of you."

He gazed up into her knowing eyes. "To be honest, I don't know if I'm ready to see her again," he admitted. "Looking at Annie lying there like that makes me want to hit something."

"You gonna take off?"

He frowned at the question. "Of course not. Why would you ask that?"

"Do you really need to ask? The last time things got tough around here, you ran."

"I was chased off," he corrected, but Maddie merely smiled.

"Matter of interpretation, I suppose."

"Well, I'm staying this time," he said.

"Just for Annie?"

He grinned. "Do you really need to ask?"

Maddie reached across the table and squeezed his hand. "She'll tell you to go," she warned.

"I'm sure of it," he agreed. "But this time I'm going to listen to what she's *not* saying, instead of *reacting* to what she says."

"Good plan."

"Do me a favor, okay?"

"Anything."

"When Dana Sue comes out of Annie's room, talk her into going home to get some sleep. She's wiped out. If I try to convince her to take a break, she'll just think I'm trying to get the upper hand with Annie or something."

"I'll try," Maddie promised. "But unless Annie's completely out of the woods, you know Dana Sue won't go anywhere."

Ronnie nodded, knowing she was right. "Then I'll see if there's an available room nearby that she can use to catch a nap."

"What about you? You look pretty beat yourself."

"I'm used to getting by without much sleep. I'll manage. I can nap sitting up in the waiting room between visits. The minute they let us stay longer with Annie, I'll be by her bed night and day till she's back on her feet." He gave Maddie a long look, fighting tears. "I love that girl. I don't know what I'd do if anything happened to her."

"*Nothing* is going to happen to her," Maddie said fiercely.

"You have an in with the guy upstairs?" he inquired.

"I have faith, yes," she said. "So should you."

"I'm trying to," he told her. "But I'm barely hanging on."

"Then hang on to me," she said. "I have enough for both of us."

"You know, Madelyn, I think I missed you almost as much as I've missed my family," he said quietly. "Even if you *were* mad as a hornet last time I saw you. You said a lot of things that night that cut right through me, but I deserved every word."

"You did," she agreed somberly, then grinned. "But I'm glad you're back. I can't wait for you to meet Cal."

"Your new husband," he said. "Annie told me. I saw him coach a couple of games before I left. You rob the cradle, Madelyn?"

She laughed. "So they say. The good part is, when I'm old and hobbling around, he'll still be able to tote my walker."

"Something tells me you'll have a lot of good years before that happens. I'm glad you're happy. I really am." Ronnie smiled at her. "I hear you have a new baby, too."

"I do," she said, her expression glowing. "And my having a baby at my age should prove to you that miracles are definitely possible."

"You think it's going to take a miracle for me to get my family back?" he asked.

"A miracle would be the easy way," she teased. "I think you're going to be on your own, but the Ronnie I knew could sweet-talk just about any woman into giving him whatever he wanted. I don't think Dana Sue's immune, despite how much she wants to be." Maddie stood up. "Come on, pal. You've postponed the inevitable long enough. You need to go back to see your daughter. Trust me, it'll get easier every time."

Ronnie rose and followed her, but at the door to Annie's room, he hesitated and looked Maddie in the eye. "You're wrong, you know. As long as Annie's in bad shape, there's no way it will get easier."

In fact, he was pretty sure now that it was possible for a heart to break more than once.

7

Dana Sue walked outside to use her cell phone after her too-brief visit with Annie, who was still sleeping most of the time. Her lack of responsiveness had been hard for Dana Sue to see, so she'd been almost relieved when the nurse had told her that her time was up.

Besides, she needed to check in with Erik and Karen to make sure they could handle things at the restaurant. She knew they'd want an update on Annie's condition, as well.

Exhausted, she sat down on a concrete bench in a garden filled with the last summery blossoms of well-tended rose bushes. A local garden club maintained the so-called serenity garden outside the main entrance, hoping the tranquility of the setting would provide comfort to the families of patients.

Closing her eyes and turning her face up to the sun, Dana Sue let the warmth soak into her. It was hot and humid, but the heat felt good after so many hours inside the air-conditioned waiting room. After the antiseptic atmosphere of the hospital, the garden's cheerful, fragrant flowers and small pond were soothing. If she hadn't been so keyed up and worried, she could have fallen asleep sitting up.

"You okay?"

Dana Sue jerked and opened her eyes at the sound of Erik's

voice. Her first instinct was to look at her watch before asking, "What are you doing here? It's almost time for the restaurant to open. You know how busy we are on Saturday."

"No need to worry," he assured her, sitting down beside her. "I went in as soon as I got your call. All the prep work's done. The waitstaff and busboys came in early to pitch in and help. Karen can hold the fort till I get back. I came to see how Annie's doing and to bring you something to eat."

"I grabbed something in the cafeteria earlier," she said.

Erik rolled his eyes. "And lived to tell the story?" He handed her a take-out box. "A wild mushroom risotto, a little pear-and-walnut salad and a slice of one of the sugar-free cakes I've been working on."

Despite her recent meal and her claim that she wasn't hungry, Dana Sue couldn't resist a peek inside the box. The aromas that drifted out were tantalizing.

"Chocolate cake?" she inquired, sniffing reverently.

"With amaretto and almonds," he confirmed. "It's moist and decadent, if I do say so myself. But you can't touch it till you've eaten the rest."

"Who's going to stop me?"

He regarded her solemnly. "No one. I'm trusting in your good judgment."

She took the fork, grinned, then took a huge bite of the cake. "Oh, sweet heaven," she murmured as the flavors burst on her tongue. "Maybe we should just turn into a bakery. You'd make us all rich."

"A decadent dessert is just the icing on a fine meal," he insisted, but he was beaming with pleasure at her praise. "Try the risotto," he urged. "I think Karen's picked up your skill with seasonings."

Dana Sue tasted the risotto and sighed. "Perfect." She took

another bite of that, then sampled the pear salad with its light raspberry vinaigrette dressing. Before she realized it, she'd finished every bite of food Erik had brought.

"I guess I was hungrier than I realized," she admitted. "Or else your cooking is just too fabulous to resist."

"When you're under a lot of stress, you need decent food to sustain you," he told her, his gray eyes filled with concern. "No more hospital meals. One of the perks of owning a restaurant ought to be delivery to your doorstep in a crisis, okay? Karen and I will see to it that you get breakfast, lunch and dinner. As soon as Annie's able to eat something, we'll work on tempting her, too."

At the sympathetic expression on his face, Dana Sue's eyes filled with tears. "You know why she's in here, don't you?"

Erik draped a comforting arm around her shoulders. "I've got eyes, don't I? It wasn't hard to figure out."

Relaxing into his solid embrace, she whispered, "I must be a terrible mother. I had no idea it was this bad."

"You're not a terrible mother," he said, giving her a little shake. "Come on. No kid has ever been luckier in the mom department."

More tears spilled down Dana Sue's cheeks. "You're being too nice. It's making me cry."

He laughed. "Sweetheart, you cry at most anything, so don't blame me for those tears. You were just due for a good cry. You've probably been holding it together all night long."

"You know, for a guy who's never had kids, you're pretty wise," she told him. "Some woman's going to be lucky to have you."

She thought she saw a shadow pass over his face, but then he rallied and met her gaze with a grin. "Maybe I already have a thing for somebody a little older. Could be I'm like Cal. He seems to be pretty happy with Maddie. Maybe you and I should…"

Dana Sue frowned at him before he could complete the ridiculous thought. Erik was the best male friend she'd ever had. She didn't want that complicated by romance. "Don't even think about it. Our relationship is perfect the way it is."

"It is," he agreed. "Still, you might not want to rule it out. How many women can honestly say their husbands are just as good in the kitchen as they are?"

Dana Sue laughed. "You wish. Now go back to work before Karen has to handle the entire lunch crowd on her own. She's getting better every day, but she's not up to that."

Erik cupped her face in his hands and studied her intently, then nodded. "Yep, color's back in your cheeks. My job here is done. One of us will bring you dinner later, okay? You let me know if you want it here or plan to be at home." He gave her a knowing look. "If you need dinner for two, let us know that, too."

She frowned at him. Was word already around town that Ronnie was back? More than likely. This was Serenity, after all. "The day I start letting you feed my ex-husband will be a cold day in hell," she muttered.

"You sure about that?" he asked. "You get this little glint in your eyes whenever his name comes up…."

"Anger," she assured him.

"Anger, passion. Sometimes it's hard to tell the difference," Erik commented.

"I know the difference," she said.

"If you say so," he said, his skepticism plain. "Anyway, you need anything, I'm just a phone call away."

"Thank you, darlin'," Dana Sue said, her eyes welling up again. "I don't know what I'd do without you. I mean that."

"Serve your customers cake from a mix most likely," he said with an exaggerated shudder. "Give Annie a hug from me, okay?"

Dana Sue nodded and watched him jog off toward the parking lot. She noted, not for the first time, that he had a very fine derriere. Far more important than his sexy body, though, was his wonderfully generous spirit. Though she knew very little about Erik's personal life before coming to Serenity, she did know he was one of the good guys, the kind of man who looked out for his friends and stood by them.

How had she ever gotten so lucky? She had two of the best friends in the universe in Maddie and Helen. Now Erik and Karen were quickly becoming like family. Ironically, she might never have met the two if it hadn't been for the breakup with Ronnie, which had forced her to think about her future and to start Sullivan's. It was astounding that something so good could have come from something so bad.

Once more she turned her face up to the sun and said a silent prayer of thanks for all she had. Then added a heartfelt plea that her daughter would recover and one day realize that she was just as blessed.

Ronnie took his turn sitting beside Annie, and tried not to weep at the condition she was in. A part of him wanted to go outside, drive to someplace in the country where he could be alone and scream at the top of his lungs at the injustice of what was happening to his little girl. Another part wanted to tear Dana Sue limb from limb for allowing it to happen, but he knew rationally that she bore only some of the blame. The rest was his. He hadn't been here to stop any of this before it got out of hand. Not that he would have been able to do any more than Dana Sue had. But if she was right about what had triggered Annie's eating disorder, maybe his presence would have made some kind of difference.

"Mr. Sullivan?"

He glanced away from Annie's pale face and saw a woman in her early forties, about his age, wearing a white lab coat over a simple pale pink blouse and hot-pink skirt. Her untamed riot of brown curls and the bright color of her skirt seemed to contradict her otherwise cool, professional appearance.

"I'm Ronnie Sullivan," he told her.

"Could I speak to you outside for a minute?" she asked, casting a pointed look in Annie's direction.

"Sure."

He followed her into the corridor.

"I'm Linda McDaniels," she said. "Annie's cardiologist asked me to look over her case and see if I could help."

Ronnie felt his heart begin to thud with dread. "Is she worse? Are there complications?"

She touched his arm gently, her expression filled with compassion. "No, nothing like that. I'm sorry. I should have explained. I'm a psychologist. I deal with a lot of girls like Annie who have eating disorders."

Ronnie still couldn't get used to hearing those words associated with his daughter. Annie had always been so level-headed. She'd always had a perfectly normal appetite for pizza, ice cream, hamburgers, fries, all the things kids her age ate. Most probably weren't good for her, but Dana Sue had always counterbalanced that with healthy meals. She'd even managed to convince Annie that carrot sticks or grapes were a good snack. And with all of her activities, Annie had never gained an extra ounce. Why she'd become obsessed with dieting was beyond him.

When he didn't respond, Dr. McDaniels regarded him sympathetically. "Do you know much about anorexia?" she asked.

"The basics, I guess. Someone develops an aversion to food, more or less. It seems to affect teenage girls most of all."

"Something like that, though the age of patients seems to be getting younger and younger, which is a worrisome trend. Most of the time it starts out as plain old dieting, either because their body image is poor or there's a lot of peer pressure to be ultrathin or even because they could stand to lose a few pounds. Then something goes awry and it becomes an obsession. Maybe something in their life goes out of whack and food intake is the one thing they can still control, so they do, to an extreme. Any idea what might have been going on in Annie's case?"

That was easy enough, Ronnie thought guiltily. "Her mom and I got a divorce a couple of years back and I left town," he said, then suddenly remembered something else. "On the day I went, when I told her I was going, she got up from the table, ran into the restroom at the restaurant and threw up. Could it have started then?"

"Possibly, at least in the sense that a major trauma in her life became associated with food. At least that gives me a starting point. If you and your ex-wife agree, I'd like to spend a little time with Annie while she's still here in the hospital. It's important to start dealing with this right away, in a controlled environment."

"The cardiologist mentioned she might need to go into a treatment facility," Ronnie said. "Is that likely?"

"I'd rather wait and see where we are after the nutritionist and I have had a few sessions with her. We don't have the kind of program here that they have at a major medical center, but we do have people who know what they're doing. If Annie's cooperative and we see some progress, perhaps get her caloric intake up and see her putting on a few pounds, then it may be possible to avoid an inpatient program. Sometimes, though, that is the best option if we're to avoid a repeat of the extreme behavior. It's just too soon to tell with Annie. Will you and your ex-wife be comfortable with sending her elsewhere, if that's what we think would be best?"

"We'll do whatever's best for Annie," Ronnie assured her. If he had to twist Dana Sue's arm to get her to agree, he'd do so. Of course, his considerable powers of persuasion might be considered suspect these days.

Dr. McDaniels gave him a knowing look. "Let's talk about you for a minute. You said you've been gone since the divorce."

He nodded.

"I imagine you're feeling pretty guilty about now," she said.

"Of course I am. If I'd been here in town…"

"Things might have turned out exactly the same way, unless your staying might have prevented the divorce."

When he was about to respond, she held up a hand. "Doesn't matter," she said. "What-ifs are a waste of time, Mr. Sullivan. Let's deal with what is and move on from here, okay? Will you be willing to participate in some sessions if I need you to? I know your presence will be a help to the nutritionist, too. We both like plenty of parental involvement in this process. Are you staying in town long enough for that?"

"I'll be here indefinitely," he said. "And I'll do whatever it takes."

"And your ex-wife?"

"She'll be there, too." Whatever reservations Dana Sue might have about being in the same room with him would just have to be put on hold until Annie was healthy again. Dana Sue was too good a mother not to go along with that.

"Fine. Then as soon as Annie's stable and alert, I'll start spending a little time with her, and I'll let you know where we go from there."

"Thank you."

"Don't thank me yet. We haven't even started the hard stuff," she warned. "I suspect you'll all have reason to hate me before we're through. Some of the emotions we're likely to touch on will be pretty raw and painful. And there are going to be times when I'll have to be tough with Annie. Prepare yourself for that." She gave him a warm smile that took the edge off her warning. "I'll be in touch soon."

He watched her walk away, then turned and saw Dana Sue staring at him, anger in her eyes. When she would have brushed right past him in an obvious snit, he grabbed her arm.

"Okay, what are you thinking?" he asked.

"That you're not wasting any time finding someone to flirt with," she snapped. "Let me go. I want to see Annie."

"Don't you want to hear what Dr. McDaniels said first?"

Her expression faltered. "She's a doctor?"

"A psychologist," he confirmed. "She's going to be working with Annie as soon as she's well enough. McDaniels also wants us to participate in some of the sessions. She says a nutritionist will want our cooperation, as well. The conversation wasn't personal, Dana Sue. It was strictly about our daughter."

"Oh," she said meekly. "Well, she's an attractive woman. You can hardly blame me for jumping to conclusions."

He bit back a smile. "No, I can hardly blame you."

But he was going to do everything in his power to see that she never had any reason to jump to such a conclusion again.

The next few days were the longest of Dana Sue's life. Not only was she worried sick about her daughter, but having Ronnie underfoot every time she turned around was unnerving. He looked better than he ever had, and he was being so darn sweet and considerate, it almost made her forget why she'd kicked him out. That momentary flash of jealousy had been a stark reminder, but he'd taken the wind right out of her sails when he'd explained who Dr. McDaniels was.

Add to that the fact that the man hadn't left Annie's side for more than a few minutes at a time. His blue eyes were clouded with worry and exhaustion, but every time Dana Sue suggested he get some sleep, somehow he turned the tables and got Helen or Maddie to take her home for a nap.

"What do you think he's up to?" she asked Maddie as her friend drove her home the first time. Maddie had added her two cents to Ronnie's argument, which was the main reason Dana Sue had agreed to go. She didn't have the strength for a fight when the two of them ganged up on her.

"I don't think he's up to anything," Maddie said. "I think he's worried about Annie."

"Sure, but there's something else going on," Dana Sue insisted. "He keeps giving me these strange, speculative looks, as if he's trying to figure out what I'm thinking."

Maddie chuckled. "I'm sure he is. He's probably waiting for you to wake up and remember what he did, then tear a strip out of his hide again. It's not as if you just said 'so long' and sent him on his way. That scene on the front lawn had the whole town talking for months. Given your volatile temperament, I'm sure he thinks it could happen again at any time."

Dana Sue grimaced. "Once was enough. It was mortifying."

"It was what he deserved," Maddie corrected.

"No, I mean I was mortified when I thought about it afterward. Thanks to my public drama the whole town knew what he'd done to me. It's little wonder Annie skipped school for an entire week after that. I wanted to hide, too."

"Well, all that's in the past now," Maddie consoled her.

"Don't you think having him back here will remind everyone?"

Maddie gave her a knowing look. "Do you honestly regret calling him?"

Dana Sue thought it over, then shook her head. "As much as it pains me to admit it, he has every right to be here. And maybe he can actually get through to Annie. I certainly haven't had any luck."

"Maybe this scare will be enough to do the trick," Maddie suggested. "Passing out is one thing. A cardiac arrest at Annie's age is quite another."

"I wish I thought you were right, but Dr. McDaniels, the psychologist, seems to think the impact will be temporary unless Annie deals with the underlying issues. She told both me and Ronnie that she wants her in therapy. I can't disagree, but something tells me Annie's going to pitch a fit."

"Let her, but see to it she goes anyway. If the alternative is being sent to an inpatient facility, I imagine she'll get with the program soon enough. And it'll help to have Ronnie as your backup."

Dana Sue blinked at that. "He's not staying. I'm sure he's just waiting for the doctors to say that Annie's out of the woods, and he'll be leaving again."

Maddie looked startled. "He's not staying in Serenity? I got the impression…" Her voice trailed off. "Maybe I got it wrong."

Panic crept through Dana Sue. "Did he tell you something different, Maddie?"

"Talk to him," her friend encouraged. "You should be discussing this with each other, not with me. I refuse to get caught in the middle."

"Oh, I intend to talk to him," Dana Sue said grimly. "Calling him the other night was not an invitation for him to move back here."

Maddie grinned. "I don't think he sees it the same way."

"Oh?"

"I believe he said something to Helen about fate stepping in."

Dana Sue sat up straight, suddenly reinvigorated and spoiling for a fight. "Fate, my behind! Get me back to the hospital right this second. I need to have a little come-to-Jesus chat with my ex."

"You sure you want to have that conversation there?" Maddie asked worriedly.

"Why not?"

"Because, sweet pea, it's a hospital. You'll have to keep your voice down."

That was a downside, Dana Sue thought, but she could manage. She'd once told off a produce vendor with fairly colorful language without anyone eating in the restaurant being aware. Of course, getting anything through Ronnie Sullivan's thick skull without shouts and shattered pottery was another matter.

Annie was so surprised to find her father sitting beside her hospital bed that she almost passed out again.

"Daddy?" she whispered weakly, in case she was hallucinating.

A smile spread across his face. "I'm here, angel. It's good to see those big blue eyes of yours open again."

"I thought I heard you talking to me, but I was sure it had to be a dream. How long have you been here?"

"Since the night they brought you in."

Everything was so fuzzy. She remembered practically gagging at the sight of all the food her mom had brought in for the sleepover. Then she and the other girls were dancing when her chest started feeling funny, like something was squeezing her heart real tight. She'd never felt anything like it before in her life, not even in phys ed, when she'd had to run. She'd decided to take a nap, and that was the last thing she remembered.

"When was that?"

"A few days ago."

"That long? Why can't I remember coming here? Or anything that's gone on since I got here? How come I'm hooked up to all this stuff?"

"The monitors are keeping track of how you're doing and the IV is getting some fluids and medicine into you. You've been mostly asleep since that night. I don't mind telling you that you gave us all quite a scare," he chided gently.

"I'm sorry. How did you know to come?"

"Your mom called me."

That meant her mom must have been terrified she, Annie, was going to die. She couldn't imagine any other reason her mom would have called her dad.

"How long are you going to stay?" she asked.

"For good," he said.

Annie just stared at him, a faint spark of hope stirring in her heart. "Does Mom know?"

"Not yet," he admitted. "Think she'll flip out?"

Annie managed a wobbly grin. "You know it."

He sighed. "Yeah, that's what I figured, too."

She reached for his hand. "Don't let her talk you out of it, okay?"

"Not a chance, angel. Not a chance."

Annie leveled a look straight into her dad's eyes to see if he was telling her the truth. He didn't even blink.

"You promise?" she asked, just to be sure.

"Cross my heart," he said, as he had after every single promise he'd ever made to her.

Annie thought back. He'd never broken one of those promises. He might have betrayed her mom, but he'd always been honest with *her,* even when it had hurt.

"Good," she whispered.

She was still clinging to his hand when she fell back to sleep.

8

The next time Annie woke up, there was a woman she didn't recognize sitting beside her bed. The white lab coat over her street clothes probably meant she was a doctor. Though her smile was friendly, the somber expression in her eyes made Annie nervous. She had a feeling she didn't want to hear whatever this woman had to say. And whenever she got scared, she used belligerence to cover her fear. Annie tried her best to stare the woman down, but she only stared back.

"Where's my dad?" Annie finally demanded, her voice laced with suspicion, as if this woman were somehow responsible for his absence. "He was here a minute ago." Annie had no idea if that was true. Given the way time was slipping by without her being aware of it, he could have left *hours* earlier.

"I don't know where your dad is right now," the woman claimed, her tone perfectly—and annoyingly—calm. "He wasn't here when I arrived."

Annie studied her with increased suspicion. "Who are you and why are you in my room?"

"I'm Dr. McDaniels. I'm going to be working with you for a while."

Alarm bells went off in Annie's head. "Working with me how? Like in physical therapy or something?"

This time the woman's smile reached all the way to her eyes. "Afraid not. I'm a psychologist. We're going to try to work on this eating disorder of yours."

"You're a shrink!" Annie said, horrified. The last thing she wanted was somebody poking around in her head, as if she was crazy. "I don't think so."

"I could show you my certification," the woman said, as if proof was what Annie was after.

"Not interested," she said stubbornly. "I don't need a shrink. There's nothing wrong with me. I certainly don't have an eating disorder."

"Really? Then why are you in the hospital?"

Annie realized she didn't know all the details about why she'd ended up here. Probably her mom and her friends had just freaked over something silly. "I got sick. No big deal," she claimed with sheer bravado. "I'll probably be out of here today."

"I doubt that," Dr. McDaniels responded. "I'd say a week to ten days if you work really, really hard."

Annie panicked at her certainty. "I'm telling you it's no big deal," she insisted. "I feel fine. I could probably run a marathon this afternoon if I wanted to."

The doctor leaned forward and looked her in the eye. "Really? You think so?"

"Sure," Annie said. "My mom probably overreacted the other night. She does that a lot."

"Not this time," Dr. McDaniels said gently. "You've met Dr. Lane, right?"

Annie nodded.

"And you know he's a cardiologist?"

He'd probably said so, but it hadn't registered. "That's a heart doctor," Annie said slowly. "Why would I need a heart doctor?"

"Because not eating can take a serious toll on your heart. That's what happened to you. You developed an arrhythmia—that's an erratic and too-fast heartbeat. Do you remember that?"

Annie swallowed hard. "I guess," she admitted. "But I feel okay now."

"Because the staff here has been working to get all of your electrolytes back into balance and to start boosting your nutrition levels. We can only do so much, though. The really hard work is up to you. Otherwise, next time, you might not be so lucky."

Annie started to tremble at the unspoken implication. Before she could control it, tears were welling up in her eyes and rolling down her cheeks. "You're just saying that to scare me," she protested. "My mom put you up to it, 'cause she doesn't like it that I'm losing weight and she's not."

"Annie, I'm not saying any of this to upset you. And your mom didn't put me up to anything. I just want you to understand that this is very, very serious, but we can fix it. If you want, I can bring Dr. Lane in here to explain exactly what happened to your heart the other night and why," Dr. McDaniels offered. "He can talk to you about how weak your heart is, what a disaster your potassium and other levels are. Or you can take my word for it that I would never lie about something this important."

Annie let her head drop back on the pillow and closed her eyes. It all made an awful kind of sense. Nothing less than a heart attack would have gotten her mom to call her dad—that was more telling than anything else. Annie was pretty sure he wouldn't have raced back home if she'd just fainted or something. But it was crazy. Kids didn't have heart attacks.

She felt a cool touch on her hand and looked up into Dr. McDaniels's sympathetic gaze. "Pretty scary, huh? I imagine you never thought that what you were doing could have this kind of consequence."

"I didn't do anything," Annie protested again, but now there was less conviction in her voice.

"We'll talk about that next time I come by," Dr. McDaniels told her. "For now, I want you to be openminded when Lacy Reynolds gets here. Work with her, okay? She has your best interests at heart."

"Who's she?"

"She's the nutritionist who's going to help make you well again. She'll regulate your food intake and teach you about nutrition."

"My mom owns a restaurant. She knows all about food."

"I'm familiar with Sullivan's," Dr. McDaniels said. "It's got a great menu. Too bad you haven't been eating what your mom serves there."

"Who says I haven't?" Annie said belligerently.

"The scales don't lie," the doctor replied gently. "And the fact that you're here is pretty telling, too."

Annie studied Dr. McDaniels for a minute. She didn't seem like the kind of person who'd be cruel or make too big a deal about something. In fact, she looked more sad than mean, as if she felt bad that Annie was here, and really wanted to help. Annie wasn't ready to trust her yet, but she couldn't dismiss her the way she'd wanted to at first.

"Could you find my mom or my dad for me?" she asked. She knew she didn't sound half as brave as she had earlier.

"Of course. I'll tell them to come by as soon as your meeting with Lacy is over," the doctor promised. "It's very nice to meet you, Annie. I think we're going to make a lot of progress together."

Annie watched her leave the room, then closed her eyes

again. There had to be some mistake, she told herself. There had to be. But somewhere deep inside, she knew that Dr. McDaniels had been telling the truth.

Without even realizing it could happen, Annie had almost killed herself.

When the door to her room opened again, Annie was hoping it would be her mom and dad. Instead, the woman who walked in, wearing white slacks, a brightly flowered uniform top and thick-soled white shoes, had spiked black hair and a pierced eyebrow. The uniform and name tag gave away the fact that she was a hospital employee. Otherwise Annie would have thought she was a college student or maybe a member of some rock band.

"Hi, Annie," she said cheerfully. "I'm Lacy Reynolds."

"The nutritionist," Annie said, surprised.

"Ah, I see Dr. McDaniels told you about me."

"Not that you'd be so young and cool-looking," Annie said candidly. "I wish my mom would let me pierce something."

"When you're my age, you can do whatever you want. See? There's something to look forward to." The woman grinned at her. "Doesn't mean I'm not tough, though, so watch out. When it comes to what goes into your mouth in this place, I'm in charge, and believe me, there's nothing that happens that I don't find out about."

Despite the warning, Annie couldn't help liking her. At least she laid everything out there so you understood the rules.

"Dr. McDaniels said you were going to talk to me about food," Annie said. "My mom knows all kinds of stuff about food and I hang out at her restaurant a lot."

"Then you know something about food, too," Lacy said. She took a small notebook out of her pocket. "Let's talk about what you've been eating lately."

Annie squirmed.

The nutritionist continued to wait, her pen poised above her pad of paper. "Well?" she prodded.

"I eat a lot of different stuff," Annie claimed eventually.

Lacy gave her a disappointed look. "Here's the first rule with me, Annie. You have to be honest. If I don't know where you are, then I don't know how far we have to go. Let's be specific. What did you have to eat the day you wound up in here?"

Annie tried to think back. She'd skipped breakfast that day except for a few sips of water. At school she'd bought a salad in the cafeteria and eaten a few shreds of the carrot on the top. When her friends had come over, she'd made a pretense of eating the pizza her mom had ordered for them, but one bite had made her feel sick.

"I wasn't feeling hungry that day," she said eventually.

"Come on, Annie. Just be straight with me."

"I had a salad for lunch and pizza when my friends came over," she said, embellishing the truth.

Lacy didn't make a single note, just kept gazing at her until Annie blinked and looked away.

"Okay, I ate some of the shredded carrot on the salad and a bite of pizza."

Lacy nodded and finally made a note. "Any idea how many calories that is?"

She shrugged. "I told you, I wasn't hungry."

"A hundred at most, and that's if you're even being honest with me. Nobody can survive on that, Annie. You do understand that, don't you?" She waited until Annie nodded before going on. "Okay, here's what's going to happen. You and I are going to work out a plan. While you're here, you're going to have three meals and three snacks a day. At first these will be very small, just a couple of hundred calories more than you were eating, but we'll increase the amount until you're up to the number of calories you should be eating."

"No way," Annie protested. The thought of all that food made her feel physically ill.

"Here's the alternative, then," Lacy said, her tone unyielding. "You're not going to starve yourself on my watch, so we'll insert a feeding tube to make sure you get the nutrition you need. You need to think of food as medicine for now. It's the thing that will make you well and allow you to go back home and live a full and happy life. I know that's what you want, and it's my goal to make sure you get it. It's up to you to decide which way we go with this."

The thought of a feeding tube made Annie cringe. "What kind of food?" she finally asked.

"You and I will decide that together, along with some input from your folks. At first it will be really simple, basic things. Maybe some fruit or crackers and juice, part of a turkey sandwich. Someone on staff will be here when you eat to make sure you eat everything you're supposed to for each meal or snack. If there's something you can't eat or can't finish, we have a nutrition shake you can have to replace the calories. You might only need an ounce or two, depending on how much of the meal you don't eat."

Annie was appalled by the regimen. She was going to feel like some kind of animal in a zoo with people watching every bite she put in her mouth. "How long does this go on?"

"For as long as it takes to get your lab work normal and your heart rate back up. Your whole team will make that decision. That's Dr. Lane, Dr. McDaniels and me. The monitoring of your food will go on even after you leave here. I'll work with your folks to see that they understand the food plan."

Annie felt tears welling up in her eyes, and turned away. "I don't think I can do this," she whispered.

"I think you can," Lacy said. "And we're all going to be here to help. We have another girl like you here right now who's almost ready to go home. You could talk to her if you want to. It might help you not feel so alone."

"No," Annie said, shaking her head adamantly. She didn't want someone else knowing her business.

"Okay," Lacy said. "Let me know if you change your mind. In the meantime, I want you to write down some of your favorite foods for me. I'll be back a little later and we can plan your menu for dinner and a snack tonight and for the whole day tomorrow, okay?"

"Whatever," Annie said, still not looking at her. How had she ever thought Lacy Reynolds was cool? She was just another adult on some kind of power trip. Maybe if she told her folks that, they would get her out of here.

She sighed when she heard the door to her room close. Who was she kidding? Her mom and dad were way too freaked to take her home. And somewhere way down inside was this nagging feeling that she ought to be freaked, too. But if she admitted that, what then? Food was the one thing in her life she'd been able to control. Dieting was the one thing she'd been really good at, though her body still wasn't as perfect as it could be. Now all these people wanted her to stuff her face and ruin everything.

Terrified by the image of herself as fat and ugly, she buried her face in her pillow and let the tears flow.

Ronnie was on his way back from the cafeteria when Linda McDaniels stopped him in the hall.

"Annie's asking for you," she told him.

He almost bolted past her, but she put out a hand to stop him.

"She knows she has a heart problem and that it was brought on by her eating disorder. The nutritionist met with her, too. Annie's in denial right now, so don't push her too hard to accept the truth. She'll come around to it on her own."

"You told her?"

"She'd figured out some of it. As I told you at the beginning, sometimes my role is to be the bad guy and lay out the hard truths. It's best to get everything out in the open, along with the plan for what happens next."

He ran his hand over his head. "What am I supposed to say to her?"

"If she has questions, answer them if you can. Otherwise leave it up to the doctors, the nutritionist or me to clarify things for her. Really, all she needs for the next couple of days is to know you're in her corner and that she's going to be okay. The rest will come in time."

"Did you tell her about the therapy sessions?"

"Only that there would be some, not how difficult or intensive they're going to be."

"How did she react?"

The psychologist grinned. "She told me she didn't need therapy, of course. Part of my job will be to convince her otherwise."

"God, how did things get to be such a mess?" Ronnie lamented.

"That's what we're going to figure out," Dr. McDaniels assured him. "We will unravel this, Mr. Sullivan."

He gave her a weary look. "She's always been a good kid, you know. Great grades. Lots of friends. A zillion different activities."

"Sounds like an overachiever," she said. "Ironically, when

that same sort of determination is turned to something like dieting, it can backfire. But let's not worry about that now. Let's just get her physically healthy and then we'll take care of whatever issues brought her to this point. Lacy Reynolds, the nutritionist, has already explained the basics of her food plan, so Annie can begin to see food in a more realistic light— as fuel for the body, not an enemy."

Ronnie nodded, grateful for the calm, reasonable approach McDaniels was offering. Without it, he had a hunch he'd be punching his fists through walls by now.

"Go to your daughter," she encouraged. "I'll see if I can track down your ex-wife and send her in, as well."

"I think she went home to get some rest," he said.

"I'll call the house, then."

"Try her cell phone," Ronnie suggested, jotting the number down for her. "She's more likely to answer that."

"Will do. Thanks. I'll be in touch later," the woman said, then strode off.

Ronnie followed her with his gaze, wishing he were half as confident as she seemed to be that Annie would come through this crisis okay. A part of him wished Dr. McDaniels would come with him to visit Annie. She knew exactly what to say to his daughter, while he didn't have a clue. The situation probably called for calm diplomacy and tact, neither of which were his strong suits. Now that the shock of Annie's appearance had worn off, now that the doctors were more certain she would recover, he wanted to blast her for the stupidity of her actions. He had a hunch that would be counterproductive.

Schooling his expression into something he hoped was neutral, he went back to her room. At first glance, Annie appeared to be sleeping again. Relieved, he took his customary place in the chair beside her bed and let his mind wander to the way she'd looked the last time he'd seen her before leaving town.

She'd appeared sad and disappointed, but at least she'd looked like a normal teenager, with color in her cheeks, a hairstyle that framed her pretty face and a body that was just beginning to round out with womanly curves. He'd been scared to death about what would happen when her interest in boys turned serious, how he would cope with the whole dating thing, but as he'd sat in his car on the street that day two years ago, he'd realized that he wouldn't even be around to play a role in whatever decisions she would soon start to make about boys.

If he'd been thinking straight then—or in all the months that followed— he'd never have left her to make her way through that hormonal minefield without a father's input. *His* input. It was a regret he'd live with till the day he died.

"Hi, Daddy," Annie said weakly, snapping him out of his memories.

"Hey, sweetheart. How are you feeling?"

"Better now that you're here. When I woke up before and you were gone, I was scared you'd changed your mind and decided to leave."

"I promised you I wasn't going anywhere, didn't I?"

She nodded.

"You can count on that, baby. I'm back for good."

She smiled and once again closed her eyes, leaving Ronnie to go back to his bittersweet memories.

Dana Sue was outside Annie's room and about to push the door all the way open when she heard Ronnie's voice. She bit back a gasp at this confirmation of what Maddie had told her earlier. Her ex was planning to stick around Serenity even after this crisis passed.

Whirling about, she marched back down the hall to the waiting room, where she'd left Maddie.

"Ronnie is staying. I heard him tell Annie he's back for good," she said, pacing agitatedly. "Why would he say that and get her hopes up?"

"Maybe because that's what he's planning to do," Maddie suggested.

Dana Sue scowled at her. "What am I going to do? I have to stop him."

"Even if this is what's best for Annie?" Maddie asked reasonably.

Dana Sue stopped in front of her. "Having Ronnie Sullivan back in her life is not what's best for Annie," she snapped, then resumed pacing.

"I wonder if Annie would agree with that," Maddie said, her tone mildly reproachful. "I think you're projecting your feelings onto Annie. *You're* the one who doesn't want Ronnie around."

Dana Sue scowled at her again and continued walking.

"Sit," Maddie ordered. "You're making my head spin. Now let's consider this rationally. Annie needs her father in her life. Even you theorized that his leaving might have had something to do with this decision of hers to obsess about her weight. Doesn't it make sense that having him back might—"

When Dana Sue was about to interrupt, Maddie held up a hand. "That it just *might* be the one thing that could turn Annie around?"

Dana Sue sank onto one of the hard, plastic chairs. "Maybe," she conceded reluctantly. "But I hate the idea. I don't want him here. I want to be the one who fixes this."

Maddie barely managed to contain a smile. "Does it really matter who fixes it, as long as Annie is healthy again?" Her gaze narrowed. "What are you really afraid of, Dana Sue? Are you scared he might actually be able to get through to Annie in a way you couldn't? That's what it sounds like you're saying."

"No," Dana Sue said at once. "That would be selfish."

This time Maddie didn't even bother trying to hide her grin. "Then it must be that you're scared he might get to you."

Dana Sue sighed. Maddie was more accurate than she wanted to admit. She was tempted to deny it, but this was Maddie, her best friend. She'd never let her get away with it. "So what if I am?" she grumbled.

"Then make this all about Annie. Set your ground rules about how involved he gets in your life. Keep your distance from Ronnie, but don't try to keep him from your daughter."

"Why do you always have to be so damn rational and reasonable and right?" she groused.

"It's a natural talent," Maddie said, laughing. "I probably should remind you that I was none of those things when Cal first came into my life. I fought that just as hard as you're trying to keep Ronnie from sneaking back into yours."

"And we all know how well that turned out," Dana Sue said wearily. She was doomed.

Unless, she thought, brightening, unless she took total charge of the situation, just as Maddie had said. She could establish the ground rules and Ronnie would just have to live with them. He would spend time with Annie on *her* timetable, under *her* conditions.

Then she remembered that one of Ronnie's favorite pastimes was breaking rules, and some of her good cheer evaporated. Still, she could try. She could raise a fuss, keep him off balance and erect enough barriers to keep an NFL lineman from getting through. She could demand he leave, and then find some compromise, so she'd come across as the reasonable one. Actually, it might be kind of fun to match wits with him again.

"We need to go outside and wait for him," she told Maddie, leaping back to her feet. "Now."

"Excuse me?"

"No, hold on," she said, pausing in midstride. "I'll go outside and wait for him. You tell him to take a break. I'll ambush him as soon as he leaves the building."

Maddie stared at her as if she'd lost her mind. "What are you going to do, Dana Sue?"

"I'm going to banish him. He'll refuse to go, naturally. Then I'll agree to some compromise, one where I set ground rules, just the way you told me to," she told her innocently. "Ronnie won't know what hit him."

"Couldn't you just walk down the hall and have this conversation with him in here?" Maddie suggested. "That's what mature adults do. They work things out."

"We're talking about Ronnie," Dana Sue said. "Quiet, rational conversation doesn't accomplish much. The decibel level required to get through his thick skull is best reserved for outside."

Maddie frowned. "Are you sure this is a good idea?"

"It's an excellent idea," Dana Sue assured her. "Just do your part. I'll take care of the rest."

When she was satisfied that Maddie would somehow manage to roust Ronnie from Annie's room, she headed downstairs and outside to lie in wait for him. The prospect of having the upper hand for once had her humming happily.

After a couple of minutes, she realized that the tune she was humming had been their favorite song way back when. She cut herself off in midnote and got busy working her temper back into the danger zone. All it took was imagining him tangled up in some motel room bed with a woman he barely knew. Maybe later Dana Sue would try to figure out why, after two years, she could still summon that image on command. Perhaps it was because it was so handy whenever she felt her resolve weakening.

Ronnie was half dozing beside Annie's bed when Maddie came into the room.

"You look beat," she said, regarding him with sympathy. "Why don't you get out of here and grab some rest yourself?"

"Someone needs to be here when Annie wakes up again," he told her.

"I'll stay, and I imagine Dana Sue will be back soon."

"You got her to go home to take a nap?"

"I tried," Maddie said.

Ronnie studied her face. "But?"

"She's back."

"Mustn't have been much of a nap."

"We never made it to her house. She decided there were things she needed to do here."

"Such as?"

"She thought she should be nearby in case Annie needs her," Maddie said, but her tone was evasive.

Ronnie regarded her quizzically. "What aren't you telling me?"

"I think maybe I'll let you figure this out on your own," she said. "All that matters is that I can sit with Annie for a while."

"Since you're here and not Dana Sue, that means she's somewhere on the premises hoping to ambush me," he concluded. He knew how these two worked as a team. He supposed he ought to be grateful that Helen wasn't in on whatever scheme they'd hatched.

"I never said that Dana Sue's return had anything to do with you," Maddie responded.

"No, of course you didn't. You'd never betray her," he said, then grinned. "But you'd set me up."

She flushed guiltily. "No comment."

He latched on to her hand. "Look, I need to get out of here for a little while, that's true. I need to find a motel room, clean up and get some rest. Annie's sleeping for the moment, so why don't you come along with me? We can take a little walk together."

Maddie balked at the door. "I should stay."

"Annie's asleep."

"Not two minutes ago, you thought someone needed to be here."

He laughed. "I don't imagine this will take all that long. Dana Sue's probably lurking right outside the front door."

"If you know that, why drag me along?"

"I want a witness to whatever she's up to," he said. "Come on, Madelyn. Protect me."

"As if," she grumbled, but she went with him.

Sure enough, just as they exited the building, Dana Sue appeared in front of him, hands on hips, her expression filled with sass and vinegar. What that woman could do to a man's libido with just a look ought to be outlawed! Ronnie thought.

"You," she began, poking a finger in his chest, "are...not...staying...here." Each emphatic word was accompanied by another jab. "I won't have it, do you understand me? This town is not big enough for the two of us. I'm not even sure the entire state of South Carolina is big enough for the two of us."

Ronnie could barely contain a smile. He managed a shrug. "I'm afraid you'll just have to learn to deal with it, sugar. I'm staying."

"Did you not hear a word I just said?" she demanded.

"I'm sure every patient at Regional Hospital heard you," he replied calmly. Then he turned to Maddie and silently mouthed, "Told you so."

Maddie looked away.

Dana Sue frowned at his comment about her volume, and the next time she spoke, her voice was lower, but no less incensed. "If I'd thought calling you was going to give you some crazy idea about coming back here permanently, I would never have picked up the phone."

"And if something had happened to Annie without me being here, I would never have forgiven you," he responded quietly. "Let's get one thing straight, Dana Sue. I love that girl. I was a fool to leave town just because it was what you wanted, and I was an even bigger fool not to demand joint custody instead of visitation, but I'm not going anywhere ever again."

He decided now was not the time to mention that he still loved Dana Sue, as well. She'd just throw those words right back in his face, accompanied by a long-winded reminder about why they were divorced.

With apparent effort, she finally simmered down a notch. "I know you love Annie. That's why I did call. But, Ronnie, seriously, I don't want you to stay."

"You've made that plain enough."

"Then you'll go?"

"No."

"Dammit, Ronnie, you can't want to be here again, not knowing the way I feel about you, not knowing that it's going to dredge up a lot of bad memories and gossip."

Once again, he was forced to contain a grin. "I can live with a little gossip and, indeed, I do know how you feel," he said. He doubted she knew it half as well as he did. She wanted to believe he was beneath contempt—and to be honest, he couldn't deny it—but that didn't mean she didn't still love him.

He probably could have proved that with a kiss, too, but then she'd have to slap him silly out of some sense of pride.

"I think we should table this discussion till things settle down a bit," he said. Then, knowing it would provoke her, he added, "I'm sure you'll be more reasonable then."

"Reasonable!" she snapped, clearly outraged by the suggestion she was out of control now. "You want reasonable? How's this? If you stay here, Ronnie Sullivan, I will make your life a living hell. I will…" She paused, apparently to consider all the vile things she intended to do to him.

He knew the only way to shut her up once she got this wound up was to kiss her, so he decided to risk life and limb to do it. He dragged her against him, sealed her mouth with his and kissed her until she turned weak in his arms. He felt none too steady himself. Dana Sue definitely hadn't lost her ability to make him see stars.

Naturally, just as he'd predicted, she slapped him when he let her go, but he was ready for it. He merely grinned. "Next time you want to rant and rave at me, sugar, think about that kiss."

"Never!" she said furiously. "It didn't mean a thing. It wasn't the least bit memorable."

He shrugged. "Then I must be out of practice. But knowing how you love to vent your anger at me, I'm sure I'll have plenty of chances to get it right. A good ole breath-stealing kiss has always been the best way I know to shut you up."

He lingered long enough to wink at Maddie. "I told you my being back was going to get interesting."

Dana Sue glared at both of them. She was still sputtering

when he slipped right on past her and went to his car. His smile spread as he considered the very promising heat in that confrontation. Damn, even under these circumstances, it was good to be home again!

9

"Well, that was…interesting," Maddie said when she joined Dana Sue and stared after Ronnie as he drove away from the hospital.

"Don't start with me," Dana Sue said sharply.

"I'm just saying—"

"I don't want to hear any of your opinions or observations about what just happened," Dana Sue said.

"I was merely going to comment on your knack for compromise," Maddie said, barely holding back a grin. "Impressive."

Dana Sue scowled at her. "Rub it in, why don't you? He didn't give me a chance to compromise. He made me so mad, all I could think about was getting him out of town as fast as humanly possible."

"I'm pretty sure he's not going anywhere now," Maddie said, her expression gloating. "What man would leave after a kiss like that?"

"Oh, go suck an egg," Dana Sue retorted. She'd never been so humiliated in her entire life. Except, maybe, for the day she'd kicked Ronnie out of her house and the whole neighborhood had come out to watch. Today was definitely a close second. She held up her hand to ward off whatever words were still on the tip of her friend's tongue. "Not another word," she warned.

Maddie grinned. "Okay."

"And don't tell Helen."

"Okay."

"Or Annie," Dana Sue added. "Especially don't tell Annie."

"Got it," Maddie confirmed. Apparently not content to leave it at that, though, she added, "I'm supposed to keep my mouth shut about your ex-husband laying a kiss on you that could have steamed up every window in the state."

Despite her annoyance, a grin tugged at the corners of Dana Sue's mouth. "It *was* hot, wasn't it?"

"You'd have to be the one to say," Maddie said piously. "I'm not supposed to comment on my observations."

"Maddie, what am I going to do?" she asked, unable to keep the desperate note out of her voice. She still wanted the man, damn him to hell.

"Am I supposed to answer that?"

"Please."

"Give it time, sweetie. Maybe he'll change his mind and leave once he knows Annie is okay."

Dana Sue met her gaze. "Maybe, if I'm being honest, I don't want him to."

Maddie's determinedly serious expression gave way to a full-fledged grin. "Something tells me he's counting on that."

She was probably right, Dana Sue thought. Maddie knew Ronnie inside out, understood him on some level that eluded her. Probably because Dana Sue never used logic when it came to Ronnie. She listened to her heart and her hormones. She'd been his partner, his lover, his grand passion, but Maddie had been his friend. In some ways, Dana Sue was jealous of that. Maybe if she and Ronnie had talked more, if they'd had the kind of relationship she had with Erik, for instance, they would have been able to work through their problems.

Instead, the breakup had been just as passionate and unthinking as the relationship.

"What if there's still this wild, out-of-control attraction, but neither of us has really learned anything?"

"You'll survive," Maddie said. "You not only survived the last time, you thrived."

"Because I had to," Dana Sue said. "I had Annie to consider. I couldn't just fall apart and let her suffer. She was in enough pain as it was." She glanced toward the hospital. "And look how *that* turned out. I did a lousy job of protecting her."

"For the hundredth time, you did not fail Annie," Maddie insisted. "If parents blamed themselves for every single foolish decision their kids made, they'd never get out of bed in the morning. Teenagers are going to make mistakes, more than likely a lot of them. All we can do is be there to pick up the pieces, and hope they learn from them."

Maddie gave her a thoughtful look. "You know, it might be easier to get through all this with Annie if you were sharing the burden with someone."

"I have you and Helen," Dana Sue said defiantly. "Even Erik has been a rock. You guys are enough."

"But daughters and dads," Maddie said, "they have a special bond."

Dana Sue thought about her too-brief relationship with her own dad, who'd died when she was only seven. She'd never felt entirely safe after that, which may have been why she'd put so much faith and trust in Ronnie. He'd made her feel that way again.

"You think I should let him stay, don't you?" she asked.

Maddie lifted a brow. "I'm not sure whether he stays or goes is your decision. Ronnie has a mind of his own. However, I do think you could find a way to look on the bright side if he does stay."

"More chances to kill him?" Dana Sue suggested, not entirely in jest.

"I was thinking of letting him share the work it's going to take to get Annie back on track. But there is a benefit for you, as well."

"Oh?"

"There are a lot of unresolved issues between you. Because he took off, you never dealt with anything."

"I threw him out. I'd say that had a certain finality to it," Dana Sue argued.

Maddie looked amused. "You threw him out in a fit of temper, because your pride had been wounded. I'm not saying it wasn't justifiable. I'm just saying it didn't give either of you a chance to work through the real issues, like why he cheated in the first place and whether there was anything he could do to prove that it would never happen again. You didn't even give him a chance to explain, did you?"

Dana Sue regarded her incredulously. "What was there to explain? The man cheated. End of story."

"With some mature relationships," Maddie said, "that would be the beginning of the hard work, not the end of the story."

"I don't recall you being all that eager to take Bill back when you found out he'd been cheating on you," Dana Sue retorted, referring to Maddie's ex-husband. Even as the words crossed her lips, she regretted opening an old wound. "I'm sorry. I shouldn't have said that."

"It's okay." Maddie didn't look half as upset as she might have a few months ago. "His girlfriend was pregnant, remember? He wanted to marry her. It was a little too late to think about working things out."

"And if Noreen hadn't been pregnant, would you have fought to keep Bill after you found out about the affair?"

"Yes," Maddie said without hesitation. "He's the father of my children and we had a twenty-year marriage on the line. A part of me will always regret that we couldn't make it work. But am I happy now? Am I glad that things turned out the way they did, that Bill left and I found Cal? Of course. Cal's incredible." A smile lit her face. "We have a new baby, something I never would have contemplated in a million years if Bill and I had stayed together. If it had been up to him we would have stopped after Kyle was born. Katie was a surprise to both of us. She turned out to be a blessing, but he was adamant about not having any more children, and I thought I was too old to consider it, anyway. Thank heaven Cal doesn't think I'm too old to do anything I want to do."

Dana Sue didn't believe her friend was being entirely honest. "You seem to have forgotten one thing."

"Oh?"

"Bill and Noreen never got married. He decided he wanted you back. You chose Cal."

Maddie's cheeks colored. "True, but there was a lot of water under the bridge by then. Even so, I hesitated for about two seconds and thought about whether I should go back to Bill because of the kids. Then I faced the fact that I was happier with Cal than I had been in a long time."

"Maybe I'm happier without Ronnie," Dana Sue suggested.

"Really?" Maddie asked.

She found the skepticism annoying. "I have Annie. I have the restaurant. I'm busier than I've ever been."

"And you've never gone out with the same man more than twice," Maddie said. "The one man who might actually be a good match for you, you keep at arm's length."

Dana Sue frowned. "Who's that?" she asked, though she already knew.

"Erik."

"I suppose you have a theory about that?"

"Of course," Maddie said. "Your heart still belongs to someone else."

"Gee, I thought it was because most of the men were jerks," Dana Sue retorted, then amended, "and because Annie freaked out over my having any dates at all."

"Not all of them were jerks," Maddie countered. "Helen introduced you to a couple of guys who were solid, intelligent men with successful careers."

"True," Dana Sue admitted.

"You found flaws in them, too," Maddie said. "Mostly because they weren't Ronnie."

"No, that was a plus," Dana Sue insisted.

Maddie rolled her eyes. "Whatever. How about Erik? What are his flaws?"

"He doesn't have any that I've noticed," Dana Sue admitted. "He's a wonderful man. I just don't feel that way about him. I would never take a chance on spoiling the friendship and the working relationship we have."

"Is it that, or is it because Ronnie was and is your soul mate, and you know it?"

Dana Sue gave Maddie a perplexed look. "I don't get it. I thought you were as furious about Ronnie's betrayal as I was."

"I was," she agreed.

"But I've seen you with him the last few days. You've given him a pass. The two of you are all buddy-buddy again, just the way you were years ago."

"Because at his core, Ronnie Sullivan is a decent guy. He made a stupid mistake, but one that a lot of men make at one time or another. He wasn't some serial cheater who chased anything in shorts and a tank top. I'm not saying he deserves a pass, just a chance to make it right."

"Helen would disagree," Dana Sue said.

"Helen's a divorce attorney. She's a lot more jaded than I am," Maddie responded. "Bottom line, it's your life, your decision. I'm just saying maybe you could keep an open mind. Whatever you decide, you know I'll back you a hundred percent."

"Even if I chase him off?"

"Even if you *try* to chase him off."

"You don't think I can?"

Maddie held up her hands. "Hey, don't you dare turn this into a challenge just to prove me wrong. It's your happiness that's on the line."

Yeah, that was the rub, Dana Sue admitted to herself. On some level she knew there wasn't another man on earth who could make her happier than Ronnie Sullivan. What flat-out terrified her, though, was that no man could make her as miserable, either.

Annie was starting to feel as if her mom was staying away on purpose. Oh, she'd breezed in and out of the ICU, told her she loved her, but she'd avoided the kind of heart-to-heart Annie had been expecting. Either that was because her dad was around or because her mom was so furious with her she didn't want to risk a fight while Annie was still lying in a hospital bed.

She hoped it wasn't because her dad was back. If it was, and her mom created some kind of ruckus with him, she was afraid her dad would take off once more. Annie didn't think she could stand it if he left again, not now when her life was such a mess.

The door to her room inched open just then and her mom peered in.

"You awake?" she called softly.

"Awake and bored," Annie said.

Her mom came into the room, brushed a kiss across her forehead and pulled a chair up beside the bed. "How are you feeling?"

"Lousy," Annie replied.

Alarm flared in her mom's eyes and she was on her feet in an instant. "What's wrong? Should I get the nurse in here? The doctor? Is it your heart?"

Annie stared at her. "Mom, chill. I just meant I was tired of all these people coming in here to poke around in my psyche and tell me what to do."

Her mom's shoulders sagged with relief. "Oh." She looked as if she wanted to say a lot more, but instead she sat back down, appearing uncomfortable.

Annie lost patience with all this tiptoeing around what was on both their minds. "Mom, why don't you just say it?"

"Say what?"

Annie's eyes welled with tears. "That I screwed up and you're mad at me."

"I'm not…"

Annie regarded her with a watery, disbelieving stare. "Come on," she said, swiping at her tears. "You know you want to yell at me. You believe what everyone around here is saying, that I was deliberately starving myself. Why not admit it? You've thought all along that I was anorexic. Now you have backup. You can say 'I told you so' for the next hundred years."

Her mom gave her a weary look. "I'd rather it weren't true, sweetie. And I'm not mad at you. I'm mad at myself for not facing it sooner and getting you some help." Her eyes filled with tears, as well. "I can't believe I was so stupid. I thought I was handling it. I thought you were smart enough to see what you were doing to yourself after you passed out at Maddie's wedding. I thought a lot of things that just weren't true. This isn't something that gets fixed by wishful thinking."

Annie was shaken by the tears spilling down her mom's cheeks. She'd never seen her cry before, not even when her dad had left. Oh, sure, she cried when they watched certain movies, but that wasn't the same. This was real. And the tears were all Annie's fault.

She reached for her hand. "I'm sorry, Mom. Please don't cry."

Her mom lifted her face, her expression filled with anguish. "We could have lost you, Annie. If Raylene and Sarah hadn't been there…"

Annie shuddered. The gravity of what had nearly happened was finally starting to sink in. Worse, if Dr. McDaniels was telling her the truth, there were no certainties that it wouldn't happen again.

"Mom, I'm scared," she whispered. "Really scared."

Her mom moved to the side of the bed and pulled her into her arms. "Me, too, baby. But we're going to fix this. All of us together."

"Dad, too?" she asked hesitantly.

She thought she felt her mom sigh against her cheek.

"Yes, sweetie, Dad, too."

Ronnie found a motel room about halfway between the hospital and the home he'd once shared with Dana Sue. Even as he pulled into the parking lot, he knew what lay ahead. The owners of the Serenity Inn, Maybelle and Frank Hawkins, had lived in town all their lives. They knew every person who came and went, including those who only passed through for a day or two. They'd known Ronnie's parents and Dana Sue's entire family, including her black-sheep uncle and his no-account sons who lived outside of town and caused more trouble with their illegal still and gambling than the Sweet Magnolias had ever dreamed of. Maybelle and Frank went to every high school football game, every basketball and baseball game. And they were regulars at Wharton's, where town gossip spread faster than a winter cold.

Still, the Serenity Inn, with its whitewashed exterior and big pots filled with geraniums, was clean, inexpensive and comfortable. And it held a few very fond memories, too....

Even though he knew this was the best of Serenity's limited options, Ronnie approached the office with a sense of dread. He plastered a smile on his face and opened the door, relieved to see that there was no one behind the desk. The sound of the bell over the door, however, brought Maybelle bustling in from the back room.

A smile lifted all the wrinkles on her round, motherly face when she recognized him. "Ronnie Sullivan, as I live and breathe. I never thought to see you in these parts again."

Before he could respond to the surprisingly warm greeting, her expression sobered and her gaze turned chilly. "I'm surprised you dared to show your face after what you did to Dana Sue. Then again, I imagine you came back because of Annie." Concern chased away her icy demeanor. "How is she doing? Is she better today?"

Almost dizzy from the rapid change in Maybelle's manner, he nodded. "She's going to be fine. It's good to see you, Mrs. Hawkins. Do you have a room available?"

She studied him with the kind of considering look a mother might give a wayward child. "For how long?"

"Until I can find a place of my own," he said.

His words seemed to catch her by surprise. "You're staying?"

"That's the plan."

"How does Dana Sue feel about that?"

He grinned, thinking back on the kiss. "She's still adjusting to the idea."

Maybelle studied him a moment longer, then finally nodded and brought out a registration form. "Fill that out. I'll give you a weekly rate for now." She wagged a finger at him. "But if I hear one word about you upsetting that girl, I will not hesitate to toss you out on your behind. Understood?"

Ronnie nodded. "Yes, ma'am," he said meekly.

She smiled at last. "Just wait till I tell Frank you're back. He still talks about that ninety-eight-yard touchdown run you made your senior year to win the homecoming game. Glory be, that was something. We all thought you'd be a star in college or the pros one day."

"You have a long memory, Mrs. Hawkins." He leaned in closer. "Don't tell anyone, but that touchdown was a fluke. I knew there wasn't a chance on earth I'd ever make a run like that again, so I decided to quit while I was ahead."

"You quit because you couldn't keep your hands off Dana Sue," she corrected knowingly. "Once you set eyes on that girl, marrying her was the only thing on your mind. And just so you know you didn't get away with anything, I know all about the two of you sneaking over here from time to time after the night clerk took over for me." She shook her head sorrowfully. "Why you'd go and mess up a thing like that is beyond me."

"It's beyond me, too," he admitted. "But it's never too late to correct a mistake, isn't that right?"

"It's never too late to try," she agreed. But there was enough doubt in her tone to warn him that she didn't think Dana Sue was going to be open to his attempts. "Here's your key. We don't allow wild partying on the premises, so behave yourself."

"Wild parties would hardly help me prove to Dana Sue that I'm walking the straight and narrow now, would they?" he said, winking at her. "I'll be so quiet you won't even know I'm here."

In fact, he was so thoroughly beat, he doubted there would be a sound louder than the occasional snore from his room for at least twenty-four hours.

After her disconcerting run-in with Ronnie and her draining visit with Annie, Dana Sue was too restless to sit in the hospital waiting room between her visits to Annie in ICU. She needed to stay busy, to do something that would drive the memory of that kiss right out of her head.

Glancing at her watch, she realized it was four o'clock, the height of the dinner prep commotion at the restaurant. Stopping at the nurse's station, she told them how to reach her if Annie needed her, then headed to work. A couple of hours chopping vegetables with a sharp knife might relieve some of her stress. She could envision Ronnie's neck beneath the blade.

At Sullivan's she stopped by her office long enough to glance at the pile of messages, grabbed a pristine white chef's jacket that would be splashed with food in minutes, and headed to the kitchen, where the noise level was comfortingly familiar.

Erik spotted her first. "Hey, darlin', what are you doing here? Come to make sure we aren't ruining your business?"

"No chance of that," she told him. "I just need to do something normal for a couple of hours. I know you and Karen have probably divvied up the workload, but there must be something left for me to tackle."

Karen glanced up from the salad greens she was distributing on plates and grinned. "I will gladly volunteer salad setup. It may just be the most boring job ever."

Dana Sue eyed the plates. "Plain old house salads?"

Karen nodded. "No time to do anything fancier."

"Do we have pears? Walnuts? Blue cheese?" Dana Sue asked.

"Of course," Erik said. "I've been making up the orders from the lists in your office. You're so organized this place could run for a year without you setting foot in it."

"I'm not sure I like that idea," Dana Sue said.

"Well, it's been a godsend the past few days," he assured her. "Doesn't mean we don't need you, so if you want to make fancy salads, go right ahead. I'll go make a note on the specials board and tell the waitstaff."

As Dana Sue settled in to slice the pears paper thin and arrange them on the greens, she sniffed the air. There was the distinctive scent of cinnamon in it. It smelled heavenly.

"What's tonight's dessert special?" she asked Erik when he returned.

"Deep-dish apple pie."

"Any of it ready yet?" she asked, her mouth watering.

"There are a couple of pies cooling on the rack now," he said. "You want a sample?"

"I want a whole slice," she said at once. "Vanilla ice cream on top."

He cast a worried look at her. "Dana Sue…" he began.

She held up her hand. "Not your job to lecture me about what I eat. I'm starved and I want apple pie and ice cream. Do I need to pull rank?"

Instead of immediately going for the pie, he pulled a stool up beside her and sat on it. "What's this about?"

"It's pie, for heaven's sake. What's the big deal?"

"You know what the big deal is," he said quietly. "Your daughter's in the hospital because of an eating disorder. Do you want to wind up in the bed beside her because you're not paying attention to your blood sugar?"

Temper stirring, Dana Sue turned on him angrily, but when all she saw in his eyes was genuine concern, she wilted. "Okay, I know you're right. I just need comfort food right now."

"There's meat loaf on tonight's menu. How about a slice of that with some mushroom gravy?" he suggested.

She finally relaxed and grinned. "May I at least have a bite of that pie afterward?"

"You may," he said, then went to fix a plate for her. When he brought it back, he regarded her with curiosity. "Anything happen this afternoon you want to talk about?"

She took a bite of meat loaf to delay responding. "My God, this is better than mine. What have you done to it?"

He gestured across the room. "Ask Karen. She made it."

Dana Sue stared at her assistant. "You made this? It's amazing."

"I just tweaked your recipe a little bit," Karen said, her cheeks flushed. "I hope you don't mind."

"Mind? Are you kidding me? I predict this will be tonight's sell-out, and our customers will insist it be on the regular menu."

"You mean it?" Karen asked.

"Of course I mean it," Dana Sue said. "If you have ideas for any other dishes, talk them over with Erik or me, if I'm around, and feel free to experiment."

"Thanks," Karen said, beaming. "I didn't want to step on your toes."

"We're a team. I may own this place, but when the food's great, it benefits all of us. I want Sullivan's reputation to get better every year. I don't want to rest on our laurels."

She turned back to Erik, who was still watching her intently. He lowered his voice. "She really needed to hear that," he said. "Now let's get back to my earlier question. Did something happen this afternoon to upset you? Is Annie doing okay?"

"She's getting better every day," Dana Sue replied. "She's had her first sessions with the psychologist and the nutritionist. I gather they weren't exactly love fests, but both women think she'll cooperate."

"If Annie's on track, then it must have been something else that sent you in here trying to stuff it down with comfort food."

"Erik, babysitting me and my moods is not your job."

"I do it because I'm your friend," he said, looking wounded. "At least that's what that pretty speech of yours a minute ago suggested."

Dana Sue felt her stomach knot. "I didn't eat the damn pie, okay? What more do you want?"

His gaze never wavered. "An explanation," he said quietly. "Did it have something to do with the kiss your ex-husband planted on you outside the hospital?"

She felt the color drain from her face. "You know about that?"

"Grace Wharton was on her way inside to check on Annie," he explained. "Apparently she made a U-turn to get back to Serenity's information central. It was the hot item over at the pharmacy soda fountain five minutes later."

"You were there?"

He shook his head. "Karen was."

Dana Sue buried her face in her hands. "I hate this. I just hate it. I should live in a big city where nobody has a clue who I am."

"You'd be miserable," he said. "So, do you want to talk about the kiss or not?"

"Not."

"Okay, then, but if it stirred you up enough to make you

want to reach for apple pie and ice cream, you might not want to repeat it too often," he advised.

"Oh, I think I can reassure you on that point," she said. "Ronnie Sullivan will not get within a hundred feet of me ever again."

Erik grinned. "Is that so?"

"Yes, that's most definitely so," she said.

"Then you might need to consider putting it in writing," he suggested, gesturing behind her.

Dana Sue whirled around and looked straight into the amused face of her ex-husband.

"Talking about me?" he inquired cheerfully.

"Go away," she retorted. "I thought you'd crawled into some cave to get some rest."

"Turns out a little catnap was all I needed," he responded. "Besides, the second I crawled into that bed at the Serenity Inn, I remembered the last time I'd slept in it—graduation night twenty-two years ago."

"You rented the exact same room?" she sputtered. "The one we…" She glanced at Erik's and Karen's fascinated expressions, then sighed heavily. "I'll have that apple pie now, please."

This time Erik didn't argue. He did, however, leave off the ice cream.

10

Annie's first so-called meal was absolute torture. The nurse brought her a tray with what looked like a mountain of food, though truthfully it was only a small salad with a tiny container of dressing and a package of crackers. It was accompanied by some kind of watery, orange-colored drink.

"It will help to get your electrolytes back into balance and keep them there," the nurse said cheerfully.

Annie had no idea what electrolytes were, and the drink looked disgusting. "Do I have to have it?" she asked, regarding the bottle with dismay.

"That's what it says on your chart," the too-perky nurse explained. "Lacy said she'd be here any second to sit with you while you eat."

Great, Annie thought. Obviously nobody in this place trusted her to actually put the food in her mouth.

Since the nurse didn't seem to be going anywhere, Annie made a great show of putting the dressing on the salad and mixing it with the greens. She opened the package of crackers and set them side by side on the tray. Then she carefully removed the top from the drink. When there was nothing left to do except eat, she tried to force herself to pick up the fork and put a bite of salad into her mouth. Halfway there, the aroma of vinegar and oil made her nauseous.

"I'm going to be sick," she said, dropping the fork and turning away from the food.

Two seconds later the nurse was beside her with a disgusting little plastic bowl just in case Annie made good on her threat. Naturally, that was exactly when Lacy walked into the room.

"How's it going in here?" she asked, then moved to take the nurse's place. "Thanks, Brook. I'll take over now."

After the nurse had gone, Lacy moved to the chair beside the bed. "That's not going to work with me, you know," she said calmly.

Annie frowned. "What?"

"Pretending that the food makes you sick."

"It does," Annie said indignantly. "That salad dressing is nothing like my mom's. It smells awful."

"Would you like me to ask your mother to bring some for tomorrow?" Lacy asked.

Tears welled up in Annie's eyes as it became clear that Lacy was every bit as tough as she'd warned she would be. "Whatever," she mumbled.

"You have thirty minutes to eat your meal," Lacy said. "Since this is your first one, we'll start the time now, rather than from the time the tray arrived."

Annie regarded her with a sense of panic. "You're going to time me? You actually want me to eat all this in half an hour?"

"That's the rule," Lacy said, her gaze unflinching. She glanced pointedly at her watch. "Starting now."

"But…" Annie couldn't think of a single argument that the determined nutritionist would buy. She put one small lettuce leaf in her mouth, chewed for as long as she could, hoping that Lacy would glance away so she could spit it into a napkin. When it became obvious that wasn't going to happen, she swallowed, gagging as the food went down.

"I don't think I can eat any more," she whispered.

"Sure you can," Lacy said. "Try a cracker or the drink."

"The drink looks disgusting."

Lacy's lips twitched, but she didn't allow a smile to form. "It actually tastes okay. Give it a try."

Annie took a tiny swallow and nearly gagged on that, too.

"Good," Lacy said, as if she hadn't nearly choked to death. "Now the cracker."

It went on like that, bite by tiny bite, sip by sip, until the half hour had passed. Annie looked at the tray and saw that she'd managed only one cracker and not even half the salad. She risked a look at Lacy, expecting to see disappointment, but instead the nutritionist gave her an encouraging smile.

"Not bad for the first time. I'll get you that energy shake I told you about to make up for the food you didn't finish."

Annie felt tears well up in her eyes again. "I have to drink a whole shake? I can't."

"Not a whole one. Just two ounces. You can do that in a couple of swallows. Remember what I said about treating it like medicine. Just drink it right down and you'll be finished until it's time for your snack."

"More food?" Annie said, sagging back against the pillows. She had no idea when eating had become such excruciating torture.

"It won't be so bad," Lacy promised. "Just half of a banana. Bananas were on that list you gave me."

Only because Annie had been coerced into writing down something or leaving the decisions to Lacy. At least making that list had given her a tiny sense that she was still in control of things.

"You won't sit with me for that, will you?" she asked hopefully.

"I won't," Lacy said. "But someone will."

"Oh," Annie said, her voice flat. "Nobody trusts me, huh?"

"Should we?"

"I guess not," she conceded grudgingly. Because she and Lacy both knew that at the first opportunity, she would flush all that food right down the toilet.

Ronnie was impressed with Sullivan's. The restaurant was cozy and inviting. It was elegant without being pretentious, and judging from the fancy Specials board posted by the hostess station, it had a diverse menu of items that would appeal to the locals, while still expanding their culinary tastes. Of course, he was so sick of hospital-cafeteria food by now that anything would have seemed gourmet caliber by comparison.

"You going to feed me, darlin', or wait for me to beg?" he inquired as Dana Sue dug into a slice of deep-dish apple pie that made his mouth water.

"We're not open yet," she said with grim finality, forking another bite of pie into her mouth.

"Not even for family?"

"You are *not* family."

"I'm the father of your daughter and the best husband you ever had," he stated.

"You're the *only* husband I ever had, more's the pity," she retorted.

After what seemed like an endless, silent stalemate, during which Ronnie just bided his time, she finally met his gaze. "You're not going away, are you?"

"Not till I'm fed," he agreed cheerfully, ignoring the fascinated glances the woman working at the stove was casting his way. He figured she could be won over to his side with a little charm. He was a bit more concerned by the stiff posture of the guy who was sticking so darn close to Dana Sue that Ronnie couldn't help wondering if there was more between them than a working relationship.

"Fine." Dana Sue flounced off her stool and marched past him. "Bring him the meat loaf special," she called over her shoulder. Then added, "In a take-out box. We'll wait out front."

Ronnie grinned. "You think my dining here will take away from the class of the place?"

"No, but I do think it will fuel the gossip already flying around town," she said. "Frankly, I don't need the aggravation. Besides, we need to get back to the hospital. Annie is your top priority, right?"

There was no mistaking the challenge in her expression. "Of course," he said. "I called to check on her right before I came here. The nurse said she was finishing her first meal under the supervision of the nutritionist. She said to come back around six-thirty." He glanced pointedly at his watch. "It's barely five-thirty now."

"I want to go back now," Dana Sue said stubbornly.

"Then by all means, we'll go now," he said, amusement threading through his voice. "You taking your own car, or can I give you a lift?"

He saw her warring with herself over the absurdity of both of them driving, when they'd be coming back to places less than a mile apart.

"I'll drive," she said at last. "You can eat your dinner in the car."

"Still have to control things, don't you, sugar?"

She shrugged. "Pretty much. Last time I let loose and trusted someone else, I got burned."

The barb struck home. "Shouldn't you be over that by now?" he asked.

She skewered him with a gaze that could have pierced steel. "Just FYI, Ronnie, women don't get over a thing like that. They suit up in body armor and move on."

He nodded. "I'll keep that in mind." When Erik came out of the kitchen with the take-out box, Ronnie accepted it. "How much?"

"This one's on the house," Dana Sue said tersely. "Now let's go."

"Before you introduce me to your friend?" He already knew Erik's name from Annie's adoring description of the man, as well as the glimpse he'd caught of him at the hospital, hanging out with Dana Sue in the waiting room and again outside.

"Oh, he knows exactly who *you* are," she said, in a way that suggested Ronnie ought to check the dinner for arsenic. "I suspect the gossip was quite specific in its description." She glanced at Erik for confirmation.

He nodded, then gave Ronnie a man-to-man, vaguely commiserating look. "I'm Erik Whitney, Dana Sue's pastry chef and second in command around here."

"Nice to meet you," Ronnie said, relieved that the introduction hadn't included anything that suggested the relationship was personal.

"I'm also her friend," Erik added pointedly. "We look out for each other."

Ronnie nodded. "Good to know. I hope to look out for her some myself."

"Have you two finished marking your turf yet?" Dana Sue inquired testily. "We need to get going."

Erik laughed and Ronnie chuckled with him.

"Maybe we'll compare notes another time," Ronnie said.

"I don't think so," Dana Sue said tersely. "Not if either of you expect to live."

Erik shrugged. "She's the boss."

"Always was," Ronnie agreed.

In the car, he met her gaze. "Must be nice to have a fierce protector like that around. He's half in love with you."

She stared at him incredulously. "He is not. He's a friend and he works for me. It's bad policy to date an employee."

"Wouldn't stop some women."

"Well, it would stop me," she said flatly.

Ronnie hid a relieved smile and said, "Yet another thing that's good to know."

He figured he'd made significant progress in discovering the dynamics of Dana Sue's life these days, including who her friends were—besides Maddie and Helen, of course—and where her loyalties lay. At this rate, it wouldn't take all that long for him to decide where he could fit in.

At the hospital, Dana Sue sailed down the hall ahead of Ronnie, determined to get to Annie's room before him. She knew it was ridiculous to be so competitive over something so small, but ever since he'd declared his intention to stick around town, he seemed to be bringing that out in her. She didn't want him to have the upper hand at anything, no matter what it cost her to best him.

When she opened the door to Annie's room in ICU and saw an empty bed, a gasp escaped before she could stop it. She whirled around and latched on to Ronnie's arm. "She's gone!"

"What do you mean, she's gone?" he demanded, peering past her.

"Look," Dana Sue said. "She's not in her bed. The room's

empty. Ronnie, if something happened to her while you and I were away, I will never forgive myself."

Stepping back, he grabbed her shoulders and looked directly into her eyes. "Calm down, Dana Sue. Annie was perfectly fine when I spoke to the nurse less than an hour ago. I'm sure there's a logical explanation. Let me check at the nurses' station."

"I'm coming with you," Dana Sue said, right on his heels. If there was bad news, she wanted them to hear it together. She didn't want it filtered through Ronnie.

A thin, blond nurse with pouty pink lips was behind the desk. Naturally, Ronnie managed to give her one of his trademark crooked smiles in an obvious attempt to charm her. Did the man have to flirt with every woman who crossed his path? Dana Sue wondered irritably. Especially now?

"Where's our daughter?" she demanded before Ronnie could speak.

The nurse—Brook, according to her name tag—beamed at both of them. "Good news," she reassured them. "The cardiologist saw her a little while ago and decided she was ready to be moved to a regular room." She glanced at a paper on the desk. "She's down on the second floor, room 206."

Dana Sue sighed with relief. "Thank goodness."

Ronnie draped an arm around her shoulder. "See, everything's fine. Let's go see our girl."

Dana Sue let his arm remain where it was for a full five seconds, drawing strength from the contact. Then she shrugged away from him. "You go. I want to call Helen and Maddie and let them know to look for us downstairs when they come by later."

He regarded her with a vague hint of disappointment in his expression, then said, "If that's what you want."

She watched him head for the elevator. Only after he was

gone did she take a deep breath and relax. She caught the next elevator and went outside to place her calls. Neither of her friends was home, so she left messages, then tried to gather her composure before going back inside to see Annie.

Dana Sue sat on a bench near the fountain that splashed water into the small pond, and let the sound soothe her. The rustling of the breeze through the palmetto trees added its own lulling music. That was where Helen found her a few minutes later.

"Everything okay?" Her friend dropped onto the bench beside her.

"I just left you a message. They moved Annie to a regular room."

"That's great," Helen said. When Dana Sue didn't respond, her gaze narrowed. "Isn't it?"

"Something tells me there's still a long way to go before anything's great again."

"With Annie? Or does this have something to do with Ronnie?"

Tears welled up in Dana Sue's eyes and spilled down her cheeks. "It's everything," she whispered, swiping ineffectively at the tears.

"Hey, come on now," Helen soothed. "Annie's going to be okay. Focus on that. Everything else will fall into place."

"Sure," Dana Sue said skeptically. "That implies that my ex-husband will go back where he belongs, which, according to him, isn't going to happen."

Helen winced. "I was afraid of that. I could take some steps to limit your contact with him. I could probably keep him away from Annie, too."

"And have her hate me?" Dana Sue responded. "Forget that. I just have to find some way to deal with this."

"I could talk to him and tell him he's making things worse,"

Helen said a little too eagerly. "I imagine I could persuade him to rethink his plan, at least once the crisis is past."

"Same problem," Dana Sue said with regret. "Annie would never forgive either of us."

Helen looked disappointed at not being allowed to use her considerable skills of persuasion. "I suppose you're right," she finally conceded. "It certainly backfired last time I managed to get him out of Annie's life on a daily basis." She studied Dana Sue. "So, what will you do?"

"I wish I knew. Maybe I just need to stop obsessing about it."

"Sounds like a start," Helen concurred. "And if you change your mind about letting me do something official, all it takes is one word from you and it's done."

Dana Sue gave her a watery smile. "Thanks. Let's not talk about Ronnie right now. Tell me what's going on with you. Are you still exercising? Did you write down your goals and give them to Doc Marshall?"

Helen flushed. "Not exactly."

Dana Sue regarded her with dismay. "Helen! Doc Marshall must have been furious. Did he put you on medication for your blood pressure the way he threatened?"

"Um, no," Helen said, not meeting her gaze.

"You canceled your appointment, didn't you?" Dana Sue guessed.

Helen gave her a guilty, barely perceptible nod.

"Are you crazy?" Dana Sue demanded. "This is important, Helen. You can't keep ignoring it and hoping your blood pressure will correct itself. Have you at least taken a day off to relax, the way you promised?"

"There was no way I could do that this week," her friend said defensively. "I've been here every second I wasn't at the office or in court."

"Okay, that's it," Dana Sue said fiercely. "Tomorrow morning we're all meeting at The Corner Spa at eight. I will even spend twenty minutes on the stupid treadmill, if you will. Deal?"

Helen regarded her with obvious reluctance, then nodded. "Fine. Deal."

"Then we set our goals," Dana Sue continued. "Maddie can type them up for us afterward so we'll all have copies. It'll help us to keep ourselves and each other motivated. I think we should even include penalties if any of us start backsliding."

"You don't think the big reward is enough motivation?" Helen teased. "I thought you really wanted that convertible."

"I do, but that's a long-term reward. I have a hunch we're going to need a lot of prodding along the way. If the most obsessive human being I know can't stick to a regimen for more than two days at a time, then the rest of us are doomed."

"I can stick to anything I want to," Helen declared.

"Then you obviously don't want to stick to this."

"And you do?" Helen said.

Dana Sue met her gaze, then sighed. "Not especially, if I'm being totally honest. But there's a big difference between not wanting to do it and knowing that I have to."

"Ditto with me," Helen admitted. "I honestly thought the challenge would make me stick to it."

"And then Annie got sick," Dana Sue said. "We have to resolve not to let *anything* interfere, okay? No begging off because of work for you and no using Annie as an excuse for me."

"You're right." Helen nodded. "Now let's go upstairs and see Annie."

"Ronnie's with her," Dana Sue said.

Her friend's eyes glittered with mischief. "Then we'll chase him away. That should be fun."

Dana Sue laughed despite herself. "You have the oddest sense of what passes for entertainment."

"Tell me the idea doesn't appeal to you, too," Helen dared her.

"Okay, it does," Dana Sue confessed. "At least a little bit. One thing, though...."

"What?"

"How's he going to get back to his motel? I drove him over here."

"All the better," Helen said. "A long walk will be good for him. Might give him time to think better of sticking around."

"Or make him mad enough to dream up a diabolical way to get even," Dana Sue said.

"Not to worry. When has any man ever been able to put one over on the Sweet Magnolias?" Helen asked confidently.

"Not often, that's true," she admitted. But that didn't mean her ex-husband wouldn't try. The prospect sent a little shudder through her. More troubling was the fact that she couldn't tell if the reaction was dread or anticipation.

Despite the earlier struggle to eat even a little portion of her meal, Annie lay back in her hospital bed feeling better than she had in months. Her dad was right there beside her, and Sarah and Raylene had come by the minute they'd found out she could have visitors. They'd told her that Ty was on his way over, too. He was coming with his mom after dinner. Annie wasn't sure how she felt about him seeing her like this, but then she remembered that he'd seen her under all sorts of embarrassing circumstances over the years and he was still her friend. Eagerness overcame her trepidation.

She'd tuned out most of the other news Sarah and Raylene were delivering. It was just a bunch of gossip from school, and right now none of that seemed important. A week ago she would have wanted to hear every word, certain that her life would be over if she missed any hot news flashes about the in crowd. Now she understood what having her life be over really meant. She felt a hundred years older than her two best friends.

"Are you even listening to us?" Sarah demanded. "You look as if you're a thousand miles away."

"I heard you," Annie swore, then grinned. "Well, some of it, anyway."

"Are you getting too tired?" Raylene asked, glancing at Annie's dad for his input. "Should we go?"

Her dad looked at her. "Annie, it's your call. You still feeling okay?"

"Maybe I *am* a little tired," she admitted finally. It was better than saying she was bored listening to the same old stuff. "Come back tomorrow, though, okay?"

"Right after school," Sarah promised. "My mom said she'd bring us whenever we want."

"Mine, too," Raylene said.

They were almost to the door when Sarah ran back and gave Annie a hug that almost squeezed the breath right out of her.

"You scared us," she said, an angry edge to her voice. "Don't you ever do anything like that again, you hear me?"

"I'm not planning on it," Annie assured her.

"But Ms. Franklin said in P.E. that eating disorders don't just go away." Sarah's expression was filled with concern. "You have to *want* things to be different, Annie."

Annie flushed with embarrassment. She was apparently being turned into some sort of example at school. "Ms. Franklin was talking about me in class?"

"She never mentioned you by name," Raylene said hurriedly. "But everyone knew. I guess she figured the opportunity to lecture us was too good to pass up."

"All I know is that if I don't see you putting real food in your mouth every single time you're supposed to, from here on I'm ratting you out," Sarah said. "I don't care if you hate me."

"Me, too," Raylene said.

After they'd gone, Annie closed her eyes, filled with shame. She'd never realized the toll her decisions took on her friends.

"You okay, baby?" her dad asked.

"Sure," she said with a sniff.

"Those two are good friends," he commented.

"I know that. I guess I put them in a pretty awful position before, huh?"

"You scared them, there's no question about that."

She shook her head. "It's more than that. Sarah knew, even though I wouldn't admit what was going on. She tried to talk to me, but I always blew her off. I did the same thing with Mom."

"I don't think either one of them will let you get away with that again," he said.

"I'm surprised Sarah even *wants* to be my friend now," Annie said.

"Why wouldn't she?"

"Because I'm so messed up." Annie choked back a sob.

"You're not messed up," her dad said, moving to the edge of the bed and gathering her into his arms. "You made a mistake, sweet pea. A real bad one, but we're going to fix it."

With her face buried against his shoulder, she murmured, "I don't know if I can."

"You can," he said with confidence. "Your mom and I will help and so will Dr. McDaniels and the nutritionist."

She knew it was useless to complain about the nutritionist, but she had to take another stab at getting the psychologist off her case. "I don't want to see a shrink."

"No choice," he said flatly. "You can't fix this by yourself."

"But you and Mom—"

"Don't know the right things to do. We're going to need Dr. McDaniels and Ms. Reynolds to help us, too. We're all in this together, Annie. You don't have to do any of it alone."

"But I'm the one who's sick. I'm the only one who can fix it, and I don't think I can."

Her dad took her shoulders and held her away so he could look into her eyes. "Yes, you can," he repeated. "You're a smart girl, Annie. You can do anything you set your mind to. It's not going to happen overnight, but it will happen. Bit by bit you'll make whatever changes you need to, in the way you eat, the way you think about yourself."

"I have a confession," she whispered, riddled with guilt.

"Oh?"

"I didn't want to eat the food they brought while I was still upstairs tonight. If I could have, I would have flushed it down the toilet." Her voice cracked and caught on another sob when she saw the dismay in her dad's eyes. "I'm sorry."

Once again, he gathered her close. "It's okay, baby. The point is that you *didn't* flush the food away, did you?"

"Only because Lacy—Ms. Reynolds—was watching me like a hawk. If I get the chance, I probably will," she admitted, resigned.

"Which is why you need a strong support system around you right now," he said reasonably. "It's going to get easier. I promise."

Annie wanted to believe him. She really did. But right now she was so terrified, all she wanted to do was run away someplace and hide. What if they made her eat and she got fat?

What if she actually started liking food again and couldn't stop eating? The thought of it made her want to puke right now.

Her dad released her eventually, and she felt the way she had on the day he'd left—abandoned somehow, even though he was still right there beside her.

"Tell you what," he said. "I think your mom has a little makeup kit in her purse. Why don't I try to find her and bring that to you? You can get all dolled up before Ty comes by."

Even though she didn't want him to leave, even for a minute, Annie nodded. "Sure. That'd be great."

He pressed a kiss to her forehead. "I'll be back before you know it," he promised.

He hurried from the room as if he couldn't wait to be gone. As the door closed behind him, Annie actually thought she heard him crying, and that scared her worse than anything. Her dad was the strongest man she knew. If he was afraid, then things had to be really bad, maybe even worse than she'd thought.

"I'm sorry, Daddy," she whispered. "I'll fix this. I swear it. Please don't leave me again."

11

Annie had been in a good place when Ronnie left the hospital the night before. Her cheeks had been pink while Ty was visiting, and she'd actually laughed a time or two, sounding like the carefree girl he'd remembered from before the divorce. Seeing her like that had been a relief. He was finally starting to believe they'd turned a corner, not just physically, but emotionally.

Believing that inspired him to take the next morning off from the hospital and head back to Beaufort. He had to quit his job there and pick up the few belongings still in his motel room. None of it would take long. While his boss liked him because he'd been reliable, experienced, and had done good work for Thompson & Thompson Construction, it wasn't as if there weren't fifty other guys who could do the job just as well. Ronnie doubted there would be much commotion over his abrupt departure, especially after he explained about needing to be close to his daughter while she recovered.

"You gonna look for the same kind of work back in Serenity?" Butch Thompson asked, hitching his faded jeans over a modest beer belly, then adjusting his well-worn John Deere cap.

For a wealthy man who owned one of the largest construction companies in the state, Butch had no pretensions at all. He worked alongside his men when he could, shared a beer with them on Friday nights after work. He handled tools as well as anyone on his crews, proving that his early years had been spent literally learning the trade from the ground up. Ronnie had never seen him in a suit and tie.

"I hear there's some new development in that part of the state," Butch added, his expression thoughtful. "I could make a few calls, check it out for you. You can count on me for a good reference."

"I heard the same thing about the construction boom over there," Ronnie admitted. "Thanks for offering, but I think I'll look for something else. I'm tired of scrambling up ladders and scampering around on rooftops."

"You know how to do anything else?" Butch asked him, his expression skeptical. "I hate to see you walk away from construction. After all the talks we've had, I had the feeling you love the work as much as I do."

"I do," Ronnie admitted. "But I have an idea that might match up my construction expertise with another business." He hesitated, then decided to ask for Butch's input. The man had started Thompson & Thompson on his own forty years ago and turned it into a profitable venture. Maybe he would be willing to offer some start-up advice to Ronnie. "If you've got a few minutes, I wouldn't mind running the idea past you."

Butch glanced at his watch. "It's lunchtime. You buying?"

Ronnie grinned. "It'd be a small price to pay for your advice."

"Not if I decide what appeals to me is a big ole T-bone steak," Butch said, grinning.

"Anything you want," Ronnie insisted.

The older man studied him for a minute and shook his head. "Not sure my input is worth that much, but I'll take the steak, just the same. My wife's been on some tear about not eating meat. I have to sneak it when she's not around to catch me. She's got my daughter spying on me, too." He shook his head. "Fine thing when a man's own daughter rats him out to his wife. I should never have brought that girl into the company."

"Making Terry a partner was the smartest thing you ever did, and you know it," Ronnie contradicted.

Butch beamed with pride, but he didn't admit to it.

They went to a place about a mile from the construction site, where the aged beef was served thick and rare and accompanied by a platter piled high with onion rings and a side of French fries. There was probably enough cholesterol in the meal to clog most of a man's arteries in one sitting.

When they'd placed their orders and the waitress had brought them both sweet tea, Butch leaned back and studied him. "Okay, out with it. You look like you're about to pop. Just how crazy is this idea of yours?"

"That's what I'm hoping you'll tell me," Ronnie said.

He took his time and tried to organize the thoughts that had been circulating through his brain ever since he'd driven through downtown Serenity for the first time on his return. Seeing the town green surrounded by empty buildings that had once been thriving businesses had saddened him. The old five-and-dime where Dana Sue had once spent her allowance on candy was shuttered, as was the dress shop where his mom had once bought most of her clothes. The barbershop where men used to gather on Saturday mornings had closed when its owner died.

Only Wharton's remained now, and only because Grace and her husband were stubborn holdouts who did enough business at the soda fountain to support the declining pharmacy sales. Once the superstores had opened less than an hour away, the dress shop, five-and-dime and other family-owned specialty shops had closed one by one. Main Street was no longer the bustling center of town it had been when he and Dana Sue were teenagers. He thought he had a way to help change that.

"Okay, here's what I'm thinking," he told Butch. "I want to open a hardware store in Serenity."

The construction company president stared at him as if he'd announced his intention to open a strip club. No, actually, he suspected Butch would consider a strip club less financially risky.

"Now hear me out," Ronnie said, before the older man could express his disdain for the idea. "Not just any hardware store. I know there's not much profit to be made in selling screwdrivers and hammers to residents of a town of four or five thousand people. That's probably why the old one went out of business."

"Then why are you even considering a dang-fool idea like this?" Butch demanded.

"Okay, you said it yourself. There's going to be a lot of development over that way," he began.

"And it'll be years before that brings in enough people to make you rich on hammers and screwdrivers," Butch scoffed.

"I'm not planning to make my money on tools for do-it-yourselfers or ten-pound bags of potting soil for gardeners," he explained, warming to the idea now that he was finally able to verbalize it to someone who might actually understand the potential. "I'll cater to them, of course, but I really want to sell to the construction companies doing all that development. If I can provide them better, faster service on their lumber, their insulation, their tools, their nails, whatever, and be right around the corner, instead of an hour or more away like the big box stores, don't you think they'd choose dealing with me? A lot of this development is west of Serenity. The superstores are way east. I'd be right on the way."

Butch's skepticism faded. He leaned forward, his gaze intense. "You think you could match the prices from the big companies?"

"I could come close if I can get enough volume," Ronnie said confidently. "The thing is, like you said, I know construction. I can anticipate what they're going to need and when, just by visiting the sites on a regular basis. I won't have to keep a lot of money tied up in wasted inventory. I can bring it in when it's needed, then turn it around quickly. Turnaround's the answer in any business, right?"

"In other words, you'll offer guaranteed, personalized customer service," Butch said slowly. "Something we sure as hell don't see much of these days in any sector."

"Exactly," Ronnie said, then sat back. "So, what do you think? Would you deal with a small local company like that, assuming it understood and could meet your demands?"

"Damn straight I would," Butch said without hesitation. "Even if it cost me a few cents more on the dollar. It would save me time and aggravation. I figure in the end it would all balance out, and I like the idea of supporting something local for a change. It would be a way for a smart developer or general contractor to make sure he becomes a real part of the community, instead of being viewed as some kind of carpetbagger who's just come to make a killing."

His expression turned thoughtful, but then he looked Ronnie straight in the eye. "Start-up wouldn't be cheap. You worked up a business plan yet?"

Ronnie shook his head. "I've only been tossing the idea around in my mind since I got back to Serenity and noticed that the old hardware store was closed. I'll need to put it on paper, see what real estate's going for downtown. A lot of it's been sitting empty for a while now, so it should be cheap enough. I've noticed the old hardware store still has some inventory sitting inside they'd probably make part of the deal. I'll have to look into what kind of loan I might be able to qualify for. I've got some savings, but it'll barely be enough to paint the interior and upgrade the shelving. I know there are bound to be a thousand things I haven't even thought of, but it feels right to me, you know what I mean? Like something bigger than just starting a little business. It could make a contribution to the town."

Butch gave him a considering look. "And impress your ex-wife?"

Ronnie grinned. "That, too." It would prove to Dana Sue once and for all that he wasn't going anywhere. She'd finally have to get used to the idea.

"So this isn't just about sticking close to your daughter, is it?" Butch said. "You want your family back."

Ronnie nodded. "Always have."

"Well, then, you give me a call when you have your plan down on paper. We'll talk again."

"Your input today has been more than enough," Ronnie said, more grateful than he could express. "I don't want to take up your time."

"Time, hell," Butch said, waving his hand. "I might want to partner up with you on this thing if the numbers look good once you've worked 'em out."

Ronnie gaped. "You're kidding."

His old boss chuckled. "Boy, don't you know by now I never kid around when there's money to be made? I know a sound investment when I hear one. Besides, I like you. You've been a good employee, even though we both know you're worth a hell of a lot more than I've been able to pay you for the kind of work I had available when you showed up in Beaufort. You're a lot more capable, too. I wish I'd been able to promote you to foreman, but I already had good men in those positions. Besides all that, you're a decent family man who made a stupid mistake, from what you've told me, a mistake you're not likely to repeat. If I'd had a son, instead of a passel of daughters, I would have wanted him to be just like you."

Ronnie grinned. He doubted Butch's oldest daughter would appreciate the implication that a son could have done anything she couldn't do. In Ronnie's opinion, Terry Thompson knew as much about construction as her father, probably because she'd been trailing after him around sites from the time she could walk and wear a hard hat. She was well respected by the men and the clients.

"How's Terry going to feel about you making a decision like this without consulting her?" Ronnie asked.

"None of her business," Butch said succinctly. "This is between you and me. It has nothing to do with the company. I'll be a silent partner, at that. Your plan. Your execution. All I want is a good return on my investment. You show me a business plan that promises that and we have a deal."

"I honestly don't know what to say," Ronnie said, hardly daring to believe the conversation had gone this well.

Butch sliced into his steak and savored a bite, then gestured toward his plate. "This beef is thanks enough. First time in weeks I've known what the hell I was eating. You try living on soy this and soy that and you'll know what I mean."

"You'll have to come over to Serenity and have dinner at my ex-wife's restaurant. Not a soy product on the menu, I can guarantee that," Ronnie told him.

Butch's eyes lit up. "Wait a minute. Are you talking about Sullivan's? *That's* your ex-wife's place?"

Ronnie nodded, feeling a burst of pride. "You've heard about it?"

"*Read* about it," Butch said. "In the Charleston paper, as I recall. Honest to God Southern cooking, that's what they said, but with a few interesting twists. As long as one of those twists doesn't involve soy anything, count me in. That's where we'll go to celebrate our partnership."

"I gather you're not planning to bring your wife along," Ronnie said.

"Sure I am," Butch said with a diabolical gleam in his eyes. "Until she got on this insane health kick of hers, Fannie actually liked decent food. Best Southern cook around, in fact. Her biscuits would melt in your mouth and her fried chicken would have made that old colonel ashamed of himself. It was one of the reasons I married her. Maybe this will remind her of what she's been missing."

"How about I throw in a gift certificate for her from Dana Sue's other venture?" Ronnie offered. "It's called The Corner Spa, and I hear they give a real good massage over there."

"I always wondered what one of those would be like," Butch said with a straight face.

Ronnie chuckled. "Sorry. You won't find out there. It's for women only."

"Well, that don't seem right," Butch said, his disappointment plain. "Oh, well, if it makes Fannie happy, I suppose I can't complain. Now I'd best get back to work before everybody spends the whole afternoon goofing off because the boss ain't around."

"Nobody goofs off on Terry's watch," Ronnie reminded him.

Butch looked taken aback for a second, then beamed. "She *is* a chip off the old block, isn't she?"

"I'd say so, Butch. You go ahead, though. I'll pay for lunch, then head on back to Serenity."

"You be in touch soon, you hear?" Butch told him, enveloping Ronnie's hand in his.

"Soon," he promised, then sat back as Butch walked away. "Well, I'll be damned."

Ronnie glanced at the bill for the two steaks, tossed forty bucks on the table and counted himself lucky. It was the best investment in his future he'd ever made.

Dana Sue sat at a table on the patio at The Corner Spa. The sun, filtering through an old pin oak tree, created a splashy pattern of light on the soft pink bricks. A breeze stirred the Spanish moss. Classical music wafted softly from overhead speakers, a touch Maddie had added since Dana Sue's last visit.

"What do you think about the music?" Maddie asked when she joined her.

"It's soothing," Dana Sue said, even though she didn't know the first thing about Bach, Beethoven or Mozart. George Strait and Kenny Chesney were more her speed.

Maddie nodded in satisfaction. "I thought so, too."

"It's classy, too," Dana Sue stated. "One more thing that sets this place apart from all the others."

"I'm glad you like it," Maddie said. "Now, do you want to tell me why you're wearing that pensive expression? You look as if you've just lost your best friend."

For once Dana Sue didn't bother trying to deny the mood she was in. She needed to bounce this off someone before she worked herself into a complete panic. "I had a call from Dr. McDaniels before I came over here."

"She's Annie's psychologist, right?" Maddie asked.

"Well, she's supposed to be, but every time she's stopped

by to visit, Annie's given her some excuse for not wanting to talk. It's been more than a week now and they're not making any progress."

Maddie didn't seem all that surprised. "I imagine the idea of therapy must be pretty scary to a sixteen-year-old. Most kids that age don't even want to tell you if they've done their homework."

"That's what Dr. McDaniels said. She told me it's not unusual for kids to be in denial."

"Then why are you so worried?" Maddie asked.

"Because Annie's life is on the line here," Dana Sue said in frustration. "If she doesn't talk, if we don't get to the bottom of what's going on with her, she could wind up right back in intensive care, and the next time we might not be so lucky. I know Dr. McDaniels is worried about that, even though she didn't say as much. Annie needs to start cooperating, not just acting all chipper, like nothing's wrong."

"Have you told her that?" Maddie asked.

"No."

"Why on earth not?"

"I suppose I was trying not to add to the pressure she's under," Dana Sue said. "Obviously that was the wrong approach."

"Maybe this isn't the best place for her to get treatment, if you're going to let her off the hook too easily," Maddie suggested gently. "Maybe it's time to consider an inpatient facility."

Dana Sue frowned worriedly. "No. I don't think I could bear sending her away, especially when she's so vulnerable."

"Not even to save her life?" Maddie asked.

Dana Sue stared at her friend. "Oh, God, Maddie, what am I going to do? Obviously she needs help."

"What does Ronnie say?"

"He hasn't said anything to me about this. I tried to call

him after I'd spoken to Dr. McDaniels, but he wasn't answering his cell phone. He's not at the hospital, either," she said, then added, "Maybe it's gotten to be too much for him and he's taken off again."

"You know better," Maddie scolded. "He'll turn up and the two of you can discuss it. In the meantime, here comes Helen, and she has that look in her eyes, the one that says she's on a mission and she's taking no prisoners."

Dana Sue grinned, despite herself. "Too bad we don't serve anything stronger than coffee in here."

"I have a leftover bottle of champagne from the opening in my office, but popping the cork on that would probably set a bad example," Maddie said, her expression wistful.

"Unless we go into your office, lock Helen on the other side and drink it before we let her in," Dana Sue said.

Apparently Helen had heard enough of what they were saying to disapprove. "No one's going anywhere to drink," she said as she sat down and opened her ever-present briefcase, then distributed legal pads to all of them. "Okay, ladies, this is the first day of the rest of our lives. Let's get busy. Ten goals in ten minutes. Start writing. We don't have all day."

Dana Sue scowled at her. "I suggest at the top of your list you write down in big, bold letters **STOP BEING BOSSY**."

Helen scowled right back at her. "Not amusing."

Dana Sue winked at Maddie. "Did you think I was trying to be funny?"

"Not so much," Maddie said.

"Okay, you two comedians, you promised to take this seriously. We need goals. We need a plan."

"Have you by any chance rescheduled your appointment with Doc Marshall?" Dana Sue inquired.

"It's tomorrow morning, as a matter of fact."

"Which explains why you're so anxious to get this in writing," Maddie concluded. "I imagine you have a notary lined up to validate our signatures on the bottom of your page when we're through."

Helen flushed guiltily. "As a matter of fact, Patty Markham has her notary seal with her. She said she'd be in here working out till eight forty-five. Which is yet another reason we have to hurry. It's already eight-fifteen and we have to agree on our goals once we've written them down. Let's get a move on."

Dana Sue exchanged a look with Maddie. "She's hopeless, you know."

"Type A, through and through," Maddie agreed.

Helen glowered at them. "Which is why I need these goals even worse than the two of you. Help me out here, instead of making fun of me."

Dana Sue sighed. "She has a point. We're not being helpful." She picked up her pen and tried to formulate her own health goals and a timetable for achieving them. Unfortunately, she couldn't seem to focus on the state of her own health, not when her daughter was in such trouble and seemed determined to fight every step of the way on her recovery.

Instead, she wrote, "Get Annie Well" over and over, as if the words had been assigned by a teacher to drill in an important lesson.

In precisely ten minutes, Helen glanced at her watch and said, "Time's up. What have you got?"

Dana Sue blinked, then looked at the paper in front of her and felt tears well up in her eyes.

Helen immediately reached for her hand. "What?" she demanded. "What's wrong, sweetie?"

Dana Sue shook her head, unable to speak. Maddie took the legal pad and looked at it, then came around the table and hunkered down beside her. "Annie will get through this," she said confidently. "She has us. She has her dad. She has Dr. McDaniels and the nutritionist."

"What if that's not enough?" Dana Sue whispered, swiping impatiently at the tears on her cheeks.

She saw Maddie and Helen exchange a worried look before Helen squeezed her hand and said in a no-nonsense tone, "It *will* be enough. We'll see to that."

Dana Sue gave her a watery smile and prayed that know-it-all Helen had gotten it right this time, too.

Two hours later Dana Sue and Ronnie were summoned to Dr. McDaniels's office.

"Any idea what this is about?" Ronnie asked as they waited outside for her to arrive.

Dana Sue nodded. "She called me this morning. Annie's not cooperating in their sessions. For the most part, she's refused to say anything at all. Dr. McDaniels told me it's not unusual, but it is troubling."

Ronnie looked stunned. "I thought she was better. She was laughing last night, almost like her old self."

"That's denial," Dana Sue said wearily. "Not a sign she's cured. She wants us to believe everything's okay."

"She needs to get with the program," Ronnie said heatedly.

"So…what? You want to go to her room and yell at her?" Dana Sue inquired sarcastically. "I'm sure that will accomplish something."

Ronnie regarded her with dismay. "I never said that. I know that yelling won't accomplish anything. It's just so damn frustrating, you know?"

"Believe me, I know," she said, thinking of her own meltdown earlier.

Dr. McDaniels arrived just then. "Sorry I'm late," she said as she unlocked the door and gestured them inside. "An unexpected crisis with one of my patients."

Dana Sue studied the psychologist's drawn face and decided she looked exhausted. Were all of her patients like Annie? she wondered. Dealing with teens in trouble was bound to take a terrible toll.

Instead of sitting behind her desk, Dr. McDaniels pulled a chair up beside them. "Okay, here's where we are. After you and I spoke this morning, Dana Sue, I visited with Annie again and got absolutely nowhere. She's still denying that there's anything wrong, though I gather she's been a bit more cooperative with Lacy. Then again, Lacy is able to give her very specific goals and watch to see that she follows through. It's more difficult to get her to talk if she's not inclined to. I think she's afraid if she admits what she's been doing, she'll have to deal with it, and she doesn't think she can."

Ronnie nodded. "She actually said as much to me the other day."

Dr. McDaniels looked surprised. "Really? I wish you'd told me that."

He squirmed. "Sorry. It never occurred to me."

"At this point, anything about Annie's state of mind is important. I need to hear it," Dr. McDaniels said.

Ronnie nodded, then said, "In that case, there's something else you ought to know. She told me she'd wanted to flush her meal down the toilet. The only thing that stopped her was that Lacy was watching her eat."

"What?" Dana Sue said, staring at him incredulously. "And you didn't think that was important?"

"She knew her attitude was wrong," he said. "I honestly think she knows better. I'm convinced she won't act on that impulse."

"Then you still don't get the fact that she lies about food," Dana Sue snapped.

Dr. McDaniels held up her hands. "Okay, that's enough. We won't get anywhere by attacking each other."

"I'm sorry," Dana Sue said. "What can we do?"

"Each of you has a unique relationship with Annie because of the divorce," the psychologist said. "She looks to each of you for emotional support. I don't know the dynamics of your relationship since your divorce, but from this moment on, I want you to present a united front."

Dana Sue felt her heart climb into her throat. "You're not saying…" she began, but she couldn't even voice the absurd idea.

The psychologist regarded her in confusion. "Saying what?"

"That Ronnie and I…" She hesitated, swallowed hard, then blurted, "That we should get back together."

Ronnie looked at her steadily, as if the idea wasn't totally insane or unappealing. Dr. McDaniels kept her expression completely neutral.

"I wouldn't presume to tell you what to do about that," Dr. McDaniels assured her. "I'm only talking about how you interact with Annie. If we agree on a plan, you both need to support it. There's no room for a good cop–bad cop approach, not between the two of you or between both of you and me. We're all on the same page. Can we agree to that?"

"Of course," she said at once.

Ronnie nodded, though his gaze was directed at Dana Sue. She could read the speculation in his eyes.

"Okay, then," Dr. McDaniels said briskly. "I've talked to Dr. Lane and he and I are agreed on this. Even though he says Annie is physically improved enough to go home, tomorrow I'm spelling out a few cold, hard facts to her. I'm going to tell her she doesn't go home unless she cooperates with Lacy and with me. Period. Can you live with that?"

"Absolutely," Ronnie said.

Dana Sue wanted to protest, but knew she couldn't, not if she wanted Annie to get well. "Agreed," she said reluctantly. "But what if that's not enough?"

"Then we talk inpatient treatment facilities," Dr. McDaniels said, her expression grim. "In the long run, that may be the best option."

"What should we be telling her?" Ronnie asked.

"She's going to want you to make me back off," the psychologist said. "She's going to plead with you to take her home, since the cardiologist says she's better. She'll make all the promises you want about doing whatever she needs to do once she's home again. You have to back me up—no progress, no release. End of story. We're in a situation that calls for tough love. Can you handle that?"

"We'll have to," Dana Sue said, her gaze locked with Ronnie's. For all of his promises to do whatever needed to be done, and her own guilt-ridden misgivings, he was the weak link in this. If anyone faltered, it would be him. He hated to see his baby miserable.

He finally winced under her scrutiny. "I can do this," he muttered.

"Even when she cries?" Dana Sue asked skeptically.

"Even then," he said with surprising resolve. "I know I was always too easy on her, but not about this, Dana Sue. Not this time."

"I hope you mean that," she told him.

Dr. McDaniels nodded in satisfaction. "Good. If you're even tempted to cave, remember one thing. Annie needs you to be her parents now, not her friends."

"When are we supposed to start this whole tough love thing?" Ronnie asked.

"No time like the present," Dr. McDaniels said. "Maybe it will put her in a more receptive frame of mind when I see her in the morning."

Dana Sue gave the doctor a wry look. "I wouldn't get your hopes up. She's got her daddy's stubbornness."

"Pot calling the kettle black," Ronnie retorted. "Let's go, darlin'. We might as well do this while we've got the backbone for it."

Dr. McDaniels chuckled at that. "Any time your backbone starts to weaken, remember I'm right here. Remember this, too. I've dealt with tougher kids than Annie. We will get through to her and make her well."

Dana Sue wanted to believe her. She *needed* to believe her.

12

Ronnie and Dana Sue were almost to the elevator when he panicked. He tucked his hand under her elbow and steered her toward the hospital exit.

"Ronnie, what is wrong with you?" she demanded. "I thought we were going to see Annie."

"We were. We will," he said. "Just not now."

She stared at him with confusion. "Why not now?"

"Because I don't know if I can do it now, that's why not," he admitted. "You were right to question me back there. If Annie looks at me with those big eyes of hers and starts to cry, I'll give her whatever she wants."

"Not with me in the room," Dana Sue said fiercely. "You *agreed* we had to be tough, Ronnie."

"And I know that's the right thing to do," he said. "But we're talking about Annie here. She's still a kid."

"She's sixteen and she almost killed herself," Dana Sue reminded him, her voice thick with emotion.

Her anger was justified, but somehow Ronnie couldn't reconcile those words with his beautiful daughter. "It was an accident," he said.

"If you mean that she didn't realize she could die from not eating, then, yes, it was an accident," Dana Sue agreed, her tone calmer but no less impassioned. "But not eating was a *decision,* Ronnie. Maybe there were a lot of factors at work that we don't understand yet, but she looked at food every single day and made a deliberate decision not to eat it, not even after she passed out at Maddie's wedding and scared us all to death."

"She passed out before?" he asked, shocked. "Why didn't you tell me? I don't give a damn how mad you were at me, I had a right to know."

Dana Sue looked vaguely guilty. "Probably so, but I was still in denial then. I was able to convince myself it was no big deal, the same way you're doing right this second. Lots of people skip meals. Lots of people faint. It doesn't have to mean they're in trouble. Sound familiar?"

Dana Sue's words resonated a little too clearly with Ronnie. He had thought all those things, even after seeing Annie lying in a hospital bed looking like a shadow of her former self. Even after grappling with the fact that a cardiac arrest had put her there.

"I hate this," he whispered. "I just hate it."

Dana Sue touched a hand to his cheek. "I know. Me, too." She started to move away and head back to the elevators. "Let's just go see her, okay?"

"No!" Ronnie said sharply. "We need to talk about this, Dana Sue. I want to know everything. Maybe then I'll be able to make some sense of it."

"I've known about it for months and I haven't made sense of it," she responded. "What makes you think you'll get it after one conversation?"

"Please, let's just get out of here for an hour and have something to eat. Then we'll come back and talk to Annie."

"But Dr. McDaniels said…"

"She doesn't know everything," Ronnie said tersely. "Apparently, neither do I. That needs to change."

Dana Sue's gaze faltered. Finally she nodded. "Okay, where do you want to go?"

"Only one place in town worth eating at, the way I understand it," he said, his tension easing now that he sensed she would go along with his request. "Admit it. You'll feel better if you check on how things are doing at Sullivan's, anyway."

She hesitated, then nodded. "I get five uninterrupted minutes in the kitchen to check on things," she bargained, then stopped herself. "Make that ten minutes."

Ronnie chuckled. "Take as long as you want, sugar. I'll still be waiting when you're through hiding out."

"Checking on things," she corrected.

"Call it what you want, as long as you know I'm not going anywhere."

She rolled her eyes. "I know. I'm beginning to think you're like a fungus. Once it comes back, it's even harder to get rid of the second time."

"Is that any way to talk about the man you promised to love for all eternity?" He was amused, despite her attempt to be insulting.

"That man's dead and buried to me," she claimed.

Maybe it was just one more thing Ronnie was wearing blinders to avoid seeing clearly, but he didn't think so. He winked at her. "We'll see, darlin'. We'll see."

Dana Sue couldn't escape into the restaurant kitchen fast enough. Despite her very best attempts to keep Ronnie at arm's length, to make him feel her disdain, he was getting to her. His genuine concern for Annie was part of it, but she'd always known he loved being a dad, that Annie was the joy of his life. It was his persistence that was beginning to undermine her defenses. Some traitorous brain cell was actually beginning to believe he'd changed, that he wanted to make amends for the past, that he wanted her back and wouldn't stop until he got her.

Of course, there were still fifty billion cells or so that weren't buying it, but that one susceptible cell seemed as if it might start dividing and eventually catch up. She had to prevent that. She needed a couple of hours with Helen's cynicism to accomplish it, but that clearly wasn't in the cards for tonight. Erik's innate protective streak would have to do.

"Did I see that ex-husband of yours come in with you?" he inquired when Dana Sue walked into the kitchen.

She nodded.

"You brought him here? Voluntarily?"

"To be accurate, he drove, but basically, yes," she said, already feeling better now that Erik was holding her feet to the fire. He might not have been around at the time of her divorce, but he knew enough of the details to make sure she didn't cut Ronnie any slack.

Erik regarded her with typical male bemusement when confronted with a female's contradictory actions. "Why? I thought you hated his guts."

Dana Sue sank onto a stool out of the way of the busboys, who were coming in with trays piled high with dirty dishes. She considered denial, but it hadn't worked with Annie. It wouldn't accomplish a thing now, either. She gave Erik a resigned look. "Apparently not so much."

He looked stunned, or maybe that was just disappointment she saw darkening his eyes. She could relate. She was pretty disappointed in her weakness, too.

"You're falling for him again?" Erik asked, as if he didn't want to believe she'd do anything so foolish.

"Maybe." She held thumb and forefinger a quarter inch apart. "Just a little bit."

"Dear God in heaven. What should I do? Sign you up for an exorcism?"

Dana Sue laughed. "Now that's an approach I've never considered. I wonder if it would work." If she thought it would, she might give it a try. But how was a woman supposed to rid herself of the feelings she'd had for a man for most of her adult life? If having him cheat on her and humiliate her hadn't done it, what would?

"I vote for telling him to get lost, and meaning it," Erik said flatly.

"Not as long as Annie's sick."

Erik's expression changed at once. "No, of course you can't do it right now. How's she doing?"

"She's being stubborn and uncooperative."

"That sounds like Annie." He grinned. "And her mother."

"Ha-ha," Dana Sue responded humorlessly. "That's why Ronnie and I are here. We're trying to come up with a way to get through to her. And he wants to hear every single detail of how she got into this shape in the first place. He's not going to be happy when I tell him I don't have all the answers."

"Then you're not here so you can get all cozy in a dark booth in the back?" Erik joked. "That's a relief."

She frowned. "I may be wavering, but I haven't jumped off the ledge yet."

"Then, since Helen and Maddie aren't here to do it, let me help drag you back from the edge of a very slippery slope," he offered. "The man cheated on you. Isn't that pretty much the scoop on Ronnie Sullivan?"

Dana Sue nodded. "For a very long time, it's been the only part that mattered."

"So, why would you even consider taking him back? I just don't get it. You're better than that, Dana Sue. You deserve a helluva lot more from the man in your life."

"You don't really know him," she began.

"I know enough," he said tightly. "I know he hurt you and Annie."

"I can't deny that," Dana Sue admitted. "But I'm just starting to remember that there's a lot more to him."

And that scared her almost as badly as what was going on with Annie.

Ronnie was chatting with the waitress about the night's specials, and awaiting Dana Sue's return, when he spotted Mary Vaughn Lewis coming in the door. When he'd left town, she'd been married to the mayor's son, the top real estate agent in the region. Knowing her driven personality, which was only one degree less driven than Helen's, he imagined she still was.

"Excuse me," he said to the waitress, a perky teenager who'd introduced herself as Brenda. "I think I'll wait till Dana Sue is free before I order. I see someone I need to speak to."

"Sure," Brenda told him. "I'll let Dana Sue know."

"Thanks." Ronnie slid from the booth and headed to the table where Mary Vaughn was already seated, her cell phone plastered to her ear. The instant she recognized him, she said something to whomever was on the phone, then snapped it shut. She stood up and threw her arms around his neck. "Ronnie Sullivan, if you aren't a sight for sore eyes," she said, giving him a smacking kiss on the lips. She lowered her voice. "You do know Dana Sue's probably around here somewhere, don't you? Are you ready to risk her coming after you with a butcher knife?"

He laughed. "Thanks for the warning, but she's well aware I'm here. That's probably why she hasn't come out of the kitchen in a while. That and the fact that she knows I'm going to grill her some more about Annie."

Mary Vaughn's expression sobered. "That poor child. How's she doing?"

"Better," Ronnie said, not wanting to get into that discussion. "Do you have a minute? There's something I'd like to talk about with you."

"Have a seat," she said at once. "I'm meeting someone, but he's always late. I doubt tonight will be an exception."

Ronnie pulled out her chair, then took the one next to her. "You look great, by the way," he told her. She had the trim build of an avid tennis player, a sport she'd taken up when she'd decided the country club would be the best place in town to meet rich potential clients.

"So," he asked, "are you still a big real estate mogul in town?"

She laughed. "The biggest. Why?"

"Are you by any chance handling the real estate that's on the market on Main Street? I didn't notice whose signs were in the windows."

"Most of it," she said. "And the one or two listings that aren't mine, I can get you into. What's up?"

"This needs to stay between you and me for now, okay?" he said.

"You know me, I'm the soul of discretion," she claimed.

Ronnie laughed. "Must have been hard for you getting to that place," he teased. "Used to be there wasn't a thing going on at the high school that you didn't know and share."

She winced at the reminder. "Not a trait that works in this

business. I know things—" She cut herself off. "Of course, if I told you, that would pretty much prove your point, wouldn't it? You can trust me, Ronnie. I swear it."

He nodded. "I'd like to take a look at the old hardware store property. When did it go on the market?"

"Only a couple of months ago," she told him. "It broke my heart to see one more business die. Rusty had a heart attack and, what with worrying about him and making sure he followed doctor's orders, Dora Jean couldn't handle the business. Not that there was much left of it, anyway. She just put a Closed sign in the window, called me and told me to sell it, lock, stock and barrel."

"When could I see it?"

She pulled out a day planner that was crammed with business cards and slips of paper. When she finally found her schedule, she skimmed a finger over the entries. "Eight in the morning tomorrow," she said finally. "Otherwise, not till after six. The day's jam-packed. I'm meeting with a developer at nine to talk about getting an exclusive on selling the homes in the new subdivision he's starting. Six hundred houses, if you can believe it. Then there's a Chamber of Commerce lunch at noon that will drag on till two. And then I'm showing properties to a couple relocating from Michigan." She rolled her eyes. "I've already shown them everything twice. I'm beginning to think they just like looking."

"Put me down for eight," he said at once.

If he liked what he heard and saw during his tour of the property, maybe he could get Mary Vaughn to consider letting him tag along to meet the developer. At the very least, he might be able to wrangle an introduction later, so he could pitch the kind of services he'd be offering to contractors once he had the doors opened. Once again it seemed as if fate had stepped in.

Just then Mary Vaughn's dinner companion, a well-dressed, older man Ronnie didn't recognize, arrived. Ronnie stood up and shook his hand as they were introduced. Though he was wearing a suit and tie, he looked as if he spent a lot of time on a golf course.

"Dave Carlson, Ronnie Sullivan, an old school friend," Mary Vaughn said.

"I won't intrude on your evening," Ronnie told him. "I was just scheduling an appointment with Mary Vaughn for tomorrow."

The man shrugged. "I'm used to it. Besides, she's one of my top Realtors, so I never complain when she's conducting business that could bring in more money."

"Ah, you're her boss," Ronnie concluded.

Mary Vaughn frowned at the man. "And ever since my divorce the man I go home with at night," she said, then added rather pointedly, "at least for now."

Suddenly Ronnie felt as if he'd stepped into a minefield. Were they married or not? It sounded as if there was tension around that issue.

He leaned down and kissed her cheek. "See you in the morning. You two have a good evening."

"Thanks," she said.

Ronnie wove his way back to his booth in about two seconds flat, picked up the menu and hid behind it.

A moment later, Dana Sue slid into the booth opposite him. "So why were you huddled with Mary Vaughn?" she asked, tilting the menu down to look into his eyes.

"Business," he said evasively.

She regarded him uneasily. "Are you about to start looking at houses, Ronnie?"

"If I were, would that bother you?"

"You know it would," she said.

"Why? Because it would mean I'm staying, just the way I told you I was?" He gave her a knowing look. "Or because it would mean I wasn't waiting around for you to invite me to come back home?"

She scowled. "Are you looking at houses or not?"

"Not," he said, then pointedly glanced at the menu. "What do you recommend tonight, sugar? The fried catfish or the scallops?"

She looked as if she wanted to recommend that he do something that was physically impossible, but she apparently thought better of it. "The catfish is one of our bestsellers," she said, her voice tight.

"Then that's what I'll have," he said cheerfully. "With a side of information."

Her expression turned wary. "About Annie?"

"No. As a matter of fact, what I really want to hear about is your social life," he said, clearly startling her. "Anybody special in your life since I left?"

"None of your business," she said flatly.

"Just trying to get a feel for the competition," he told her, enjoying the quick rise of color in her cheeks.

"You are so not in the race," she claimed.

"You so do not want to challenge me like that," he retorted with amusement. "Not unless you're ready for the consequences."

"What consequences?" she asked, a hint of alarm in her voice.

Below the table, he touched his knee to hers. In the booth's close quarters, there was no place for her to flee, not without causing a scene. His gaze locked on her mouth. Then, before she could snatch her hand away, he picked it up and rubbed his thumb across her knuckles, then lifted it to his lips and skimmed a kiss across skin that had been nicked more than once by a paring knife. Though she did her best to feign indifference, he could feel her pulse scramble in her wrist, and saw her eyes darken with the first stirring of desire.

Satisfied that he'd gotten the hoped-for reaction, he lowered her hand to the table and winked. "That, for starters."

Her hand shook as she picked up her glass of water. She took a long swallow, seemed to debate tossing the rest in his face, then murmured, "You're a pig."

"You've called me worse," he noted.

"You've deserved worse."

"No doubt about it," he agreed. "Now that we've established that, let's go back to your social life. Who's in your bed these days, Dana Sue?"

"I am not discussing this with you," she said heatedly. "Either we order right this second or I am out of here."

"Let's order," he said at once. "I can eat and ask you questions at the same time. Maybe food will improve your mood. It used to."

She glared at him, beckoned to the waitress and placed an order for the chocolate decadence cake and nothing else. "He's having the catfish," she said tersely when Brenda rushed right over, clearly eager to impress her boss. "And a side of rat poison, if Erik knows where it is."

The girl's pen paused in midair and her eyes widened. "What?"

Dana Sue gave her a weak smile. "Just kidding. The catfish, fries and vegetables will do."

"Okay," Brenda said, and hurried away.

Two seconds later, Erik came storming out of the kitchen and arrived at their table with an intimidating scowl on his face. "What the hell is going on here?" he demanded, his gaze on Ronnie.

"Your boss is in a snit," he answered. "Not to worry. I'm used to her moods."

"If she's ordering the chocolate decadence cake for herself, she's not in a snit. She's trying to kill herself."

"Erik!" she warned.

She spoke in a tone that even Ronnie recognized as meaning she was way past the end of her patience. Erik didn't seem fazed, however, which Ronnie thought was something in his favor.

"Well, dammit, I am not contributing to your downfall by bringing you that cake," Erik said. He whirled on Ronnie. "And if you gave a damn about her, you wouldn't have let her order it."

Ronnie knew he was missing something here, something important. He faced Dana Sue. "What's he talking about?"

"Something that's none of his business or yours," she said, tossing her napkin on the table. "Men!" she muttered, as if it were a four-letter word. She rose and stalked off.

Ronnie was relieved to see that she'd headed for the kitchen, rather than out the front door.

"Maybe you should tell me what's going on," he told Erik.

"Yeah, I should, but I need to get back in there and stop her from doing something stupid. Your catfish will be right out."

Ronnie stared after them and debated following. He wasn't entirely sure if he'd just witnessed some weird sort of lovers' tiff or something else entirely. Whatever it had been, it was clear that those two had something between them. Ronnie honestly didn't think it was a relationship, not a sexual one, anyway, but they were clearly close enough that they confided in and protected one another.

So what secret did Dana Sue have that she didn't want to share with him? Until a couple of years ago, Ronnie had known everything there was to know about her. He knew how she couldn't start her day without coffee. He knew she wore socks to bed when the weather turned cool. He even knew exactly where every one of her erogenous zones were, including one that had never been on a chart in any sex manual he'd ever seen.

And though she'd never said a word about it, he knew how desperately she missed her mom and how terrified she was that one day she, too, would develop diabetes.

At that thought, a lightbulb went off in his head. Diabetes! No wonder Erik had freaked when she'd ordered the cake and nothing more. Since Ronnie had been gone, Dana Sue had apparently started having problems with her blood sugar, problems she didn't want him to know anything about.

He could call her on it, or he could pretend that her argument with Erik had simply gone over his head. For now, maybe it would be better to do the latter. Give her time to tell him herself. In the meantime, he could keep an eye on her, see if she was taking proper care of herself. Not that he knew what that looked like, but he could find out. The Internet was a godsend when it came to researching that kind of stuff. And the Serenity Library had computers he could use to do it. Old Mrs. Harrington, the most tight-fisted widow ever to walk the earth, had shocked everyone by donating them.

At the memory of Dana Sue's mother and the diabetes complications that had led to her death, Ronnie found his appetite had fled. When his meal came, it could've been sawdust. He ate it anyway. As proud as Dana Sue obviously was of the food at Sullivan's, he didn't want to even try explaining why he'd left so much as a bite on his plate.

Then, plastering a smile on his face, he risked poking his

head in the kitchen. At first glance, he didn't see Dana Sue, but Erik gestured silently toward the stove.

She had her back to him. She'd tied on an apron and was sautéing five different dishes at the same time, then serving them up onto plates that already had garnishes in place. She added a decorative swirl of sauce, then tapped a bell to call for a waiter.

She lined up three more orders in clips hanging just above her head, and started the process again. Her movements were efficient and fast, her concentration intense.

Ronnie slipped over to Erik. "Do you need her here?"

He shook his head. "Karen was handling that till Dana Sue came in. She's just taking a break."

"Good. I'm going to get her out of here. We need to go back to the hospital to see Annie." Ronnie met the pastry chef's troubled gaze and decided the time had come to attempt to make him an ally, rather than an enemy. "Did she eat?"

Erik seemed surprised by the question. "I talked her into having the meat loaf again." He shrugged. "Comfort food usually works."

Ronnie decided not to press the issue further, but he had a hunch that Erik knew he'd figured out what was going on with her.

"I won't get her that upset again," he promised in an undertone, then sighed. "Okay, I probably will, but I'll keep her away from anything she shouldn't eat."

Erik's gaze narrowed, but like Ronnie, he didn't give anything away. Instead, he merely nodded. "I hope you stick to that."

"I'll do my best."

Dana Sue's voice cut through the noise around them. "Are you two planning to stop whispering anytime soon?" she demanded, her back still to them. "It's getting on my nerves."

Erik grinned. "Then by all means we'll shut right up. If there's one thing I hate in the kitchen, it's an edgy woman with knives."

She handed off the next batch of orders to Karen, then came to join them. "Something you might want to remember more often," she told Erik, patting his cheek. Then she faced Ronnie. "Ready to go back to the hospital?"

"Sure. Are you?"

"Ready as I'll ever be."

Ronnie knew the feeling. Every time he thought about Annie's uphill battle, it made him want to sit down and cry. Add in the battle Dana Sue was secretly waging, and he wondered if anything was going to be normal for any of them again.

13

Dana Sue was relieved to find Annie surrounded by her friends when she and Ronnie got back to the hospital. It meant they could put off giving her the lecture Dr. McDaniels had suggested. Maybe having company—especially Ty, who was slumped down in a chair in a corner, watching Annie with a worried frown on his face—would even improve Annie's mood enough that she'd be more receptive to whatever her parents said to her later.

Dana Sue glanced at Ronnie and noted that he looked just as relieved as she felt.

"We probably should kick them out so we can talk to her," he said, not showing much enthusiasm.

"They'll go soon enough," Dana Sue said. "Besides, if we're the ones responsible for making them leave, she'll be too upset to want to hear anything we have to say."

"Why are you two standing outside Annie's door whispering?" Helen asked when she arrived a few minutes later.

"Strategy session," Dana Sue told her.

"Oh?" Helen looked from her to Ronnie and back again. "Bad news?"

"Only if Annie doesn't listen to what we have to say." Ronnie's expression was grim.

Alarm flared in Helen's eyes. "Is she worse?"

Dana Sue slipped an arm around her waist. "No. It's just what I was telling you about this morning at the spa. She's still giving the psychologist a tough time."

"Denial," Helen said sagely. "Who amongst us hasn't grappled with that from time to time?"

Dana Sue studied her and recognized the tension in her posture. She suspected not all of that came from concern for Annie. "Are you okay? Did you see Doc Marshall today?"

Helen frowned at the question, then cast a pointed look at Ronnie.

Dana Sue got the message. "Excuse us," she said to her ex, then dragged Helen off toward the waiting room. The instant they were seated in a relatively secluded corner, she demanded, "Tell me what happened."

Helen snapped open her briefcase and dragged out a prescription pill bottle. "These happened," she said dully.

"Blood pressure pills?" Dana Sue guessed.

"Water pills," Helen said, regarding them with disgust. "People don't take water pills till they're old. Who wants to spend the whole darn day running to the bathroom? Can you picture me stopping a trial every ten minutes to say, 'Excuse me, Judge, but I need to use the restroom, *again*'? I'll be the laughingstock of the courthouse."

Dana Sue bit down hard on her lower lip to keep from chuckling. Obviously, to Helen this was more about aging than it was about admitting she needed to treat her blood pressure more aggressively.

"Your blood pressure's not high because you're old, for goodness' sake," Dana Sue said. "It's high because you're completely overwhelmed, you work too hard, you don't exercise and eat right." She gave her a hard look. "But you know all that, don't you?"

"Of course I do," her friend said impatiently. "I told Doc Marshall I was dealing with things. I showed him my goals, the very ones you and Maddie signed off on this morning. One day off every week. Aerobic exercise for one hour three days a week, weight training for two. Sign up for a meditation class. A healthy dinner at a regular time every night. *Yada-yada-yada.* There were ten goals on that paper. It was *notarized.* What more does he need?"

"He didn't tell you?"

"Actually, he said it was too little too late," Helen grumbled. "He said that my blood pressure was up from my last visit, and until I could come to him with a lower blood pressure reading and prove that I was achieving those goals, they were only words on a piece of paper." She was all but quivering with indignation. "As if I'd lie about my intention to keep them."

"You have before," Dana Sue reminded her mildly.

Helen scowled at her. "Whose side are you on?" she snapped.

"Yours, always, but he has a point," Dana Sue said, ignoring the irony of her being the one to voice support for the doctor's firm stance. She certainly hadn't listened to a word he'd told *her,* or more precisely, acted on his advice. "How long have you been making promises that you'd deal with this by exercising and eating properly?"

"I do exercise. I do eat properly," Helen said, then winced under Dana Sue's skeptical scrutiny. "Most of the time, anyway. Look at me. I don't have an extra ounce of weight on me."

"Because you work most of the time and get stressed over it when you're *not* working," Dana Sue said. "He's not giving you those pills to insult you or quarrel with your intentions. Doc Marshall wants you healthy. That's it."

"I wouldn't be so quick to defend him if I were you," Helen retorted. "He'll probably come after you next."

Helen's prediction was definitely valid, which was one reason Dana Sue hadn't scheduled an appointment with him. She didn't want to face him and find out that she was one step closer to needing pills or insulin to regulate her blood sugar. She felt fine—most of the time, anyway. And when she remembered to check her blood sugar, the level wasn't that bad.

Recognizing the rationalization for what it was, she winced. They were all pathetic, she concluded wearily. They'd rather ignore their problems than deal with them head-on. How could she come down hard on Annie when she was just as bad? Maybe denial was a natural state for her, but it was dangerous for Annie and just as risky for Helen. Right now Dana Sue needed to focus on them.

"Let me ask you something," she said. "If a client comes to you with a problem, what do you do?"

"Give them the best advice I can," Helen answered, looking confused. "What does that have to do with anything?"

"Bear with me a minute," Dana Sue said. "Do you expect them to take it?"

"Of course," she stated, as if anything else was inconceivable.

"When you see Doc Marshall, you're expecting him to give you his expert professional advice, right? You don't want him just to tell you what you want to hear, any more than you'd tell one of your clients only what they want to hear."

Helen's frown deepened. "You're starting to get all reasonable and obnoxious like Maddie," she accused.

Dana Sue grinned. "I'll regard that as a compliment." She took the bottle of pills from Helen's clenched fist. "'One a day,'" she read. "Seems a small price to pay if it'll help get your blood pressure in check."

"It's the principle," Helen complained, clearly not yet ready to give in.

"No, it's your stubborn pride," Dana Sue corrected. "You don't like admitting you need help. Just think how great you'll feel the day you can toss these things in the trash forever."

Helen sighed then and reached for the bottle. "Fine. I'll take the damn pills, but don't you come grumbling to me when he hands you medication for your diabetes. I'll throw all this calm, logical crap right back in your face."

Dana Sue laughed. "Feel free."

Only after Helen had gone to stick her head in Annie's room and say good-night did Dana Sue sink back on the uncomfortable plastic chair and sigh. She was such a fraud. When push came to shove and she was faced with a prescription proving that she couldn't control her blood-sugar levels on her own, she was going to be just as impossible as Helen. Worse, even.

But just as she'd been there for Helen tonight, Helen and Maddie would be there to remind her of the goal—to stay alive and well.

Thinking of that reminded her that she and Ronnie needed to do that very same thing for Annie tonight. Pulling herself together, she marched down the hall, prepared to endure tears, anger or whatever else their daughter threw at them.

She found Ronnie alone in the room with Annie. They were playing checkers, which had been one of their favorite after-dinner pastimes since Annie had been old enough to understand the rules.

"She's still beating the daylights out of me," he said as Dana Sue pulled a chair up beside his.

Annie beamed. "I am, but I don't think you're really concentrating," she said. She immediately jumped his remaining three men to win yet another game.

Ronnie sighed dramatically. "See what I mean?" He turned to Dana Sue. "She's ruthless."

"You taught her that, so don't start complaining about it now," Dana Sue said. When Annie started to set up the board for another game, Dana Sue stopped her. "Let's put it away for tonight, sweetie. We need to talk."

Annie's expression turned wary. "About?"

"Your sessions with Dr. McDaniels," Ronnie said.

Dana Sue gave him a grateful look, relieved that he wasn't going to leave this whole conversation up to her.

Annie's good mood vanished in a heartbeat. "I don't need a shrink," she said sullenly. "I don't know why she keeps coming back. I've told her I'm fine."

"You're not fine," Dana Sue insisted. "Look where you are, sweetie. No girl your age winds up in the hospital with heart problems unless there's something serious going on."

"But I'm well now," Annie argued. "I've been eating the stuff Lacy and I agreed to, except when it's totally disgusting. And then I drink those stupid little shakes to make up for it. Ask her. She'll tell you that she's gotten my calorie count almost up to normal, or what passes for normal in her world. I feel great. Dr. Lane says I'm getting stronger every day. I bet he'll let me out of here tomorrow or the next day."

"It's not entirely up to him," Ronnie said, his tone unyielding. "And just so you know, he agrees with Dr. McDaniels that you can't leave unless you start cooperating with her."

"They're sticking together?" Annie asked incredulously. "That sucks."

"You should be grateful to them," Ronnie said. "If you don't get to the bottom of what happened, Annie, you'll wind up right back in here again—and next time you might not be so lucky."

Annie locked gazes with her dad and tears welled up in her eyes. "But I'm okay now, really. Please, Daddy, just take me home. This will never happen again. I swear it."

Dana Sue saw the muscle working in Ronnie's jaw and knew he was struggling with himself.

"Taking you home before Dr. McDaniels says it's okay is not an option," he said at last. "I don't care how many tears you shed or how many promises you make. Until we know with absolute certainty that you're not going to stop eating again, we can't risk it, Annie."

She looked stunned by his refusal. "You don't get to come back here after abandoning me, and tell me what to do," she said bitterly. "If you loved me, you wouldn't have left, and you wouldn't make me do this."

Though he was visibly shaken by the accusation, Ronnie's resolve didn't waver. "Your mom and I *do* love you, more than anything on this earth. I think you know that. We don't want to lose you, sweetie."

"But I'm fine," Annie protested, her voice rising. "Fine!" She leaped out of the bed. "Here, I'll prove it," she said, spinning around and dancing to some tune that was playing only in her head.

"Stop it right this second!" Dana Sue commanded. "Get back into bed."

The no-nonsense tone brought Annie up short. Blinking back a fresh batch of tears, she sat on the edge. Dana Sue moved over to sit beside her. Thinking about what Ronnie had revealed earlier in the day, she asked, "I need to know the truth about something. Have you been eating the meals they're bringing to you? Are you really consuming all those calories they think you are?"

"I'm not flushing anything down the toilet, if that's what you're asking," Annie said defensively. "Somebody sits here to make sure of that."

"That's not exactly what I asked," Dana Sue said gently. "Are you eating every bite?"

Annie avoided her gaze.

"Are you?" she persisted.

"It's too much food," Annie protested, but she looked ashamed.

"Have you eaten any of it?" Dana Sue said, not giving her an inch.

"Some," Annie said.

"And the rest? Do you leave it on the tray so the nurses can decide if you're following the rules? Before you answer, remember that I know just how sneaky you can be when you want someone to believe you're eating properly."

Annie's chin set and she remained stubbornly silent.

"I didn't think so," Dana Sue said wearily.

"I told you, they watch me like a hawk," Annie grumbled. "It's not like I can get away with cheating. It's no wonder I don't have any appetite."

Dana Sue wasn't convinced she hadn't found another way around the rules. "If you're not flushing it down the toilet, what then? Are you hiding it somewhere till after they're gone?"

She stood up and reached for the trash can, but before she could dig around in it, Annie began to cry in earnest.

"Mom, stop it," she pleaded. "Not you, too. Doesn't anybody trust me?"

Dana Sue found a napkin in the bottom of the trash with half a turkey sandwich wrapped in it. Her heart aching, she held up the damning evidence. "Baby, don't you see, this is exactly why you need to talk to Dr. McDaniels. It's barely been a week since you've been out of ICU and you're already falling back into the same old pattern."

"What about you?" Annie retorted, her tone scathing. "How many times have you pulled a pint of ice cream from the fridge since Dad came back to town? Talk about old patterns."

Dana Sue felt heat climb into her cheeks. "Not the point," she said, avoiding Ronnie's gaze. "You're the one in a crisis now, not me."

"Your mother's right," he said, his voice surprisingly harsh. "And I don't ever want to hear you speak to her that way again. Understood?"

Annie looked as if she wanted to lash out at both of them, but instead she nodded. "I'm sorry, Mom," she said, her tone meek.

"Apology accepted." Dana Sue brushed Annie's hair back from her face. If she needed reminding of just how bad things were and why they were doing this, touching those brittle strands were enough to bring the point across.

"I'm tired," Annie said, crawling back beneath the covers and turning away from them.

"Then we'll let you get some rest," Dana Sue said, exhausted herself. "Please think about what we've said. When Dr. McDaniels comes tomorrow, talk to her. She's not the enemy. She's on your side."

Annie didn't respond.

Dana Sue cast a helpless look at Ronnie, then stood up to wait as he leaned down to kiss Annie.

"'Night, sweet pea," he said. "Love you."

"Love you, too," Annie murmured, her voice catching on a sob.

Dana Sue had to leave the room before she, too, burst into tears. When Ronnie followed her out, she looked into his distraught face.

"Do you think any of that got through to her?" she asked him.

"I wish to hell I knew," he said. "We did the best we could."

She met his gaze and voiced her worst fear. "What if it's not enough?"

"It has to be," he said simply. "It just has to be."

Though Ronnie was excited about getting into the old hardware store to see its potential, he couldn't shake the scene with Annie from his head. Would today go better than previous days when she met with Dr. McDaniels? And if it didn't, what would happen next? The possibility of having to send Annie away loomed over everything. He knew Dana Sue was no happier about it than he was. Both of them were praying it wouldn't come to that.

Pushing that worry aside for now, he paced the sidewalk in front of the hardware store, fifteen minutes early for his meeting with Mary Vaughn. He was already a nervous wreck when she drove up and parked right behind his car. A lot was riding on what he saw inside and the figures she was going to give him.

"I like a client who's eager," she told him with a smile as she found the right key in her purse and unlocked the door. "It usually means I can wrangle a better deal for the seller."

Ronnie laughed at her candor. "I'm interested, not stupid," he told her. "If I decide to buy—big *if*, by the way—I'll be as fair to Dora Jean and Rusty as I can be, given the limitations of my funds."

"Sounds reasonable," she said. "You need me to go through here and give you a spiel, or would you rather look it over on your own?"

"On my own, if you don't mind. Then we can go over any questions I have."

She nodded. "I'll wait outside, then. I have calls I need to make, anyway. The street's the only place to get a decent cell phone signal around here. My calls were cut off three times last night while I was at Sullivan's. I should have known better than to try to take them in the first place."

"Make your calls. I'll be fine," Ronnie said, eager to get inside.

The place was musty from being closed up for even just a couple of months. Ronnie walked up and down the aisles, a thousand memories crowding in as he thought of all the times he'd come inside and pestered Rusty for advice about tools and the various projects he was doing around his parents' house. The forty-year-old house had had its charms, but there'd always been something breaking or requiring paint or patching. His dad had been clueless and his mom impatient. Ronnie had enjoyed the work, and doing the odd jobs himself had the added bonus of keeping his mom off his dad's case. He'd earned a fair amount of pocket money from his grateful father, who'd insisted they move to a maintenance-free condo in Columbia when they retired.

Today the shelves were no longer as fully stocked as they'd once been. And there was so much dust! Still, the remaining inventory was good quality and would give him a head start. He imagined Rusty would put him in touch with suppliers. Maybe he'd even want to come in and work from time to time if his health permitted. Ronnie liked the idea of having the old guy around. It'd give the place some continuity.

The large back room of the building held a limited supply of lumber, insulation and other building supplies, but Ronnie knew he'd need a warehouse for the kind of operation he was envisioning. Still, this place could be the anchor, with plenty of room for, literally, the nuts and bolts of the business.

He walked behind the counter and fingered the old, intricately molded brass cash register. He'd probably need to replace it with something more modern and electronic, but there was a charm to this one that made him wish it could be otherwise.

Looking outside, he could see the town square through the grime-covered window. He imagined that glass sparkling in the sun, a clever display of some sort on the built-in shelf below, or glittering with lights at Christmas. It felt so right that if Mary Vaughn had come back in at that precise second, he would have agreed to any terms she laid out for him.

Which was why it was a good thing she was still outside, her cell phone plastered to her ear. He went out to join her and she immediately ended her call. When she emerged from her car, he noticed that she took her time, making sure he got a good view of her shapely legs. He couldn't help wondering if that was part of her sales strategy or if the relationship she was in was as rocky as he'd suspected the night before. Mary Vaughn on the prowl was a complication he didn't need.

"Well?" she asked, studying his face.

"Walking through there brings back a lot of memories," he said. "You have the specs and asking price with you?"

She nodded at once and pulled them from her briefcase. "I also have a contract with me if you want to make an offer."

Ronnie was so tempted it took everything in him not to go for it, but he shook his head. "I need to look over these papers," he said. "And there're people I want to discuss this with."

"Don't wait too long," she said, but they both knew there wouldn't be a lot of competition for the property, not until someone took the lead in bringing life back to downtown.

"I'll be in touch," Ronnie promised. "How's Rusty doing now? I'd like to speak to him if he's well enough for company."

Mary Vaughn's gaze narrowed suspiciously. "You wouldn't

go behind my back and try to make a deal directly with him, would you?"

Ronnie returned her gaze evenly. "I think you know me better than that," he said, annoyed that she'd even felt the need to ask.

She flinched at his tone. "Sorry. It just makes me nervous when buyers want to set up little tête-à-têtes with sellers."

"Understandable," he said. "But I imagine there are things Rusty could tell me about this place that you can't. Besides, I'd just like to talk old times with him."

Mary Vaughn visibly relaxed. "He's probably chomping at the bit for some company by now. Dora Jean's had him on a very short leash."

Ronnie nodded. "I'll drop by, then. You and I will talk again."

"Any idea when?"

He needed to pay that visit to Rusty, then talk again with Butch. Considering the amount of time he needed to devote to Annie, as well, it would be at least several days. "End of the week," he suggested. "Maybe not till the first of next."

The Realtor looked vaguely disappointed, but made a note in her day planner. "I'll call you if I haven't heard from you by then."

"Of course you will," he teased, then brushed a quick kiss across her cheek. "You didn't get to be queen of real estate around here without trying to make things happen."

He was about to walk away when he remembered her other meeting this morning. The fact that he'd forgotten something so important was testament to how distracted he was by Annie's rebellious attitude.

"Would you do me a favor?" he asked Mary Vaughn.

"Of course."

"When you're talking to your developer friend this morning, mention my name, okay?"

"Mind if I ask why?"

"Let's just say it's all part of this plan I have in the back of my mind."

As if sensing that it might help her to close the deal for the property, she said, "You could come along with me now. I'm sure he wouldn't object. He's a pretty laid-back guy."

Ronnie debated with himself, then decided against it. "I need to get my ducks in a row first," he told her. "Just speak kindly of me if the opportunity arises."

"Done," she said at once. "Now I'd better run. Being late never makes a good impression."

Ronnie watched her climb into her cream-colored Lexus and drive off. He cast one last look back at the hardware store and once again felt that burst of excitement deep inside. He shoved the papers Mary Vaughn had given him into his pocket and headed straight back to his motel. It was time to start running some numbers to see if this dream of his had a chance in hell of succeeding.

Annie scowled at Dr. McDaniels, trying to hold back her anger. She knew the woman had ratted her out to her parents, and now they were going to be all over her until she cooperated. The whole thing sucked, big-time.

Annie remained stoically silent, even though the shrink was regarding her with an expectant expression, just waiting for her to open up and spill her guts. So what if her parents had been telling her the truth, that she couldn't get out of the hospital till she started talking. The truth was, she was scared. What if she blabbed every one of her deepest, darkest secrets and the doctor decided she was a basket case? Nope, she couldn't take that chance.

"I've got nothing for you," she told the shrink eventually. "I don't eat because I'm not hungry."

"Never?" Dr. McDaniels asked skeptically.

"Nope, never."

"And yet you know the human body has to be fed in order to survive," Linda McDaniels said. "You know it's important to drink plenty of fluids, so you won't get dehydrated. I imagine they taught you all that in school."

"Sure," Annie said. She didn't add that Lacy and Dr. McDaniels themselves had been over the same information a zillion times in the last week or so. It was getting really old.

"Then not eating or drinking is a conscious choice on your part. You must be making a decision to starve yourself to death. Why?"

Annie shrugged. "I dunno."

"I think you do," the shrink chided.

"Then maybe you should tell me," she said. The woman might as well work for her seventy-five bucks an hour!

As if she'd guessed Annie's unspoken challenge, Dr. McDaniels merely smiled. "I think I'll let you come up with your own answers, Annie. Think it over and we'll discuss it further tomorrow. Same time."

"I thought I was going home tomorrow," she said, even though she'd been told it wouldn't happen as long as she wasn't talking to the shrink.

Dr. McDaniels shook her head. "Not unless I feel you're giving me your full cooperation. Lacy says you're still trying to fool the nurses about how much you're eating, as well. I heard all about that turkey sandwich you managed to hide in the trash can, Annie. That you would do something like that when you're in the hospital tells me you still don't grasp the seriousness of this."

"Did my mom and dad blab about that?" Annie demanded.

Dr. McDaniels regarded her evenly. "They didn't have to. There's not much we don't find out about around here. Think of this as a tiny microcosm of Serenity. News travels very fast on the hospital grapevine."

"That sucks," Annie said sullenly.

"No, it just means there are a lot of people around here who are dedicated to seeing to it that you get well. But you have to want that, too, Annie. You have to acknowledge that you have a problem before we'll ever be able to deal with it."

"What happens if I don't talk?" she asked. "You going to keep me locked up here forever?"

"Your parents didn't explain the alternative to you?"

Annie shook her head. "No."

"Okay, here's what I told them," she said, leveling a look at Annie that made her squirm. "If you don't address this in a meaningful way, I'll have no choice but to recommend that you go to an inpatient treatment facility."

"No way!" Annie cried.

"Yes, way," the shrink responded. "So here are your choices, Annie. We start to make some progress here, and you eat everything on the menus that you and Lacy plan, then I'll release you, and we'll continue to have sessions every day after school. Or you go to a treatment facility that specializes in eating disorders. There are a couple in the state that I recommend."

"I'd have to go away from Serenity and leave all my friends?" Annie asked incredulously. "For how long?"

"As long as it takes."

Annie shook her head. "My parents will never agree to me being sent away."

"They already have," Dr. McDaniels said. "So what's it going to be?"

Annie stared at her in dismay. "I'd have to keep these stupid appointments every day after school?"

"Until you get a grasp on why you're doing this, yes. We can't fix the problem until you acknowledge and understand it, and we come up with a plan for getting you healthy again. The sooner we get started, the sooner you'll be well, and free of me."

Nobody had explained that part of the deal to her. It totally sucked, Annie thought. "What if I, like, have some kind of breakthrough?"

"That would speed things along," the shrink conceded. "I think we'll all be a lot happier if you understand what pushed you down this path in the first place. That way it's less likely to happen again. So, tomorrow, same time. If your attitude's improved and you've gotten real with Lacy, too, then we can talk about you going home."

"Yeah, whatever," Annie grumbled. Her chances of getting out of here were next to nothing unless she talked. She might as well accept that. Her mom and dad were on the doctors' side. They were totally united for once.

It was kinda cool, in a way. She had a hunch if it went on long enough, they'd wake up and see what Annie already knew—that they still loved each other. She'd figured that out the first time she saw the way they looked at each other after she woke up. Maybe, eventually, she'd have her family back. If that happened, this totally lame stay in the hospital would be worth it.

14

"How did Annie do in her therapy session today?" Maddie asked Dana Sue, who'd stopped by The Corner Spa the next morning. "If you have time for tea, let's go outside and sit on the patio. The weather's gorgeous and you look as if you could use a break."

"I honestly don't know if I'm coming or going," Dana Sue admitted, pouring herself a cup of strong Earl Grey tea from one of the pots in the spa café, then heading to the patio. "I go by the hospital for a while in the morning, then again in the afternoon and evening. In between I'm trying to keep up with the paperwork at the restaurant."

"Isn't Ronnie at the hospital a lot, too?"

Dana Sue nodded. "And believe me, that just adds to the stress." She closed her eyes and turned her face up to the sun filtering through the trees. The warmth felt heavenly. If she could have, she would have sat right here all day long.

"You could always divvy up the visiting times, so neither of you needs to be there as much," Maddie suggested, studying Dana Sue intently. "You wouldn't cross paths as much, either." Her expression turned smug. "If that's what you really want."

"In theory that's a great idea," Dana Sue said. "But right

now it seems to be taking both of us coming at Annie at the same time to get any point across. Otherwise she just tries to play us off against each other. Heck, she tries that when we're both in the same room. She attacks me to stir up my guilt, then turns on the tears for Ronnie."

"Would you cave if he wasn't there for backup?"

"No," Dana Sue said. "I've finished pretending that everything will work itself out on its own."

"Would Ronnie give in if you weren't around?"

"Now that's the million-dollar question," Dana Sue said. "He's been amazingly stern with her so far, but I know it's killing him." She shook her head, determined to give him more credit. "No, he wouldn't give in. He knows how important this is."

"Does he have any idea of the kind of stress you're under and how bad that is for you?" Maddie asked worriedly.

Dana Sue shook her head. "No. At least, I haven't said anything about my health. Unfortunately, the other night at the restaurant, Erik was tossing out all sorts of hints. I'm not sure whether Ronnie caught on or not. Every now and then, though, he gets this look in his eyes that makes me wonder. And he gets all weird if he thinks I haven't eaten three meals a day. If he *has* figured things out, I don't want to know. I couldn't cope with his pity on top of everything else."

"It might be genuine *concern,* not pity," Maddie corrected. "He still has feelings for you, Dana Sue. You know he does."

"I can't cope with that right now, either." She regarded her friend wearily. "I'm just so damn tired. I would give anything for one decent night's sleep. I don't think I'll get one, though, till Annie's back home again."

"Any idea when that will be?"

"If she'd just wake up and get with the program, it could

be tomorrow or the day after, but she's stubborn to her core," Dana Sue said ruefully. "From what Dr. McDaniels told me, she was only marginally more cooperative today, even after Ronnie and I ganged up on her last night."

When Maddie started to respond, Dana Sue held up her hand. "I can't talk about this anymore right now, okay? I'm at the end of my rope. Besides, I came over here to thank you for getting Ty to go by to visit with her so much. I'm sure a hospital is the last place he wants to be, but he's been really good about stopping by."

"He's worried sick about her," Maddie confessed. "In fact, his reaction caught me by surprise. I think he's feeling guilty for some reason. I've tried to talk to him. So has Cal. We've told him what happened wasn't his fault."

"That's true, but he was there the night it happened," Dana Sue told her. "Did you know that?"

Maddie looked stunned. "I had no idea."

"Not actually *when* it happened, but earlier," Dana Sue explained. "Annie was having that sleepover we'd talked about, and Ty and some other guys came by the house, even though I'd strictly forbidden Annie to invite any boys. I saw them leaving. With everything else that's happened, I haven't confronted her about it yet."

"I'll speak to Ty tonight," Maddie said, frowning. "He knows he has no business being at a party of any kind when the parents aren't home."

"Knowing how he feels about Annie, as if she's another kid sister, he probably felt he should have been looking out for her that night," Dana Sue mused. "I have no idea what went on while he was there—a lot of dancing, I suppose— but he might feel responsible for what happened later, even though he was long gone. Please tell him again that none of this was his fault, that it all started a long time before that night."

Maddie nodded. "I also think I'll have another serious chat with him about spending time at any of his friends' houses when the parents aren't around. Kids his age need adult supervision. He knows that's the rule, even if it *is* your house and he's always treated it like a second home."

"Just don't stop him from spending time with Annie," Dana Sue pleaded. "She adores him. He's an important part of her support system right now."

Maddie smiled. "I know. I've watched her looking at him as if he hung the moon."

"I wish he looked at her the same way," Dana Sue said, then added wistfully, "Wouldn't it be great if sometime down the road the two of them got together?"

"Sometime *way* down the road," Maddie replied. "But, yes, it would be great. Right now, though, all Ty really cares about is baseball. And all I care about is getting him into a good college. Cal and I are still at odds over that, since he thinks Ty could go pro straight out of high school, and that scout he invited to watch him play agrees. So far, Bill's remaining neutral, which means it's up to me to convince Ty that college is important. You'd think Cal, of all people, would understand the importance of a college education, since it came in darn handy for him when his baseball career ended so abruptly."

Dana Sue regarded her with a wistful expression. "I wish those were the kind of things going on with Annie right now— nice, normal, teenage stuff."

"Oh, sweetie, this crisis will pass," Maddie said, regarding her with sympathy. "A day will come when all you'll worry about will be whether Annie's home on time from a date and whether her grades are good enough for the college she wants to attend."

"That day can't come soon enough for me," Dana Sue exclaimed earnestly. "I need to go. I want to stop by the restaurant before I head back to the hospital. I'm going to owe Erik and Karen huge raises after the way they've pitched in, but there are some things I have to do myself. I would give anything to spend an evening there cooking. I miss it."

"Well, even if you don't have time to cook, eat a decent meal while you're there," Maddie advised. "I hear the food's outstanding, even with the owner away."

Dana Sue smiled. "Thank goodness for that." She leaned down and gave her friend a fierce hug. "Thanks for listening."

"Anytime," Maddie said. "Ronnie's a pretty good sounding board, too, you know. And he has as much of a stake in the outcome of all this as you do."

"I know," Dana Sue murmured. She just didn't want to start relying on him, and find out that all his promises about sticking around Serenity meant no more than the vows he'd taken on the day he'd married her.

Annie was feeling pretty battered and bruised after another unproductive session with Dr. McDaniels. It was getting harder and harder not to give in to the psychologist's entreaties, especially knowing that she could be stuck here for days if she didn't cooperate, or worse, wind up in some dump far away from home, where they'd pester her until she caved in. There had to be rules about torturing a kid, right? Maybe she should ask Helen about that.

There was a hesitant tap on the door of her room, then it inched open. Ty stuck his head in, his expression tentative.

"Is it okay to come in?"

Annie brightened at the sight of him. He was such a hunk, especially in jeans and an old Atlanta Braves T-shirt. "Sure," she said eagerly, wishing she'd done something to fix herself up earlier. She probably looked pretty disgusting. "Shouldn't you be in school?"

"I cut classes," he admitted, pulling a chair up beside the bed.

She stared at him in shock. "To come see me?"

He nodded, looking uncomfortable. "It's just that every time I've come, the room's been filled up with other kids, and your folks or my mom. I wanted to talk to you alone."

"Your mom's going to flip out when she finds out about this, you know. Coach Maddox probably will, too. Isn't he real strict about players being in class?"

"Oh, yeah," Ty admitted. "But he's my stepdad now. I can probably get him to cut me some slack."

"Dreamer," she teased. "He probably thinks he has to be harder on you than anybody else, so you'll be an example, even if you are his star player."

Ty shrugged. "Doesn't matter. I needed to talk to you about what happened."

"You mean the night I got sick," she said, her enthusiasm for the visit waning.

"Yeah, that," he said. "And the fact that me and those other guys were over there. I feel like we contributed to what happened."

"That's crazy," she said. "You'd been gone forever when I passed out."

"Maybe so, but that's the second time I was around and you keeled over."

"It wasn't the same as it was at your mom's wedding," Annie insisted. "I just got a little dizzy that time."

"From not eating," Ty said. "And we both know it wasn't

just some little thing. I know all about anorexia from school, Annie. It's not something to fool around with. I'm worried about you."

She stared at him, startled that he would admit to such a thing. "Why?"

"You almost died, dammit, that's why," he said, his voice rising. "Don't you know how scary that is for everyone around you? Sarah and Raylene are terrified. I get sick thinking about what could have happened. And all of us feel guilty because we've seen what you were doing and haven't stepped up to say anything." His somber gaze clashed with hers. "So I'm stepping up, here and now. You're my friend. Heck, you're practically family. We've known each other since we were babies."

"I know," she whispered, shaken by the barely concealed anger and fear in his voice.

"Then here's the deal," he said, his gaze not wavering. "Either you get help for this right now or I'll be on your case morning, noon and night until you do."

Tears welled up in her eyes and spilled down her cheeks. "It matters that much to you?"

"*You* matter that much. Not just to me, but to a lot of people."

She regarded him incredulously. "But I'm so fat," she whispered. "I don't know how you can even stand to look at me."

Ty stared at her in shocked disbelief. "Are you crazy?" He jumped up, yanked open a bedside drawer and fumbled around until he found a compact. "Look at yourself," he demanded, holding up the tiny mirror. "Take a good, hard look, Annie. You used to be beautiful, but now you look like a skeleton."

Annie couldn't bear to look in the mirror. She began to cry in earnest at the harsh words.

Ty tossed the compact back in the drawer, then took her hand in his. "I want the old Annie back. I want to see your dimples again. I want to hear you laugh again. I want all of us to go out for pizza and burgers and not see you pushing the food around on your plate and only pretending to eat it."

Annie clung to his hand, stunned that any of this mattered to him. "I don't know if I can be that way again," she told him.

"I think you can be," he said with confidence. "I'll bet the shrink does, too, or she wouldn't be wasting her time. But you have to want it, Annie. You have to want it enough to fight for it. I know all about how you're stonewalling the doctor right now. My mom was telling Cal about it last night at dinner. You act like none of this is a big deal, but it *is*."

Annie closed her eyes so she wouldn't have to see his disappointment. Having Ty come down on her like this had caught her totally by surprise. She wished she could tell him what he wanted to hear. Did he think she wanted to die?

"Hey," he said, squeezing her hand. "Look at me." He waited patiently until she finally relented and met his gaze. "I know you're scared. And I know what the teacher said in health class about anorexia being some kind of weird control thing." He smiled at her. "So here's how I see it. If you were strong enough to control your eating that way, then you're strong enough to turn things around. You just have to want it."

His smile spread. "And until you want it enough for yourself, consider me your conscience. I'm going to be on your case like white on rice."

Annie wasn't sure she could see a downside to that, but she knew there was one. Having Ty underfoot every time she turned around was like a dream come true. Knowing he was there for one reason only, to see to it that she ate, well, that wasn't so terrific. In fact, it was kinda humiliating.

"I can do this on my own," she told him, not wanting him to know how scared she was that she couldn't.

He nodded. "I believe that. Just the same, I think I'll keep a close eye on you until all the votes are counted."

"Did your mom send you over here?" Annie asked.

He blinked at the question. "No, why?"

"My mom?"

He shook his head.

Annie lay back against the pillows, pleased that he'd done this completely on his own. Maybe he *did* care about her, at least a little. Not like he was in love with her or anything, but this was the start she'd always longed for.

For the first time since her life had started spiraling out of control, she felt motivated to fix it. Maybe the next time Dr. McDaniels came by she'd have something to say to her.

Ronnie had been just down the hall when he'd seen Ty slip into Annie's room. Given the time of day, it was pretty clear the kid had cut classes to come. His reason for doing that must have been pretty important.

Ronnie had waited a good, long time before wandering down the hall and hanging around outside the door. He'd caught only snatches of what Ty had said to Annie and almost none of her replies, but he'd heard enough to feel a surge of admiration for Ty.

He was still standing there when Ty finally emerged from the room.

"Ronnie," Ty said, looking vaguely guilty. "I didn't know you were around."

"Just got here," Ronnie fibbed. "I appreciate you coming by to spend some time with Annie."

"I've been worried about her," the teen said with a shrug.

"Me, too." Ronnie debated saying more, then decided the boy needed to know how grateful he was for some of the things he'd said to Annie, hard truths that the rest of them had been tiptoeing around in some ways. "Look, Ty, I wasn't trying to eavesdrop, but I heard a little bit of what you said in there. I think you may have gotten through to her in a way none of the rest of us have been able to do. I can't tell you how grateful I am."

Ty stood a little taller. "I meant every word," he said.

"I know you did. That's why I'm so impressed. You've turned into a very mature young man."

Ty grinned sheepishly. "I'm not so sure my mom's going to agree with that when she finds out I skipped school to come by here."

Ronnie draped an arm over his shoulder. "Let me deal with your mom."

Ty regarded him with relief. "My stepdad, too? He's the baseball coach and he has all these rules about cutting class."

"I'll speak to him, too," Ronnie promised. "In fact, why don't we take care of that right now? You have any more classes this afternoon?"

Ty shook his head.

"Then I'll call your mom and see if she and your stepdad can meet us for a milk shake at Wharton's. Sound good?" he asked, heading for the exit.

"Sure," Ty said. He looked away, then gave Ronnie a shy glance. "I don't know everything that happened when you left town, but I'm glad you're back. You and Dana Sue were always cool together. To me, you were like another set of parents, you know?"

Ronnie felt the warm sting of tears at the comment. "Thanks. I always felt like that, too." Before he could embarrass himself or Ty by actually shedding a tear, he pulled out his cell phone, then realized he had no idea what the number was at The Corner Spa. He held the phone out. "Why don't you give your mom a call?"

Ty regarded it as if it were contaminated. "No way. School's not out for another ten minutes."

"Ah," Ronnie said. "Then tell me the number."

"A *much* better idea," Ty said.

When Maddie answered, Ronnie chuckled at the impatience in her voice. She was obviously swamped with whatever it was she did over there. "Sounds to me like I called in the nick of time," he told her.

"Ronnie?"

"Yep."

"This place has been crazy all afternoon. Sorry if I sounded snarly."

"Not a problem. Have you got time to play hooky?" he asked, grinning conspiratorially at Ty as he did so.

"Do I sound like I do?" she said.

"No, which is precisely the reason you should take a break. Everything will seem much less stressful when you get back to it."

"I don't know," she protested. "My desk is piled high."

"Will that change if you're gone for an hour?"

"Probably not," she admitted.

"Then meet me at Wharton's. I've been craving a chocolate milk shake. So has your son."

There was a long silence on the other end, before she said cautiously, "Excuse me?"

"Meet you at Wharton's in ten minutes, Madelyn," he said. "Invite your new husband to come along."

"You want me to include Cal when my son has apparently skipped school this afternoon? Are you crazy?"

"I don't think so. See you in ten minutes." Ronnie hung up before she could pester him with a lot more questions.

Ty regarded him worriedly. "You really think you can pull this off? Keeping me out of trouble, I mean?"

"Not to worry. By the time I've finished spinning this story, you'll sound like a cross between Mother Teresa and Dr. Phil."

Ty stared at him for a long time, then grinned. "Cool."

Ronnie nudged Ty into the booth at Wharton's, then slid in beside him so the kid couldn't bolt. He concluded it had been a good move when Maddie came flying in, looking part Mother Hen and part Terminator.

"Cal coming?" he asked cheerfully as she sat down opposite them. Next to him Ty squirmed and avoided his mother's fierce gaze.

"Somebody had better explain what's going on," Maddie said tightly. "The sooner the better."

Ronnie was glad he'd ordered the second he and Ty had gotten there. He shoved Maddie's milk shake a little closer. "Have a sip. You'll feel better."

"Plying me with ice cream is not going to work," she groused, but took a sip just the same. She'd never been able to resist milk shakes or hot-fudge sundaes. In fact, as Ronnie recalled, they were her drugs of choice when she was upset. Odds were she'd be calmer any minute now.

A few moments later, after she'd stared hard at Ronnie, then at Ty, as if trying to decide which of them to strangle first, her expression brightened slightly.

"Hey, darlin'," the man she'd married in Ronnie's absence said, dropping a kiss on her cheek, then turning to Ty with a far more dangerous expression. "Tyler."

"Uh-oh," Ty murmured beside Ronnie.

"Maddie, are you going to introduce me to your husband?" Ronnie asked hurriedly.

"Ronnie Sullivan, Cal Maddox," she said tersely. "Now start talking. Why wasn't my son in school this afternoon and why is he with you?"

Ronnie gave Ty an encouraging glance, then met Maddie's gaze. "Actually, he was with Annie."

Maddie looked startled. "At the hospital?" She turned her gaze to Ty. "You've been going by at night. Why would you cut class to go?"

"Because at night there are too many people around," Ty said. "I thought maybe if I could really talk to her—you know, get in her face—maybe I could make her see how screwed up she is."

Maddie sat back, clearly stunned. Beside her, Cal looked as if he was torn between exasperation and pride. He finally broke the silence.

"And?" he said. "How did it go?"

Ty looked toward Ronnie for support. "Pretty good, I guess. I think she really heard me."

"He was amazing," Ronnie said. "I was in the hallway and overheard some of it. You should be very proud of him, Maddie. He didn't cut Annie an inch of slack. He said stuff to her that I've been scared to say." He looked at Cal. "He quoted a lot of stuff from school about anorexia."

Cal nodded slowly. "I'm relieved to know that one lesson sank in, but—"

Ronnie cut him off. "Look, Cal, I know Ty was wrong to cut class, but this one time I think he did it for all the right reasons. Couldn't you maybe give him a break?"

Cal was clearly torn between the rules and his understanding of the good Ty had done.

Apparently, he reached a decision, because he smiled at Ty. "I am not condoning what you did…" he told him.

"Me, neither," Maddie added sternly.

"…but I'm really proud of you," Cal continued. "And since, technically, it isn't baseball season for several more months, I don't suppose I need to suspend you from a game for violating the rules."

Maddie's expression softened. "And I will give you a note for your teacher explaining that you had permission to cut because of a family matter, and that it was my fault for not giving you the note in advance."

Ty's relief was unmistakable. "Thanks. I promise I won't do anything like this again. I just thought it was important, and I was afraid you'd both say no if I asked."

"It *was* important, which is why we're not coming down on you," Cal said. "But don't get it into your head that you can pull a stunt like this again and then expect our approval later. Next time, ask."

"Yes, sir," Ty said solemnly. "Could I maybe get a burger? I skipped lunch to get to the hospital."

"Tell Grace I'm buying," Ronnie told him, moving to let him out of the booth.

After he'd gone, Ronnie faced Maddie. "He's grown up since I left."

Her gaze followed Ty before she turned back. "Some days I regret that, but I have to say that today I've never been more proud of him."

"Same here," Cal said. "Do you really think he got through to Annie?"

"I'll know more after she has her next session with Dr. McDaniels," Ronnie said. "But I really think he did. If that's the case, I'll owe him for the rest of my life."

Maddie reached over and squeezed his hand. "We all will."

Now that he'd helped to smooth things over for Ty, Ronnie sat back and took a long, considering look at Cal Maddox. "So, Coach, tell me how you snagged the second-best woman in Serenity?"

"Second-best?" Maddie protested.

Ronnie grinned at her. "Dana Sue's at the top of *my* list, darlin', but you sure do come in close behind her."

Cal looked at Maddie with enough heat to make Ronnie wish Grace Wharton would turn on the air-conditioning. "Sorry to contradict you," he told Ronnie. "But in any poll I take, *Maddie* comes out on top."

She tucked her arm through Cal's and grinned at Ronnie. "And that, in a nutshell, is how he got me."

"I guess we'll just have to wait and see if I think he deserves you," Ronnie said.

Maddie laughed. "You don't get a vote."

Cal leaned across the table and met his gaze. "Maybe we should be talking about how you let a woman like Dana Sue get away."

Ronnie didn't flinch under Cal's direct gaze. "That's an easy one. Stupidity, pure and simple." He winked at Maddie. "And just for the record, I'm much smarter now. It won't happen a second time."

Maddie's gaze was serious as she told him, "I'm counting on that, Ronnie Sullivan. I really am, because if you break her heart again, I won't be responsible for what I do to you."

"And I'll back her up," Cal said.

Ronnie grinned at the two of them, impressed by their united front. "Not to worry. I have a plan."

"Care to share it?" Maddie asked, her curiosity obviously aroused.

"Not till all my ducks are lined up in a nice, neat row," Ronnie told her. "And even then, I think Dana Sue should be the first to hear about it."

"Does this plan of yours involve the old hardware store?" Maddie asked.

Ronnie frowned. "How the hell do you know about that?"

"Sweetie, this is Serenity. Have you forgotten that gossip travels with the speed of light around here?"

He shouldn't have, Ronnie conceded. News of his affair had certainly spread like wildfire. Of course, this time he thought he'd sworn Mary Vaughn to secrecy.

"Wipe that frown off your face," Maddie advised. "Mary Vaughn didn't say a word. At least half a dozen people drove by while you were looking the place over the other day. And Grace's antennae flew up the second she saw you and Mary Vaughn get out of your cars down the block. If you'd wanted to keep it secret, you'd have had to go in there in the dead of night."

"I'll remember that next time," Ronnie said. "I'd better pay Grace and get out of here. Now that at least part of the cat is out of the bag, I'd better kick my timetable up a notch. I have some calls to make."

"Don't keep Dana Sue in the dark too much longer. She's bound to have heard the same gossip I have," Maddie warned him.

And, Ronnie suspected, she was probably already turning his silence into some big conspiracy to keep her out of the loop. "I'll tell her the minute there's something to tell," he promised.

Maddie winced. "You might have different definitions of when that is."

Ronnie sighed. "More than likely, but that's the best I can do. If she says anything to you…" he began.

Maddie grinned and held up her hands. "I know nothing."

Cal, who'd been silent through the exchange, spoke up. "Want my advice?"

"Sure," Ronnie said.

"Tell her whatever there is to tell right now. I may not have the same long history with Dana Sue that you do, but most women resent being the last to know, especially when the news involves someone who's trying to patch things up with them."

"Even if nothing's final?" Ronnie asked doubtfully. "Even if it could all fall apart tomorrow?"

"Even then," Cal said, glancing at Maddie for confirmation.

"He's right," she said. "Talk to her now, Ronnie. The sooner you make her a part of your plan, the sooner she'll start to feel like you're a team again."

"Good point." He nodded. "I'll talk to her first chance I get." With any luck it wouldn't already be too late.

15

When Dana Sue walked into the kitchen at Sullivan's around four o'clock, Erik greeted her with a frazzled look.

"What's wrong?" she asked at once.

"Karen's babysitter bailed," he said, as he frantically tried to do half a dozen things at once. He dredged catfish in a spicy cornmeal mixture, layered it in a pan, then shoved that in the refrigerator and pulled out the salad greens. Precut green beans were ready for the steamer, slivered almonds were in a bowl for garnish and he had okra stewing on the stove.

Dana Sue immediately nudged him out of her way. "I'll take over with the salads. What are tonight's specials?"

"Thank goodness it's the middle of the week. I think we can get away with only having one. I'm going to go with a shrimp scampi over linguine," he said. "It's quick and easy."

"Perfect. Dessert?"

He regarded her with dismay. "I've got nothing. It hadn't even crossed my mind. I've had to concentrate totally on this mental checklist I've been going over for the main dishes and the sides."

For a pastry chef, that was an admission of just how stressed out he was. "Warm walnut brownies with ice cream," she suggested, knowing it was something he could prepare in his sleep. "One big batch cut into squares and you're done. I think there's one of your apple pies in the freezer, too. I'll grab it now, so it can get to room temperature by the time we open for dinner. Pop a slice in the oven, add a scoop of cinnamon ice cream to that and we're set."

Erik didn't argue, though normally he would have fought her over serving something that hadn't been prepared that day. "Do we have any of the cinnamon ice cream left?" he asked.

"If we don't, vanilla will do. I know we have that," Dana Sue said. It was such a staple that she made sure they never ran out. Even so, she double-checked while she was at the freezer.

"Why didn't you call me the second you heard from Karen?" she asked as she retrieved the pie and set it on the dessert rack to thaw.

"You have enough on your plate," Erik said. "I thought I could handle this. It's one night and not even one of our busiest ones. It shouldn't be a big deal."

She grinned at him. "There's a reason we have an assistant," she commented. "Sometimes there's even a need for all three of us to be here. You know that. You're not Supercook. And this place is my responsibility. Next time there's a crisis, call me."

"Believe me, I will," he said, looking a bit less harried as he began the more familiar task of mixing the ingredients for his moist, decadent brownies. "There's one other thing you probably should know."

"Oh?"

"One of the waitstaff called in sick two minutes before you walked in the door. I haven't had time to phone around for a replacement yet."

"Which one?" she asked.

"Paul."

Dana Sue winced, trying to envision the staffing chart. Midweek they often got by with just two waitstaff, plus the busboys. Paul could handle a crowd on his own. No one else could. "That means Brenda's it, right? She's been here awhile, but just part-time, and always with someone more experienced. Darn, this couldn't have happened on a worse night, with Karen off, too. I won't be able to pitch in on the floor."

"Tell me about it," Erik commiserated.

"I'll figure something out," Dana Sue promised, just as she glanced up and spotted Ronnie in the doorway. She studied him with a narrowed gaze and made an impulsive decision that would save some time. She'd worry later about whether it was smart.

"I know you haven't done it since we were kids, but do you remember anything at all about waiting tables?" she asked him.

"Get the orders right and don't spill the food on the customers," he said, regarding her with a puzzled expression. "Is this a test? Did I pass?"

"Close enough," she said. "Grab a menu and study it. I'll show you which tables to cover in a few minutes."

"You want me to wait tables here? Tonight?" he asked incredulously, though he didn't turn tail and run.

Erik appeared to be equally dismayed. "Are you sure, Dana Sue?"

"He's a warm body and he's here," she said crisply. "And he owes me."

"Now there's a criteria for staffing I've never heard before," Erik commented, then shut up in response to Dana Sue's wilting look.

"Why?" Ronnie asked, though he'd already grabbed a menu that had been left in a rack by the door. He pulled a pair of reading glasses from his pocket and put them on.

"Crisis," she told him, refraining from commenting about the glasses. "If you're not sure about something, ask me, or better yet, ask Brenda."

"That kid who waited on us last time I was here?" he asked.

Dana Sue grinned. "Tonight that kid is only one step below me on the totem pole, pal. Do whatever she tells you."

Ronnie shrugged. "If you say so."

For once, Dana Sue was grateful for his laid-back personality.

When most of the prep work was finally under control and Erik no longer looked so frazzled, she ducked into her office and called Annie.

"Hey, sweetie," she said when her daughter picked up the phone.

"Hi, Mom. Where are you?"

"At the restaurant. We have a little crisis over here tonight, so I'm not going to be able to get by to see you. I'm so sorry. I'm sure either Helen or Maddie will drop in later. How are you doing?"

"Better," Annie said, and for once she actually sounded as if that were the truth. "Ty came by today."

"Really?"

"I'll tell you about it when I see you," Annie promised. "He said a lot of stuff that made sense."

"I'm glad."

"Do you know where Dad is? He hasn't been here this afternoon, either."

"Actually, he's with me," Dana Sue said. "I've got him waiting tables."

Annie laughed. "You're kidding, right?"

"Nope. He looks kinda cute with an apron tied around his waist." She lowered her voice. "You know something else?"

"What?" Annie asked, obviously intrigued.

"He put on reading glasses to check out the menu," she confided.

"No way!"

"He looked cute."

"You thought so?" Annie was obviously encouraged.

Dana Sue considered censoring herself to avoid giving her daughter false hope, but decided just this once to be candid. "Even if he is your dad and I'm still annoyed with him, it doesn't mean I can't see what a hottie he is."

Annie giggled. "Mom, you're so funny."

Satisfied that she'd been able to make Annie laugh, she said, "I have to go, sweetie. If it's not too late, I'll call you when things slow down for the night. Otherwise, I'll be by first thing in the morning."

"Love you," Annie said. "Tell Dad I love him, too."

"Will do," Dana Sue promised, then hung up. She felt hopeful for the first time in a long time. Maybe it was because her daughter had sounded so upbeat, or maybe it was the prospect of working side by side with Ronnie for an evening. Whatever it was, it felt darn good.

Ronnie was not the fastest waiter in the universe. He blamed that partly on the fact that every single person who recognized him wanted to chat about why he was back in town. He'd caught up with a lot of old friends between balancing trays of water glasses, bread and drinks. He'd only mixed up two orders all evening, which had to be some kind of coup, considering he hadn't waited tables in over twenty years.

It had been fun, too, and enlightening to see how smoothly Dana Sue was able to balance her duties in the kitchen with charming the diners. He caught a lot of speculative looks cast their way every time they crossed paths and paused to chat, even if the chat was about nothing more than an update on the availability of the night's special.

The crowd finally thinned out around nine. Ronnie was about to take a breather when Helen breezed in and headed straight for one of the tables in his section.

"I came to see if the rumors were true," she said, regarding him through narrowed eyes when he approached her table.

"Which rumors would those be?" he inquired.

"That Dana Sue is now employing the man who cheated on her," she said. "Just how low do you plan to sink, Ronnie?"

He bristled at the accusation. "There are so many things wrong with what you just said, I'm not sure where to begin. Maybe I should let Dana Sue explain to you, since I'm sure you'd never believe a word I said."

"I can spot a lie a mile away," Helen countered. "I want to hear your version."

"First, I am not working here," he said. "I pitched in to help Dana Sue out of a jam. There was no discussion of pay. I don't need her money. Now, are you ordering? The kitchen's about to close. And before you ask, we're out of the special, so if that's what you came for, you might consider coming earlier next time."

Helen blinked at his rapid-fire response, then sighed. "I'm sorry," she said, surprising him. "When Annie told me Dana Sue had put you to work, I jumped to conclusions."

"Yes, you did," he said. "That's something you might want to watch. It's a bad habit, especially for a lawyer who's been trained to postpone judgment till all the facts are presented."

"You're right," she said with apparent sincerity. "I really am sorry."

Ronnie glanced around to be sure his tables were still

empty, then pulled out a chair. "Look, you and I need to make peace. I appreciate the fact that you're only looking out for Dana Sue, but I am not the enemy. Not anymore."

"I'll withhold judgment on that," she muttered dryly.

"Fair enough."

Before he could say anything more, Dana Sue came hurrying out of the kitchen and headed straight for their table. "Brenda told me you were here," she said to Helen. She cast a worried look from one to the other. "Good. No bloodshed."

"Not tonight," Helen said.

"We're negotiating a truce," Ronnie added.

Dana Sue looked doubtful. "How's that going?"

He grinned. "About as well as you'd expect with Helen as one of the negotiators. She's tough."

"It's a good trait," Helen said defensively.

"Most of the time," Dana Sue agreed.

"Somebody has to hold his feet to the fire," Helen said.

"I'm perfectly capable of doing that," Dana Sue assured her.

"She is," Ronnie confirmed.

Helen finally sat back and relaxed. "As long as you know I'm keeping an eye on you," she said.

He winked at Dana Sue. "That's a given. So, are you eating or not?" He glanced at his ex-wife. "What about you? Have you eaten anything?"

She shrugged. "No time. I'm not hungry, anyway."

"You need to eat," Helen said sternly. "I'll have the salmon. Bring her the same thing."

In the kitchen, Ronnie gave Erik the orders, put water and bread on a tray, then walked back to the stove, where Erik was already spooning vegetables onto the plates alongside salmon that had been drizzled with olive oil and herbs.

"Last customers?" he asked Ronnie.

"Dana Sue and Helen, actually." He paused. "Can I ask you a question?"

Erik regarded him warily. "Okay."

"I know Dana Sue's family history," Ronnie said. "I was around when her mom died from complications of diabetes. I know Dana Sue has always been terrified that the same thing would happen to her. Has she been diagnosed with diabetes?"

Erik shook his head, but before relief could flow through Ronnie, Erik added, "The doctor's warned her, though, that she needs to be careful, eat properly and exercise, or she'll need medication to control her blood sugar. It's already inching toward dangerous territory. She's supposed to check it at least once a day, keep track of it and report in to him once a month. But I don't think she's doing it, at least not daily, and probably even less since Annie's been in the hospital."

"Which is why you freaked over the chocolate decadence cake the other night?"

Erik nodded. "And that's all I'm saying. You want to know anything else, ask Dana Sue."

"Thanks. It confirms what I'd already guessed. And just so you know, I'll watch out for her."

Erik gave him the first genuine smile since the day they'd met. "You already have been. I've seen that. It's been the only reason I haven't offered to beat you to a pulp."

"One more question," Ronnie said. "The two of you...you seem close."

"We are," Erik agreed. "I could let you interpret that to mean that there's something going on, but I won't. Dana Sue and I are a team in here, but that's it. And so you know, that's not because I haven't tried to convince her otherwise from time to time."

"We're not going to have to duel at dawn or something, are we?" Ronnie asked him.

Erik held up his hands. "Not me. I'm a pacifist. As long as you're good to her, I have no issues with you."

Ronnie nodded, appreciating his candor. "I'd better get these meals out there before the owner takes exception to the service. Then again, she's probably well aware that she's likely to get what she pays for and I came dirt cheap."

Erik chuckled. "Make sure Dana Sue doesn't come back in here to clean up. I've got that under control."

"I'll be back to help you."

"No need. You could join her and Helen."

"Something tells me it would be smarter to hide out in here till Helen leaves," Ronnie said. "She's not my biggest fan."

"And you don't think you can win her over?" Erik asked, clearly amused.

"Not in one night," Ronnie told him. "I had years when I was around and on good behavior, and she wasn't all that thrilled with me then."

And even though he'd made progress with winning over Dana Sue, in the end he had a hunch she was going to be an even harder sell than her best friend, at least when it came to taking that final leap of faith.

Annie wasn't exactly eager to see Dr. McDaniels in the morning, but for the first time her stomach wasn't twisted into knots at the prospect of a session with the shrink. Maybe she could tell her a few things, and if the doctor didn't get all weird on her, then maybe she could tell her the rest. It wasn't like not admitting she was anorexic was getting her anywhere. Everyone knew it, even Ty. Having him confront her without acting like she was a freak had finally given her the courage to say it out loud. She'd actually practiced getting the words out when no one was around. After a couple of times, she'd been able to say it without feeling sick to her stomach.

When the door to her room opened, she half hoped it would be her mom, but it was the shrink, right on time.

"Good morning, Annie," Dr. McDaniels said in the same cheerful tone that always grated on Annie's nerves. "You look better this morning."

Annie regarded her with a shy smile. "The nurse helped me wash my hair and blow it dry."

"It looks good. You have some color back in your cheeks, too."

"Blush," she admitted.

"Nothing wrong with a little makeup," Dr. McDaniels said. "And it shows me you're starting to take an interest in your appearance again. Any particular reason?"

"Ty— he's my friend—was here yesterday and he made me start looking at some things in a different way," Annie told her.

"How so?"

"He kinda yelled at me for being so dumb and not caring enough about myself."

Dr. McDaniels tried to hold back a grin. Annie could see her struggle with it, but the corners of her mouth turned up.

"He yelled, huh? Maybe *I* should have tried that."

Annie shook her head. "I think I had to hear it from him. Ty's, like, this really great guy. He's the star of the baseball team. We've known each other forever. When he told me how scared he was for me, it made me look at everything from his perspective, not just mine. I mean, I'd heard that from my folks and Sarah and Raylene—they're my best friends—but this time I really got it."

"Ty made you realize that your actions affect all the people who care about you," Dr. McDaniels suggested.

Annie nodded. "He did something else, too. He held up a mirror and made me look in it."

"And?"

"I didn't like what I saw, because I saw myself through his eyes. He didn't see the fat person I do. He made me realize I don't look so good."

"Sounds like you had quite a breakthrough," Dr. McDaniels said, obviously pleased. "You ready to get to work to change the behavior that brought you here?"

Annie knew exactly what the woman wanted to hear. She wanted more than an agreement to change. She wanted an admission that Annie recognized she had a problem.

She forced herself to look the psychologist in the eye. "You mean my being anorexic?"

Dr. McDaniels beamed. "That is exactly what I mean."

Annie swallowed hard. "What if I can't change it?"

"You can," she said emphatically. "I believe that. So should you. The biggest step is admitting the problem. I'm not saying it won't be hard and there won't be days when you hate me and Lacy and every nurse monitoring your food intake. There will be times when you'll think it would be easier just to bag the sessions, or days when you look at food and the idea of putting one single bite in your mouth makes you sick. But you can do this, Annie. I'm here to help you. Lacy's on your side, too. Your folks will do anything in the world to support you. And it sounds as if your friends Ty, Sarah and Raylene will help you, as well."

Annie grinned. "Ty said he was going to stick to me like white on rice to make sure I eat."

"Good for him. Now here's what I want you to think about for tomorrow," Dr. McDaniels said. "The only way to be sure you don't go back to your old pattern is to figure out how you ended up there in the first place. I want you to think back to how all of this started. Maybe you wanted to lose a couple of pounds before a big dance. Maybe it was something bigger than that. Think really hard and see if you can isolate the turning point when food suddenly became the enemy. Can you do that?"

Annie nodded. She could have answered the question right now, but she didn't feel like talking about it. She didn't even like thinking about it.

Dr. McDaniels regarded her intently. "Annie, do you already know the answer to that? Do you want to get into this now? I can stay longer."

"No," she said hurriedly. "I don't."

The shrink looked vaguely disappointed, but she didn't press her. "Fine. We'll talk more tomorrow," she said, just as the door to Annie's room started to open.

Seeing her mom in the doorway, Annie breathed a sigh of relief. Now she was off the hook for sure. Of course, the downside was that she had almost twenty-four hours to dread her next session.

When Dana Sue found Dr. McDaniels in Annie's room, she immediately felt guilty for interrupting.

"Sorry. I didn't realize you were having a session," she said, trying to gauge from the psychologist's expression how the session was going. "I'll be in the waiting room when you're finished."

"No need," Dr. McDaniels said. "Why don't you come in now? We've just finished."

"Are you sure?" Dana Sue asked. "Don't cut it short on my account."

"I'm not. Annie and I have been chatting for a while," the

doctor told her with a warm smile. "We've made some progress this morning, right, Annie?"

The teen nodded, though she didn't look quite as cheerful as the psychologist.

"That's wonderful," Dana Sue said.

"In fact, we've made enough progress in the right direction," McDaniels announced, "that I think we can release Annie from the hospital tomorrow, as long as she agrees to continue seeing me every day in my office."

Annie's expression brightened. Obviously, this was the first time she'd heard the news. "Really? I can go home?"

"If Lacy and Dr. Lane agree, you can leave right after our session tomorrow," Dr. McDaniels told her.

She turned to Dana Sue. "And then I'd like to schedule a family session for the next day, if that's okay with you. Can you and Mr. Sullivan be there?"

Dana Sue nodded at once. "Absolutely."

"We'll use that time to go over all the guidelines you'll need for Annie's recovery, and maybe talk a little bit about what each of you can do to help her stay on the right track," she told them. "I think I'll ask the nutritionist to be there for that session, as well."

"What about her first day home?" Dana Sue asked. "Is there anything we need to do then?"

Dr. McDaniels glanced at Annie. "Do you want to fill your mom in after Lacy and I go over everything tomorrow?"

Annie nodded eagerly, clearly pleased that the doctor trusted her to be honest about the rules.

Dr. McDaniels stood up. "You did good work today, Annie. I'm proud of you."

"It wasn't as hard as I thought it was going to be."

"It'll get harder," the doctor warned her. "And there will

be setbacks. You need to understand that, so you don't just throw up your hands and give up."

Annie nodded. "Okay."

"Then I'll see you in the morning," she said.

After she'd gone, Dana Sue crossed to Annie to give her a hug. "I'm so proud of you, sweetie. And I cannot wait to have you home again. I don't think I've slept the whole time you've been gone."

"Even though my music hasn't been blasting?"

Dana Sue shrugged and admitted ruefully, "I guess I've missed that, too."

She sat down beside Annie on the bed. "You want to have a little homecoming celebration? Just Maddie, Helen, your dad and maybe Ty, Sarah and Raylene?"

"That would be awesome," Annie said. "But, Mom, not a lot of food, okay? Could you just invite them to stop by after dinner? I'll feel weird if everybody's watching to see what I put in my mouth."

"If that's what you want," Dana Sue agreed. Maybe it was too soon to expect Annie to be comfortable around any occasion involving food.

Or maybe, Dana Sue thought with concern, it was a sign that she was already thinking of ways to slip back into her pattern of avoiding meals with other people, so no one would notice that she wasn't eating at all.

Hating that she didn't trust her daughter's motives, Dana Sue resolved to check with Dr. McDaniels about what her own expectations ought to be regarding her daughter's behavior, and about the warning signs that would tell her that Annie was regressing. This time Dana Sue didn't intend to ignore anything.

16

Ronnie had just spent an hour on the phone with Butch Thompson, who'd agreed to come to Serenity in the morning to look over the hardware store and Ronnie's business plan.

"Then I want that meal you promised me at your wife's restaurant," Butch had told him.

"You bringing *your* wife along?"

"Not this time. We'll set that up once we have all the paperwork finished and signed. Shouldn't take longer than a week or two."

Having Butch respond as if their deal were a foregone conclusion had left Ronnie elated, so when the phone rang again he was more cheerful than he'd been in a while.

"Ronnie?" Dana Sue asked, as if she wasn't quite sure it was him.

"Hey, sugar. How are you?"

"Good," she said. "You sound pretty chipper yourself. Something going on?"

"I'll tell you about it later," he promised, then remembered he'd gone to the restaurant the night before specifically to fill her in. Once he'd gotten caught up in her staffing crisis, he'd forgotten all about it. He didn't dare put it off much longer, but he wanted to tell her face-to-face so he could gauge her reaction.

"Why'd you call?" he asked.

"Can you meet me at the house in an hour?"

"Sure," he said, though he was surprised by the invitation. It must be important if she was willing to let him cross that threshold again. "You want to tell me why?"

Dana Sue hesitated, but she'd never been any good at keeping secrets. Ronnie gave her time to reach the bursting point.

"Annie's coming home tomorrow!" she said at last. "Isn't that fantastic?"

Relief flooded through him, along with a bit of caution. "Fantastic doesn't even begin to describe it," he said. "The doctors are sure she's ready?"

"I saw Dr. McDaniels myself just a few minutes ago. She seems to think Annie's finally turned a corner. She's set up a family counseling session for all of us day after tomorrow."

"It must have been the visit from Ty," Ronnie speculated.

"What visit was that?" Dana Sue asked, sounding puzzled. "I mean, Annie mentioned he'd been by yesterday, but with everything going on at the restaurant last night I completely forgot about it."

"And I forgot to mention it for the same reason," he said. "I'll tell you everything when I see you at the house."

"Yes, you will," she said, sounding grimly determined all of a sudden. "I expect to be told everything you know that concerns our daughter."

"I wasn't deliberately keeping it from you," he said, knowing how her mind worked. She could turn this into some major slight at the drop of a hat, just as she could his failure to mention his plans for the hardware store.

"Okay, if you say so," she conceded eventually, though her tone was still cool. "I know I'm probably overreacting. I'll see you in an hour and we'll settle this then."

It wasn't until Ronnie had hung up that he remembered his appointment tomorrow with Butch. A couple of years ago he would have tried to juggle it all. Now, with his priorities where they belonged, he knew that as critical as that meeting was, Annie's homecoming was more important. He called the man on his cell phone.

"Butch, it's me again. Can we postpone for a couple of days? I just found out my daughter's getting out of the hospital tomorrow. I want to be with her. And the following day we're supposed to meet with her doctor. Since I don't have the details yet, it might be easier if we just rescheduled for the end of the week."

"Not a problem," Butch said at once. "I'll see you Friday, same time. How does that sound?"

"Perfect. Thanks."

"No need to thank me. The way you care about that girl is one of the reasons I like you so much."

Relieved that he'd done the right thing and it had turned out okay, Ronnie whistled as he showered and changed into clean clothes, before heading over to the house that had been his home for nearly twenty years. He wasn't entirely sure how he was going to feel crossing the threshold again after all this time. He was just glad that Dana Sue was finally willing to let him inside, instead of greeting him on the lawn with a cast-iron skillet in her hand.

Dana Sue figured she had ten minutes to make the house look reasonably presentable before Ronnie saw it again. Since Annie had been in the hospital, she'd kicked her shoes off just inside the front door and left them there. Plates and glasses from late-night snacks were strewn around. There was a layer of dust over everything. She wasn't the most attentive housekeeper under the best of conditions, but even by her low standards, it was a mess.

She'd managed to toss her shoes into the closet and get the dishes into the kitchen and in the dishwasher before she heard Ronnie's pickup pull into the driveway. To avoid any awkwardness over whether he should just walk in or knock and wait at the door of the house he'd once lived in, she met him at the entry.

"Thanks for coming over," she said, standing aside to let him in.

As he brushed past her, he dropped a quick kiss on her forehead that left her feeling completely disconcerted. It had been so innocent, so casual, he could have been kissing a distant cousin. It was nothing like the soul-searing kisses they'd once engaged in the second he came through the door. The lack of passion in this kiss stirred the daredevil in her, the woman who'd once grabbed what she wanted and held on for dear life.

Apparently puzzled by the fact that she hadn't followed him inside, Ronnie turned around and stared at her. "You okay?"

Was she? she wondered. Was it okay for her to be struggling with the desire to bunch his shirt in her fist and drag his face down to lock lips with him? Or was that insanity?

Even as heat and need rushed through her, she convinced herself it *was* crazy. It was nothing more than an instinctive reaction to having him back under this roof, back in this room where they'd made love more times than she could count, both of them too eager and frantic to wait to climb the stairs to their bedroom. They'd been more circumspect once Annie had come along, but this room still held an astounding number of tantalizing memories.

"Dana Sue?" he asked, still watching her with a bemused expression.

She shook off the memories and forced a bright smile. "Sorry. Just a momentary lapse."

She started to breeze past him and take refuge in the kitchen, but he snagged her arm and met her gaze. "I remember, too," he said softly.

"Remember what?" she said, a false note of cheer in her voice.

He grinned at her attempt to pretend they hadn't been thinking about the exact same thing. "Everything," he said succinctly, his gaze locked with hers. "I used to lie awake at night in my motel room and think about the way we were together, the way it didn't take more than a look or a casual touch to set us on fire."

"Don't," she pleaded.

"Don't tell you or don't remember?" he asked.

"Either one," she whispered. "We can't go back, Ronnie."

"No," he agreed, still holding her gaze. "But we can start fresh, make new memories."

"How? The image in my mind, the one I can't shake, isn't so pretty."

"The affair," he said bluntly.

"Yes, the affair."

"It was a meaningless one-night stand," he told her. "That doesn't make it okay, but is that enough reason to give up on us forever?"

"I thought so," she said, then realized she'd used the past tense, which might be just enough to give him the encouragement he was obviously seeking. "I still do," she added. "Apparently you did, too, since you left town."

"You really do not want to go there," he told her quietly. "I left because you didn't give me much of a choice."

"Oh, please, I hardly banished you."

"No, you just made it very clear how miserable you'd be if I stayed. I went because I already felt guilty for the pain I'd put you through. The last thing I wanted to do was prolong it and make it harder for you and Annie."

"Then why are you so insistent about staying now?"

"Because I've finally seen what a mistake it was for me to go," he said, then grinned. "And despite what you've said, I don't think you want me gone."

"I do," she said, but her answer was halfhearted.

"Do you really?" he asked. "Aren't you beginning to mellow just a little bit? Didn't you notice how well we worked together last night, as if we could read each other's minds? Haven't you noticed how well we've worked together to present a united front to Annie? Individually, we're both pretty good parents, but together we're awesome."

She'd noticed all of that, but she didn't trust it. She couldn't. "I won't have this conversation with you," she said, jerking her gaze away before she could fall under his spell and into his arms. "You're only here right now because of Annie. I thought you could help me plan her homecoming."

He backed down at once, clearly sensing that she was reaching the end of her patience. "I'd love to do that. And there's something I'd like to tell you about if there's time."

"Let's sit in the kitchen," she said, hoping there would be fewer memories in there since it had always been her domain. "Let's focus on Annie's homecoming, okay? I'll fix us some sweet tea."

His narrowed gaze suggested he knew it was the last thing she ought to be drinking. "I'll use sugar substitute," she said.

"Did you hear me say a word?" he asked.

"No, but we both know you know something, or think you do. Since I don't want to discuss it, you'll just have to take my word that I know what I should and shouldn't put in my mouth."

"I'm sure you do," he said placatingly. "And you're smart enough to follow the doctor's orders, I'm sure."

"I am," she said. At least when she remembered, or wasn't driven to indulge in comfort food to suppress her exasperation with this man.

She put water on to boil, pulled tea bags from the cupboard, then grabbed a handful of sweetener packets. "Satisfied?" she asked as she tore them open and dumped the contents in the water, then added the tea bags.

"Thrilled," he commented wryly.

Scowling, she looked him in the eye. "One thing about you I've noticed hasn't changed."

"Oh?"

"You're still annoying as hell."

He grinned. "I prefer to think of myself as a good jump-start to your metabolism."

"You wish," she scoffed, but she had to bite back a chuckle.

There were times, though she would rather eat dirt than admit it, when having Ronnie around again reminded her of what she'd felt like when she was totally and completely alive. To her chagrin she hadn't felt that way—not even once—since he'd left.

She put such thoughts out of her mind.

Annie wasn't sure what made her happier, being home again or seeing her mom and dad under the same roof and making a genuine attempt to get along, even if they were only doing it for her sake.

They'd gotten home just before lunchtime, and her mom had insisted they all sit down together for sandwiches and tea.

She'd made turkey on whole-grain bread, then cut them diagonally into quarters, the way Annie had liked them when she was little. Instinctively, she'd known to put the sections on a plate in the middle of the table, rather than placing a huge sandwich in front of Annie.

Annie knew both of her parents were watching her like a hawk as she took one little section and put it on her plate, then added a tiny scoop of her mom's potato salad. There had been a time when she could have eaten the whole bowl, but a taste was about all she could manage now without wanting to run from the table and hurl. Still, it was progress, and she guessed from their expressions that her mom and dad got that. To her chagrin, Annie also knew that Lacy had given them a very precise list of what she was to eat and at what time, every single day. The regimen wasn't going to change just because she was out from under the watchful eye of the nurses at the hospital.

"Erik sent over some of his cinnamon ice cream for later," her mom told her. "He thought maybe we could have that when everyone drops by."

"Awesome," Annie said, surprised that the idea actually held some appeal. Erik's homemade ice cream was amazing. When he'd been working on getting the recipe down pat at the restaurant, Annie had only tasted it, but she bet her mom had eaten five gallons. "You didn't invite a lot of people, did you?"

"Just the ones we talked about," her mom assured her. "And they won't stay long. They're coming around seven, after dinner, just the way you wanted."

"Thanks." She took a bite of the sandwich and forced herself to swallow. To her surprise, it tasted pretty good, better than the sandwiches in the hospital, somehow. Maybe because her mom had made it. Annie took another bite.

"You should get some rest after lunch," her dad said. "You don't want to overdo things on your first day home."

Annie frowned at him. "All I did was walk in from the car," she protested. "Even at the hospital, they made me go in a stupid wheelchair. It was totally lame."

Her dad grinned. "You didn't seem to complain much at the time. I noticed the orderly was pretty cute."

Annie rolled her eyes as she ate another bite of the sandwich, finishing off the little section. "Puh-leeze. Kenny's, like, twenty-three. I'm pretty sure he flunked out of high school. That's probably the best job he'll ever have."

"Nice to know you have high standards," Ronnie teased. "Just don't be too quick to judge people. You never know what hidden talents they might possess."

"If Kenny has any talents, believe me, they're hidden so deep no one will ever discover them," she scoffed, then noticed that she'd absent-mindedly put another section of sandwich on her plate. Shrugging, she went ahead and took a bite.

"You sure about Kenny's lack of talents?" her dad asked.

Annie studied him. "What do you know about him that I don't?"

"Just that he's a talented carpenter," her dad said. "He's been making furniture most of his life and selling it on consignment in a few galleries that specialize in hand-crafted pieces by local artisans. I predict you'll hear big things about Kenny one of these days."

Her mom looked as surprised as Annie felt.

"How do you know this?" Dana Sue asked.

"I actually took the time to talk to him," Ronnie said. "He's shy, not dumb." He gave Annie a pointed look. "Another lesson, by the way."

"Are you trying to fix me up with him or something?" she asked, after swallowing more food and chasing it down with unsweetened tea.

"Of course not," her dad said at once. "He's too old for you."

"Then why are we even having this discussion?" she demanded, irritated that she'd missed the chance to get to know a guy who sounded a lot more interesting than she'd guessed. Maybe she was a snob, just the way her father had hinted without saying it.

"I think I know," her mom said, regarding her dad with an amused expression. "He's distracting you, so you won't think about food. You'll just eat it. Worked like a charm, too."

Annie stared at her. "What do you mean?"

"You've eaten a whole sandwich, sweet pea."

Annie stared at the plate and saw that all the sections were gone. Her dad might have scarfed down more than his share, but not all of them. And her mom didn't even *like* turkey sandwiches.

"I ate a whole sandwich?" she asked, still doubtful even after her dad confirmed it with a pleased nod. But wouldn't that have made her feel sick? Annie didn't feel ill, though. She felt okay. She'd actually had a whole meal with other people and hadn't freaked out. An odd sense of triumph washed over her. She grinned at her dad. "Cool. Sneaky, but cool."

"I think that about sums up your dad," her mom said, but she was laughing, so it didn't sound mean at all.

Annie recalled a lot of meals around this table, and almost all of them had been like this, filled with teasing banter and some serious talk about life and stuff. She'd missed that more than anything when her dad had gone. Her meals with her mom, the few times they'd even bothered, had been silent and lonely, even with both of them sitting right here. Lately, her mom was at the restaurant most nights, and never had time to sit down and eat with Annie.

"I'm really glad you're here," she told her dad, not caring if it made her mom crazy to hear it. Maybe if her mom finally realized how much it meant to her to have her dad back in her life, she would do something to make sure he stayed.

"Me, too," he told her. "I've missed being in Serenity."

"Not just that," Annie said, anxious to get her point across. "I meant here with us."

"Annie..." her mom cautioned.

"I'm just saying it's great he's here." Annie's tone had a touch of belligerence. "That's how I feel. Dr. McDaniels says I need to own my feelings."

She stood up. "I'm going to take a nap now. Make sure I wake up way before everyone gets here, especially if we're going to have dinner first. I want to look really nice so they won't worry I'm gonna collapse or something."

"I'll make sure you're up in plenty of time," her mom promised.

Annie looked at her dad. "And you'll still be here, right?"

"I'll be here," he confirmed.

"Couldn't you just *stay* here?" she asked, knowing even as she posed the question that her mom was probably freaking out.

"I'm close by," her dad said. "We'll see each other all the time."

Obviously, he wasn't going to put her mom on the spot, but Annie wasn't afraid to do it. And she thought she knew the perfect way to pull it off. She'd bring it up at tomorrow's family counseling session. She had a feeling neither one of them would want to deny her what she wanted if she kicked up enough fuss about it with Dr. McDaniels. Okay, it was manipulative. But she could live with that if it pushed her mom and dad one step closer to getting back together. Sometimes adults just needed a hard push to get them to do what they secretly wanted to do, anyway.

"Don't even think about it," Dana Sue muttered fiercely the instant Annie left the room.

"Think about what?" Ronnie inquired innocently, though he knew perfectly well what she was referring to.

"You're not moving back in here and that's final," she said. "Not even for Annie's sake."

"She's going to bring this up at that family counseling session tomorrow," Ronnie predicted.

Dana Sue stared at him with alarm. "She wouldn't dare."

"Of course she would," he said. "Didn't you see that gleam in her eye? Our Annie is on a mission and she knows she has leverage."

Dana Sue sank back in her chair, then reached for a spoon and began eating the remaining potato salad.

"Should you..." Ronnie began, only to fall silent at her withering look. She did toss the spoon back into the bowl, though.

"Well, this is one time she's not getting her way," Dana Sue said forcefully—though she didn't look as if she believed that. "You're just going to have to back me up on this."

"What if I think she has a point?" he asked.

"Then you're crazy," she said bluntly. "It would be lunacy for you to move back in here under any circumstances."

"There is a guest room," he reminded her. "And I'm wasting money staying at the inn."

"The guest room is about five hundred miles closer to my room than you ought to be," she snapped. "Isn't it time for you to go back to Beaufort or...or wherever you've been?"

"Afraid not," he said. "I quit my job over there."

She regarded him with dismay. "Why would you do that?"

"It wasn't fair to ask them to hold it for me when I had no intention of going back."

"But you have to go back," she said, sounding desperate. "Because?"

"You know perfectly well why. You cheated on me, Ronnie, and I will not have you underfoot every time I turn around, reminding me of that."

Obviously this still wasn't the right time to bring up the hardware store. "What do you suppose folks in Serenity remember most—that I cheated, or that you threw everything I own onto the front lawn and then chased me off before I could gather up half of it?"

She winced. "It's probably a toss-up," she said stubbornly, though they both knew that wasn't true. People could forget a man's foibles, but they weren't likely to forget a woman in the throes of a very noisy revenge. A commotion like that made a lasting impression.

He grinned at her. "Care to take a poll?"

She stared at him. "What are you talking about?"

"Let's go for a walk and ask everyone we pass what they remember most about the two of us."

She shook her head. "You're pathetic."

"How is that pathetic?"

"You know there are only women home this time of day, and all you have to do is ooze a little of that charm of yours and they'll all side with you. If you get really lucky, one of *them* might ask you to move in."

"I thought women stuck together when it came to things like this."

"They do," she said, then amended, "Mostly. Look at Maddie, though. She's already back to being your best buddy. She always was a sucker for that crooked smile of yours. At least Helen isn't so easily duped."

"Helen's turning bitter about men," Ronnie observed. "She needs to find the right one quick, before all those nasty divorces make her too cynical."

Dana Sue bristled. "That's a lousy thing to say."

"Don't tell me you haven't thought the same thing," he chided. "You're too good a friend not to see what's happening to her."

Dana Sue sighed. "Okay, you have a point. She is a little jaded and she does need somebody in her life who can mellow her out. I just don't know if the kind of man she needs can be found in Serenity."

"She works all over the state," Ronnie reminded her, relieved to have distracted Dana Sue from their own relationship for the moment. "Surely somewhere in South Carolina there's an eligible man who's smart enough and brave enough to take her on."

"She does meet some nice men," Dana Sue said. "She even fixed me up with a few of them."

A streak of pure jealousy shot through Ronnie at the thought of Dana Sue with some stuffy, white-collar guy. "You and Helen don't have the same taste in men," he commented darkly.

"And look where that got me," she retorted.

"More than twenty years of bliss, if you go back to high school," he said, undaunted by the barb.

"And two years of pure misery," she responded.

Ronnie bit back a smile. "If you'd given me half a chance, the misery wouldn't have lasted that long."

She balled up her napkin and threw it at him. "Not going to happen."

"We'll see," he murmured. "We'll see."

Dana Sue might not want to admit it, but they were already making progress.

17

Dana Sue lingered in the dining room, her gaze caught by the sight of Ronnie and Cal off in a corner talking sports or something like old pals. Ronnie had never gotten along that well with Bill, Maddie's first husband, despite having known him since high school. In fact, Ronnie had been the first to recognize that Bill was all wrong for Maddie. It turned out that his perception of Bill as selfish and unfeeling had been right on target.

Not that he'd ever spoken up, Dana Sue recalled. Not to Maddie, anyway. And he hadn't wanted Dana Sue to share his impressions, either.

"Maddie's married to him," Ronnie had said on more than one occasion. "What I think of Bill doesn't matter. For her sake, I'll make the attempt to get along with him, the same way Helen does."

At the time, Dana Sue had been surprised by the implication that Helen was no more enamored of Bill than Ronnie was. But it turned out that she, too, had been keeping quiet for Maddie's sake. She'd never been nearly as reticent about Ronnie. Practically from the day they'd met, Helen had always expected the worst from him, and hadn't kept silent about her fears.

Only Dana Sue had seen how Bill's treatment of Maddie had bothered Ronnie. She had a hunch he was the only one of them who wouldn't have been surprised to learn that Bill was having an affair with a nurse in his office. But of course, by then, Ronnie had been gone.

Watching him now, she noticed that he didn't seem to have the same kind of issues with Cal, despite the age difference between Cal and Maddie that had set tongues wagging all over town a year or so ago.

When Ronnie glanced up and caught Dana Sue looking his way, he winked. A few minutes later he crossed the room and joined her.

"You and Cal seem to have found a lot to talk about," she said, not entirely sure how she felt about the two of them turning into pals. It would be just one more thread weaving Ronnie into the fabric of her life.

"I like him," he said. "He's grounded and down-to-earth. He adores Maddie and the new baby, and Ty, Kyle and Katie clearly look up to him. He's obviously been good for all of them."

"Then you approve of her choice this time?"

"Not that it's my business, but yes. He told me Bill wanted Maddie back once his relationship with his nurse fell apart. Is that true?"

Dana Sue nodded. "Thank goodness Maddie turned him down. She's been happier with Cal than she ever was with Bill."

Ronnie searched the room till his gaze landed on Maddie. "She's glowing, isn't she? Marriage and being a new mom suit her. With the other kids, she just looked tired, probably because Bill expected her to deal with everything at home while he concentrated totally on his career. I doubt that man ever changed a diaper or stayed up with a sick kid, despite being a pediatrician."

When Ronnie turned back to Dana Sue, his expression softened. "You were beautiful when you were carrying Annie. You positively glowed."

She regarded him doubtfully. "That must have been during the five seconds a day when I wasn't throwing up."

He stroked her cheek. "Don't do that, Dana Sue."

"Do what?"

"Put yourself down. You're a gorgeous woman. Pregnancy only added to it."

Dana Sue impulsively touched her rounded hips. "Now I have the extra pounds, but there won't be any baby to show for them."

Ronnie frowned at her. "I like the way you look."

"Sure," she scoffed. "Every man dreams of his wife gaining weight."

He regarded her with obvious dismay. "I don't get where this is coming from. Did you expect to be some tiny size your entire life, especially with your height? You look like a woman, Dana Sue. A healthy, attractive one who happens to have curves. If you ask me, that's the way a woman ought to be."

She wanted to believe him, wanted to see herself through his eyes, but all she could think about were the extra pounds she saw every time she stepped on the scale. There had been three more this morning. Having Ronnie back and getting under her skin had driven her to comfort food a little too often.

"You can't mean that," she protested.

Heat flared in his eyes and he stepped closer. Dana Sue instinctively backed up. He kept pace with her until her back hit the wall. There was no place left to go, and the determined glint in his eyes sent a shiver down her spine.

"You're still the most desirable woman I've ever known,"

he said quietly, his mouth hovering just over hers. "And I still want you."

Dana Sue swallowed hard at the sincerity in his voice, which was accompanied by the darkening of his eyes. She knew that smoldering look, knew exactly where it usually led. But they had a houseful of people right now. Surely he wouldn't…

With his hands on the wall on either side of her, trapping her in place, he leaned forward. Her mouth turned dry. When she opened it to utter a protest, his covered it. The shock of the kiss was familiar, the sensations ricocheting through her dangerous. Weak-kneed, she reached for him and held on for dear life as his tongue plundered and sent her head spinning.

It couldn't still be like this between them, she thought, with one last attempt to cling to sanity. It was wrong to want him this badly, to want his hands to make good on the promises being made by his kisses, to want him inside her, bringing every part of her to life again.

But it felt so damn right, she admitted, as his body pressed against hers, surrounding her with heat and undeniable evidence that his desire was as powerful as hers.

Long before she was ready, he dragged himself away, looking as dazed as she felt.

"Remember that the next time you question how any man—how *I*—could want you," he said, his voice a low rumble next to her ear.

"Uh-huh," she said, her thoughts so scrambled she couldn't come up with anything more.

Then he was gone, leaving her to sink onto the nearest chair and reach for a bottle of water chilling in a cooler filled with ice. If there hadn't been a dozen people around, she would have poured it right over her head without a thought to the damage it would do to her hardwood floors. Instead, she settled for taking a long, slow swallow that did nothing to cool the heat still simmering inside her.

"Quite a performance," Maddie commented, pulling up a chair and sitting beside her. "Those steamy kisses are getting to be a habit. I was afraid for a minute I was going to have to dump this ice over the two of you."

"Why didn't you?" Dana Sue asked, a plaintive note in her voice. "It might have snapped me back to my senses."

"Doubtful," Maddie said. "It's going to take more than ice to put a chill on what's going on between you two."

"Don't say that," Dana Sue pleaded.

"It's true. Why not accept it and run with it? You know you haven't been happy without him."

"And I was miserable because of him," Dana Sue retorted.

"He made one terrible error in judgment," Maddie said. "He learned his lesson."

"How can I be sure of that?"

Maddie started to respond, then shrugged. "Maybe you can never be sure of anything, sweetie." She glanced around until her gaze fell on Cal, who was chatting with Erik, Katie half-asleep in his lap. "Maybe you just have to grab on to what makes you happy now and then work like crazy to hold on to it."

"I thought that's what I was doing when we were married," she said. "And he still slept with another woman."

"Have you asked him why?" Maddie asked.

Dana Sue shook her head. "I'm not sure I want to know. What difference would it make, anyway?"

"It might reassure you that it had nothing to do with you," Maddie said.

"He was my husband. I'd say it had a lot to do with me," Dana Sue said, her tone sarcastic.

"I meant that it might not have been about you at all. Sometimes men just lose their heads for a minute and do something incredibly stupid."

"And that makes it okay?"

"Of course not. But do you give up on your marriage because of it any more than you would give up on your marriage because one of you wrecked the car?"

Dana Sue frowned at her. "It's hardly the same."

Maddie sighed. "I'm not explaining this very well. All I'm suggesting is that to Ronnie that one-night stand might have held no more long-term importance than some accident that smashed up a car. It happened. It's over with. No long-running affair, no emotional entanglement, the way there was with Bill and Noreen. Ronnie's one-night stand was about sex. The other was about a relationship, a real, ongoing intimacy between two people that took away from what Bill and I shared."

"I suppose," Dana Sue said, not entirely convinced. "But it hurt just the same."

"Of course it did. And it was wrong, no question about it. But, sweetie, weigh it against the big picture. Ronnie loves you with everything in him. What happened was one little blip, barely noticeable when you look back over twenty years together." Maddie patted her hand. "Just think about it, okay? Don't let your pride rob you of what you really want."

"It's not about my pride," Dana Sue said defensively.

Maddie's brow rose. "Isn't it?"

Dana Sue turned away from her knowing look. "I need to check on Annie. She could be getting tired."

"Annie's fine," Maddie said, gesturing toward the porch. "She's out there with Ty, Sarah and Raylene. But we probably should get going, just the same. What time is your family counseling session in the morning?"

"Ten o'clock," Dana Sue said. "I have to admit, I'm scared."

"What of?"

"What's going to come out in there," she confessed. "What if all this turns out to be my fault?"

"I don't think it's about casting blame. I think it's about moving forward so Annie won't fall back into the same destructive pattern."

"I know you're right," Dana Sue conceded.

"Then what are you really worried about?"

"Annie wants Ronnie and me back together. And right now, I would do almost anything in the world to make her happy," Dana Sue explained. "But that?" She shook her head. "I can't go back to Ronnie because it's what Annie wants."

Maddie grinned. "Maybe you should do it because it's what *you* want."

Before Dana Sue could protest again, Maddie pressed a kiss to her cheek. "Talk to you tomorrow. I'll gather up my crew and get out of here. That should signal the others it's time to go, too."

"Thanks," Dana Sue said gratefully.

Of course, with everyone gone there would be no one to serve as a buffer between her and Ronnie. The memory of the kiss he'd laid on her a short time before stirred her blood all over again.

But when she looked around as everyone was leaving, there was no sign of him anywhere. She glanced at Annie as she closed the front door behind the last guest.

"Where's your dad?"

"He cleaned up the kitchen, then left," Annie said, her expression knowing as she watched Dana Sue for a reaction. "Disappointed, Mom?"

"No, of course not," she insisted. But she was, and that most definitely was not a good thing.

"Liar," Annie accused with a grin. "If you'd let him move back in, he'd still be here."

"Not an option," Dana Sue said tersely.

"Maybe it should be," Annie taunted. "'Night, Mom. See you in the morning."

"Good night, sweetie. I am so glad you're home again."

"Me, too."

Annie started toward the stairs, then came back and wrapped her arms around Dana Sue's waist. "I love you. Thanks for sticking by me."

"Always," she answered. "No matter what."

She just prayed there would never be another crisis like the one they'd just been through and, in the months to come, that they'd all have the strength to navigate the bumps in the road to Annie's recovery.

Ronnie's hasty exit the night before had been deliberate. He knew how much his kiss had rattled Dana Sue. He'd been just as shaken. He'd also known that to expect anything more right now was out of the question. Better to slip away than to make a move that would alienate her just when they were making real progress.

He'd also wanted to get a good night's sleep before this family counseling thing. He had no idea what to expect or how much of the blame for Annie's problems was going to come down on his head. He was prepared to accept some of the responsibility, but Dana Sue bore some of it, as well. In fact, she seemed inclined to heap all of it on her own shoulders, right along with condemning herself for her weight gain.

An hour before the appointment, he pulled into the driveway at the house, noting that the trim on the brick house was in need of a coat of paint. Maybe he could get to that this weekend. It would be yet another peace offering to Dana Sue.

The kitchen door opened and Dana Sue emerged. "You coming in?" she called.

He left the car and headed inside.

She eyed him warily as he entered. "Have you eaten? I could scramble some eggs for you."

"No, thanks. I don't have much appetite this morning." He let his gaze travel over her very slowly. "Except for things I shouldn't have."

Her cheeks immediately turned pink. "Ronnie!"

"It's true. I thought about that kiss all night."

"You shouldn't have."

"Then you shouldn't have made it so memorable," he said, then deliberately changed the subject to something more neutral. "Where's Annie?"

"Getting dressed."

"Are you as scared about this morning as I am?" he asked, and saw a hint of relief in her eyes.

She nodded. "Crazy, isn't it? It's like being called to the principal's office."

He laughed. "I definitely know more about that than you do, but yes, it's exactly like that."

"I don't think it's supposed to be," she said. "I mean, we're all after the same thing, right?"

"Seems that way to me," he agreed. "Why don't you go hurry Annie along so we can get out of here? The sooner we're there, the sooner it'll be over with."

"Good idea," she said at once, and headed upstairs.

While she was gone, Ronnie poured himself a cup of coffee and took a long, satisfying swallow. Dana Sue still made the best coffee he'd ever tasted.

Two minutes later, she was back, looking shaken.

"What?" he asked. "Is Annie okay?"

"She was in the bathroom," Dana Sue said, her voice catching. "Ronnie, she was throwing up. I heard her. She'd eaten every bite of her breakfast. I sat right here with her to make sure. Then she went upstairs and threw up." There was panic in Dana Sue's eyes when she met his gaze. "What are we going to do?"

He wrapped his arms around her and held her close, feeling as helpless as he had the first time he'd seen Annie in the hospital. "Whatever it takes," he said grimly. "Did you confront her?"

Against his chest, he felt Dana Sue's quick head shake. "No," she whispered.

"Probably just as well. We'll deal with it with Dr. McDaniels. You stay here. I'll go up and get her, make sure she's okay."

He took the stairs two at a time. A part of him was angry, so angry he wanted to punch something, but overshadowing that by far was the terror that they were heading into a whole new territory with Annie. Was she about to replace one eating disorder with another? Did kids do that?

Before he could make himself crazy with more unanswerable questions, he spotted Annie coming out of the bathroom. She gave him a halfhearted smile.

"Hi, Daddy."

His heart flipped over in his chest at her woebegone expression. "Hey, baby. You okay?"

She gave him a knowing look. "Mom heard me, didn't she? I know she came upstairs a few minutes ago."

He nodded.

"I wasn't throwing up on purpose," she said, leveling a gaze into his eyes that begged him to believe her. "I wasn't! I just got scared all of a sudden and then I felt sick."

"It's okay," he soothed. "You feeling better now?"

"I guess."

"We'll talk about this some more when we see Dr. McDaniels."

She seemed to wilt a little. "You don't believe me, do you?"

He tucked a hand under her chin and looked into her eyes. "I want to, baby. I really do."

"It's the truth. I swear it. I couldn't make myself do that," she said with a shudder. "I just couldn't."

Ronnie had no response for that.

Annie regarded him with regret. "I know I have to earn your trust again, yours and Mom's, but it's hard, you know?"

"I know. Something tells me this is like a lot of other things that just take a while to sort out. We'll have to take it one step at a time."

"Like you and Mom?" she asked.

Ronnie smiled. "Yes, just like me and your mother."

Suddenly Annie grinned, and all of his heartache vanished at the beauty of it.

"I saw you kiss her last night," she told him. "Way to go, Dad!"

He winked at her. "Like I said, one step at a time."

"I don't know," she replied, an impish glint in her eyes. "A kiss like that oughtta be a giant leap, at least."

"Your mother's a stubborn woman and my mistake was a whopper," he reminded her. "It wouldn't be smart to take anything for granted."

"Just don't give up, okay?" she said.

"Never," he assured her. "Not on her and not on you. Not in a million years."

* * *

Annie was starting to feel sick to her stomach again. Everyone was staring at her so expectantly, like they wanted her to say something profound that would make everything okay. But nothing was okay. Nothing had been okay since her dad left.

Could she say that? Wouldn't it just make things worse if she said food was all mixed up in her head with the way she'd felt when he'd told her he was leaving that day at Wharton's? What if she said she'd stopped eating so she wouldn't gain weight like her mom had? That was part of it, too. At least she thought it was.

But if she blurted any of that out, wouldn't they just feel worse? Would it really solve anything? This was her problem, not theirs.

"Annie," Dr. McDaniels said, giving her an encouraging nod. "It's okay to say whatever you're thinking. That's the only way to put the past behind you and move on."

"Maybe we could talk about this morning instead," Annie said hesitantly.

Dr. McDaniels looked surprised, but nodded. "If that's what you want. What happened this morning?"

"My mom heard me throw up and I know she freaked about it, because she sent my dad upstairs. He looked all worried and scared."

"Can you blame him?" the shrink asked.

Annie shook her head. "But I didn't do it on purpose," she said, looking directly at her mom. "I was just nervous about coming here, and I got sick. I don't want you guys to go crazy every time I get sick to my stomach. If I ever get the flu, you'll probably send me straight to some treatment facility."

"Did you get sick to your stomach a lot before you developed an eating disorder?" Dr. McDaniels asked.

Annie nodded. "Whenever I had to stand up in school and give a report, I'd throw up in the morning. Remember, Mom?"

Her mother nodded slowly, a faint hint of relief in her expression. "That's true," she said.

Dr. McDaniels nodded, too. "Then let's assume for the moment that this was more about nervousness than food. Maybe next time you feel that way, Annie, you can ask for some ginger ale or crackers or something that might help to settle your stomach, okay? Not only might that make you feel better, but it might reassure your parents."

Annie suddenly had an image of the way her mom ate when she felt bad. She stuffed herself with whatever she could get her hands on. "No!" she protested sharply, before she could stop herself. "I won't do that!"

"Do what?" Dr. McDaniels inquired, her voice calm despite Annie's obvious agitation.

"It'll be like Mom," Annie blurted.

She saw the color rise in her mother's cheeks and knew she'd said exactly the wrong thing, even if it was the way she felt.

"What does that mean, Annie?" the shrink asked, waving off Dana Sue when she would have responded.

"When she's upset, she eats. She gained a lot of weight, probably twenty pounds, even before my dad left. More since then."

"Your mother looks fine to me," the psychologist said. "Why is her weight gain so upsetting to you?"

Annie knew she'd started something that she couldn't stop if she wanted to. She had to say it all. "Because if she hadn't gained it, my dad wouldn't have slept with another woman and my mom wouldn't have kicked him out," she lashed out, despite the stricken expression on her mom's face. "I hate that you did that! I hate it!"

"Hold it," Ronnie commanded, his voice harsher than

Annie had ever heard it. "I did not sleep with another woman because your mom had gained a few pounds."

"Then why did you?" Annie retorted. "It must have been *something* she did."

Her dad looked from her to her mom, then shook his head. "I honestly can't explain why I did what I did, but I do know it had nothing to do with your mom's weight. I think she looks incredible."

Annie wasn't buying it, but then she thought about the kiss she'd witnessed just last night. He'd definitely been into it. He'd certainly acted as if he thought her mom was pretty hot then. "Really?" she asked uncertainly. "It wasn't about that?"

"Absolutely not," he said firmly. "It's the one thing I'm one hundred percent sure of."

"Annie, do you think this had something to do with your decision to stop eating?" Dr. McDaniels asked. "Or maybe you were punishing your mom for what you saw as a failure to take care of herself?"

Annie considered both possibilities. "I don't know," she said eventually. "Maybe."

"Doesn't that sound pretty self-destructive?" the psychologist prodded gently. "Who got hurt the most?"

"Me," Annie admitted.

"Exactly," Dr. McDaniels said. "Think about that between now and tomorrow. We'll pick up where we left off."

"Do you want us here again?" her mom asked.

"No, I think the next couple of sessions will be just Annie and me. Why don't we schedule another family session for two weeks from now?"

Her mom and dad both looked relieved. Annie couldn't blame them. She knew she'd made them feel bad today. She had a suspicion the ride home was going to be pretty tense.

"By the way," Dr. McDaniels began as they were about to go out the door, "for now let's keep what's said in here in this room."

"You don't want us to talk about it?" her mom asked incredulously. "Won't that be like having an elephant in the room that everybody pretends not to notice?"

Dr. McDaniels smiled. "More than likely, but better that than reacting in the heat of the moment and saying something you might regret. Let's deal with all the issues in here for now."

Annie regarded her with gratitude. "Thanks."

"Don't get too excited," Dr. McDaniels warned. "I want you to be able to say whatever's on your mind in here, no matter how hurtful it might be, but your folks will get their turn to respond, too. The goal is to get everything out in the open without censorship or retaliation, so we can figure out a healthier way to handle issues when they come up. We need to undo the whole tangle of emotions and food, and I think that's best done in a structured setting, okay?"

She gave Annie a stern look. "And remember, you have an appointment with Lacy tomorrow right after we meet. She's going to want to see your food notebook—don't forget that your mom or dad needs to initial every page, okay?"

Annie rolled her eyes. "Jeez, do I have to have *two* people ganging up on me?" she said, only partly in jest. "It hardly seems fair."

"Two?" her mom said, smiling again. "Add in your dad, me, Maddie, Helen, Ty and Erik, and you don't stand a chance, kid. Get used to it."

To her surprise, Annie didn't feel resentful, at least not much. In fact, it was kinda nice knowing there were so many people on her side. She just hoped she wouldn't let them down, because something told her the hardest part was yet to come.

18

When Ronnie offered to take Annie home and stick around to spend the day with her, Dana Sue agreed. She needed time to herself to absorb what Annie had said during the session. She'd known all along that on some level Annie blamed her for Ronnie's cheating and for his leaving, but hearing her actually make the accusation aloud had shaken her.

Rather than going to the restaurant, Dana Sue headed for The Corner Spa. For once, though, she didn't go to Maddie's office for solace. Instead, she went straight to the locker room and changed into the workout clothes she kept there, but all too seldom wore. Grimly determined to start making some of the changes on her list of goals once she'd finally made it, she headed for the hated treadmill, turned it on and started walking.

She'd been at it for fifteen minutes, her pace slow but steady, when the tranquil view of the woods and stream out back began to work its magic. Her legs and joints were starting to ache, but she felt infinitely calmer than she had when she'd arrived. She pushed herself to walk a little longer.

She'd actually walked two miles when Maddie found her there. Dana Sue stopped the machine, feeling triumphant. "Look," she said, pointing to the computerized controls that kept track of everything from distance to calories burned and pulse rate. "Two miles. That must be some kind of record for me."

"Congratulations!" Maddie said. "Usually I can't get you anywhere near these machines. What's different about today? Are you thinking about winning that convertible all of a sudden? Maybe Helen was right about those prizes being good motivation, although she still hasn't been in here the way she's supposed to be."

"The list was only part of it," Dana Sue responded.

"What was the rest?" Maddie pressed. "Did you have a sudden urge to come in here to ogle Elliott? If I weren't married to the sexiest guy in town, I'd spend a lot more time staring at our personal trainer's hot bod myself."

Dana Sue mopped her brow and rolled her eyes. "Nope, this isn't about Elliott, hot though he is," she said, sneaking a peek in his direction just the same. "The truth is my daughter announced at her session today that I'm fat and that's why Ronnie cheated on me."

Maddie regarded her with sympathy. "That must have hurt."

Dana Sue shrugged. "It's not like she hasn't said it before, the part about my weight, anyway. Hearing her actually say aloud that she thought it was the reason Ronnie cheated really ripped me apart, though. If she really believes that, I'm astonished she doesn't hate me."

"You know Annie could never hate you," Maddie objected. "What did Ronnie have to say to all this?"

"He was pretty great, actually. He told her that what he did had nothing to do with that, that he thinks I look incredible. He sounded pretty convincing today, and he's told me the same thing before."

"So have I," Maddie reminded her. She patted her rounded stomach, which still hadn't gone away since her pregnancy.

"At our age there aren't too many of us who couldn't lose a few pounds to be healthier, but we're not obese or unattractive by any means. I certainly haven't lost the extra weight from my pregnancy as quickly this time as I did with my first three kids."

Dana Sue regarded her curiously. "And you're not worried about that?"

"If Cal thought I was beautiful at nine months pregnant, with crow's-feet around my eyes and a belly the size of a whale, he's not going to be put off by some extra pounds that settle on my hips," Maddie said confidently, her expression serene. "That doesn't mean I want them there, but I'm not going to obsess about it. I made that list of goals for me." She grinned. "And because I'd really, really like to go to Hawaii with my husband."

"I wish I had your body image and self-image," Dana Sue lamented. "I'm afraid a part of me agrees with Annie."

"Even though Ronnie told you otherwise?" Maddie asked.

She waved off the question. "He has no idea why he slept with that woman, so how am I supposed to believe that subconsciously it didn't have something to do with my being overweight and less attractive?"

"Because it's the one thing he does know," Maddie suggested. "Why would he lie?"

"Because he's trying to win me over," Dana Sue said readily. "He'd hardly admit something like that now, would he?"

Maddie regarded her thoughtfully. "You know, listening to you has given me an idea."

"Oh?"

"I'm going to call that psychologist you guys are seeing and ask if she'd be interested in teaching some classes here on body image and self-image."

Dana Sue was skeptical. "You think anyone would take them?"

Maddie grinned. "You would, because I'm not going to give you a choice."

"Ah, bossy Maddie is back," Dana Sue said, laughing. "Nice to see you again. I was afraid marriage was turning you all mellow and sweet."

Maddie gave her a sour look. "Not much chance of that, especially when I still have swollen ankles at the end of the day and an endless craving for nachos with jalapeños that hasn't gone away just because the baby's here."

"You're kidding! You ate nachos and jalapeños while you were pregnant? I never saw you do that. And that could explain the swollen ankles, by the way. All that salt."

"Believe me, I know it. And you never saw me because I forced Cal to make them for me in the middle of the night." Maddie shrugged. "I hesitate to think what that might say about Jessica Lynn's personality. Cal still shudders every time he makes them for me."

"But he does make them?"

Maddie smiled smugly. "What can I say? He's a very devoted husband. If I said I wanted pizza at 3:00 a.m…well, did you ever see that airline commercial with the husband who flies all the way to Chicago to get a pizza for his pregnant wife? That's Cal. He seems to view catering to my whims as his obligation, given his role in creating this baby."

"You could really take advantage of a man who thinks like that," Dana Sue said. "So is there anything you've been dying to have, any need that's unsatisfied?"

Maddie's expression was gleefully wicked. "Believe me, my needs are very satisfied these days. He considers *that* his responsibility, too, and he embraces it pretty eagerly, I might add. And he's so cute with the baby. Every time he holds her, the most amazed expression crosses his face. I was hesitant when he first suggested we have a baby together, but now I'm so glad we did."

Dana Sue sighed. "I envy you."

Maddie's expression sobered. "Because of the baby?"

"No, because you have a man in your life who adores you. It's Helen who's envious of the baby."

Maddie frowned. "She is? She's never said anything."

"She wouldn't want to put any sort of damper on your happiness, but I think she's starting to realize what she's missed out on," Dana Sue said. "To be honest, I think that's what's really behind these goals of hers. She wants to get healthy so she can have a baby. Not that she's ready to admit it, but I can see it in her eyes when she looks at Jessica Lynn."

"Amazing," Maddie said. "How'd I miss that?"

Dana Sue grinned. "You've been too busy to worry about how envious your friends are of your happiness."

"Well, you certainly have no reason to be. You could have a man in your life, if you wanted one," Maddie reminded her. "All you have to do is open your heart to the possibilities."

"Easier said than done," Dana Sue responded. She wondered if she'd ever get to a point where she trusted Ronnie enough to let him back into her heart and into her life.

By Friday morning, Ronnie was anxious to get his meeting with Butch Thompson over with. He'd run numbers until he was seeing them in his sleep. He'd sketched out a business plan, then used Annie's computer to put it down on paper. He was sure it lacked the kind of expertise Butch was used to seeing, but Ronnie had tried hard to balance reality against what he envisioned.

He was nervously awaiting Butch's arrival at Wharton's

when Mary Vaughn came in. She spotted him and immediately headed for his table.

"I thought I'd hear from you by now," she said. "You haven't answered any of my calls."

"Patience, Mary Vaughn," he chided. "I'll call when things have fallen into place, hopefully before the end of today."

Her expression brightened. "Oh? Shall I call you later?"

He grinned at her eagerness. "No, I'll call *you*. Either way. I promise. Now scoot on out of here. I have a business meeting, and the gentleman just walked through the door."

Mary Vaughn turned to look and a huge smile immediately spread across her face. "Hey, Uncle Butch, what are you doing in Serenity?"

Ronnie stared as she threw her arms around Butch and pressed an enthusiastic kiss to his cheek. "You two know each other?" he asked.

Butch grinned. "This little gal is my favorite niece."

"I'm your *only* niece," she corrected.

"Still my favorite," Butch said. "Her mama's my big sister."

Ronnie shook his head. "Small world, isn't it?"

When Butch sat down, Mary Vaughn dragged a chair over to the end of the booth without waiting for an invitation. "Okay, spill it. What kind of business are you two doing together? I'm asking as family."

Butch gave her a chiding look. "And I'm telling you, as family, to get lost and let us menfolk do our thing."

"If I didn't know there's not a sexist bone in your body, I'd be offended by that," she grumbled, but she stood up. Turning to Ronnie, she said, "We'll talk later, you hear?"

"I'm sure we will," he said, grinning.

After she'd gone, Butch regarded him curiously. "How does my niece fit in with this idea of yours?"

"She's the Realtor for the property I want to buy here in town," Ronnie explained.

"Ah, so she's hot on the trail of a big deal," Butch said approvingly. "That girl always was a go-getter. I'm surprised she walked away just now."

"So am I, to be honest," Ronnie replied. "But I think we can count on the fact that she won't let this drop."

Just then Grace Wharton walked up to take their order. "Coffee for you, I imagine," she said to Ronnie, then smiled at Butch. "What about you? You in the mood for breakfast? We make a mighty fine omelet here."

"I ate breakfast hours ago," Butch told her. "Coffee's fine."

Grace continued to hover. "You and Dana Sue going to the fall festival this weekend?" she asked Ronnie.

He stared at her blankly. "I hadn't even thought about it, to tell you the truth. Since Annie's been sick, I've lost track of everything."

"Well, the three of you should go," Grace said. "You remember how Annie used to talk you all into buying her something from just about every vendor there because she felt sorry for them if it looked like they weren't doing much business?"

Ronnie grinned. "That child ended up with a lot of junk that way. Half of it always wound up in our next garage sale," he recalled. "You're right, Grace. I'll talk to Dana Sue and Annie about going."

Grace beamed at him. "I'll get your coffees right now," she said, bustling away.

After she'd brought the coffee, Butch settled back in the booth. "You have some facts and figures for me?" he asked.

Ronnie took the folder from the seat beside him and handed it across the table. Nerves on edge, he sat silently while Butch went through the paperwork.

At one point, the older man's eyes widened. "There's this much development in the area?"

Ronnie nodded. "If anything, that's a conservative number. Those are just the projects that have already gotten governmental approval and permits. I got the list at city hall. There are at least one or two more with proposals before the planning commission."

"Impressive," Butch said. "And you think you can make deals with them?"

"Some of them, anyway," Ronnie said. "I'll know more when I speak to some of the developers directly, but I didn't want to do that yet, not until my idea is a go."

Butch nodded. He reached the last piece of paper in the file. "This your bottom line, then?"

Ronnie nodded. He'd tried to keep the figure conservative, too, but even so, it was a lot of money—though maybe not to a man like Butch.

The older man lifted his gaze and studied him. "You kept this low so I wouldn't turn tail and run, didn't you?"

"I tried to be realistic about what I could get by with for start-up costs," Ronnie corrected.

"You'd be out of business in six months," Butch said flatly. "Start-up never goes as smoothly as anticipated. Clients never pay exactly when you expect them to. You need a cushion in here, so you don't go bankrupt before you've had a chance to prove yourself. Worst mistake a start-up company can make is to be undercapitalized."

"I didn't want to—"

Butch cut him off. "You didn't want to presume on our friendship," he said. "But this is business, Ronnie. If my investment's going to pay off for both of us, we have to approach it that way. No shortcuts. No attempt to get by on less than you'll need."

He took out a pen and wrote on the bottom of the page, then pushed it across the table. "I'd say that's a more realistic figure, wouldn't you?"

Ronnie gaped. It was forty percent above his own estimate and more than he'd ever dreamed of asking for. "Are you sure?"

"I'm sure that's what it'll take if you want to do this right," Butch said. "That'll give you enough cushion for a couple of years so you can get yourself on solid ground."

"You have that much confidence in this idea?" Ronnie asked, hardly daring to believe that Butch would provide so much backing.

"And in you," he confirmed. "Now where's this building you want to buy? Is it close enough we can take a look at it?"

"Down a block and across the street," Ronnie told him, his head spinning. "I'll pay for the coffee and we can take a look. Of course, we can't see inside without Mary Vaughn."

"Then call her," Butch said. "Might as well satisfy her curiosity. She'll be able to get started on the paperwork that much sooner."

The next two hours were a blur to Ronnie. Butch moved fast when he was on a mission. Inside the hardware store, he barked out comments about immediate changes Ronnie ought to consider, then gave Mary Vaughn a figure to take to the owners that was well below the asking price.

Ronnie winced when he heard the offer. "I don't want to lowball Rusty and Dora Jean," he protested. "They spent their whole lives with this business."

"Here's a lesson you need to understand," Butch responded. "There's no room for sentiment when it comes to business. I believe in being fair, not idiotic. That offer is thousands more than they paid for this place and thousands more than they have in their pockets right now. Getting out from under any overhead they have should be worth the difference between their asking price and our offer."

Mary Vaughn met Ronnie's gaze. To his surprise, she nodded. "He's right. It's a good offer."

"Okay, then," Ronnie said. "But before you take it to Rusty, let me have a word with your uncle, okay?"

"I'll be outside filling out the paperwork," she said.

After she'd gone, Ronnie leveled a look into Butch's eyes. "I thought you were planning to be a silent partner in this."

Butch immediately looked chagrined. "You're absolutely right. I'm so used to taking charge and getting my own way, I got carried away for a minute there. I swear it won't happen again."

Ronnie regarded him skeptically.

"Okay, it probably will," Butch admitted. "But feel free to tell me to butt out. I'll put that in writing if you need me to. I am not going to try to micromanage this business of yours."

"I think I will get that in writing," Ronnie said. "Just to be on the safe side."

"You're going to do fine on your own," Butch told him approvingly. "Now, how about that lunch you promised me? Maybe Mary Vaughn will have some news for us before we've finished eating."

"Don't you want to take care of all the paperwork on our deal before she presents that offer to the owners?" Ronnie asked.

"I keep my word," Butch told him. "So do you. We'll get it all down on paper to keep the lawyers happy, but as far as I'm concerned we have a deal right now that you could take to court." He scrawled his signature across the bottom of Ronnie's papers, just below the figure he'd added. "You sign there, too. Then we'll let the lawyers make it all nice and tidy."

Ronnie nodded. "I look forward to doing business with you,

Butch. I really do. And even though I made a big deal about you being a silent partner, I know I'm going to be turning to you for advice so much you'll get sick of hearing from me."

"Couldn't happen," Butch assured him. "Nothing I like more than talking business to a guy who's interested in learning something. Now, let's tell my niece she can do her thing, then get some lunch. Spending money always makes me hungry."

Ronnie realized he was starved, as well. "We'll take my car. Sullivan's is about a mile from here."

As they made the quick drive, Ronnie realized he'd never gotten around to filling in Dana Sue on his plans. Once Mary Vaughn made an offer on the hardware store, the news was going to spread like wildfire. He just prayed he'd get to Dana Sue before she tapped in to the Serenity grapevine.

When Dana Sue walked into the kitchen at Sullivan's through the back entrance, Erik looked at her with surprise. "I didn't think you were coming in till later."

"I was getting antsy at home and I think Annie was getting sick of my hovering," she explained. "I made sure she ate her lunch, then slipped away to check on things here."

"Your ex is having lunch in the dining room," Erik said.

"By himself?"

Erik shook his head. "He's with a man I've never seen before, and about five minutes ago, Mary Vaughn joined them."

Dana Sue bristled. She'd known Mary Vaughn most of her life. Usually they got along, but ever since Mary Vaughn's divorce from Howard Lewis, Jr., the mayor's son, she had been on the prowl. Lately she'd been living with her boss, but rumor had it that the relationship was already in trouble. The last few times they'd eaten at Sullivan's, the tension was so thick it could have been cut with a knife. Dana Sue had a sudden image of Mary Vaughn making Ronnie her next target. She didn't like it. With Dana Sue telling anyone who'd listen that she didn't want Ronnie back, Mary Vaughn would see him as fair game.

"I'll be back," she said tightly, stalking into the dining room and scanning the crowd until her gaze caught Ronnie's. He gave her a distracted wave, then turned back to listen intently to whatever Mary Vaughn was saying. Dana Sue had a sudden urge to plunge a butcher knife straight into the woman's heart. Or maybe into Ronnie's.

Her reaction was so intense, it scared her. Not because she thought she would ever act on it, but because she'd even *thought* such a thing. It meant Ronnie was starting to matter to her again. It also meant she still didn't trust him.

Cursing herself for being a fool, she ignored the temptation to bust up their little party, and headed for her office and shut the door. At least she'd had the presence of mind not to slam it and let Ronnie and everyone else know she was annoyed. Inside, she buried her face in her hands.

"Idiot, idiot, idiot," she muttered. It was obvious she could not get involved with Ronnie again, not without turning into some kind of suspicious shrew. Not for the first time, she prayed he would solve the problem for her by leaving town. Yet that thought made her unbearably sad.

She forced herself to return phone calls and concentrate on the pile of paperwork on her desk. She'd been at it for an hour when the door to her office opened and Ronnie poked his head in. There was an excitement in his expression she hadn't seen in years. If it had anything at all to do with Mary Vaughn, Dana Sue would have to kill them both, she thought direly.

"Is this a good time?" he asked, then came in without waiting for an answer. He looked around for a place to sit, shook his head at the clutter, pushed a stack of catalogs aside and perched on the edge of her desk, his knee nudging her thigh.

"What?" she asked impatiently. Damn. The man always made her so blasted jittery.

"I thought you ought to know what I'm planning before word spreads all over town," he said at last.

"Your departure?" she inquired hopefully.

"I told you that wasn't happening."

"You've said a lot of things over the years, then had a change of heart. Forsaking all others was one of them," she said, unable to keep the bitterness out of her voice.

"Old news," he said blithely.

"But not forgotten," she said. "Look, I'm busy. Just tell me whatever's on your mind and go away."

"I just bought the old hardware store," he announced, as if it were no more important than buying a new pair of jeans.

Dana Sue stared at him, stunned. "The hardware store? Why?"

"I'm going to open it again," he explained.

"Are you crazy? They closed it because the big chains were killing them."

"They closed it because Dora Jean couldn't handle it after Rusty got sick," he corrected. "And I imagine he got sick from the stress of trying to figure out how to compete with the big chains, so you're probably half-right."

"What makes you think you can do any better? And where'd you get that kind of money, anyway? I thought you kept on working construction after you left here. Did you buy a winning lottery ticket I never heard about? And what does Mary Vaughn have to do with this? Please tell me she's not your partner." Then Dana Sue really *would* have to kill one of them.

Ronnie held up his hand. "Hey, one thing at a time. There's going to be a lot of building in this area over the next few years. I've been working construction since I left here, and because of that, I think I know how to deal with these developers and contractors who are going to be swarming all over the place. If I provide them with what they need at a competitive price, and give them the convenience of being a little closer by, especially with fuel costs being so high, I'll do just fine. And getting another business on Main Street going again will make a contribution to the town. As for the money, I have a backer. My boss, Butch Thompson, from over in Beaufort, sees real potential in the idea. He's partnering with me to do this. And Mary Vaughn is handling the sale of the store. That's it. Oh, she's also Butch's niece, but I had no idea about that till a couple of hours ago. Have I covered everything?"

Astonished, Dana Sue could only stare. It was a far more ambitious plan than she would ever have envisioned for Ronnie, and it required a long-term commitment, one she'd thought him incapable of making. Obviously he intended to prove her wrong.

"Aren't you going to say anything?" he asked eventually.

"I still think you're crazy," she said at last, but there wasn't as much conviction in her tone. Truthfully, she rather admired his audacity.

"Why? You've made a success of this restaurant when everyone told you fine dining was the last thing anyone in town cared about. You, Helen and Maddie have created something terrific with The Corner Spa. Half the men in town are grumbling because you won't let them in there. Why shouldn't I be part of Serenity's revitalization, too?"

"Because owning a business sounds so…so stodgy and traditional," she said eventually. "You'll be tied down."

Ronnie grinned. "You scared I'm not going to knock your socks off with my wicked unpredictability anymore, sugar?"

She met his gaze. "Maybe," she said, though the truth was far more complicated than that.

He stood up, pressed a kiss to her mouth that pretty much made mincemeat of her fear, then headed out the door. Just when she was beginning to catch her breath, he stuck his head back in.

"Have I mentioned lately that I love you?" He winked. "Just thought you should know." He started to leave once more, then turned back. "Fall festival's tomorrow. I think we should go. I'll be by at nine to pick up you and Annie."

And then he was gone, leaving Dana Sue's head spinning and her resolve to avoid him in tatters.

19

For the first time since Ronnie had come back to Serenity, Dana Sue was scared—really scared—that he was going to make good on his threat to stay. Buying the hardware store, starting a business—those weren't whims. They took money and commitment. Neither were things she'd associated with Ronnie, at least not recently. She'd made herself forget about the many years they'd been together when he *had* been faithful, in favor of remembering the one night when he hadn't been.

Punching in Helen's number after Ronnie left her office, she managed to catch her friend between meetings.

"Can we get together tonight?" she asked. "Your house."

"Sure," Helen said at once. "You want to tell me what's going on? You sound a little desperate. Why my place? Shouldn't you be sticking close to Annie?"

"I'll make sure someone's with Annie, but I don't want her to hear any of this," Dana Sue said. "I need advice."

"Is Maddie coming, too?"

"I'm calling her next. I wanted to make sure you were available." She needed both their perspectives if she was ever to make sense of her own mixed emotions—Maddie's romanticized version of her relationship with Ronnie and Helen's far more skeptical one. "Seven-thirty okay?"

"Fine with me," Helen said. "My client's here, so I need to run. I'll see you tonight."

Five minutes later, Dana Sue also had Maddie's agreement to meet her at Helen's, and a commitment that Ty and Cal would drop in on Annie, bring her favorite Chinese takeout for dinner and make sure she ate every bite on the menu plan. Satisfied, Dana Sue sat back and tried to relax. There was nothing she could do to stop Ronnie from buying the hardware store or restarting a hardware business on Main Street, but maybe Helen and Maddie could tell her how to avoid falling for this latest evidence that her ex-husband was a changed man. She needed to know tonight, so she could be prepared for spending an entire day with him at the fall festival tomorrow, a command performance she could see no way around if she wasn't to disappoint Annie.

Focusing now on this grand scheme of his, she tried to recall a single time in all the years she'd known him that Ronnie had so much as hinted that he wanted to operate his own company. He'd always been perfectly content to work construction jobs that brought in good money, but didn't tie him down.

Of course, he could have said the same thing about her. She'd worked in various restaurants from time to time, waiting tables in some, working as a hostess in others, then finally gravitating toward the kitchen, which had felt right from the first moment she'd tried it. She'd literally learned the business from the ground up and finally found a way to capitalize on all the years she'd spent in the kitchen with her grandmother and mother making old-fashioned Southern dishes for family gatherings. Dana Sue was a self-taught chef who'd developed not only her instincts about food, but a head for business.

If she hadn't split up with Ronnie, she doubted she would ever have found the courage to strike out on her own and open

Sullivan's. It was only after Helen and Maddie encouraged her to take a chance, worked with her on her business plan and helped her to secure the loans that she'd finally trusted herself enough to try. The success that had followed had been beyond her wildest hopes and dreams. Why shouldn't Ronnie be ready for the same kind of risks and potential rewards? And why did she find it so disconcerting?

Those were the questions Dana Sue asked Helen and Maddie when they were all settled on Helen's patio that evening. She and Helen had margaritas, their drink of choice for serious discussions, while Maddie sipped a nonalcoholic frozen fruit drink since she was still nursing the baby.

"He's really going to do it?" Maddie asked, looking delighted. "That's fantastic. It's just the shot in the arm Main Street needs. With only Wharton's in business, it looks so sad now."

"I think you're missing my point," Dana Sue complained. "It means he's definitely staying."

Maddie grinned. "And that surprises you? Isn't that exactly what he's been telling you since he got here?"

"I didn't believe him," Dana Sue admitted, then corrected herself. "I didn't want to believe him."

"Or maybe you were scared to believe him," Maddie suggested, her tone gentle.

Dana Sue shrugged. "That, too." She turned to Helen. "What's your take on this?"

"I have to admit, he's caught me off guard. This plan of his is exciting and ambitious and it just might work. Where's he getting the money? Does he have it?"

"Apparently so. He said something about his partner being his boss from Beaufort and Mary Vaughn's uncle."

Helen regarded her with surprise. "If they were right there, why didn't you go over to the table to find out what was going on?"

"Mary Vaughn," she said succinctly. "It was making me a little crazy to see her with Ronnie. Of course, that was before I knew they were talking real estate. But still, I wouldn't put it past her to set her sights on him."

Maddie rolled her eyes. "Would you listen to yourself?" she asked impatiently. "You're making up excuses to keep from grabbing the man, even though you know you want him back. Ronnie's not interested in Mary Vaughn. He never was, not even when she threw herself at him back in high school. He chose you then and he's chosen you now. You're the only one too blind to see it."

"I'm not sure I believe it, either," Helen said.

Maddie scowled at her. "Because you're jaded. You really need to start practicing another kind of law. Divorces are giving you a very cynical outlook when it comes to love. If it keeps up, you'll never give a relationship even half a chance."

"I believe Cal loves you," Helen responded, a defensive note in her voice. "Besides, I'm not the issue here. I think I have good reason to distrust Ronnie's feelings for Dana Sue. So does she."

Maddie groaned. "People make mistakes. People regret them. People change. You show me a human being without flaws and I'll show you the most boring individual in the universe."

Dana Sue watched Helen struggling to come up with a response to that, and decided to say what she knew the other woman was thinking. "Helen thinks she's perfect," she said. "Isn't that right, sweetie? And we know she's not boring."

Helen frowned at her. "Of course I'm not perfect. I've made mistakes."

"Really?" Dana Sue feigned shock. "You have?"

"Okay, stop teasing," Helen grumbled. "I know nobody's perfect, but some mistakes are bigger than others and don't deserve to be forgiven."

Maddie nudged her with a bare foot. During her pregnancy she'd gotten used to kicking off her shoes because her feet were swelling. Now, she'd told them, she did it for the pure enjoyment of it. "Not your decision to make in this case. It's up to Dana Sue." She turned to her. "Do you really want to keep holding on to the anger and resentment?"

"No," Dana Sue said wearily, then corrected herself. "Yes."

Maddie smiled. "Which is it?"

"I don't know, dammit. It's hard holding on to it, especially when he's being so sweet, but letting go is scary."

"Living is scary," Maddie reminded her. "The only time it's not is when you stop taking risks." She leaned forward. "I certainly can't guarantee you that Ronnie will never hurt you again. I doubt he could guarantee you that, either. But is the bland, safe existence you've had since he left a good trade-off for the excitement and unpredictability of being with him?"

"My life isn't bland or safe," Dana Sue protested. "I started my restaurant. I've made new friends. We opened the health club. Life's been pretty darn good with him gone."

"That's right," Helen chimed in. "A woman doesn't have to have a man around to lead a satisfying life."

"Of course not," Maddie agreed. "But I'm here to tell you that all those achievements are a thousand times better if there's someone to share them with, someone who'll rub your back late at night or listen to you when things are going wrong." She gave Dana Sue a penetrating look. "Can you honestly tell me that it hasn't been easier to cope with what happened to Annie because Ronnie's here to help and to share the anguish and worry?"

"He's been incredibly supportive," Dana Sue conceded grudgingly. "And yes, it's been nice to know I'm not in this alone."

"But you're still afraid to start counting on him," Maddie guessed.

Dana Sue nodded.

"Then don't," Maddie advised. "Take it one day at a time. It's not as if he's asked you to marry him again. All he's asking for is another chance to prove that things can be different. Can't you give him that much?"

It sounded so reasonable when Maddie said it. One day at a time. No big deal. But there was a flaw in that. A big one. Dana Sue was still in love with him. Every day she let Ronnie back into her life, every second she spent with him, took her closer to the point of no return.

And if Ronnie let her down yet again, this time she wasn't sure she'd bounce back.

Besides, she thought, there was Annie to consider. If Dana Sue and Ronnie tried to make it work and failed, their daughter would be devastated a second time.

"I can't take the chance," Dana Sue said miserably. "It's not just about me and what I want. Annie almost died because of what happened between me and her dad. I don't think she would survive if Ronnie and I got back together and things didn't work out."

Not even the eternally optimistic Maddie seemed able to come up with a response to that. And because she couldn't, Dana Sue knew she was making the right decision. No matter how much she might want things to be different, she couldn't let Ronnie back into her life. Unfortunately, that didn't mean she could keep him out of Annie's. Which meant Dana Sue was going to have to find some way to build a wall around her heart.

* * *

The annual fall festival had been moved from the town square to the park since Ronnie had gone away. Once, it had been as much a boon to the local businesses as it was to the artists, produce vendors and food booths. But with the changing times the city fathers deemed it pointless to keep the event downtown, with only Wharton's left to benefit. And, Annie had told Ronnie, there was a lot more room in the park for the increasing number of people who came to town for the festivities.

"Dad, there's Sarah. Can I spend some time walking around with her and Raylene?" Annie begged just as soon as they arrived.

Ronnie cast a glance at Dana Sue, trying to gauge her reaction. She'd obviously come along grudgingly this morning, and he anticipated that any minute she was going to start making excuses to head for Sullivan's. If Annie left the two of them alone, it was going to make it that much easier for Dana Sue to take off. Still, he refused to use Annie to keep Dana Sue around.

"It's up to your mom," he said at last.

Dana Sue looked surprised, but nodded. "Go," she told Annie. "But you have to find your dad and me before lunch. We're all going to eat together."

Annie groaned. "You're going to watch me today, too?"

"You know the rules," Ronnie said. "But you can have Sarah and Raylene join us, if you want."

Annie's sullen expression faded. "Cool! Okay, I'll meet you at noon by the gazebo—that's where all the food booths are."

After she'd run off, he glanced at Dana Sue and saw her studying him with a thoughtful expression. "You handled that very well."

"By reminding her of the rules?" he asked.

"No, by including her friends for lunch. I wish I'd thought of that."

He grinned. "You were probably too distracted by the prospect of spending a couple of hours all alone with me. You afraid I'll do something outrageous right out here in public, sugar?"

Dana Sue shrugged. "I wouldn't put it past you."

"Sorry, darlin', I intend to be on my best behavior. I don't want to give you any excuses for bolting."

"Actually, I wanted to talk to you," she said, her face turning somber.

Ronnie knew that expression. It meant he wasn't going to like whatever it was she had to say. The only way around that would be to keep her from saying it.

"Not till we've looked at all the art," he said, reaching for her hand and drawing her toward the first booth.

"Ronnie," she said, a protest obviously on the tip of her tongue.

"It's the fall festival," he said. "The weather's gorgeous. Not a cloud in the sky. We're surrounded by folks we know. Annie's getting back to her old self. So, no serious conversations allowed today." He gestured toward the watercolors on display. "What do you think?"

"I think you're impossible," she muttered, but she turned her attention to the art. "Pretty, but bland."

"My thought, too. Do you suppose Maddie's mom has a booth this year? I think a couple of Paula Vreeland botanical prints would be lovely in the foyer at Sullivan's."

Dana Sue regarded him with a startled look. "You know, you're absolutely right. I can't imagine why I never thought of that. When we opened, I decorated on a shoestring, but I can afford more now, and they'd be perfect against the dark-green wall just inside the door."

Ronnie winked at her. "See, contrary to popular opinion, I do have a tasteful bone in my body."

As they strolled among the vendors in search of Maddie's mom, who'd built a national reputation for her art and a local reputation for her eccentricities, Ronnie kept Dana Sue's hand tucked in his. For once, she didn't try to pull away.

The instant Paula Vreeland spotted them, she cut off a conversation she was having with the artist at the next booth and came out to greet them. "Ronnie, it's good to see you back in town," she said. "And to see you with Dana Sue."

"Thanks, Mrs. Vreeland. You're even more beautiful than you were when I left," he said. "And just in case you're not aware of it, your art is all over the place in Beaufort. I can't tell you how many homes I visited that had one of your paintings on the wall."

"And Ronnie thinks I've shown an amazing lack of good sense by not having a few prints hanging in the foyer at Sullivan's," Dana Sue stated. "For once I actually agree with something he has to say."

"Take a look around," Paula Vreeland said. "And if you don't find what you want here, come by my studio next week. I have more there. I usually don't bring the originals here, because the cost is prohibitive for this crowd, but with the discount I'll give you, you could afford to buy them for Sullivan's."

Dana Sue regarded her with dismay. "I couldn't ask you for a price break," she protested.

"You didn't ask," Mrs. Vreeland corrected. "I offered, and not just because you've been such a wonderful friend to my daughter, either. Having my paintings in your restaurant will bring me tons of new sales. You've drawn a very classy clientele, Dana Sue. I'm as proud of you as if you were my own."

Ronnie noticed Dana Sue blinking back tears, so he drew her toward a delicate painting of a magnolia blossom. He could almost feel the velvet texture of the creamy petals. "I think this would be perfect for a business owned by one of the Sweet Magnolias," he said. "What do you think?"

Dana Sue studied it, then nodded. "It is perfect," she said, a catch in her voice.

"Then consider this one my gift to you. I wasn't here for the grand opening, so I owe you one."

"Ronnie, please, you don't have to do that, especially not with all the expenses you're going to have when you open your new business," she said.

"Maybe I'm hoping you'll give me a break on catering the opening party," he teased. "Don't argue with me, sugar. I want to do this. Now see if there are any others you want."

While she looked at the other paintings, Ronnie chatted with Maddie's mother, then paid for the one he'd chosen as his gift for Dana Sue. She wrote a check for two others she liked.

"Can we pick them up later?" Ronnie asked. "When it's time to go home?"

"Absolutely," Mrs. Vreeland told him. "I'll put Sold stickers on them right now. You two run along and enjoy yourselves."

From then on their progress was slow going because the crowd had grown and it seemed everyone in town had heard about Ronnie's plans for the hardware store and wanted to congratulate him and to thank him for doing his part to make downtown the hub of the community again. Even the mayor put in his two cents, telling Ronnie to let him know if there was anything the town could do to support the business.

"Just shop there," Ronnie told Howard Lewis. "And tell your friends about it."

"When do you anticipate opening?" the mayor asked.

"If we can get all the details ironed out, I'd like to open before Christmas," Ronnie answered, drawing yet another startled look from Dana Sue.

After Howard had moved on, she eyed Ronnie warily. "You can do it that fast?"

"If I throw myself into it nonstop for the next six weeks or so," he said.

"I guess that means you won't have much time for Annie."

Ronnie frowned at her. "I will always make time for Annie, and for you. You know yourself that getting a business off the ground is hard work, but I intend to balance that with the other important things in my life."

"Sure," she said, radiating skepticism. "You say that now, but when time starts running short, I'm sure spending time with Annie will be the first thing you sacrifice."

Ronnie stopped in his tracks and gave her a penetrating look. "Are you trying to pick a fight with me?"

She blinked at the hard edge in his voice, then sighed. "Probably," she admitted.

"Care to explain why?" he asked.

"I need you to go back to being the villain," she said. "It would make my life so much easier."

Ronnie relaxed. "Not going to happen, darlin'. Now, let's go pick out a couple of pumpkins. I'll carve the one with the happy face and you can do the one with the scary frown."

She gave him a sour look. "Is that supposed to be funny?"

Ronnie shrugged. "I thought it had the potential to coax a smile out of you. Guess I'll just have to keep trying."

"Even if having you be nice is making me nuts?" she asked.

He nodded. "Yep, afraid so."

Her lips twitched at his response, but she turned away before he could see if it turned into a full-fledged smile. It didn't matter, though, because he wasn't going to stop trying until they were back to laughing all the time, the way they once had.

There was something weird going on with her mom and dad, Annie decided after being out of the hospital for two weeks. They were still watching her every move, making sure someone was with her for every meal, making sure she stuck to the routine they'd worked out with the dietitian. But the two of them were never around at the same time. They seemed to have some uncanny knack for avoiding each other. It was almost as if they'd worked out a schedule behind her back.

Tonight her dad had barely walked out the door when her mom walked in. Annie regarded her with a perplexed expression. "Did you wait down the block till you saw Dad leave before you came home?" she demanded.

"Why would I do that?" her mom asked, her guilty expression revealing the truth.

"Because you don't want to see him," Annie said dryly. "What's he done now?"

"He hasn't done anything," she said. "He's busy these days. So am I. You know I've been neglecting the restaurant and the health club. I need to make up for the time I've missed."

She made it sound pretty reasonable, but Annie wasn't buying it. "Will you both be at the family counseling session tomorrow?"

When her mom regarded her with a startled expression, Annie knew she'd forgotten all about it. "You can't get out of it," Annie declared. "The whole point of family counseling is for all of us to be there. Dad's coming. I reminded him tonight." In truth, he hadn't seemed any more eager to be there than her mom, but he'd agreed.

Her mom sighed. "Of course I'll be there. It just slipped my mind, that's all."

The sessions the shrink had had with just Annie hadn't been so bad. Dr. McDaniels was pretty cool, after all. She got the things Annie tried to explain to her, and she didn't make a lot of judgments. She just pushed and prodded till Annie started to look at situations differently.

Like her parents' marriage, for instance. She knew now that there was probably nothing any of them could have done to keep it from falling apart after her dad had cheated. But whatever the real reason was that he'd slept with that bimbo, it was *his* issue, not her mom's and certainly not Annie's. And her not eating was a pretty dumb way to go about protesting her dad leaving town.

Not that she'd realized at the time that was what she was doing, some sort of stupid hunger-strike thing, but that was what it amounted to. She might not trust herself to eat right all the time yet, but she was pretty sure she'd never be that dumb again.

In her attempt to figure out what was going on between her mom and dad, Annie had forgotten to share the good news she'd had that morning.

"Guess what?" she said, unable to contain a grin. "Dr. McDaniels said if the cardiologist says it's okay when I see him day after tomorrow, I can go back to school next week."

Her mom beamed. "Wow, that is good news! You've worked really hard to get better. I know it'll be great to be back in class and with your friends again."

The best part would be seeing Ty every day, Annie thought, but she didn't tell her mom that. He'd been coming by a lot while she'd been at home, but she couldn't wait to see if he would spend time with her at school. Not that he was acting like a boyfriend or anything. He'd never kissed her, except on the cheek, the same way he kissed her mom. But Annie thought it would say a lot if he treated her like a friend in front of all the guys on the baseball team and the other seniors. Like she was special.

"Are you all caught up with your assignments?" her mom asked.

Annie nodded. "Sarah and Raylene have been bringing them and I've sent all the homework in with them. I might have to take some tests I've missed, but it shouldn't be too hard to catch up. Ty said he'd tutor me if I need it."

Her mother regarded her intently. "That was nice of him. He's been a good friend, hasn't he?"

"The best," she said, feeling her cheeks heat.

"You aren't counting on anything more, are you?" her mom asked, looking worried.

Annie knew the point she was trying to make—that Ty was her friend, not her boyfriend. But she didn't need reminding of that every minute. "No way," she said. "Why are you making such a big deal about it?"

"I just don't want you to be disappointed."

"It wouldn't be the first time in my life I've been disappointed," Annie told her.

Her mom frowned at that. "Are you talking about me and your dad?"

"Exactly," Annie said.

Her mom suddenly looked tired and incredibly sad. "And look at how you dealt with that," she said gently. "I couldn't bear it if Ty hurt you, and it sent you down that path again."

"Did it ever occur to you that maybe he *won't* disappoint me?" Annie demanded heatedly. "Thanks for believing in me, Mom." Hurt and anger were all mixed up inside her as she ran upstairs to her room and slammed the door behind her.

She heard her mom call after her, but she just buried her face in her pillow. She knew what she'd said was mean, and it wasn't even true, not really. Her mom had always believed in her. In fact, she was her biggest booster. Annie knew in her heart that she was the one who didn't believe that she was good enough for Ty. Which was why her mom's warning had touched a nerve.

When Ronnie walked into Dr. McDaniels's office in the morning, the tension was palpable. Annie and Dana Sue were barely looking at each other and Dana Sue was deliberately avoiding his gaze. He opted to take a seat beside his daughter.

Leaning in close, he whispered, "Did you have a fight with your mom?"

She shrugged. "Sort of."

"About?"

"Stuff."

He sat back with a sigh, then glanced at Dana Sue, whose posture was stiff as a board. "What about you? You want to tell me what the fight was about?"

"Not really."

"Then the next hour ought to be a lot of fun," he murmured, relieved when Dr. McDaniels came in and closed the door. Maybe a neutral party could sort out the problem.

"How is everyone?" the psychologist inquired, regarding them all cheerfully.

The murmured responses from either side of him were so unenthusiastic that Ronnie felt compelled to make his own hearty. Dr. McDaniels gave him a grateful look.

"I sense some tension here," she said.

"You think?" Annie muttered.

Dana Sue sighed heavily. "All I did was tell her not to get

her hopes up about a young man she likes. I just didn't want her to be disappointed if he didn't live up to her expectations."

So that was it, Ronnie thought. This was about Ty and—Ronnie would be willing to bet—about him. Locking gazes with Dana Sue, he said, "Is this really about Annie not putting her feelings at risk with Ty, or about you being scared to risk yours with me?"

Dana Sue scowled at him. "Your name never came up," she said tightly.

"I'm sure it didn't," he retorted. "That doesn't mean you weren't projecting your fears onto Annie and Ty."

"Okay, hold on a second," Dr. McDaniels said. "One of you needs to fill me in. Who is Ty? I believe you've mentioned him before, Annie. Want to tell me a little more about him?"

Annie leaned forward eagerly and painted Ty in glowing terms. "I like him," she concluded, casting a defiant glance at her mother. "A lot."

"Which is why I was concerned," Dana Sue said. "Ty's older. He has his own friends, his own interests. He's been wonderful with Annie, but I'm not sure they're on the same page when it comes to their feelings."

"So you want to protect her from being hurt," the psychologist said.

"Well, of course I do. I'm her mother," Dana Sue said.

"You can't protect kids from growing up and making their own mistakes," Dr. McDaniels said. "What if Annie is hurt? Would it be the end of the world? Every girl has her heart broken at some point."

"Not now, dammit," Dana Sue said forcefully. "She's too fragile. She needs to get healthy and strong again before she has to face something like that."

The psychologist turned to Annie. "You know you're taking a chance, right? You know that putting your heart on the line might be risky?"

"Sure," Annie said. "But it's okay. How will I feel if I play it safe and never even get a chance to be happy with Ty?"

"Out of the mouths of babes," Ronnie muttered, his gaze on Dana Sue.

Dr. McDaniels seized on his comment. "You're seeing some parallels here to your relationship with Dana Sue."

"Plain as day," he said.

"How about you?" she asked Dana Sue. "Do you think Ronnie's right? Are you projecting your own insecurities onto your daughter?"

"Absolutely not!" Dana Sue snapped, then closed her eyes. "Maybe," she whispered.

Instead of pressing her, the doctor turned back to Annie. "What's the worst thing that might happen if you put your heart on the line with Ty?"

"He might not like me back the same way," she said at once.

"And you could cope with that?"

"Better than I could deal with not knowing," Annie stated.

"That sounds like a pretty mature attitude to me," Dr. McDaniels said. "What do you think, Dana Sue?"

"I think she has no idea how devastating it will be if he doesn't."

"And you know that from experience, right?" the psychologist prodded.

Dana Sue nodded.

"But you survived, didn't you? You got through all the heartache and made a new life for yourself. Seems to me you've accomplished a lot you can be proud of."

"Well, of course I am," Dana Sue said, looking puzzled.

"Then what makes you think Annie couldn't be just as strong?"

"She's anorexic," Dana Sue said.

"And she's working on changing that," the doctor countered. "Anything else?"

"Well, no," Dana Sue admitted.

"And what about you? Are you likely to be any less strong if you take a risk and it doesn't work out?" Before Dana Sue could answer, the psychologist held up a hand. "Let me ask that another way. As I understand it, after you and Ronnie split up, you were pretty upset, right?"

"Of course."

"You thought your life was over?"

"In some ways, yes," Dana Sue admitted.

"Yet you risked quite a lot to open Sullivan's," the doctor reminded her. "Were you prepared for the possibility it might fail?"

Dana Sue nodded.

"But that didn't stop you from trying, did it? Why?"

"Because I knew I was strong enough to handle it if it did fail," Dana Sue said.

"Yet you said you were feeling pretty fragile at the time," Dr. McDaniels said.

Dana Sue met her gaze. "I see your point."

"Do you? Do you understand that life is filled with risks? Unless you face them head-on and try, you may as well resign yourself to sitting on the sidelines."

Ronnie waited with bated breath. He had a hunch his entire future hinged on whatever conclusion Dana Sue reached right now.

"You're right," she finally said, looking startled by the admission.

"Well, then, there's no reason I can see not to reach out for whatever it is you want in life," Dr. McDaniels said.

Dana Sue regarded her warily. "Are you saying I should give Ronnie another chance?"

"Only if that's what you want to do," the doctor said neutrally. "Your decision, not mine. Not Annie's. Any more than it's your decision whether she puts her heart on the line with this young man she likes."

Suddenly Annie was grinning at her mom. "Not so easy realizing that your fate's in your own hands, is it, Mom?"

Dana Sue chuckled. "Basically it sucks," she confirmed.

"But isn't it just a little bit empowering?" Dr. McDaniels asked.

Dana Sue finally risked a look in Ronnie's direction. He thought he saw a spark of the old daredevil in her eyes and took heart.

"You know," she said at last, "I think it is. In fact, this could turn out to be fun."

"I'm not entirely sure I like the sound of that," Ronnie grumbled, mostly in jest.

"Well, get used to it, pal," Dana Sue said. "A new day is dawning."

Annie beamed at both of them. "Cool."

Yeah, Ronnie thought. It was pretty darn cool, and maybe just a little scary knowing that now it might be up to him not to blow the second chance Dana Sue was finally willing to give him.

20

Dana Sue was feeling pretty good about her breakthrough during the family counseling session. She was finally ready to move on, convinced she could handle whatever came next. If she and Ronnie tried and things didn't work out, well, so be it. She'd gotten over him—sort of, anyway—once before. She could do it again. And after listening to Annie's mature remarks in the session, she was starting to believe her daughter could weather a failure, as well.

After they'd dropped Annie off at home, she suggested a walk. As she and Ronnie started walking aimlessly, she deliberately slipped her sunglasses on—to shade her eyes from Ronnie's scrutiny, perhaps—then met his gaze. "So, what now?" she asked.

Ronnie's crooked smile spread slowly across his face. "I don't have a plan. Do you?"

She frowned at him. "That is so typical," she complained. "You've been hinting around for weeks now about wanting me back, and when I call you on it, you don't have any idea where we go next."

"Sugar, you took me by surprise back there. I've gotten so used to you putting up walls between us and me having to use all sorts of sneaky tactics to get around them, I hadn't considered what I'd do if you decided to flat-out knock them down."

"I didn't knock them down," she countered. "I created a tiny little crack, but you need to figure out how to wriggle through it. Let me know when you have a strategy."

She whirled around and walked away. No plan, indeed! The man was impossible. Maybe she'd just been a challenge to him, simply an instance of Ronnie wanting what he couldn't have. Now that the game was over, he probably didn't even want her anymore. He had his new business. He had his daughter back in his life. And he had Mary Vaughn fawning all over him. Flirting required a whole lot less commitment than a real relationship. That was probably more than enough to satisfy him.

Dana Sue had made it halfway down the block, her spine stiff and her temper stirring, when he caught up with her, spun her around and captured her mouth in a kiss that was hotter than the South Carolina sun at high noon. It wiped every thought, every trace of anger, right out of her head.

When he finally released her, she had to cling to his shoulders to remain upright. That and the need throbbing through her infuriated her all over again. She immediately lashed out at him.

"Making a public spectacle out of me is not the answer," she said irritably.

He grinned, his own sunglasses now firmly in place so she couldn't read the amusement no doubt glinting in his eyes. "That wasn't a spectacle, darlin'. That was a public declaration that we're back together."

Dana Sue bristled. "You're putting your brand on me like I'm some piece of Grade A beef?" she demanded indignantly.

His lips twitched. "I wouldn't put it exactly that way."

"No, it's not something I'd want to admit to, either," she said. "But that's what it amounted to, isn't it?"

"You know," he said casually, "it works both ways. You kissed me back, so now all the world knows I'm yours, too."

"Including Mary Vaughn?" Dana Sue asked, warming to that idea. If he thought she'd tolerate that budding friendship or collaboration or whatever it was, he needed to rethink that right now.

He stared at her blankly. "What does Mary Vaughn have to do with anything?"

"I've seen the way she is around you," Dana Sue said. "She wants you, Ronnie. Everyone in town knows her current relationship is on the skids and she's looking for a replacement. Seems to me like she's picked you."

He continued to look bemused. "Isn't she living with that guy? I think she said he's her boss."

"Technically, yes," Dana Sue conceded.

"What does that mean, 'technically'? Either she is or she isn't."

"It's sort of the way you were technically married to me when you went cruising around for someone else to sleep with," she retorted. "Like I said, the relationship is over, even if he hasn't moved out yet."

"Okay, that's it," Ronnie said, rising predictably to the bait. "Let's go." He latched on to her arm and started half dragging her down the sidewalk.

She tried digging in her heels, but he was bigger and stronger and obviously more irritated. "What is wrong with you?" she asked. "Where are we going?"

"To my motel room," he told her.

"I am not going to your motel room," she said, horrified by the prospect of that news spreading around town by lunchtime.

"Do you really want to go back to the house and have this fight in front of Annie?"

"I don't want to fight with you at all!"

"Well, when we're finished fighting and want to make up, I don't think we should be doing that around Annie, either," he said.

The heat that shot through Dana Sue had nothing to do with anger and everything to do with anticipation. That was more exasperating than anything else. Surely in two years she ought to have built up more of an immunity to this man.

"What makes you so sure we *will* make up?" she asked.

"Because it's what we do," he said dryly. "We fight. We make up. It's a cycle, one we might want to consider breaking one of these days. But I'm willing to tackle that notion later, if you are." His gaze challenged her. "Now, are you coming willingly, or do I have to throw you over my shoulder?"

She stared at him with shock. "You wouldn't dare," she began, then shook her head. "No, of course you would. Okay, I'm coming, but just to talk."

"Right," he said, his skepticism plain.

At the Serenity Inn, when Dana Sue would have stopped to chat with the owners, Ronnie's hand in the middle of her back steered her straight past them and toward his room.

"That was rude," she huffed.

"Did you really want to stand there and exchange small talk with them so they'll have even more hot news to report when they go to Wharton's for lunch?"

"Do you honestly think that rushing past them is going to stop that? Now they'll just tell everyone that we were so anxious to get to your room, we barely said hello. I'm sure folks will draw their own conclusions about that."

"Let them," Ronnie said tersely as he pushed open the door to his room. "Since you're so convinced that Mary

Vaughn is after me, maybe the news of our reunion will call a halt to any wild ideas she might be having."

"You're dreaming if you think that," Dana Sue replied as she followed him inside. "It'll just make you more of a challenge. Don't you know her at all?"

He grinned. "Not half as well as I know you."

She concentrated on surveying the room. To her surprise, it was reasonably tidy. There were no clothes strewn about, no towels left lying on the floor where he'd dropped them after his shower. The decor was a little flowery and feminine, which made Ronnie look all the more masculine by contrast.

Impulsively, Dana Sue sat on the edge of the bed, rather than in the room's only chair. Since she had a hunch about how this was going to go, she might as well not have far to move.

"Okay, what did you want to talk about?" she asked, her hands folded primly in her lap.

Ronnie looked amazingly uncertain, now that he had her here. His eyes traveled over her slowly, darkening with passion during the journey.

"You want anything to drink?" he asked, his voice oddly choked. "There's a vending machine just outside."

She shook her head. "I'm good."

"Candy? Chips?"

Now she knew he was nervous. Otherwise he would never be suggesting junk food. Ironically, she found that unfamiliar hint of uncertainty charming. Her annoyance began to fade.

"Maybe we should change the agenda," she suggested.

His gaze narrowed warily. "Oh?"

"You could join me on the bed, instead of hovering by the door, and we could make love. Then we could talk later." She shrugged. "You know, about whatever you had on your mind when you dragged me over here."

He shook his head. "No, I am not getting anywhere near that bed until you hear what I have to say. I want to put that betrayal of mine to rest once and for all."

She regarded him with regret. "That may not be possible."

"Then maybe we don't have a future, after all, Dana Sue," he said, so flatly that it left her shaken. "I won't go through the rest of our lives having you throw that in my face every time you get mad at me. I won't have you going into a tail-spin and imagining the worst every single time some woman looks at me twice."

"I know you're right," she said, feeling more scared than she'd been in years. Could they get this close to a reconciliation, only to blow it because of her stubborn inability to forget about the past? "I don't know why I can't just let it go."

"I imagine it's because I've never explained why it happened," he suggested. "And that's probably because I can't. I've tried telling you this before, but I'll do it again. There is no excuse, Dana Sue. I was drifting. I was looking for excitement without even realizing it. Something. I honestly can't explain it. I loved you with all my heart. I loved our life. I adored Annie, but on that night, when that woman came on to me, I felt a spark of something I hadn't felt in a long time. Maybe it was the danger, the risk of getting caught. I do know it had nothing to do with her and nothing to do with you. It was like she lit a match and touched it to something I didn't even know was flammable. It was the first and only time I was even remotely tempted to be unfaithful."

Dana Sue didn't know what to say to any of that. None of it made her feel any better. "If you don't know why that night was so different, how can you be sure it won't happen again?"

"Because in the last two years I finally learned to value what we had, instead of taking it for granted," he said candidly. "Practically from the day we met, I knew you were crazy about me. I guess I thought you'd forgive me anything. Or maybe I wanted to find out if you would." He shrugged. "I just don't know. I do know that I will never take a chance on ruining our relationship again. I want our life back, Dana Sue. I want *you* back."

The sincerity behind his words was real. She believed that's what he wanted, today, anyway. But what about tomorrow and the day after that? If what they'd had was so fantastic, and still he'd cheated, what would happen when they hit a bump in the road?

Life was all about taking risks, she reminded herself. She didn't have to take a giant leap of faith, just one small risk today and another tomorrow, until the days added up to something she could trust. Maybe she could do that much. She'd told Dr. McDaniels she could less than an hour ago. Was she already willing to make a liar of herself?

She held out her hand. "Come here," she said softly.

Ronnie stood where he was, regarding her worriedly. "Are we through talking?"

She smiled. Maybe he was no more of a risk-taker than she was, after all. "You'll have to take a chance," she told him, her hand still extended. "Come here and find out."

The mattress sank down when he lowered himself beside her, careful to keep some space between them.

She lifted the hand he'd ignored to his cheek, felt the quick rise of heat, the tense tic of a muscle working in his jaw.

"If you don't kiss me right now, Ronnie Sullivan, I think I'll explode," she said, her breath hitching.

"I'm afraid I'll explode if I do, especially if you change your mind."

"Not going to happen," she said with certainty. Not today, anyway. She realized she couldn't promise tomorrow yet any more than he could. And that was okay. Right now was all anyone really had.

"I love you," she whispered.

His smile was tinged with relief. "I love you, too," he said.

Then his mouth was on hers, his hands were sliding under her blouse, and the whole world went spinning.

Ronnie remembered now why Dana Sue was etched in his heart forever. No woman could possibly be more unselfish in bed, more passionate, more exuberant. Once she'd reached this point, she wasn't holding back. She was as eager a participant as he was, her hands wandering, her mouth a wicked tease against his skin.

Now that they were here, still clothed, but tangled together in his bed, their bodies fitting together so perfectly it took his breath away, he couldn't imagine why he'd ever sought out anything else. Not even the thrill of the unknown was any match for this.

Dana Sue seemed to hesitate when he reached for the buttons on her blouse. He lifted a brow. "Changing your mind?"

She shook her head, and this time he recognized that the color in her cheeks was from embarrassment, not passion. It was her weight again. He could see it in her eyes, the faint fear that he wouldn't like the body she had now.

His gaze locked with hers as he reached again for the top button on her blouse. This time he skimmed a finger along the bare skin at the base of her throat, felt her pulse jump. "One button?" he suggested.

"You never stop with just one," she said, her breath a little ragged.

Ronnie grinned. "Then let me get on with this," he said. "I love *you,* Dana Sue, every inch, every pound. If I wanted some skinny young thing, I'd be with her now, instead of here with you."

Still, she brushed his hands away from her blouse. "I should never have let my weight get so out of control," she said. "Especially when I know it's not good for my health."

Ronnie tucked a hand under her chin and forced her to face him. "If you're not happy about the way you look, then you can do something to change it. I'll stand behind you all the way. But don't make it about me, darlin'. I love looking at you. I love touching you and watching you come apart. You were a sexy, desirable girl when I met you, you were a sexy, desirable woman when I married you, and nothing about that has changed in the past twenty years. *Nothing!*"

There was so much hope in her eyes as she listened to him, it broke Ronnie's heart. "If you don't believe what I'm saying, let me show you," he pleaded.

At last she nodded, and this time when he slowly undid the buttons on her blouse and pushed the fabric aside, she shivered, but she didn't try to stop him. Ronnie couldn't seem to tear his gaze away. If anything, her body was lusher and more womanly than before. He traced the curves with his scarred and work-roughened fingers, feeling her skin burn beneath his touch. The faint scent of lavender filled his head, as familiar and intoxicating as the texture of her skin.

She was wearing an unadorned white bra, and her nipples were already hardened peaks beneath the material. He closed his mouth over one and heard her cry out in pleasure, then moan as he sampled the other one. She didn't protest when he unhooked the front closure and removed the bra, then gave her full breasts more attention. There'd been a time when she could come just from that—from his mouth teasing and taunting her sensitive nipples. Even now, her hips bucked against the mattress.

He shifted until he was covering her, her instinctive movements making him even harder, but he waited to reach for the snap on her slacks, waited until she was all but pleading before he slid down the zipper and reached inside to touch her hot, wet core. This time when she bucked, he felt her coming with an orgasm that ripped through her and almost shattered his own self-control.

Grinning, he met her gaze. "Now we can take our time and do this right," he teased, sliding her slacks and panties off, then lingering to caress her rounded hips and thighs so there would be no question that she still turned him on, that he still found her everything a woman should be.

Only then did he stand and shed his own clothes, coming back to her in less than a heartbeat, burying himself in her with a thrust that felt like coming home after a long, long absence. Locking gazes with her, he began to move, slowly, watching her eyes darken again, feeling her body respond to him, knowing the precise moment when control was about to slip away, and what to do to make it happen.

"I love you," he told her, even as he felt the waves of another climax wash through her, setting off his own.

And for the first time in two years, with Dana Sue wrapped in his arms, Ronnie finally felt at peace, as if his life made sense again.

Ronnie was still asleep when Dana Sue scrambled out of his bed and yanked on her clothes with jerky movements. She'd finally done it. She'd finally lost her mind and crawled back into bed with her ex-husband. And she'd done it wide-awake, stone-cold sober and in the middle of the day. That left her with no excuses, not a single one.

That was not the way this reconciliation was supposed to

go. She'd figured they'd date for a while, maybe he'd spend some time at the house with her and Annie. Then, after weeks and weeks of reassuring herself that he was a changed man, she'd take that final leap of faith and let him back into her bed.

It had been a foolish notion, she realized now. This afternoon had been inevitable from the second he'd shown up at the hospital. For two people who were supposedly mature adults, they never had possessed an ounce of restraint, not when it came to sleeping together. The only reason she'd still been a virgin up until graduation from high school was that Maddie and Helen had hardly ever left her alone with Ronnie, knowing she had absolutely no willpower when she was around him. That and Maddie whispering in his ear that the way to keep Dana Sue was to never let her get the upper hand, she remembered ruefully. He'd done his part to keep her at arm's length, at least until graduation night, when they'd come to this very motel room.

Sneaking out the door now, she closed it quietly and all but ran down the block, hoping to avoid any prying eyes.

How could she have been so stupid? She'd promised to give him a chance, not an invitation back into her bed, or his, to be more precise.

Maybe she was being ridiculous, she thought. Why not admit the man still had the ability to make her toes curl? And it *had* been reassuring—more than reassuring—to see that nothing had changed, even though she no longer saw herself as being sexy. Still, she'd had high hopes that they would put off this step till she'd lost weight and firmed up.

Instinctively, she headed for The Corner Spa. "That's sort of like closing the barn door after the cow is out," she muttered as she marched past Maddie's office and dragged on her workout clothes.

This time, instead of the treadmill, she headed for the weight machines. Unfortunately, she didn't have the slightest clue how to work them properly. She'd probably wind up pulling a muscle instead of toning it, she decided.

Frustrated, she looked around until she spotted Elliott, the only male allowed to cross the threshold of the women-only spa. A personal fitness trainer with abs like steel, dark hair and chocolate-brown eyes, he worked individually with quite a few of the spa's members and provided eye candy for all the rest. Until this moment, Dana Sue had been part of the latter contingent.

Crossing the gym, she waited until he'd finished instructing his current client, a white-haired woman of seventy who was curling ten-pound weights as if they were feathers. He winked at her when she'd finished the assigned repetitions.

"Nice work, Hazel," he said. "See you next week."

Hazel, bless her heart, pressed a little kiss to his cheek and rubbed her hand down the hard muscle of his forearm. "Elliott, you make me feel like a girl," she teased. "I swear if I were forty years younger, I'd be beating down your door."

Elliott laughed. "And what would your husband say about that?"

"Oh, that old coot," she said dismissively. "His cataracts are so bad he can't even see what's going on right in front of his nose. He'd never know a thing." She turned to Dana Sue. "You watch out for this one, honey. He is pure temptation."

Dana Sue grinned at her. The only man who tempted her was back in a motel room sound asleep. "I'll keep that in mind," she promised anyway.

Elliott turned his attention to her. "What's up, Dana Sue? You finally going to let me spend some time working with you?"

She knew he was teasing, because she'd already turned

down every offer he'd made to give her free personal training as thanks for the spa recommending him to its clients.

"As a matter of fact, yes," she said, clearly catching him
off guard.

"Now?" he suggested with an eagerness that amused her.

"You afraid I'll change my mind if we wait?" she asked.

"It wouldn't surprise me."

"Then let's do it," she said. "Remember, though, I have no
muscles to speak of."

"Thus the need for my help," he responded. "Let's start
with free weights. Pick up a couple of different weights and
tell me what feels comfortable."

She automatically reached for the two-pound weight.

"Oh, no, you don't," he scolded. "Try for five pounds at
least. You saw that Hazel was working with ten. Are you
going to let a senior citizen humiliate you?"

"I'm not proud," Dana Sue said, but she picked up the
weight he suggested.

Thirty minutes later, she'd decided she hated Hazel and Elliott, as well as Helen and Maddie. Every muscle ached, including ones she didn't know she had.

"Why do people do this to themselves?" she moaned, sitting on a bench and mopping her brow with a towel Elliott
handed her.

"To shape up and live longer," he said. "It'll be easier
next time."

"Maybe there won't be a next time," she responded.

He sat down on the opposite end of the bench, his skin taut,
his muscles bulging. "What brought you in here today?" he
asked. "I've been after you since this place opened its doors,
and you've blown me off every time."

She thought of the shame she'd felt when Ronnie had seen

her naked for the first time. Not that he'd shown even a hint of revulsion, but she'd felt her own self-loathing deep inside. Only Ronnie's kindness and her own grim determination not to bolt had kept her in that bed. Okay, and the need that had been burning inside her, too.

"I just decided it was time," she said eventually.

"I heard about that contest you have going with Maddie and Helen. I know regular exercise was on your list of goals. Maddie let me sneak a peak. Have you decided you want to win?"

Dana Sue thought of the convertible she could claim if she did, then shook her head. "Actually, that's the least of it."

"I see." Elliott gave her a knowing look. "New man in your life?"

"Old one, if you must know," she said, knowing the news would be all over town in no time, anyway.

"One motivation is as good as another, as long as you don't give up," he said. "It would be better, though, if you were doing this for yourself, to make you healthier and more fit."

"Maybe I'd better focus on Ronnie for the time being," she retorted candidly. "Because if it were up to me right this second, you'd never see me again."

"Okay, then," he said briskly. "It's all about Ronnie. I can live with that. See you on Monday, same time?"

A thousand excuses came to mind, but she shoved them all back down. "Sure," she said grudgingly. "Is it okay if I hate you, though?"

"You won't be the first," he assured her. "Just know that I live for the day when that attitude changes, and it will, Dana Sue. It will."

"In this lifetime?" she asked doubtfully.

"Give it two months," he said. "By Christmas you're going to think I'm the best thing to happen in your life since Annie was born. And I've seen you with your daughter. I know how you dote on her."

"Right now, I have to tell you that the pain you've inflicted on me is more comparable to childbirth."

"Two months," he repeated. "I'll take you shopping for a slinky new dress myself."

Dana Sue's skepticism didn't fade, but once again she thought of the bet she had going with Helen and Maddie. If Elliott was right, maybe that convertible wasn't as far out of reach as she'd thought. An image of her skinny new self driving around town with the top down and Ronnie by her side came to mind. Yeah. Maybe she could do this, after all.

21

With Annie much improved and about to go back to school after taking six weeks off, the kitchen at Sullivan's became Dana Sue's safe haven. Grateful to be back in a familiar routine, she was spending more and more time there, when she wasn't at the gym working with Elliott, or meeting with Helen and Maddie. The three friends got together for coffee or tea, and an update on the progress each was making toward their goals, at least three mornings a week. Sometimes Maddie's new baby came along on the days when she couldn't bear to leave Jessica Lynn with a sitter.

So far, all of them were doing better with meeting their exercise goals. Dana Sue had lost five pounds and Maddie had toned up her abs.

On this late-October morning the focus was on Helen, who'd just announced she had turned down a client in Charleston because the case would have taken too much of her time.

Maddie and Dana Sue stared at her in astonishment before toasting her achievement with tall glasses of unsweetened, caffeine-free iced tea.

"Way to go, Helen!" they chorused.

"How did it feel to say no?" Maddie asked.

"It made my stomach hurt," she admitted. "What if word

gets out that I'm not taking new cases, and I wind up with no clients at all?"

"What if it enhances your reputation that you are now taking on only a select few clients?" Dana Sue retorted. "People in need of the best will be clamoring to see you. You'll be able to charge a fortune."

"I already charge a fortune," Helen said, the corners of her mouth twitching upward.

"Still, this is very, very good," Maddie told her. "We'll help you come up with exactly the right marketing spin to use."

Then, before Dana Sue could get too comfortable being out of the spotlight, Maddie turned to her. "And you—how many pounds have you lost?"

"None since last time," Dana Sue confessed, trying to hide her disappointment at the scale's refusal to budge beyond the five pounds she'd lost fairly quickly. "But speaking of spin, I *am* toning up. Elliott keeps reminding me that muscle weighs more than fat and inches are what count. My chef jackets are getting looser. Pretty soon, they'll be too big. I'm going to have to take up sewing."

"Just buy new ones when you need them," Maddie said. "I remember the disaster you made of that skirt in home ec back in high school. I recommend you not even pick up a needle and thread."

Dana Sue laughed. "Mrs. Watkins said she'd never seen a more crooked hem, and I never could get the zipper aligned so it would close."

"My point exactly," Maddie said. "You need a professional jacket to impress your clientele. You look great, by the way! I imagine Ronnie's very excited about the new you."

Dana Sue blushed. "He seemed to like me well enough before."

"Any talk about what happens next with you two?" Maddie asked, then looked away when Jessica Lynn whimpered in her carrier. Maddie picked the baby up and patted her on the back.

Dana Sue shook her head. "It's like a twelve-step program in reverse. We're taking it one day at a time, but instead of trying to live without something, we're trying to see if we can live *with* each other."

Helen gave her a penetrating look. "If it's going all that smoothly, why are you hiding out at Sullivan's all the time?"

"I own it. I'm not hiding out there," Dana Sue said, immediately defensive. "I relied on Erik and Karen too much for too long. Now that Annie's a little better, I need to get back on the job. Besides, Karen seems to keep having little crises with her kids. I know that's the risk of having a single mom on staff, but her repeated absences are starting to worry me. Erik can't handle everything on his own, so I really do need to be there."

Helen shook her head. "Not buying it. I think you're avoiding Ronnie. What I don't understand is why."

"Maybe he's avoiding me," Dana Sue said tightly.

"Hold on a sec," Maddie said, looking from one to the other. "I thought things were working out. The whole town knows you're back together." She paused and raised a brow. "Well, except for Mary Vaughn, but she tends to be delusional when she has a man in her sights. As long as Ronnie's your ex and not your husband, she'll see him as fair game."

Helen frowned. "Gee, that must be reassuring for Dana Sue to hear."

"Sorry," Maddie said. "But we all know how Mary Vaughn operates. Including Ronnie. I don't see him falling for it." She turned back to Dana Sue. "Besides, for a couple of weeks there you and Ronnie were inseparable. What changed?"

Dana Sue blinked back unexpected tears. "I have no idea. All of a sudden it's all about his new business. He's at the hardware store for hours and hours every day. Annie's in there helping him, now that she's back on her feet. When he's not painting and cleaning and going through wholesale catalogs, he's running around with Mary Vaughn."

Maddie and Helen exchanged a look.

"I knew that's what this was about," Maddie said. "You're jealous. You're terrified that Mary Vaughn will sink her claws into Ronnie, and instead of protecting your turf, you're walking away from the fight. Why don't you just let him move back in?"

"It's too soon," Dana Sue said, then sighed. "Besides, that won't solve anything. Every time I lay eyes on the two of them with their heads together, I lose it. If I'm in the kitchen at Sullivan's, I don't see what's going on."

"How's that working for you?" Helen asked. "Are you any less jealous? Any less scared? Hasn't it occurred to you that if there *was* anything going on between those two, it wouldn't be happening right under your nose? Ronnie may be a lot of things, but he's not stupid. After what occurred two years ago, he's not going to be in your face with some other woman. I may not be his biggest fan, but even I can see this has to be innocent, at least on his part. Besides, you said yourself that Annie's over there with them. Do you honestly think he'd flaunt a relationship with Mary Vaughn around her?"

"You could have a point," Dana Sue conceded grudgingly.

"Maybe you should just march over to the hardware store and ask what you can do to help," Maddie suggested. "Make yourself part of his dream."

"I don't know the first thing about hammers and bolts and toilet-repair kits," she said.

"You could learn," Maddie said. "I doubt that Mary Vaughn gets all warm and fuzzy at the thought of tools, either. But she obviously gets all turned on by your ex-husband."

Helen shot a warning look at her. "Not helping," she said. "Next thing you know Dana Sue will be over there with a carving knife."

"Believe me, I've been tempted," she admitted.

"What's held you back, aside from the law?" Helen asked.

"Just like you said, Ronnie has sworn to me that Mary Vaughn means absolutely nothing to him, that she's just helping him to make some business contacts. I might be white-knuckling it, but I am trying to trust what he says."

"Trust is all well and good, but I'd want to see the evidence for myself," Helen said. "I'd be in their faces twenty-four-seven if that's what it took to reassure myself that those two aren't collaborating on anything besides business."

Dana Sue shook her head. "I have to start trusting him sometime or it will never work between us."

But even as she said the words, she realized that she simply wasn't there yet. Not wanting to dwell on her insecurities for another second, she turned to Maddie.

"How are you feeling? It looks as if you've lost a few pounds of pregnancy weight."

Maddie shrugged. "It's very slow going, but I'm trying not to let that discourage me. I keep reminding myself that chasing after a toddler will take off whatever weight I haven't lost in the meantime." She held Jessica Lynn up in the air. "This is the only weight-lifting I do, right, baby girl?"

The baby gurgled happily.

"I always thought I'd be chasing after a couple of rug rats by now," Helen said, her expression surprisingly wistful.

Dana Sue shot an I-told-you-so look at Maddie.

"You've never talked about wanting children before," Maddie stated. "Not in all the years we've known you."

"What was the point?" Helen said. "Everybody knows I'm married to my career. It's too late now."

"It most definitely is not too late to have a baby, if you want one," Maddie told her gently. "Look at me."

"But you have a man in your life," Helen responded. "I have a client list in mine."

"If you want a baby, you can make it happen," Maddie insisted. "There are lots of options. You could find a willing partner, you could have artificial insemination or you could adopt."

Helen shook her head. "I always thought I'd do it the old-fashioned way, but time just got away from me."

Dana Sue could relate to that. She covered Helen's hand with her own. "Don't give up yet. The right man could be just around the corner. Your situation's not like mine. Ronnie and I couldn't have another baby even if we wanted to. It would be too dangerous."

"Because of the diabetes," Maddie said. "I hadn't thought of that."

"It was always there," Dana Sue admitted. "Even when I had Annie, there was some concern. My blood sugar spiked then, but they figured it was gestational, and we kept it under control. Now that it's a real threat, there's no way I can risk another pregnancy. And with everything else going on— Ronnie's new business, keeping up with Sullivan's, keeping an eye on Annie—another baby simply isn't in the cards."

She hadn't realized until just now how much she regretted that. She held out her arms. "Give me a turn with that sweet little thing." She cradled Jessica Lynn and was carried back sixteen years to when she'd held a freshly bathed and powdered Annie. "God, this brings back memories."

"My turn," Helen said, reaching eagerly to take the baby, and cooing at her. Jessica Lynn, her blue eyes wide, gurgled happily back at her, then grabbed for a chunk of Helen's hair and tugged. Helen patiently extracted the little fist.

"I want this," she whispered, her face filled with raw emotion. "Why didn't I know before now just how badly?"

"Because you haven't let yourself think about anything except your career for years," Maddie told her. "Now that you're trying to get some balance into your life and you've opened yourself to other possibilities, there it is."

She reached out and patted Helen's hand. "Don't give up. A lot of us had dreams when we were young that we put on the back burner, only to wake up one day and realize it may be too late. I went to college and got a business degree, but it was nothing more than a piece of paper for nearly twenty years while I spent all my time supporting Bill's career and raising a family." She gestured around them. "Now, thanks to the two of you, I'm a part of this. It's not the same as realizing you want a baby, but I get where you're coming from."

Helen returned her sympathetic look with a wounded expression. "Why didn't you tell me? Why weren't the two of you all over my case before now?"

Dana Sue could barely swallow the laugh that bubbled up. "What would you have done if we'd tried?"

"Which we did, by the way," Maddie added. "How many men did we try to get you to take more seriously, or at least to go out with more than once?"

Helen sank back in her chair. "I told you to butt out, didn't I?"

"About a thousand and one times," she confirmed.

"Sometimes you're kind of hardheaded," Dana Sue commented.

"Kind of?" Maddie said.

Helen regarded them with a faint spark of hope in her eyes. "You really think it's not too late?"

Maddie gave her a wry look. "I just wouldn't spend the next year doing a pros and cons analysis, the way you usually do. However you decide to approach it, this is a project that needs to be on the front burner, okay? Make an appointment with Doc Marshall."

Helen looked horrified. "I can't talk to him about this. He's still freaked about my blood pressure. He'll just tell me no."

"If that's an issue, any other doctor will tell you the same thing," Dana Sue said reasonably.

Helen's jaw set determinedly. "I'll consult a high-risk-pregnancy specialist," she said at once, handing Jessica Lynn off to Maddie. She dragged out her day planner and jotted down a note. "I'll do it as soon as I get to the office."

"Do you actually *know* a high-risk-pregnancy specialist?" Maddie inquired tactfully.

"No, but I can find one. In case you haven't heard, research is one of my specialties."

Dana Sue grinned at Maddie. "She'll know the medical malpractice records of every ob-gyn in the state by noon."

"And have references on the rest by midafternoon," Maddie added.

"Mock me if you must," Helen said, taking a final sip of her iced tea. "I can still tell it's decaf," she said, making a face, then sighing. "Remind me tomorrow that I'm giving up caffeine completely, even the one cup of coffee I've been allowing myself in the morning. It's probably not good for babies, right?"

"You could be getting a little ahead of yourself," Dana Sue said, but at Helen's daunting look, she held up a hand. "No more caffeine. Got it. It's not good for you in any case."

After Helen had breezed out of the spa like a woman on a mission, Dana Sue exchanged a glance with Maddie. "Do you think she's really serious about this?"

"I think she hit the biological clock panic button this morning," Maddie said, a worried frown on her face. "Knowing Helen, the alarm will keep going off till she's solved the problem to her satisfaction."

"And that means taking a bouncing baby home from the hospital," Dana Sue concluded.

"Seems that way to me."

"Maybe we should remind her that a few weeks ago all she could talk about was going on a wild shopping spree in Paris," Dana Sue suggested.

"I think maybe we just need to stand by and support her in whatever she decides," Maddie said. "That's what she's done for us."

Dana Sue nodded. "You have a point, but I keep envisioning a two-year-old with a briefcase in one hand and a cell phone in the other."

The disconcerting image made both of them smile.

Ronnie had made an appointment with Helen two weeks earlier. He had a hunch if he'd spoken to her directly, he'd never have made it onto her calendar, but her secretary seemed oblivious to any issues between them.

When he was finally admitted to her office, he wasn't sure what sort of welcome to expect, but it wasn't the feverish, distracted look on the lawyer's face as she waved him to a chair.

"I just have to finish this search," she murmured, her gaze immediately returning to the computer on her desk.

Ronnie sat down and waited. And waited.

"Um, Helen, would it be better if I came back another

time?" he asked, after fifteen minutes of hearing nothing but
the click of her fingers on the keyboard.

She blinked and looked at him with surprise. "Ronnie?
What are you doing here?"

That wasn't what he'd expected, either. "We have an appointment, remember?"

She blinked again. "Why? I'm Dana Sue's attorney. I can't
represent you."

"Not even on this business deal I'm doing?" he asked.

"Why would you want me to?" she said. "You're not exactly my favorite person."

"I'd say that's an understatement, but I was hoping that
might be starting to change. Besides, you're the best attorney
in the area and that's what I need."

The compliment seemed to catch her attention. "Okay, talk
to me. I'm not saying yes, just that I'll listen. You have ten
minutes. I have another appointment at three-thirty."

"Since you wasted fifteen minutes of my appointment
doing whatever you were doing on the computer, I'm sure you
won't mind if we run over," he retorted.

She gave him a startled look, then grinned. "You've
changed. You're tougher."

"I prefer to think of it as more businesslike, something you
should appreciate."

"I do, actually. Okay, start talking."

He explained his arrangement with Butch Thompson, then
handed over a file. "Here are the contracts his attorney drew
up. I trust Butch implicitly, but I also know enough not to sign
anything until it's been looked over by someone representing
my interests."

"Absolutely," she said.

"And so you know, this isn't a one-shot deal. If everything

goes the way I'm hoping, there will be contracts with developers throughout the region that will need to be drawn up. I'd like you to do that, as well."

Helen nodded and turned her attention to the contract, jotting notes to herself as she read. "It's a fair deal," she said at last. "At least on the surface. I'd like to go through it again tonight. Can I bring it by the hardware store tomorrow? I'd like to see what you're doing there, anyway."

"Of course," he said, relieved she hadn't shown him the door. "By the way, can I ask what you were doing when I got here? You seemed awfully absorbed in your Internet search. Big case?"

To his astonishment, color bloomed in her cheeks. The ever-confident, often arrogant Helen actually looked embarrassed. Was she trying Internet dating, perhaps?

"Just a personal project," she admitted, which made the whole computer dating thing seem even more likely, if unexpected.

"Okay," he said, not pushing it. He wondered if Dana Sue knew anything about whatever Helen was up to.

As if she'd read his mind, she gave him a hard look. "Don't try prying it out of Dana Sue, either. It's personal."

"Got it," he said, and grinned. "Whatever it is has put a real sparkle in your eyes. I hope it works out."

She regarded him with surprise. "You almost sound as if you mean that."

"I do. Why wouldn't I?"

"I was pretty hard on you during the divorce and since you've been back in town," she said.

"You were protecting Dana Sue," he countered. "I can appreciate that. And by the way, I don't intend to hurt her again."

Helen sat back and studied him, then asked, "Okay, assuming I give you the benefit of the doubt about that, where does Mary Vaughn fit in?"

"She doesn't," he said without hesitation.

"Really? I hear she's spending a lot of time at the hardware store."

"She volunteered to give me a hand. If I'm going to open before Christmas, I need all the help I can get. Should I have turned her down?"

"That depends on how serious you are about not hurting Dana Sue again. Just a word of advice? If Mary Vaughn really isn't an issue, you might want to work a little harder to make sure Dana Sue knows that," Helen said. "Mary Vaughn, too. Otherwise I'm afraid I might have to defend your ex-wife on an assault and battery charge."

"Really?" he asked, taken aback. "She's that jealous?"

"You never heard it from me," Helen told him. "And if I were you, I'd wipe that smug expression off your face before you say anything to her about it."

"Duly noted," he said. "I'll take care of that tonight."

"It might bear repeating. This is Dana Sue, after all."

He laughed. "From now till doomsday, if that's what it takes."

She actually smiled. "There must be something wrong with me," she said. "I'm starting to like you, Ronnie Sullivan."

"Ditto, Helen Decatur."

"I'll see you tomorrow," she promised. "Now tell my secretary to send in my next client. Otherwise I'll wind up being here till midnight, and I've made a vow to stop doing that."

"Who's holding you to that?" he asked curiously.

"Your ex-wife, for one. Maddie, for another."

"Take it from a man who's learned a little something about vows," he said. "It'll go better when you start holding your own feet to the fire."

* * *

Annie felt like an idiot. She was going back to school today, and her mom was hovering as if she was going off on a trip to Mars.

"Mom, it's not like it's my first day of kindergarten," she protested. "I've been to school before. I know the kids. I know the teachers. I've done my homework. So chill, okay?"

"It's a big deal," her mom protested. "You haven't been there in six weeks."

"Summer vacation's longer than that and you don't go all weird when I go back in September."

"This is different," she insisted.

"The doctors all tell me I'm ready," Annie said in exasperation. "Even Dr. McDaniels, and you know she doesn't cut me any slack. You're the only one who's not ready for this."

"Your dad's a little nervous, too," her mom told her. "He'll be here any minute."

Annie regarded her with dismay. "And then what? Are you two going to hold my hands and walk me to school?"

Her mom grinned. "Don't give me any attitude or we might decide that's a wonderful idea."

"Mom!"

"We just thought it would be nice if we had a family breakfast before you left."

Annie felt her stomach clench. "I don't need you to watch me to make sure I eat," she said irritably. "We are so past that."

"This isn't about your anorexia. It's about the three of us being together on an important day," her mother responded. "You know we always made a big deal about this kind of thing."

Annie regarded her suspiciously. "And that's all this is?"

"I swear it," she said, sketching a cross over her heart.

"You look nice, by the way. That blue is a great color on you. It matches your eyes."

"You don't think it's too tight?" Annie asked worriedly. "I've gained some weight since I bought it."

"No, it's a perfect fit now. Very flattering."

Annie spun around in front of the full-length mirror on the back of her bedroom door, something she wouldn't have done a few months ago. She felt a momentary pang of uncertainty, a faint flicker of the old fear of being too fat, but then she looked—really looked—at herself, the way Ty had made her look in the mirror at the hospital. There was no question that she looked healthier now. If anything, she was still a little on the thin side, but her color was better and her hair had more shine and bounce since her mom had sprung for the works at a salon in Charleston Helen recommended. The three of them had gone together. Her mom had even gotten a few highlights in her own hair. They made her look younger.

Impulsively, Annie turned and gave her mother a fierce hug. "I know I get mad when you and Dad are on my case, but don't stop, okay?"

"We will never stop looking out for you," her mother promised, returning her hug.

Annie stepped back and surveyed her with interest. "You've lost weight."

"More inches than weight," her mom corrected, then held up her arm and flexed her bicep. "Look, a real muscle."

Annie laughed. "Awesome. Are you working out at the spa?"

"Every day except Sunday," her mom confessed. "Treadmill three days, weights the other three. Elliott's pushing me hard."

"The personal trainer?"

"Yes."

"Whoa!" Annie said. "Has Dad gotten a look at that guy?"

Her mom looked puzzled by the question. "No, why?"

"Because he's seriously hot. I don't know if Dad would want you hanging out with him."

"It's not your dad's decision," she retorted.

Annie reconsidered the situation. "You know, it could be a good thing. If Dad got a look at Elliott, he might hurry up and ask you to marry him again."

"Hold on," her mom protested. "Your dad and I are not even close to discussing getting married again."

"You should be," Annie declared. "Everyone knows you belong together. You're just wasting time."

"We're being cautious," her mom countered. "It might have been a good idea if we'd taken things slower way back when."

"But then you might not have had me, or I'd be, like, twelve or something."

"True," her mom said. "But things turned out exactly the way they were supposed to turn out. And," she added pointedly, "they will this time, too."

"I still think you ought to make sure Dad gets a look at Elliott," Annie said. "It could speed things along."

In fact, since her mom seemed so reluctant to stir things up, maybe it was something *she* could handle. When people got as old as her mom and dad, they didn't have time to waste.

22

All thoughts of matchmaking for her mom and dad fled the instant Annie set foot inside her school. On some level, she felt the way she had on her first day of kindergarten, and she almost wished her parents had insisted on coming with her, after all. Everything seemed kind of surreal and unfamiliar, as if she'd never met any of these people or attended a single class. Even the smells seemed different, though floor wax and chalk dust still permeated the air.

Worse, she felt as though everyone was staring and whispering. In fact, she *knew* they were, because of the silence that fell as she passed by. She told herself it shouldn't matter, that the kids who knew her and cared about her had already been around to show their support. The rest were simply eager to have something to talk about—the girl who'd nearly died from not eating. She just happened to be *today's* news; it was scarier than most because it could have happened to any of them.

Still, even though she understood, there was a huge temptation to bolt just to get away from the speculative stares. The second she considered doing exactly that, Sarah and Raylene materialized beside her.

"You ready for the history test?" Sarah asked, as if this was any other day and not a whole six weeks since the last time Annie had been in class.

"Not me," Raylene responded, moaning. "I hate history. Who can remember all those dates? And why should we care, anyway?"

Annie grinned at Sarah and together they recited the teacher's favorite saying, "Those who don't understand history are doomed to repeat it."

Raylene merely rolled her eyes. "As if I'm going to be in a position to declare war on anybody."

"You could be in Congress some day," Annie said. "You're smart enough."

"Puh-leeze," Raylene said with a toss of her hair, then grinned. "Of course, I could be *married* to a congressman."

"You just set women's lib back by twenty years," Sarah said with a groan. "Don't you have any ambition for yourself?"

"To marry well," Raylene said. "Ask my mother. It's the only thing that counts, which is why I am going to have to go through with this whole stupid debutante thing." She stuck her finger in her mouth. "Gag me."

Annie regarded her with surprise. "You're going to have a ball and all that kind of stuff?"

"That's what they tell me. My grandparents in Charleston have it all arranged. I even have to take some stupid classes in the 'social graces,' whatever those are."

Sarah giggled. "Do they have any idea what a challenge it's going to be to turn you into a lady?"

Raylene scowled at her. "Bite me."

"It could be fun," Annie said thoughtfully. "I'd do it if I had the chance."

"No way," Sarah said.

Raylene grinned. "She just wants a chance to ask Ty to some fancy dance."

Sarah nodded. "Now, that I can believe."

Annie grinned back at them. "So bite *me*," she said, suddenly feeling like a normal kid again.

"I wish we could do it together," Raylene said wistfully. "If we did, maybe I could get through it without puking."

Sarah grinned at her. "I imagine one of the first things they'll teach you is to stop talking about puking in public."

"It's better than *doing* it in public," Raylene countered. "Come on, guys, we'd better get to class. Mr. Grainger takes off points if we're late, and I'm going to need all the points on this test I can get."

Both girls linked their arms through Annie's as they hurried down the hall. It made walking into class a thousand times easier, Annie thought, grateful to both of them.

"Welcome back," Mr. Grainger said when Annie had taken her seat.

That was it, and then he was handing out test questions, and Annie was officially back in school. It didn't mean there wouldn't be times the rest of the day when she was aware of stares and whispers, but the worst was behind her. Best of all, there was the chance she would run into Ty at lunch. And her dad was back in town for good. Life was better than she'd ever imagined it could be a couple of months ago.

Dana Sue stared at Ronnie across the kitchen table. "How do you think she's doing at school?" she asked for what had to be the tenth time.

"Probably a whole lot better than she was when you were hovering over her an hour ago," he said.

"Of course I was hovering," she exclaimed. "Don't try to

convince me you didn't want to keep her right here where we could keep an eye on her."

"Never denied it," he said. "But now that she's gone, you and I could use this time to do something for ourselves."

She studied him with a narrowed gaze. "Such as?" she asked warily. "If you're thinking about sex at nine o'clock in the morning, there must be something wrong with you."

"I think about sex whenever I look at you," he said. "Doesn't matter what time it is. But actually, I was thinking we could go down to the store and you could pick out some paint for the trim on the house."

She stared at him blankly, vaguely disappointed. Despite her comment, sex was never far from her mind lately, either. "This house? You want to paint the trim on this house?"

"It needs it, in case you haven't noticed."

"But painting it is not your responsibility," she said. "I just haven't gotten around to hiring someone."

"Why hire a painter when I'm here and willing, and I own a hardware store where I can get the paint wholesale?"

"That's too much logic in one sentence coming from you," she said. "It makes me nervous."

"Me offering to paint the house makes you nervous? Why?"

"Because something tells me it's like the camel getting his nose under the edge of the tent. Next thing I know you'll decide the bedroom needs paint and right after that you'll want to test the mattress."

Ronnie laughed. "You haven't let me anywhere near our bedroom since I got back to town. I have no idea if it needs painting or not."

"It does, but you're not going to do it," she said stubbornly. "I'll get around to it eventually."

"Eventually might be soon enough for the bedroom, but it's

not for the exterior. Stop getting all weird over a few cans of paint and come with me to pick it out."

"You're determined to do this, aren't you?"

"Yes, I am," he said somberly. "Very determined."

"You could pick it out yourself," she suggested.

"And risk your wrath if I get it wrong? I don't think so," he countered. "Besides, maybe you should give this some thought. Be daring. Paint the trim shocking pink or something."

Despite her reluctance to go forward with this project at all, a memory of the first time she and Ronnie had worked side by side to fix up the house came back to her and had her smiling. "As I recall, the first time you and I painted the trim, we got more paint on ourselves than we did on the house."

"Which is why I'd paint it all by myself this time," he teased. "You were too much of a distraction in your cute little shorts and tank top."

Dana Sue rolled her eyes. "Okay, you can paint it, but I think shocking pink might be a little over-the-top."

"Ah, you're still in your stodgy, traditional phase," he noted. "I thought you'd be past the stage when our house has to look like every other house on the block."

"I am not stodgy," Dana Sue said.

"Oh, please, who are you trying to kid? Annie had to plead with you before you agreed to paint the shutters bright blue instead of black."

Dana Sue frowned. "I don't remember that."

"Then you've conveniently blocked it from your memory," he said. "Come on, sugar, there's a whole color palette down at the store with your name on it. Besides, you haven't even been by to see the changes I've made. I want to know what you think."

She was surprised by the hint of hurt in his voice. "Really? It's the first time you've invited me."

"Silly me," he said. "I thought maybe you'd be interested enough to drop on by with Annie."

"Maybe we both need to stop assuming things and just ask for what we want," she said.

"I want you to stop dillydallying and to come with me," he said plainly.

She grinned. "Okay, then, let's go look at paint. And just so you know, I will try really, really hard not to tell you how to rearrange the displays once I've seen them."

"Thank God," he said with exaggerated relief. "Helen's already offered her two cents. She would have had the whole place torn apart and reorganized, if Annie hadn't hustled her out the door."

"Helen's seen it?" she asked, surprised.

"She brought by some papers the other day," he said. "Didn't I tell you she's handling the legal work for the business?"

Dana Sue frowned. "You didn't mention it and neither did she."

"You don't object, do you?"

"No, why would I?"

"You sound a little ticked off," he commented.

"Because neither of you saw fit to tell me," she said. "Is Maddie somehow involved in all of this, as well? Maybe you're thinking of hiring her as manager?"

Ronnie leaned down and kissed her hard. "While Maddie would be an excellent manager, I can't afford her. Stop feeling slighted. You're the only one who's had a personal invitation to tour the place before the grand opening, and the only one for whom the owner is going to paint a house personally."

"That's something, I guess."

"Based on my usual rates for that kind of job, it's quite a lot," he taunted. He held the kitchen door open and waited impatiently as she hunted for her purse and followed him out. "Shake a leg, sugar. If we don't hurry up, the window of opportunity for me to make good on the offer is going to slam shut. I have almost no time for myself now and once I open the store, my time's not going to be my own for a while."

"I see," she said, feeling somehow deflated by the news and by the fact that he didn't seem the least bit disappointed that there would be no time for the two of them.

He glanced over at her after he got behind the wheel of his pickup. "Stop fretting, Dana Sue. You and Annie will still be my number-one priority."

"You sure about that?" she asked doubtfully.

"Oh, that's right, I was thinking of sneaking off to Myrtle Beach with Mary Vaughn for a couple of weeks," he said.

Dana Sue scowled at him. "You are so not funny."

"And you so don't have anything to worry about," he countered. "I…love…you. Only you, okay?"

She finally allowed herself to relax. "Okay," she said meekly. "If that changes—"

"It's not going to change," he said, cutting her off. "Not ever."

Impulsively, she reached across the console and linked her fingers through his. Some of his strength and certainty seemed to seep into her then.

"You know," she said, tracing a slow, tantalizing circle in the middle of his palm. "The paint will still be there in an hour, won't it?"

He gave her a startled look. "You want to…?"

"Oh, yeah," she said.

Ronnie whipped his pickup around the turn to the Serenity Inn so fast she was almost thrown from her seat.

"I guess that's a yes," she said, grinning as he skidded to a stop in front of his room.

A day that had started with worry and uncertainty had just taken a substantial turn for the better.

Just as he'd warned might happen, Ronnie was so caught up with staying on Annie's case and getting his business up and running that he barely crossed paths with Dana Sue during the first two weeks of November. When they did happen to meet, he forced himself to do little more than kiss her senseless and keep on moving. The kisses were reminders of everything good between them. He figured it was going to take him opening the store and making a go of it to prove to her that he wasn't going anywhere again. Even though their relationship had heated up considerably, he was smart enough to know that it would take more than hot sex to make her accept him back into her life for good.

Somehow he had to find a way to prove to her that everything he needed was right here in Serenity—a career he could get excited about, a daughter he was crazy about and the only woman he'd ever craved with every fiber of his being. A woman who most definitely was *not* Mary Vaughn.

By working practically around the clock himself, and with a lot of help from Annie and the ever-present Mary Vaughn, who wouldn't take his hints discouraging her, he was actually running ahead of schedule. He was opening the business on Saturday, almost a whole week before Thanksgiving, rather than the pre-Christmas launch he'd been envisioning. Maybe after this weekend he could get serious about his pursuit of Dana Sue.

"Dad, when are you going to ask Mom to marry you again?" Annie asked as she put up the crepe-paper streamers she'd insisted on for the store's grand opening.

"Maybe I thought I'd wait till she asks me," he teased.

Sherryl Woods

"Are you nuts?" Annie demanded, regarding him with a thoroughly disgusted expression. "Don't you know her at all? She will never do that. It's not romantic enough. You need to sweep her off her feet."

He grinned at his daughter, grateful to see that she was no longer just skin and bones. She'd gained a few pounds and her cheeks had a healthy glow. The glow seemed to increase a thousandfold whenever Ty was around, which he would be any minute now. She'd apparently coerced him into helping her decorate. Ronnie would have opened the doors without fanfare, but Annie and Dana Sue had conspired on the decorations and on catering the whole thing.

"You're wrong about what your mom needs," he told Annie. "She doesn't need grand gestures and romance from me. She needs to see I'm in this for the long haul. And she needs to believe I'm not going to start looking elsewhere just because she's gained a little weight, or for any other reason."

Annie frowned at him. "Haven't you even noticed that she's toning up?"

"Well, of course I have," he said, though he wasn't about to explain to his sixteen-year-old daughter that a man knew just about all there was to know about his wife's body. Okay, ex-wife, but that was a technicality he'd remedy when the time was right.

"Have you seen her trainer yet?" Annie asked, carefully avoiding his gaze. "Mom works with him a lot. He's a real hunk."

"Is that so?" Ronnie said neutrally, even though his blood pressure spiked at the image.

"A total hottie," Annie confirmed gleefully.

"You wouldn't be trying to make me jealous, would you?" he inquired, regarding her with amusement. "Because jealousy is actually a very damaging trait in a relationship, especially for your mom and me."

"Why?" Annie asked, frowning.

"Because of what happened before," he reminded her. "Trust is a pretty big deal with us right now. I wouldn't start messing with that, if I were you."

Annie regarded him guiltily. "I never thought of that. Sorry."

He gave her shoulder a squeeze. "Not to worry. It's just something you should think about before you start trying to matchmake."

"I just want you guys back together before you're too old to do stuff, you know?"

Ronnie almost choked at the comment, but recovered without giving himself away. "I don't think that's something you need to worry about," he said when he could get the words out without chuckling.

"Well, what's holding things up?" she demanded, handing him the end of a streamer while she climbed nimbly up a ladder. "You love her, right? And I know she still loves you." Annie stretched and slapped the streamer up with some tape, then scampered right back down.

"We're still working on the whole trust thing," he said. "And she needs to know that I am not going anywhere ever again, at least not without the two of you."

Annie nodded sagely. "Okay, I get it. *That's* why you're opening this place, instead of just getting another construction job."

"Exactly."

"I think a flower shop might have impressed her more. She loves flowers, but I don't think she gets all that worked up over hammers and paint," Annie said, her expression filled with doubt as she looked around the store. "I mean, this place is painted beige, for goodness' sake. How boring is that?"

"What would you have suggested? Purple?" He grinned. "As for a flower shop, can you honestly see me making up bouquets of posies?"

Suddenly Annie was laughing, her expression more care-free than Ronnie had seen it in years. If nothing else, his coming home had been good for her.

And very soon, he thought hopefully, Dana Sue might finally see it was good for her, too.

Dana Sue was setting out hors d'oeuvres on tables that had been tucked in various corners of Ronnie's store when the bell over the front door chimed. From where she was, she couldn't see who had come in, but the next thing she heard was Mary Vaughn's chipper voice.

"Ronnie, sweetie, I'm here," she called out. "I came early to see what I could do to help."

Dana Sue set her basket of light-as-a-feather cheese straws down with a thunk and marched around the end of the display unit. "Hello, Mary Vaughn."

The Realtor's eyes widened, but she was too good a sales-woman to appear rattled. "Dana Sue," she said warmly, giving an air kiss somewhere in the vicinity of Dana Sue's ear. "I had no idea you'd be here."

"Sullivan's is providing the food," Dana Sue said without elaborating. Some devilish little imp inside her wanted to deliberately give the impression that she was nothing more than the hired help.

Mary Vaughn seemed to relax. "Oh, of course, I believe Ronnie did mention something about you catering the grand opening. I suppose I assumed you'd just drop off the food and leave. Or perhaps send Erik. This must be uncomfortable for you."

Was the woman living in a cave? Dana Sue wondered irritably. The whole town had been speculating for weeks about the reconciliation between her and Ronnie. Mary Vaughn had apparently turned a deaf ear to it simply because it didn't suit her. Or perhaps she was so confident in her own powers of seduction, she'd assumed Dana Sue wouldn't stand a chance against her. Knowing Mary Vaughn's ego, Dana Sue found it easy to imagine that she could blow off all the gossip as premature or misguided.

"Why would I be uncomfortable?" Dana Sue inquired innocently. "Ronnie and I were married for a lot of years. We have a daughter. We've spent a lot of time together since he came back to town."

"Because of Annie, of course," Mary Vaughn said, though she was starting to look just a little uncertain.

"Of course," Dana Sue said sweetly.

Just then Ronnie emerged from the back room, took one look at the two of them squared off facing each other and turned pale. To his credit, he apparently sized up the situation in a glance, because he strolled over, bent down and kissed Dana Sue with so much heat she worried that some of the nearby hors d'oeuvres might get singed.

With his arm still firmly around her waist, as if he feared she might take off, he smiled warmly at Mary Vaughn. "Thanks for coming. Have you tried any of the food yet? Dana Sue and Erik outdid themselves."

Mary Vaughn evidently didn't need to be hit in the head with a baseball bat to get the picture when it was spelled out right in front of her face. She managed a weak smile and said, "I was just thinking I'd love to try one of those cheese straws. A party in the South wouldn't be complete without them."

"So true," Dana Sue confirmed, refusing to take offense at the implication that they were unoriginal. "I believe you'll find that mine are a slight variation on the traditional cheese straws."

She bit back a grin when Mary Vaughn swallowed her first bite and nearly choked, then grabbed for a bottle of water. "Jalapeños," she whispered, waving a hand in front of her face.

"Didn't I mention that?" Dana Sue said. "Sorry. Most everyone in town knows Ronnie likes things a little spicy."

Ronnie gave her a look, then gently nudged her toward the front. "Let's give Mary Vaughn a chance to catch her breath," he said. "You can help me greet people."

"Whatever you need," Dana Sue said, casting a smug look back at the other woman.

Up by the old-fashioned cash register, which Ronnie had insisted on keeping, he regarded her with amusement. "I thought men were the only ones who marked their turf," he said.

"You've got to be kidding," Dana Sue replied. "Women are just more subtle about it."

He laughed at that. "Sugar, if that was subtle, I'd hate to think what you'd do if you wanted to make things any plainer."

"Are you complaining that I put my brand on you back there?" she asked.

"Not a bit. I just wish you believed that it wasn't necessary."

"Maybe not for you," she conceded, "but Mary Vaughn doesn't respond to anything less than a two-by-four hitting her between the eyes, so to speak."

"So I've noticed," Ronnie said wryly. "And given the number of two-by-fours out back, I suppose I'm lucky you didn't decide to get your message across literally. Are you going to relax and have fun now?"

"Absolutely," she assured him. "But I think I'll keep my eye on her, just the same."

Ronnie cupped Dana Sue's face in his hands and kissed her again. "Just one more to help you get the message," he said when he released her. "You don't need to worry about Mary Vaughn."

"Maybe I should," Dana Sue said, grinning. "Especially if it means you'll keep on kissing me like that."

"Darlin', I'd do that anyway. Anytime, anyplace you'd like."

The front door opened before she could reply, and Maddie and Cal came in, followed by Annie and Ty.

"We'll finish this conversation later," she told him. "Go say hi to your first customers. Cal could probably use some help buying tools to put together all that unassembled baby furniture he bought the other day. He decided his daughter needed more than a bassinet, and bought out the entire baby department at some fancy store over in Charleston."

"You just want to brag to Maddie about putting Mary Vaughn in her place," Ronnie teased in a low voice, before heading off to greet Cal.

"Well, of course I do," she called after him. "What's a victory if you can't share it with your friends?"

Maddie frowned as she joined Dana Sue. "What are you gloating about?"

"Nothing I can talk about here," Dana Sue told her with a pointed glance toward the back. "Could I show you some nails or bolts or something?"

"No, you can show me the food," Maddie said. "You promised there would be food."

Dana Sue laughed. "One of these days you're going to regret this free-for-all eating you're still doing. Nachos in the middle of the night, now this. At our age, the pounds don't come off that easily. Besides, do you really want to give Helen and me this much of an edge in our contest? I'll have you know I didn't sample one little hors d'oeuvre that I made."

"Good for you," Maddie said serenely. "And don't worry about me getting too far behind you and Helen in reaching my goals. I have every intention of behaving myself once I stop nursing the baby, but until then I am going to enjoy every mouthful."

"What about our goals? Does Helen have any idea you're secretly slacking off?"

Maddie looked vaguely uneasy. "No, which is one reason I need to get to the food now before she's here to lecture me."

"Then I recommend you start with the mini crab cakes," Dana Sue advised. "Erik outdid himself with those. He insisted that the crab meat be flown in from our supplier in Maryland. Since it's out of season, it cost an arm and a leg. They'll be the first things to go."

Maddie grabbed three and put them on a plate, then added a couple of cheese straws. "So, when is Helen supposed to get here?" she asked, glancing nervously toward the front door.

Dana Sue grinned. "Actually, you might want to sit down for this."

Maddie regarded her with alarm. "What? Has something happened to her?"

"Not exactly," Dana Sue said. "But she volunteered to help Erik in the kitchen at Sullivan's today, since Karen called in with another emergency and I needed to be here."

"And you let her?" Maddie asked incredulously.

"It was my idea, as a matter of fact," Dana Sue said blithely. "It's only for a few hours. How much damage can she do to the place's reputation in that amount of time? Erik's keeping a close eye on her."

"But who's keeping an eye on Erik to make sure he survives?" Maddie asked. "You know how Helen is. She's even more of a control freak than you are. Doesn't matter if she has a clue what she's talking about. She'll probably start telling him how he ought to do things, and who knows where that could lead? Murder? Mayhem?"

Dana Sue grinned. "I know. It kind of boggles the mind, doesn't it?"

"And you're okay with the potential for bloodshed?" Maddie asked.

"As long as they clean the place up before I get back there, I think it will be good for both of them to butt up against another immovable object."

"Erik already has you for that," Maddie reminded her. "This could be more than he can take."

"Not a chance," Dana Sue said calmly. "When it comes to a battle of wills between those two, my money's on Erik."

Maddie stared at her, suddenly looking suspicious. "What are you really up to, Dana Sue?"

"Not a thing," she swore innocently. "Just making sure the restaurant's covered for a couple of hours."

If something else heated up in that kitchen, well, that would just be nature taking its course.

23

Since opening his store, Ronnie had been working night and day. He'd had no idea how time-consuming owning his own business would be, especially one that required him to get out and meet with developers several times a week. He did his best to schedule those meetings over dinner, so he could spend at least a little time with Dana Sue and Annie at the end of the day, but it didn't always work out that way. Too often several days would pass without him catching so much as a glimpse of either of them. He began to wonder if he'd been a little too ambitious for his own good.

How was he going to prove anything to Dana Sue if he almost never crossed paths with her? Even Annie seemed to be losing patience with the number of times he'd had to cancel plans with her because of a last-minute business meeting with a potential client.

Serenity Hardware & Supplies had been open for three weeks and he was well ahead of his most ambitious projections, when Butch called on Tuesday to schedule a Friday-night dinner meeting with him at Dana Sue's restaurant.

"I know Christmas is just around the corner and you probably have a million things to do, but we need to talk," the older man said, his tone ruling out any excuses.

The unexpected command performance made Ronnie extremely nervous. Was Butch unhappy about something? Ronnie didn't see how he could be, given the way things had been going, but until they sat down and he could look into Butch's eyes and judge the man's mood for himself, he was going to be a wreck.

Maybe Butch was already losing patience with his promise to be a silent partner. If Butch didn't like what he was seeing on the bottom line, would he try to wrest some of the control away from Ronnie? Helen had closed tight any potential loopholes in their contract that might have allowed that, but he was still on pins and needles.

That night, as he waited for Dana Sue to close up, he sat in a booth nursing a beer while Annie did her homework next to him. They'd begun insisting that she have dinner at the restaurant every night, then hang around until closing. Ronnie made it by as often as he could, though not nearly often enough to suit him.

He knew that Annie resented their keeping watch over her eating habits, but she seemed resigned to it. She also seemed willing to balance her annoyance at their hovering against her desire for family time. The holidays had always been special for all of them, and she plainly wanted to recapture that.

Sullivan's was decorated for the season. White lights sparkled on the outside patio. Inside, several trees had been tucked into various corners, each glittering with tiny white lights and gold ornaments. The hostess station was surrounded by a sea of bright red poinsettias, with more lights nestled among the blooms. It was all very festive and tasteful. Ronnie was impressed with Dana Sue's talent for making the restaurant so welcoming.

Main Street was brightly lit once again, after several years of neglect. Ronnie had talked to the Whartons, and together they'd gone to the mayor and encouraged him to have workers once again weave lights in the trees on the town square and resurrect the giant snowflakes that had once hung from the lampposts. Next year Ronnie thought he'd see if he could round up some support for holding a Christmas market, or at least bringing back a tree-lighting ceremony on the green. The downtown needed community events like that to encourage more businesses to return.

As he brooded about his meeting with Butch, and all the energy it would take to revitalize downtown Serenity, he realized Annie was studying him warily.

"Dad, are you okay?" she asked eventually. "You look kind of freaked about something."

"Nothing for you to worry about," he assured her. "How are you doing with your English essay?"

"Done. I'm doing algebra now," she said, wrinkling her nose. "Do you have any idea why I need to take algebra?"

"It will come in handy someday, I'm sure," he said, just as he'd been told.

"You took it, right?"

He nodded.

"And you're over forty. Has it *ever* come in handy?"

He laughed. "All those ratios and formulas have helped me figure out a few things from time to time."

She regarded him skeptically. "You're kidding."

"Nope. For instance, if I have a budget of ten thousand dollars for lumber, and two-by-fours are so much per ten-foot piece, how many can I get for my money?"

"It's like word problems in math," she said with amazement.

"Exactly. And I think traffic investigators use formulas like that to calculate the speed of cars involved in a crash. See, there are all sorts of practical uses."

Her expression turned thoughtful. "Maybe it's not such a waste of time, after all."

"I think they try really hard not to make education a waste of time. Even if you're sure some fact will never, ever come in handy, it might turn up in a crossword puzzle someday," he teased. "That alone should make it worth learning."

"Dad!" she protested, giggling.

"How are things between you and Ty these days?" he asked. "I haven't seen much of him lately."

Her eyes lit up. "He calls almost every day after school. He's studying really hard for all the tests we have before the holidays. He got early admission at Duke, but they need to have the midterm grades before his acceptance is final."

"So, Duke is his first choice?"

She shook her head. "His first choice would be going with a pro baseball team. Cal says he's good enough, and so did a scout for the Atlanta Braves, but his mom says he has to go to college first."

"And his dad?" Ronnie asked. Bill Townsend, Maddie's ex, had always pushed baseball with Ty. It had been a passion the two of them had shared.

"Ty thinks his dad would let him go pro, but his dad won't go against his mom. You know, the way you and Mom gang up on me."

"For your own good," Ronnie said.

"Yeah, right." Annie rolled her eyes. "That's what parents always say."

"Because parents are wise," he stated.

"You and Mom can't be that smart. You're still not living under the same roof."

Ronnie was frustrated by the situation, too. Not that living at the Serenity Inn was a hardship in any way, but it was kind of like living in a fishbowl. Every time Dana Sue sneaked into his room, it was all over Wharton's by lunchtime. He wouldn't be surprised if the regulars over there were placing bets on what time of night she slipped in and what hour of the morning she slipped out. If not, they surely had a pool going on over when he'd finally pop the question.

"Some things can't be rushed," he told Annie.

Dana Sue came out of the kitchen just in time to overhear his comment. "What can't be rushed?" she asked. "I'm sorry if I took too long."

"Not you," Annie told her. "You and Dad. You're like a couple of snails creeping toward the finish line. You'll make it when you're, like, sixty or something."

Dana Sue flushed. "Do you see us both every day?"

"You, yes. Dad, not always."

Dana Sue shrugged that off. "Okay, but it's not like he's not around at all. And you know we love you. You're not lacking for anything, right?"

"I'm not worried about me," Annie countered, leaning forward, her expression intense. "It's you two, Mom. You act as if you have all the time in the world."

Dana Sue frowned at her. "Who says we don't?"

Suddenly, to Ronnie's dismay, tears welled up in Annie's eyes. As it often did with teenagers, her mood had turned from light to serious in the blink of an eye. Clearly, this was something she'd been worrying about for a while now.

She shoved her way out of the booth. "What if you turn out to be like Grandma?" she asked Dana Sue, her voice small and filled with fear as she stood beside the table, her gaze accusing. "What if you *die?* Look at all the time you'll have wasted."

"Annie, I'm not going to die," Dana Sue said, reaching for her hand. "Not for a long time."

"But you could if you don't take care of yourself," Annie argued. Snatching her hand away, she headed out the door, leaving both of them sitting there in stunned silence.

Ronnie cast a worried look at Dana Sue, who had turned pale. "You okay?" he asked.

She nodded. "I'm fine. Go after her. I had no idea she was so upset about this. She's never said a word."

"I'll bring her back," he promised. "Get something to eat. You look as if you might pass out."

"Just go," she told him.

Outside, Ronnie didn't have to go far to find Annie. She was huddled in the passenger seat of his pickup, her knees pulled up under her chin.

"I'm sorry," she whispered with a sniff when he opened the door and slid in behind the wheel. "I shouldn't have said any of that. Is Mom really upset?"

"She's worried about you," he told her. "She didn't realize this was on your mind. You've never mentioned it before."

"I have, but she blows it off. I know she doesn't want to talk about it." Annie shrugged. "It's just that I think about Grandma sometimes, and I know Mom doesn't take care of herself the way she should, and I get scared."

"Your mother is not going to die," Ronnie said emphatically.

"She could," his daughter said stubbornly. "Grandma did. Diabetes can get really bad and the complications can kill you. We learned all about it in school, plus I looked it up on the Internet after you guys told me how Grandma died."

Ronnie wondered if he was the best person to be having this conversation. Maybe he and Dana Sue should be doing it together. But he was here, and Annie was obviously too upset to be put off.

"It's true that your grandmother died of complications

from diabetes," Ronnie said slowly. "But she'd had it for years and never took care of herself. She didn't listen to the doctors. She ate what she wanted. Her blood sugar was always out of control, so she was in and out of the hospital. Your mom's not like that."

"Not yet," Annie said direly. "But she gained weight and that's bad. I know she's lost a few pounds and she's been exercising, but she still grabs something sweet whenever she gets nervous or angry. You weren't around, Dad. After you left, she ate everything in sight. Pizza, cake, ice cream, chips—you name it, she gobbled down every bite. You all act like I'm the only one in the family with an eating disorder. At least I got help. Mom hasn't seen Doc Marshall in months now. I've heard him trying to get her to make an appointment for herself, but she hasn't done it. When we go, it's all about me."

Ronnie was more disturbed than he wanted to admit, but he needed to defend Dana Sue's actions. He knew exactly what she would say—that she was, first and foremost, a mom, and good mothers put their children first. "Because you had a major crisis, Annie. We couldn't ignore that."

"But I'm better now," Annie said reasonably. "Why isn't somebody on Mom's case about all this stuff? Erik tries to keep an eye on her here, but Mom just blows him off if he gets in her face too much. Helen and Maddie try to talk to her, and they have some sort of bet thing going at the spa, but I don't think it's enough."

Ronnie was distraught about the picture Annie was painting of Dana Sue's health. He was also concerned that his daughter was so upset about it. The last time she'd needed to find some way to control the things going on in her life, she'd become anorexic. She might be better, but she wasn't out of the woods. Worrying about her mom was the last thing she needed, when her own recovery was still so precarious.

"How about this?" he suggested eventually. "I promise you that I will insist your mom see Doc Marshall and make sure everything's okay. I'll drag her to the office if I have to."

Annie gave him a wry look. "Good luck with that."

"I meant it literally, baby. If that's what it takes, I will carry her in there."

He'd hoped for a smile, but Annie merely looked relieved. "When?" she pressed.

"As soon as we can make an appointment."

She leaned across the console and threw her arms around his neck. "Thank you."

"I should be thanking you. I knew your mom needed to pay attention to her blood sugar—Erik and I have even discussed it—but I had no idea things might be really bad."

"Maybe they're not," Annie said, a wistful note in her voice. "I don't want her to be sick, but wouldn't it be better to know?"

Ronnie nodded. It would definitely be better to know. He'd just have to pull out every persuasive tactic at his disposal to make Dana Sue see that. Or maybe her seeing Annie freaking out tonight had been enough to do the trick.

"Let's go back in and get your mom," he said at last. "It's time to go home."

"Would it be okay if I hitched a ride with Erik?" she asked. "He won't mind dropping me off. Then you and mom could have more time to talk."

Ronnie nodded. "Run into the kitchen and make sure it's okay with him. Then let us know when you leave."

"Okay," she said, opening her door and dashing for the back door of the restaurant.

Ronnie was slower to exit the pickup. He had a hunch Dana Sue wasn't going to be happy about his attempt to interfere in her life. And though he'd vowed to drag her to the doctor if necessary, he didn't want this to become a bone of contention between them, just when their relationship was finally on peaceful ground. But if push came to shove, he wouldn't hesitate to do whatever it took to make sure her health wasn't in jeopardy.

Dana Sue nibbled on the plate of cheese and veggies Erik had brought her in lieu of the chocolate cake she'd requested. He hadn't even flinched when she'd scowled at him, just spun on his heel and returned to the kitchen.

Why hadn't she noticed how worried Annie was about the whole diabetes thing? Maybe because she tried so hard to ignore the problem herself, as if ignoring it would make it go away. Obviously she'd mastered the fine art of denial when it came to her daughter's health and her own. She'd been trying to take off the blinders where Annie was concerned. Maybe it was time to do the same thing with her own health.

When Ronnie finally came back and slid into the booth opposite her, she pushed the plate of snacks in his direction.

"How'd it go? Where's Annie?"

"She's in the kitchen asking Erik if he can give her a lift home."

"Why can't she go with me?" Dana Sue asked.

"She wants us to have time alone to talk."

Her gaze narrowed. "About?"

"How much trouble are you in with the whole blood-sugar thing, Dana Sue?"

"It's no big deal," she insisted. "I've always known I was at risk. Doc Marshall's been watching it."

"Has he put you on any medication?"

She looked toward the kitchen as the door swung open, hoping it would be Erik or Annie coming to save her from getting into this with Ronnie. Instead, Annie merely waved. "Erik's giving me a ride," she said, and let the door swing shut.

"Well?" Ronnie prodded.

"I'm not on insulin," Dana Sue said, but she avoided his gaze.

"Any other medications?"

"Not yet," she said with a touch of defiance. "I'm monitoring my blood sugar. That's all."

"Are you really?" he asked, with such skepticism it made her hackles rise.

"Why would I lie?" she countered irritably.

"Because it's convenient," he suggested. "You don't want to deal with this in a meaningful way, so you'll tell me lies or half truths just to get me off your case."

"Maybe that's because it's not your problem!" she snapped.

Ronnie leveled a look at her that made her squirm.

"I love you," he said quietly. "That makes it my problem. Annie loves you. That makes it her problem, too. And frankly, in case you haven't noticed, Annie can't cope with many more problems right now."

"I'm fine," Dana Sue said.

"I think Annie and I would both feel a lot better if we heard that from Doc Marshall," he replied, not backing down an inch.

"Oh, for heaven's sale, if that's what it will take to get you two off my back, I'll make an appointment."

"Tomorrow," he prodded.

"As soon as he can fit me in," she said.

"Tomorrow," Ronnie repeated. "Understood?"

"Whatever."

He met her gaze. "Dana Sue, don't take this lightly," he pleaded. "Annie's really scared. Now that she's explained why, I have to admit I'm a little scared myself. This is not something you can ignore. Surely you, of all people, know the seriousness of uncontrolled diabetes."

"I do, and I say you're both worrying about nothing," she insisted, even though she knew better. She was only slightly more informed than her mother had been. And almost as stubborn. Dana Sue pushed down the memory of how that attitude had turned out for her mom, because she couldn't bear to think about it.

Well, she was going to be different. She was not going to get full-blown diabetes; she certainly was not going to die from its complications. Right this second she hated her daughter and her ex-husband for even raising the possibility and forcing her to face it. She needed them to believe in her, not to question her every decision.

She frowned at Ronnie. "Haven't you noticed that in the last few weeks I've been sticking to my exercise program at the spa? And I'm watching what I eat."

"Tell me you didn't order cake or pie or ice cream the second I went out of here after Annie," he said mildly.

She gestured toward the cheese and veggies. "Obviously I didn't get any of that."

He gave her a wry look. "Your choice or Erik's?"

"Look, I'm doing the best I can," she said. "Why isn't that enough for you?"

"It's enough if Doc Marshall says it's enough," Ronnie stated. "Call me in the morning and tell me what time your appointment is. I'll pick you up and go with you."

"That's ridiculous," she said. "I'm perfectly capable of getting to the doctor's office on my own."

"It's not a question of whether or not you're capable of doing it," he said. "It's a matter of whether you will."

"I have to say I'm not crazy about the way you're treating me. I'm not some irresponsible child, Ronnie."

His hard stare never wavered. "Then don't act like one." He held out his hand. "Come on. I'll drive you home. Annie shouldn't be by herself tonight when she's as upset as she was when she left here. You two need to talk."

"You're right about Annie, but my car's here," she said. "I can drive myself home."

"Humor me," he retorted. "That way you'll have to call me in the morning because you'll need a ride."

"You're not the only person in this town I could call for a lift," she grumbled.

"But I am the only one who will hunt you down if I don't hear from you when I expect to," he warned.

She sighed and went with him, turning out the inside lights and locking the front door behind them. She paused on the patio. Normally being surrounded by the fairyland of lights made her smile, but tonight her mood was too dark to enjoy the moment.

As they crossed the parking lot, Ronnie draped his arm across her tensed shoulders. When they reached his pickup, he pinned her against the side and framed her face with his hands.

"I love you, Dana Sue. I want you around for a long, long time. I won't let you do anything that could cut that time short."

She regarded him wearily. "You say that as if you think I'm trying to kill myself."

"Not trying to," he said. "Just not doing all you can to make sure it doesn't happen. If I have to, I'll bully you the way we've had to bully Annie."

"I could wind up hating you for it," Dana Sue threatened.

He grinned. "Annie said that a time or two, as well. It didn't make us back down. Some things are just too important for me to worry about how mad you might get."

Just as Annie had, Dana Sue wanted to lash out, but it was one thing for their sixteen-year-old to throw a tantrum. It was something else entirely for a mature woman to do it.

"I'll make the appointment," she promised.

"And call me first thing in the morning to let me know what time to pick you up," he reminded her yet again.

"Yes, fine," she said impatiently. She knew she should appreciate his concern, and Annie's, too, but right now all she felt was pressure. And fear. What if there *was* reason to worry? What if she was much sicker than she'd realized?

Ronnie winked at her in an obvious attempt to lighten the tension. "If you're a really good girl, I'll bring you a sugar-free lollipop."

Dana Sue rolled her eyes. "Trust me, you're going to have to come up with a better reward than that."

"Well, there is one other possibility," he said. "And since you're being so agreeable, I could give you a preview tonight."

Despite her annoyance at the moment, she regarded him with real regret. "Annie," she reminded him. "Home alone."

"Darn, I knew there was something I was forgetting. Too bad I can't just come home with you."

"You could, but I hear the guest room mattress is really uncomfortable. Didn't you insist on that so your folks and mine wouldn't stay too long when they visited?"

"What was I thinking?" he grumbled good-naturedly.

"Probably that there would never be a time when I'd make you sleep on it," Dana Sue said as they pulled up in front of the house. In the window, the huge tree Ronnie had helped them lug home and decorate was sparkling with colored lights. That was yet another sight that normally cheered her, but failed to move her tonight.

"Good night, Ronnie."

"'Night, sugar. Sleep well."

He waited until she was inside and had switched off the porch light before backing out of the driveway.

After he was out of sight, Dana Sue leaned against the door with a sigh. Coming home from an evening with Ronnie, as if they were seventeen and had just been on a date, was getting old.

Before tonight she'd have said he was getting close to putting them both out of their misery by asking her to marry him, but now that he knew about her health issues, she wasn't so sure. What if he was scared off? Just one more reason to avoid Doc Marshall as long as possible.

Of course, avoiding Ronnie if he found out she hadn't made an appointment was going to be a whole lot trickier.

24

Annie could hardly wait to get her session with Dr. McDaniels over with. Ty had driven her to the psychologist's office and was waiting for her outside. They were going to Charleston to do some Christmas shopping afterward.

"You seem awfully eager to get out of here," Dr. McDaniels said, regarding her with amusement. "It wouldn't have anything to do with that young man I saw with you in the parking lot, would it?"

Annie beamed. "That's Ty."

"I thought it might be. How's that going?"

"Well, it's not like we've had a real date yet, but we talk almost every day, and I think maybe he's going to ask me to a party over the holidays."

"Will you be okay if he doesn't?" Dr. McDaniels asked.

"Yeah, I guess so," Annie said, then met the shrink's gaze. "Can I ask you something that isn't about food?"

"Of course."

"Why are boys so hard to understand?"

Dr. McDaniels laughed. "They say the same thing about girls, you know."

Annie didn't believe that for a minute. "I'm serious. I don't get why Ty hasn't figured out how great we'd be as a couple.

We can talk about everything. We've known each other forever. We're practically best friends."

This time Dr. McDaniels didn't laugh or even crack a smile. She took the question seriously. It was something Annie liked about talking to her.

"Sometimes it's hard to change an old pattern," she told Annie. "Or maybe Ty is afraid if you two start dating and it doesn't work out, it'll ruin the friendship you have. Given how close your families are, that could be really awkward."

Annie nodded slowly. "I see what you mean. Does that mean I should just give up?"

"Absolutely not. Just keep your expectations in check and don't be in too big a rush to change things. Best friends often have the best relationships in the long run. Weren't your mom and dad friends for a long time before they got serious about each other?"

Annie grinned. "That was just because my dad knew it was the smart way to keep my mom interested."

"Well, going slowly worked out okay for the two of them. Maybe you and Ty will follow the same path. One day things will just click. Can you be patient and wait for that?"

"I can wait for Ty for as long as it takes," Annie said. "He's definitely worth it."

"*You're* definitely worth waiting for, too. Don't forget that," Dr. McDaniels said. "Now, one last thing before you go. Do you have any questions at all about how to get through the holidays with all the food that's going to be around? Sometimes it's really hard to see so much food. It can make you feel as if you might lose control and eat everything in sight. Some people panic and revert to avoiding everything, not just the food, but all the social interactions and parties that might involve it."

"I don't think I'll do that," Annie said. "But if I start to get anxious or anything, I'll call you."

"Good. That's exactly the thing to do. Or talk to your mom or dad. Or come to one of those support-group meetings we've talked about. You have the schedule."

Annie had been to one meeting at Dr. McDaniels's insistence. It had felt kind of good to know there were other kids who'd been through what she had, but she hadn't been back. Going there made her feel as if she was still sick, as if she had to focus on the anorexia all the time, when all she wanted was to put it behind her. Seeing Dr. McDaniels once a week was reminder enough.

Apparently her expression must have given her away, because the doctor said, "I know you don't want to join a support group, Annie, and I've gone along with that because you seem to be doing well on your own. It can be a really good resource, though, especially when you're facing a social occasion with a lot of food—the kind that come up during the holidays. You'd be welcome at any meeting."

"I'll remember," Annie assured her. "Are we finished now?"

"Yes, you can go," Dr. McDaniels said, smiling. "Enjoy your afternoon with Ty."

"Thanks, I will."

Annie turned and bounded out the door. She skidded to a stop before she walked into the parking lot. She didn't want Ty to think she was too excited about this shopping trip.

Halfway to the car, she could hear the music blaring from the radio, tuned to their favorite rock station. Thank goodness they had the same taste in music. A lot of kids at school liked rap, but Annie just found a lot of the lyrics disgusting.

She tapped on the window of the car, then opened the door

and got in. Ty grinned at her and immediately turned the music down. "How'd it go?" he asked, starting the car.

"Okay," she told him.

He turned and studied her before putting the car into gear. "You sure?"

Annie nodded.

"You'd tell me if you were having problems again, wouldn't you?" he asked.

She flushed under his scrutiny. "Do we have to talk about this?"

He frowned at her sharp tone. "I'm just saying you can talk to me about stuff."

"I know that," she said impatiently.

He cut the engine. "Okay, spill. What's going on?"

"Nothing," she insisted, not sure why her mood had turned sour when she'd been so excited and optimistic earlier. Maybe it was the reminder that Ty couldn't seem to forget she had an eating disorder. Sometimes she wondered if the concern he had for her health was the only thing between them.

"Annie, I know you," he persisted. "There's obviously something on your mind. If it doesn't have anything to do with your session, then what is it?"

"It's my mom," she said, seizing on the first thing that came to mind so she wouldn't have to explain that she was frustrated because he still didn't see her as a potential girl-friend. "She's not taking care of herself the way she should."

"Have you told her you're worried?"

"Last night. My dad talked to her, too."

"Well, my mom and Helen have this whole bet thing going with her. Maybe they're on top of things."

"I don't think so," Annie said wearily.

Ty reached for her hand and gave it a squeeze. "I'll tell my mom to talk to her again, okay?"

Annie could hardly breathe for fear Ty would drop her hand. She liked the way his felt, all warm and strong, the skin rougher than her own. His holding her hand wasn't such a big deal, but he'd never done it before.

"Annie?"

"Hmm?" She lifted her gaze from their clasped hands to his face.

"You're all flushed," he said, dropping her hand to touch her cheek. "Is something else wrong?"

"Nothing," she said with an exasperated sigh. She reached for the knob on the car stereo and turned up the music.

Ty turned it back down, regarding her with a confused expression. "Are you mad at me?"

Annie decided to be honest. "Not mad, frustrated," she said.

"Why?"

"I like you."

He still looked befuddled. "I like you, too."

"No, I mean I *really* like you, and you treat me like your kid sister or something."

"Oh."

Annie shook her head. "I knew I should keep my mouth shut," she said, filled with self-disgust. "It's okay that you don't like me that way."

He glanced at her, appearing far more uncertain than she'd ever seen him look before. "Maybe I do," he said quietly.

Annie's pulse scrambled. "You do?"

His gaze met hers. "I just don't want to mess things up between us, you know?"

She nodded, filled with relief. "I know. Me, too."

"And I'll be going away to school next year," he reminded her. "It would be crazy to start something and then have to leave."

"You're probably right," she agreed, her hopes deflating.

"Still, maybe we could spend some time together," he said, as if he was working it out in his own mind as he spoke. "Like today, this shopping trip. We could think of it like a date, sort of." He regarded her hesitantly. "What do you think?"

"I think it's a really good place to start," she agreed.

A grin spread across his face and he reached for her hand again. "You mind?"

"Not at all," she said, then winced. "But you're supposed to drive with both hands on the wheel."

He released her reluctantly. "That's one of the things I like about you. You follow the rules."

"Not always," she said. "But I have learned that some rules are there for a reason." She gave him a quick sideways glance as he started the car. "But you could hold my hand when we get to the mall. I can't think of a single rule that would break."

Ty's mouth curved into that smile that made her knees weak. "Me, neither," he said.

Annie felt as if she were floating on air. She'd taken a risk and it had paid off. She and Ty were a couple. Or almost a couple. Better than just friends, anyway. Heck, she didn't know what they were, but it felt good.

Ronnie was spitting mad. Dana Sue had successfully evaded every single attempt he'd made to get her in to see Doc Marshall. Tuesday's promise had turned into Wednesday's, then Friday's. He'd spent most of each day trying to catch up with her, but it seemed no matter where he looked or called, he'd just missed her. Either she was slippery as an eel or her friends were covering for her. And he had too much respect for her professionalism to barge into the kitchen at Sullivan's and make a scene—though he was only a hairsbreadth away from doing so.

In fact, the only thing that would prevent the two of them from having a major blowup at the restaurant tonight was the presence of Butch Thompson. If Butch hadn't especially requested dinner at Sullivan's, Ronnie wouldn't have gone within ten miles of the place, fearing what he might say or do when he finally crossed paths with Dana Sue.

Butch and his wife were already seated at a table when he arrived. Ronnie forced a smile, greeted Jessie Thompson with a kiss on the cheek, then shook Butch's hand.

"Sorry I'm late."

"We were early," Butch said. "I've been itching to get a look at this menu all day long. Even Jessie's declared a night off from her no-meat rule."

Ronnie chuckled. "Then I highly recommend the meat loaf. It's one of the specialties here. With red bliss mashed potatoes, you'll think you're back in your mama's kitchen."

"Not my mama's," Jessie declared. "She couldn't cook worth a lick. That's why I learned so young, so the family wouldn't starve to death or die from eating too many things turned to charcoal. I did everything the old-fashioned, Southern way, too. It's a wonder our blood can still find a way through our arteries."

Butch patted her hand. "You've made up for it, Jessie. We're eating real healthy now. In fact, I'm sure all that oatmeal has sopped up any cholesterol that's slipped past you. A break tonight won't hurt either one of us."

She laughed. "It's not that bad," she told Ronnie. "Butch likes people to take pity on him." She gave Ronnie a knowing look. "The way you did when you took him out for that steak a few months back."

"Whoops!" Ronnie murmured. "I guess she caught us."

"Said she could smell it on my breath," Butch confessed. "But I think it's just some sixth sense she has about when I've strayed from the straight and narrow."

Butch winked at his wife, reminding Ronnie of what a lasting marriage could be—two people who might bicker and tease, but who loved each other despite all their foibles.

"So, Ronnie, are you going to lure your ex-wife out of the kitchen so we can meet her?" Jessie asked.

He stiffened. "We'll see," he said tightly.

Butch gave him an odd look, obviously picking up on the tension in his voice. "Things going okay on that front?"

"We've hit a little impasse over something, but we'll fix it," Ronnie assured him, his gaze drifting toward the door to the kitchen, where he was hoping to catch a glimpse of Dana Sue as the waitstaff went in and out.

Brenda bounced up to the table just then and grinned at him. "Hi, Mr. Sullivan. Does Dana Sue know you're here?"

"No, and don't bother her. I'm sure she's busy."

"It's crazy in there," Brenda confided. "Karen called in and bailed on her again. Third time this week. Dana Sue's looking pretty frazzled."

Frazzled wasn't good, Ronnie thought. If he could have, he would have canceled this meeting and gone to lend her a hand. Instead, he forced a smile for Butch and Jessie. "You ready to order?"

"The meat loaf's come highly recommended," Butch said. "I'll have that."

"Make it two," Jessie chimed in.

"Might as well be three," Ronnie said.

After the waitress had gone, he looked at his partner. "Any particular reason you wanted to meet tonight?"

"Aside from the prospect of a good meal, you mean?" Butch said. "I just wanted to congratulate you on the way things are going. I've looked over those reports you've been faxing to me, and you're well ahead of projections. That tells me you're working hard."

"Trying to," Ronnie said. "Things should really start hopping after the first of the year. I want to justify the faith you had in me."

"Maybe you're trying a little too hard," Butch suggested, his expression one of concern.

Ronnie stared at him. "What do you mean? How can I possibly be trying too hard?"

"This business wasn't the only thing that brought you back to Serenity, was it?"

"You know it wasn't," Ronnie said.

"How much time have you spent with your daughter and your ex-wife since you opened the business?"

"Not as much as I'd like," he admitted.

"Don't take your eye off the real prize here," Butch told him. "What good is a thriving company if you don't have someone to share your life with?"

Jessie smiled. "Listen to him, Ronnie. He's the voice of experience. I said something very much like this to him thirty-five years ago. He took it to heart, which is one reason we're still together. I wouldn't have given you two cents for the likelihood of that after our first five years of marriage, when he lived and breathed that construction company from early morning till late at night."

Butch covered her hand with his, then turned to Ronnie. "What did you see when you looked at those reports you've been sending?"

"A positive bottom line," he replied. "Four-month goals being met in one-quarter of that time."

The older man nodded. "Looked real good, too, didn't it?"

"Sure," Ronnie said, though he wasn't at all certain where this was heading.

"But how many late nights did it translate into?" Butch asked. "How many times did you blow off the chance to spend time with your daughter or Dana Sue, so you could have an extra business meeting in the evening?"

Ronnie sighed as the point sank in. "Too often," he admitted.

"I set you up with enough capital for the five-year plan we put down on paper. Succeeding in less time than that would be great, but not if it takes a toll on your personal life. Balance, son. Don't underestimate the value of balance when it comes to setting your priorities."

Ronnie got the message. Once again, he thought of what Brenda had told him about the situation in the kitchen. He glanced that way.

"You worried about what the waitress said earlier?" Butch asked. "About someone not showing up for work tonight?"

Ronnie nodded. "Dana Sue's too stubborn to call for help, but on a Friday night this place turns into a zoo."

"If you'd like to pitch in and give her a hand," Jessie said, "we'll be just fine."

"That's right," Butch confirmed, his gaze locking with hers. "It's not often I get my wife all to myself anymore. You go ahead and do whatever you can to help. I think I've gotten my point across, am I right?"

"Absolutely, and thank you," Ronnie said. "I really appreciate it. Don't forget that your dinner's on me. It's the least I can do after all you've done for me."

"No need for that. We're partners, son," Butch reminded him. "You're doing plenty to keep your end of the bargain. Now, go on in there. I want to see if I can convince Jessie to stay at a motel with me tonight and pretend we're honeymooning."

Ronnie left the two of them with their heads together and a look in Jessie's eyes that suggested Butch wasn't going to have to do much persuading. Apparently she wasn't half as hardheaded and impossible as the woman in Ronnie's life.

Dana Sue wasn't sure exactly when she noticed that she was feeling a little queasy and light-headed. It must have been right as the dinner rush kicked into high gear. Karen had bailed on her for the umpteenth time lately, which meant Dana Sue was going to have to deal with the headache of replacing her, something she'd been loath to do, knowing how difficult things were for Karen as a single mom. Still, she couldn't have an assistant who was this unreliable.

Amazingly, Ronnie had once again come to her rescue. He'd breezed in the door a few minutes ago, plucked an apron from the hook in the pantry and asked for an assignment. He'd done it without commenting on her failure to schedule a doctor's appointment, but she doubted she was off the hook. When she risked a look in his direction, she noticed he was chopping vegetables and making salads like a pro. She'd just turned to thank him for pitching in when she broke out in a sweat.

This wasn't the first time it had happened. On each occasion she'd found a way to dismiss the symptoms, just as she'd dismissed them when her hand had felt a little numb and she'd had to put aside a knife and stop chopping until sensation came back. Adding up all the incidents suddenly frightened her in a way that each individual occurrence hadn't.

She grabbed a stool and sat. Frightened by the light-headed feeling, which still wasn't going away, she called Ronnie's name, her voice little more than a frightened whisper. He whipped around and was at her side in an instant.

"You okay?" he asked, his hands on her thighs. "What's going on?"

"I think her blood sugar must be all out of whack," Erik said, immediately joining them, his expression worried. "She hasn't been paying attention to what she's eaten lately. Her blood-testing kit is in her office. I'll get it."

"No," she protested, not wanting Ronnie to witness whatever evidence might show up in the results.

Ronnie looked into her eyes. "Sugar, we had this conversation the other night. You know you can't play games with this, not if you have diabetes."

"I don't have it," she said, shooting a disgusted look at Erik for ratting her out about her eating habits, and for being so quick to volunteer to get her testing kit. "Not yet, anyway."

"Do I need to get you to a hospital, call 911, what?" Ronnie asked, calm and reassuring, but grimly determined.

Erik handed her a slice of cheese. "This should help. I'll go get your kit."

Within a few moments, Dana Sue could feel her body slowly returning to normal. "That's better," she said, regarding Erik gratefully as he returned. "No need to test now."

"Either run the test or go to the hospital," Erik said flatly.

"I'm with Erik," Ronnie said. "Two choices, Dana Sue. We either call Doc Marshall and ask him to meet us at his office, or we go straight to the emergency room."

She shook her head. "I'll be okay. Besides, we've got a full house tonight. I don't have time to go anywhere."

"Annie could pitch in," Erik suggested. "She's learned some of the basics from you. And Helen said she'd come by anytime we need her. Believe it or not, she takes directions in here pretty well."

"Call them," Ronnie told Erik, then scooped Dana Sue into his arms. "Let's go get you checked out, sugar."

"Put me down, you idiot," she snapped, even though it felt good to be cradled against his chest. "And don't you think, under the circumstances, that calling me 'sugar' is a bad idea?"

Ronnie grinned. "You *are* feeling better, aren't you?"

"Yes, dammit, which is why I don't need to see a doctor."

"Too bad. Maybe if you'd made that appointment earlier in the week the way I asked you to, it wouldn't have come to this," he said, exchanging one of those superior-male looks with Erik that made her want to clobber them both over the head with a cast-iron skillet. Erik was grinning when Ronnie marched out the back door with her still in his arms.

"Ronnie Sullivan, I have been taking care of myself for quite some time now," she began, only to have him cut her off with a look that said she hadn't done a particularly good job of it. She frowned and admitted, "Okay, maybe I've let a few things slide. I've had a lot on my mind."

"Annie's better now," he said. "And you deliberately ignored me when I asked you to call Doc Marshall and make an appointment. You know you're in the wrong. That's why you've been avoiding me ever since the night you made that promise."

"You didn't ask me to do it. You ordered me to," she reminded him.

"Sorry. My mistake. I was just thinking about your health."

"Not your problem," she said tightly.

"I think we had that discussion the other night, too." He plunked her down in the passenger seat of his pickup, then got behind the wheel and backed out of his parking place as if in a race. "I'm going to worry about you. Get used to it."

As soon as they were on the road, he glanced at her and said firmly, "Maybe we need to get something straight. I'm back for good. I thought opening the business would prove that, but I guess you're going to need constant reminding. In addition, I intend to marry you again. The timing's up to you, but the outcome's a given. That gives me worry rights."

Even though his claim made her heart leap, she scowled at his arrogance. "The outcome is not a given," she retorted. "You have a lot of nerve coming back here and making assumptions about me."

"I'm making assumptions about us, actually. We belong together, Dana Sue. That is never going to change."

She desperately wanted to believe him. "Even now?"

He studied her blankly. "What do you mean, even now?"

"I've gained weight. I'm dealing with the possibility of diabetes. I'm a mess," she said, choking back a sob at how completely out of control she felt even after all the changes she'd tried to make.

He regarded her with dismay. "Honey, you are so far from a mess," he chided. "You're the best thing that ever happened to me. I don't care about a few extra pounds as long as they don't hurt your health. As for the diabetes, if you have it, we'll deal with it. If you need insulin, I'll even learn to give you shots."

"You're terrified of needles," she objected.

"I'll get over it," he said emphatically. "There is nothing I wouldn't do for you. I love you. I love your high spirits, your generous heart, your beautiful face, even your ferocious temper. I'm not quite as crazy about your stubborn streak, but I can live with it."

Dana Sue held his gaze and saw nothing that would make her doubt what he was telling her. Not even the flicker of an eyelash to suggest he was using sweet talk to get something he wanted, rather than speaking from his heart.

"Okay," she said at last, giving in to him, to her own heart. She should have done this when he first came back to town, and saved them both months of aggravation, but that stubborn streak he'd mentioned had stopped her.

Ronnie's gaze narrowed. "Okay what? You'll go to the doctor without complaining?"

She shook her head. "No—though I'll do that, too. I'm telling you I'll marry you."

He looked stunned. "You're saying yes," he murmured, as if he couldn't quite believe it. The tires squealed as he swerved into a parking space at the hospital and cut the engine. "Yes?"

"I'm saying yes, and believe me, no one is more surprised by that than I am."

"You're saying yes when I'm about to haul you into an emergency room," he muttered with a shake of his head. "That pretty much knocks the romance right out of the moment."

She grinned at his frustrated tone. "You had something else in mind?"

"Christmas morning," he admitted. "A pretty velvet box under the tree. Me declaring my undying devotion, while Annie cheered. Something like that."

"It is a pretty picture," Dana Sue admitted, wrapping her arms around his neck as he lifted her out of the car. "But something about all this suits us."

He regarded her with a bemused expression. "A hospital parking lot suits us? How?"

"It's unpredictable. A little crazy."

He covered her mouth with his and kissed her till the dizzy sensation came back, this time in a good way.

"I think I'll include that in our wedding vows," he told her when he finally pulled away, ending the kiss.

"What?" she asked, still too dazed to think straight.

"I'll promise to keep things crazy and unpredictable all the days of our lives."

A smile spread across Dana Sue's face. "Now that's a promise I know you're capable of keeping, Ronnie Sullivan."

And something told her that once she had her little slice of heaven back again, she wouldn't have any desire to sneak a slice of Erik's pies or decadent cakes. Maybe this time Ronnie would turn out to be good for her heart *and* for her health.

Epilogue

"Mom, would you stand still?" Annie pleaded. "Your veil is crooked."

"I shouldn't even be wearing a veil, much less a white dress," Dana Sue grumbled. "I can't imagine what I was thinking, letting you talk me into having a fancy, formal wedding."

"I don't think it had anything to do with me," Annie said smugly. "I think it's because you realized you could still get into your old wedding dress and you wanted to show off."

"Okay, smarty-pants, that did have something to do with it," Dana Sue admitted. It had been a revelation when she'd found the box with the dress in the attic in January as she was putting away Christmas decorations. The even bigger surprise had been that the dress still fit. All those sessions with Elliott Cruz had paid off. Well, that and having her family and friends watching every bite of food she put in her mouth. Now she understood how Annie felt when they hovered over her. Still, it had been worth it. Dana Sue's blood-sugar readings had been normal for weeks now, and she hadn't had to start insulin.

She glanced at Annie, who had climbed onto a chair to rearrange her veil. Looking at her now, it was hard to believe that just a few months ago she'd nearly died from anorexia complications. Her skin was glowing with health, her hair hung down her back in a wave of natural, shimmering golden highlights. She was still below optimum weight for her age and height, and some days were more of a struggle than others, but she was trying, and that was all Dana Sue and Ronnie could ask. If Annie ever had a relapse, which Dr. McDaniels had warned them was a possibility, Dana Sue knew she and Ronnie would be on top of it.

When the veil was arranged to Annie's satisfaction, she jumped down from the chair and stood behind Dana Sue in front of the mirror. "You look beautiful, Mom."

"*We* look beautiful," Dana Sue corrected. "The bridesmaid dress Maddie wore the last time I married your dad fits you perfectly."

Annie grinned. "I know. It freaked her out. She says since she had the baby she's the size of a cruise ship. She said she's nowhere close to achieving those goals you guys set. What's really cool, though, is I don't think that's how Cal sees her at all."

"Nope," Dana Sue agreed. "In his eyes, she's the most beautiful woman on earth. That doesn't mean Helen and I aren't about to get tough with her for ignoring those goals."

Annie regarded Dana Sue intently. "Do you think you and Dad will have another baby, the way Maddie did when she married Cal?"

To her dismay, Dana Sue's eyes welled up with tears. "I wish we could. I would give anything to have another child, especially if he or she was even half as wonderful as you. But it's not possible, sweetie."

"Because of the diabetes risk," the teen said, her expression sympathetic.

"That and my age," Dana Sue said.

"But you're no older than Maddie," Annie argued. "So it's the diabetes that's the real danger."

She sighed. "Yes, I suppose it is."

Annie hugged her. "I'm sorry, Mom."

"Me, too."

"What about Helen? Do you think she'll ever have a baby?"

It was all Helen talked about lately, but Dana Sue didn't think that was something she should discuss with her daughter. If and when Helen weighed all the pros and cons and made a decision, it would be her news to share.

"You never know," Dana Sue said evasively.

"She'd be a great mom," Annie said. "Ty, Kyle and Katie think so, too. She's, like, the best surrogate aunt in the world."

"Why don't you tell her that?" Dana Sue suggested. It might help Helen to know there were four kids who considered her excellent mother material. To Dana Sue's surprise, the ever-confident Helen seemed to be filled with self-doubts on that score.

Annie grinned. "Maybe I will. My last project turned out okay."

"Project?" Dana Sue said.

"You and Dad," Annie told her, that smug expression back on her face. "You didn't think you two came up with this idea all on your own, did you?"

She laughed. "Of course not. Just because we somehow managed to come up with the same idea over twenty years ago doesn't mean we could have been that ingenious again."

"Exactly," Annie said. "I'd better go check on Dad. You know how bad he is at tying his tie."

"You do that," Dana Sue encouraged. "I'll see you in a few minutes at the back of the church."

"Don't be late—Dad's enough of a wreck without that."

"I won't be," Dana Sue promised. She'd waited too long for this moment as it was.

To Ronnie's relief, the ceremony went off without a hitch. Dana Sue looked every bit as breathtaking as she had on their first wedding day. The reception at Sullivan's was packed with well-wishers, including his folks, who'd driven over from Columbia. He'd seen the fleeting sadness in Dana Sue's eyes at not having her own parents with them anymore, but she'd recovered quickly. Annie had flitted around, taking charge of any detail that Maddie and Helen didn't get to first. Erik had prepared enough food for everyone in Serenity and then some. The entire menu had been conscientiously scanned to be sure there was nothing on it that Dana Sue shouldn't have. Even the amazing, towering wedding cake was sugar-free.

Ronnie had insisted on hiring a band, something they hadn't been able to afford at their first wedding. He drew Dana Sue onto the dance floor for one last spin before they left on their two-week honeymoon to Italy, where Ronnie had scheduled them both to take cooking classes in Tuscany. It was a surprise, sort of a busman's holiday for Dana Sue, but one he knew she would love. It was a dream she'd had for years, but claimed she no longer had time for. He intended to make sure they always took the time to do the important things.

"You could take the tie off now," Dana Sue said, regarding him with an amused expression as he ran his finger around the too-tight collar of his shirt.

"I can stand it for five more minutes," he replied. "You know there are going to be pictures when we take off from here. I don't want you complaining years from now that I looked like I was at some barbecue."

She touched his cheek, an impish gleam in her eyes. "You know I prefer you in nothing at all."

Ronnie laughed. "Ditto, but that's dangerous talk when we have a flight to catch out of Charleston in a few hours."

"I'll bet you could make it worth it if we did happen to miss the flight," she said.

He shook his head. "I'm sure I could, but I'd never hear the end of it, so just rein in your libido, sugar. We'll be in Italy before you know it."

Across the room, he spotted Annie dancing with Ty. He pointed them out to Dana Sue. "Those two seem to be getting closer, don't they?"

She nodded.

"Think I need to have a man-to-man talk with him?"

"And humiliate your daughter?" Dana Sue teased. "I don't think so. She and I have talked about Ty a lot recently. I think she really has her head together where he's concerned. Because he's going away to school in the fall, they've agreed to take things really slowly."

"They'd better," Ronnie said grimly.

She patted his cheek. "You are such a dad."

He winked at her. "I am, aren't I? Always will be." He glanced at his watch. "Any last goodbyes you need to say before we go?"

"Not a one. Annie's thrilled about staying with Helen. Erik has everything under control here, or if he doesn't, I'll never hear about it. Karen's been on the job more regularly lately. I think we're good."

"Then let's go and start the rest of our lives," Ronnie said, leading her toward the exit.

Before he could open the door, they were once again surrounded. Somehow Maddie and Helen were ahead of them, expectant grins on their faces.

"What do you think they're up to?" he whispered to Dana Sue.

"I have no idea," she said, then gasped as she looked past them to the street. "My car!" she shouted. "You bought my car!"

She was gone before Ronnie could ask what the devil she was talking about. Then he spotted the sassy red Mustang convertible parked by the curb, a huge bow on the hood. Beside it, Maddie and Helen were grinning, and Dana Sue was hugging them both fiercely.

"What's going on?" he asked when he joined them.

Dana Sue turned to him with eyes that shone. "I won my car!" she said, looking awestruck. "We had a bet and I won."

"Are you talking about those goals the three of you set? This is your prize?" he said incredulously.

"She met every goal on her list," Helen confirmed.

"And one that wasn't on there," Maddie added. "She took you back. That was on *my* list for her, not that anyone will give me any credit for it."

"Poor Maddie," Dana Sue said. "But I don't feel all that sorry for you, because I won!"

Ronnie chuckled at her unbridled delight in her triumph. "Gloating's not nice, sugar."

"I don't care," she said. "For once in my life I actually beat both Helen and Maddie."

"Given the prize, I'm not surprised you worked so hard to win." He glanced at her friends, neither of whom looked all that disappointed at having lost. "What were you two supposed to get if you won?"

"A trip for two to Hawaii," Maddie stated.

"A shopping spree in Paris," Helen said with a shrug. "I'll get there sometime and pay for it myself."

Dana Sue regarded her two best friends with tears in her eyes. "You know," she suggested slyly, "we could just set new goals. I'm starting to feel pretty lucky."

Helen's eyes lit up at once. "New goals? I like that."

Maddie groaned and frowned at Dana Sue. "What were you thinking?"

"That I want to see both of you as happy as I am right this second," Dana Sue responded.

Maddie linked her arm through Cal's and smiled serenely. "I *am* that happy."

"But Helen will never try to meet her goals if we don't challenge her," Dana Sue said. "We owe her. And something tells me she has a new goal she's just dying to add to her list."

"Yeah, I do," Helen said. "In the meantime, I can practically hear those shops along the Champs-Élysées calling my name."

"Two weeks from tomorrow we meet at The Corner Spa at eight, then," Dana Sue said, then grinned up at Ronnie. "Hop in, pal. I'm about to take you on the ride of your life."

He laughed at her exuberance. "Sugar, there was never a doubt in my mind about that."

* * * * *

Please turn the page for an exciting preview of
FEELS LIKE FAMILY
Book three of the Sweet Magnolias
on sale in April 2007

It was nearly seven when Helen finished with her last client. Barb had left an hour earlier, so she turned off the lights and closed up the office, relieved to have the workday behind her.

Outside she weighed the prospect of going home to her empty house against dropping in at Sullivan's for a decent meal and a few snatched minutes of Dana Sue's time. Maybe she could lay some groundwork before she and Karen met with her formally tomorrow. Barb had already set up that appointment for two o'clock, after the lunch crowd thinned out.

Sullivan's won out easily. The restaurant, which specialized in what Dana Sue called new Southern cuisine, was packed, as it was most nights. Though Serenity's population was only 3500 or so, the restaurant's reputation had spread through the entire region thanks to excellent reviews in the Charleston and Columbia newspapers.

Helen was greeted at the door by Brenda, the harried waitress. "I should have a table opening up in a few minutes," she told Helen. "Do you mind waiting?"

"Not at all. Do you think I'll be risking life and limb if I stick my head in the kitchen to say hello to Dana Sue?"

Brenda grinned. "I'd say that depends on whether you're

prepared to pitch in and help. She and Erik have their hands full tonight. It's been crazy ever since that review in the Columbia paper. If it's going to stay this busy, she needs to hire some additional prep staff for the kitchen and some more waitstaff. Paul and I have just about run ourselves to death tonight, even with the busboys pitching in. And just so you know, we ran out of all the specials an hour ago."

"I'll keep that in mind," Helen said, then headed for the kitchen.

When she pushed open the door and stepped in, she saw Dana Sue at the huge gas stove. Face flushed from the heat, Dana Sue juggled half a dozen different sauté pans, then slid the contents onto waiting plates, added the decorative sauces and spicy salsas, and moved them to a pickup area for the waitstaff.

Her expression filled with relief when she spotted Helen. "Grab an apron," she ordered. "We need you. It's nuts in here."

"Looks to me like what you need is more trained help. Where's Erik?" Helen asked as she whipped off her suit jacket, hung it on a peg in the pantry, then found an apron and put it on over her two-hundred-dollar designer silk blouse.

"Right behind you," a deep voice rumbled. "Watch your step. I'm loaded down."

She turned and found him carrying a tray laden with pies fresh from the oven. She could smell the heady aromas of peaches, cinnamon and vanilla.

"If you'll give me a slice of that, I'll be your slave for the rest of the night," she said.

Erik grinned at her. "I'll save you a whole pie, but you don't have time to eat it now. I need you to mix up another batch of the mango-papaya chutney for the fish." His gaze skimmed her outfit and he shook his head. "You realize that blouse is heading straight for the dry cleaner's after this, don't you?"

Helen shrugged. She had a dozen more in her closet. It wouldn't be a huge loss. "Not a problem."

His dark eyes warmed. "That's what I love about you. No pretensions. Underneath that icy courtroom demeanor that I hear you possess lies the soul of a woman ruled by a passion for food and a willingness to help out a friend in distress, no matter the personal cost."

The compliment caught her off guard. When the usually taciturn Erik popped out with something unexpected or insightful, as he occasionally did, it made her wonder what his story was. She winked at him. "I'm only this cavalier because I figure with the size of tonight's crowd, Dana Sue's good for the cost of another blouse."

"Don't," he protested. "You're ruining my illusions. Do you remember how to make the chutney?"

Helen shook her head. "But don't worry. I know where the recipes are. I'll get that one and find the supplies in the storeroom. I'll have another batch whipped up in no time. You don't need to supervise."

"As if," Dana Sue called out from her station by the stove. "Erik is so thrilled to have someone to supervise for once, he's not going to pass up the chance."

Within moments, Helen had fallen into the frantic rhythm of the kitchen. When she could, she snatched glances at Erik, admiring the efficiency with which he moved almost as much as she craved the desserts which he excelled at making. Though he'd been hired primarily as a pastry chef right after graduating from the Atlanta Culinary Institute—which he'd attended after apparently leaving some other career he never mentioned—his role in Sullivan's kitchen had been expanded over time. Dana Sue relied on him as her backup and had officially named him as assistant manager just a few weeks earlier.

In his late 30s or early 40s, he had a wry wit, a gentle demeanor and was fiercely loyal to and protective of Dana Sue. Helen liked that about him, almost as much as she liked his pastries and occasionally lusted after his six-pack abs and competent hands. That she lusted after him at all was a surprise, because she'd always preferred polished, executive types over the strong, silent, athletic types.

Helen was relegated to the most basic duties for the next two hours, but she liked being part of the hustle and bustle of the kitchen. The aromas were delectable, the excitement and stress palpable. If cooking at home were half this much fun, she might do it more often. Instead her culinary endeavors ran to scrambled eggs, when she remembered to buy any, and the occasional baked potato. She did make a damn fine margarita, though, if she did say so herself. That was the result of a few summers in Hilton Head working as a bartender during law school. She'd made great tips, great contacts and learned a lot about human nature.

By the time the last meal had been served and only a few customers were lingering over coffee and dessert, she was exhausted from being on her feet for so long, to say nothing of being half-starved.

"Okay, you two, that's it," Erik said, hustling them toward the door to the dining room. "Get in there and sit down. I'll bring you both dinner in a few minutes."

Dana Sue shook her head. "Only if you're going to join us," she told him. "You haven't had a break all night, either."

"Sure," Erik said. "But you need to eat now and Helen needs to kick off those ridiculous heels she insists on wearing."

Vaguely miffed by the comment, Helen stuck out her foot in its sexy high-heeled sandal, her most extravagant indulgence. "What's wrong with my shoes?"

Erik's gaze lingered on her foot with its perfectly manicured pink toenails, then traveled slowly up her leg to the hem of her skirt, now hitched up to show a couple of inches of thigh. "Speaking as a man, there is nothing wrong with those shoes," he told her, regarding her with amusement. "Speaking as someone who's watched you hobbling around in here for the past couple of hours, I'd say they're inappropriate for being on your feet for very long."

Mollified, she grinned. "You may have a point."

From *New York Times* bestselling author

SHERRYL WOODS

The Sweet Magnolias

February 2007	March 2007	April 2007

SAVE $1.00 off the purchase price of any book in *The Sweet Magnolias* trilogy.

Offer valid from February 1, 2007 to April 30, 2007. Redeemable at participating retail outlets. Limit one coupon per purchase.

Canadian Retailers: Harlequin Enterprises Limited will pay the face value of this coupon plus 10.25¢ if submitted by customer for this product only. Any other use constitutes fraud. Coupon is nonassignable. Void if taxed, prohibited or restricted by law. Consumer must pay any government taxes. Void if copied. Nielson Clearing House ("NCH") customers submit coupons and proof of sales to: Harlequin Enterprises Limited, P.O. Box 3000, Saint John, N.B. E2L 4L3, Canada. Non-NCH retailer—for reimbursement submit coupons and proof of sales directly to: Harlequin Enterprises Limited, Retail Marketing Department, 225 Duncan Mill Rd., Don Mills, Ontario M3B 3K9, Canada.

52607602

U.S. Retailers: Harlequin Enterprises Limited will pay the face value of this coupon plus 8¢ if submitted by customer for this product only. Any other use constitutes fraud. Coupon is nonassignable. Void if taxed, prohibited or restricted by law. Consumer must pay any government taxes. Void if copied. For reimbursement submit coupons and proof of sales directly to: Harlequin Enterprises Limited, P.O. Box 880478, El Paso, TX 88588-0478, U.S.A. Cash value 1/100 cents.

5 65373 00076 2   (8100) 0 11383

® and TM are trademarks owned and used by the trademark owner and/or its licensee.
© 2006 Harlequin Enterprises Limited

MSWSMT07

REQUEST YOUR FREE BOOKS!

2 FREE NOVELS
FROM THE ROMANCE/SUSPENSE
COLLECTION PLUS 2 FREE GIFTS!

YES! Please send me 2 FREE novels from the Romance/Suspense Collection and my 2 FREE gifts. After receiving them, if I don't wish to receive any more books, I can return the shipping statement marked "cancel." If I don't cancel, I will receive 4 brand-new novels every month and be billed just $5.49 per book in the U.S., or $5.99 per book in Canada, plus 25¢ shipping and handling per book plus applicable taxes, if any*. That's a savings of at least 20% off the cover price! I understand that accepting the 2 free books and gifts places me under no obligation to buy anything. I can always return a shipment and cancel at any time. Even if I never buy another book from the Reader Service, the two free books and gifts are mine to keep forever.

185 MDN EF5Y   385 MDN EF6C

Name	(PLEASE PRINT)	

Address		Apt. #

City	State/Prov.	Zip/Postal Code

Signature (if under 18, a parent or guardian must sign)

Mail to **The Reader Service:**
IN U.S.A.: P.O. Box 1867, Buffalo, NY 14240-1867
IN CANADA: P.O. Box 609, Fort Erie, Ontario L2A 5X3

Not valid to current subscribers to the Romance Collection,
the Suspense Collection or the Romance/Suspense Collection.

Want to try two free books from another line?
Call 1-800-873-8635 or visit www.morefreebooks.com.

* Terms and prices subject to change without notice. NY residents add applicable sales tax. Canadian residents will be charged applicable provincial taxes and GST. This offer is limited to one order per household. All orders subject to approval. Credit or debit balances in a customer's account(s) may be offset by any other outstanding balance owed by or to the customer. Please allow 4 to 6 weeks for delivery.

Your Privacy: Harlequin is committed to protecting your privacy. Our Privacy Policy is available online at www.eHarlequin.com or upon request from the Reader Service. From time to time we make our lists of customers available to reputable firms who may have a product or service of interest to you. If you would prefer we not share your name and address, please check here. ☐

BOB07

SHERRYL WOODS

32363 STEALING HOME	___ $6.99 U.S.	___ $8.50 CAN.
32336 WAKING UP IN CHARLESTON	___ $6.99 U.S.	___ $8.50 CAN.
32238 FLIRTING WITH DISASTER	___ $6.99 U.S.	___ $8.50 CAN.
32149 THE BACKUP PLAN	___ $6.99 U.S.	___ $8.50 CAN.
32048 DESTINY UNLEASHED	___ $6.50 U.S.	___ $7.99 CAN.
66815 ABOUT THAT MAN	___ $6.50 U.S.	___ $7.99 CAN.

(limited quantities available)

TOTAL AMOUNT	$ _____
POSTAGE & HANDLING	$ _____
($1.00 FOR 1 BOOK, 50¢ for each additional)	
APPLICABLE TAXES*	$ _____
TOTAL PAYABLE	$ _____

(check or money order—please do not send cash)

To order, complete this form and send it, along with a check or money order for the total above, payable to MIRA Books, to: **In the U.S.:** 3010 Walden Avenue, P.O. Box 9077, Buffalo, NY 14269-9077; **In Canada:** P.O. Box 636, Fort Erie, Ontario, L2A 5X3.

Name: _____

Address: _____ City: _____

State/Prov.: _____ Zip/Postal Code: _____

Account Number (if applicable): _____

075 CSAS

*New York residents remit applicable sales taxes.
*Canadian residents remit applicable GST and provincial taxes.

MIRA®

www.MIRABooks.com

MSHW0307BL